THE
APOSTLE
KILLER

ALSO BY RICHARD BEARD

THE
APOSTLE
KILLER

RICHARD BEARD

MELVILLE HOUSE
BROOKLYN · LONDON

THE APOSTLE KILLER

First Melville House Printing: September 2016

Melville House Publishing   8 Blackstock Mews
        46 John Street   and   Islington
    Brooklyn, NY 11201   London N4 2BT

mhpbooks.com   facebook.com/mhpbooks   @melvillehouse

Library of Congress Cataloging-in-Publication Data
Names: Beard, Richard, 1967– author.
Title: The apostle killer / Richard Beard.
Description: Brooklyn, NY : Melville House, 2016.
Identifiers: LCCN 2016022377 (print) | LCCN 2016028473
    (ebook) | ISBN 9781612195797 (hardcover) | ISBN
    9781612195803 (ebook)
Subjects: LCSH: Apostles—Fiction. | Murder—Investigation—
    Fiction. | Jesus Christ—Resurrection—Fiction. | GSAFD:
    Christian fiction. Y Mystery fiction | Suspense fiction |
    Historical fiction.
Classification: LCC PS3552.E167 A66 2016 (print) | LCC
    PS3552.E167 (ebook) | DDC 813/.54—dc23
LC record available at https://lccn.loc.gov/2016022377

Design by Marina Drukman

Printed in the United States of America
1   3   5   7   9   10   8   6   4   2

With the Lord one day
Is as a thousand years,
And a thousand years
As one day.
(*2 Peter 3:8*)

CONTENTS

THE
APOSTLE
KILLER

I

Judas

———

"BURST ASUNDER"

First, find the body.

Male, early thirties, bearded. Distinguishing features: extensive trauma injury, severe to hands and feet. Decomposition consistent with springtime conditions in an arid territory. So follow the smell of a four-day-old death, the black fruit stench of human decay. The corpse is out there somewhere.

Find it. Then the occupying army, representing human progress, will investigate. These people have forensics, a rational system of criminal justice, and will ensure that those guilty of stealing a body from a burial site are tried and punished. Whoever they may be.

Cassius Marcellus Gallio, counterinsurgency, switches on the recording equipment and speaks out loud the precise date, the exact time, the full names of those present. This is how it usually begins. Then he switches the machine off, watches the green recording light fade and die. In this city he has the title of Speculator. He expects to get results.

'What I'm wondering, what I really want you to tell me, off the book, if you can, is how much you knew in advance.' Cassius Gallio will be polite for as long as possible. The interview room often does the rest—a single metal table and a folding metal chair. No one wants to wind up in the fortress, in the Antonia. Outside, down in the streets, a turncoat can convince himself that his loyalties are divided. In the Antonia they are not. Inside the fortress the time has passed for 'and,' for 'both.' The choice now is either/or, the occupiers or the occupied, reason or superstition.

'If you can remember, if the information is alive in your brain, and not too much trouble to share.'

Despite the hard chair and the bare room, the Judas is not in a talkative mood. Cassius Gallio flips open his notebook and draws a circle. An imperfect circle, so he has another go. Same intended shape, different imperfections. Nothing is going right for him today.

'I'm withholding half your fee.'

'I did what we agreed.'

Valeria, Gallio's colleague, sits on the front edge of the table with one foot on the floor. She picks her fingernails with the corner of a laminated guide explaining emergency procedures in the event of fire. Her nails are clean. She taps the stiff edge of the card on her knee. Tap tap. On her knee, the back of which would fit perfectly the inside of Cassius Gallio's elbow.

Gallio concentrates. Not today, he thinks, of all days. He doesn't have time for the inconvenience of Valeria's knee.

'Judas?'

4

The man flinches at the sound of his name. He gnaws at the inside of his cheek, bites at the skin of his fingertips. Let him, let the traitor eat away at himself. At the barred window Gallio looks down on the early Jerusalem streets: a normal Monday morning, visibly untouched by miracles. A boy runs down an alley, a tray of loaves on his head. He dodges a rasping scooter, which hits the main drag and accelerates away through traffic. Life goes on.

'Where's the body?'

Cassius Gallio had reacted to yesterday's rumour, of course he had. He came in late on a Sunday to follow up the lead, a sighting on the Emmaus road to the north of the city. Not the body but the man himself, apparently alive, a dead man walking. Gallio had sent Valeria to make enquiries, but it turned out to be nothing, peasant gossip about an executed convict and his seven-mile hike for lunch.

If they were regular police, Gallio thought, he would have charged someone for wasting regular police time. Speculators were not regular police. He needed that body.

First thing Monday morning he ordered a citywide search. He prepared his people for the worst—the shrunken lips, the livid meat—but the certainties of a dead body would put an end to any mystery. All through the day uniformed troops moved house to house, going in hard on the Lower City. Cellars, attics, any darkness that could conceal a folded adult corpse. Freezers. Gallio makes sure his people look inside the freezers, chest and wardrobe. The body could be whole, could be dissected. Check bathtubs for acid corrosion, and treat plastic sheeting as suspicious. Pick through building sites, anywhere with recently poured concrete.

The forces of order know what to do. Sadly, this is neither the first nor last time they'll search for a missing body.

Gallio sends five-man cordons to walk the mountain scrub. No sign yet of a shallow grave. Valeria supervises the dive team at the reservoir and the Bethesda pool, where she clears out the cripples who've come for a cure. She finds no trace of weighted human remains dumped into the water. Gallio opens a series of tombs, an inspired hunch as a hiding place. The body isn't there.

Until further notice every cart and truck leaving Jerusalem will be security-checked at the city gates. Still no result. Think. Gallio orders raids on apothecaries suspected of trading in human body parts, eyes and spleens for the more costly curses and spells. Nothing. Think again. If anyone wants to move the body then spices or perfume would mask the smell. Gallio turns over shipments of nard and aloe, and at this troubled time Passover in Jerusalem smells like heaven.

And of burned meat from the Temple sacrifices, and a haze of two-stroke. Maybe a night downstairs in the Antonia will put Judas back in touch with reality.

'A local source tells me the way you betrayed him was foretold.'

Gallio perches on the steel table-edge, next to Valeria. He licks the end of his biro, to remind Judas he's expecting solid information worth noting down. Then he draws an irregular triangle like a head above one of the imperfect circles from yesterday. Saliva doesn't help, smears the ink.

'Judas?'

He's not listening. Valeria slices him across the cheek with her laminated card. In an occupied territory the army are the cops, and the army cops have their own secret service, the Speculators. They don't like their time being wasted. Valeria shapes for another hit, but making Judas flinch is enough.

'His other followers knew what was going to happen, Judas.' Gallio will have to spell it out to him. 'The missing body was written in the prophecies. Ergo, you, Judas, also knew what would happen.'

Instructions in the Event of Fire has opened a cut below his eye, and blood seeps through. Gallio rolls his eyes. Earlier than he'd have liked he leans back and flips a switch on the intercom. He says: 'Chicken, now.' In the starkness of the interview room his words sound like a code, as if he's lost the habit of saying anything straight. Saying it twice may help. 'Chicken, as soon as you can.'

Judas has spent a night downstairs in the Antonia. He's dirty and hungry. But also, Gallio concedes, the chicken does have a double meaning. Good cop. Judas is the asset, and the asset's cover is blown. His eleven former companions, his ex-friends, despise him. He'll appreciate every kindness.

'Judas!' Val stabs the stiff end of the card into his shoulder. Bad cop, an act but she's a natural. 'He knew what was going to happen and he planned every move, didn't he? You might have warned us, said a little something in advance.'

'I'm hungry,' Judas says.

They wait. A rotisserie chicken in a white and silver bag, an underpaid local recruit: he carries the bag past the security barriers, into the lift, out of the lift, through the manned gate to the reinforced door of the interview room. Keypad, authorised personnel only. Gallio goes to open the door, takes the bag that smells of grease and freedom. He says thanks, in good cop character, swings the door shut, hands the hot roast chicken to Judas.

Cassius Gallio has a heart of gold, but Judas peers cautiously inside. A cloud of chicken steam billows to the ceiling. The chicken is not a trap, Judas, or a trick. Everything is as it seems.

Judas pulls out the browned carcass, snaps it open and bites out the liver. Hungry. As he chews, the meat gives him strength. He breaks off a drumstick and points, jelly glistening on the hanging skin.

'I kept you out of it. They trusted me.'

Judas is an innocent, Judas is a baby. Obviously they didn't trust him, or he'd know how they'd subverted a public execution. If he had their trust he could explain why the disciples, his former friends, were spreading misinformation about the dead man being alive. Judas had yet to volunteer a satisfactory answer as to why they were doing that.

'They played you.' Valeria keeps her amber eyes fixed on Judas, skims the laminated card onto the table, where it slides across the metal and drops to the floor. 'Played us too. You're nervous, Judas. Why is that? What reason do you have for being so nervous?'

Valeria is a people person, who enjoys the intimate questions. Who are you? What are you afraid of? Will you ever leave your wife?

'Your leader is dead, Judas,' she says. 'We watched him die, and it wasn't pleasant, but he can't hurt you now. The others, however, have worked you out. They recognized the signal you gave to trigger the arrest.'

'We should have thought up something more subtle,' Gallio adds. 'Sorry, our mistake.'

'They'll be wondering where you are,' Valeria builds the fear. 'You're seriously outnumbered.'

'Eleven against one.'

'Honestly,' Judas says. He holds the chicken carcass in both hands. 'We never discussed stealing the body. From the start of this you promised to protect me. It was the first thing you said.'

He rips at the chicken breast with his teeth, chews and swallows, bites, chews, all body, no brain. He reduces life to the basic function of taking on fuel, hoping to block out the last few days, and the feeling that life and death have stopped following the basic expectations.

'Judas. Look at me.'

On the edge of the table, next to Valeria, Gallio is as close to his former inside man as can be. He leans forward and brings his blue eyes to bear. Sweat beads on the bridge of Judas's nose. 'Put down the bird, Judas.'

Gallio lays his wrists on the man's shoulders, his metal watchband hard against Judas's collarbone, and he leans, making Judas heavier, a burden on his shoulders weighing him down. 'Stop chewing, Judas. Good. Good boy. Mouth closed. Now look at me, Judas, look into my eyes. We want the truth about what happened this weekend, and don't be frightened. We're the good guys. We won't let them fuck you up.'

Gallio himself takes plainclothes shifts at the hotel. He sits at the bar with his laptop and types out notes for a provisional report. Low priority, no cause for alarm. What they have here is an unusual but annoying theft. That is what this is. What it can't possibly be, and what he refuses to contemplate, is died, risen, coming again.

Unfortunately, being unreasonable is not against the law. The disciples can't be arrested for their delusions, but they need to know they're in trouble and under constant surveillance. Gallio wears the same jacket every day, so they'll notice him, has his shoes shined in the lobby when they come down to breakfast because he wants them to know he's watching. He makes a show of staring, hardly blinking, at eleven out-of-towners with plenty of hair and delicate fingers. They do not dress well, favouring lighter colours in the range between beige and cream. Cult uniformity, which is why Judas had to single out their leader: they all look alike.

The disciples are agitated, glance left and right, know that Jerusalem is full of spies. 'Agitated,' Gallio adds to his notebook, next to the intricate lines of a diamond formation. He blocks out the letters, especially the capital A: years of training for this. He is supposed to make connections, work out how conspiracies against the civilized world fit together, but in this case he simply doesn't know.

Over the following days he chases leads with increasing desperation. In one tip-off the dead man is supposed to have appeared to his mother, alive and disguised as a gardener. Gallio rounds up the city's registered gardeners. They vow to make a formal complaint to the Prefect, which is fine, but none of them remembers speaking to a distressed middle-aged lady on the day in question at or near the crime scene.

So Gallio brings in the mother, because close family members are always suspects. Instead of a lawyer she insists on coming accompanied by one of the disciples, John. John recommends she exercise her right to remain silent.

'Have you seen your son since the day of the execution?'

She exercises her right, but John is ready to fill the silence. He's a young man with barely enough beard to look the part, and thick glasses he pushes up his nose to punctuate the nonsense he likes to spout. According to John a man died, was in a tomb for three days, and then on the Sunday he came back to life and walked away. A god is involved.

'That figures.'

'He came back from the dead,' John says. 'Oh, fuck off.'

But Cassius Gallio doesn't have the evidence to prove John wrong. He lets them go, and in the fortress Gallio bans all discussion of resurrection as a potential line of enquiry. As an occupying force they have arguably imported some questionable laws, but there's nothing debatable about laws of nature. The Complex Casework Unit will expect a rational explanation. Anything else is going to sound, coming from Cassius Gallio, like an excuse. A terrible excuse, especially from him, after the embarrassment of what happened with Lazarus.

He still doesn't understand how they did that. Lazarus died from multiple diseases. Cassius Gallio himself witnessed the wreck of the man in his final hours, and then the burial, but four days later Lazarus was alive again and dazed by sunshine in front of his tomb. Gallio couldn't explain the mechanics, the trick, and since failing to come up with answers he'd been put on a caution. Complex Casework is taking an interest. He can't afford to fail again.

The Jewish leadership also lack patience for the gimmicks of Jesus. Without providing evidence they spin the disciples as thieves who'd steal a body from a tomb. Maybe so, but the disciples give nothing away, supply no reasonable cause for arrest.

Gallio follows them, and on the steps of the Temple they tout an organized line, devoting themselves to a falsehood about an executed criminal who is alive, healthy and a surprise visitor at their city-centre hotel. Delusion, Gallio reminds himself, is not an arrestable offence. Their dead leader appears behind closed doors, they say, of course he does, but comings and goings are easy to check: no one fitting the description of Jesus enters or leaves the hotel within the specified time frames.

'Could you have missed him?' Gallio has made Valeria responsible for the surveillance teams, and anyone can make mistakes. 'Could you have confused him with one of his followers?'

'I don't think so, we don't know.' Valeria covers for her operatives, who are working double shifts. 'They all look similar. It's possible.'

CCTV is inconclusive. The disciples are in and out. From above, with fisheye angles and in corridor light, the men are interchangeable. Except the dead one among them would be limping. He would limp, if he could walk, but probably he couldn't even walk. He's not alive, he's crippled and he's dead.

Gallio confines Judas to a safe house in the Upper City, a flat in a modern block beside the museum where the street fills daily with a useful confusion of human traffic. Gallio tells Valeria to give Judas what he wants, within reason, and he stays indoors and comfort-eats. He likes his bottles of wine, but when Gallio asks Valeria what she makes of him she shrugs, flicks open her notebook like a blank ID. In the centre of the page is a penciled square, heavily shaded at the edges and empty in the centre. She pushes the notebook close to Gallio's face.

'I need more than that.' Gallio bats her hand away. They touch, for a split second. 'Has he tried to contact anyone? How frightened is he?'

'That's all I've got. I've thought it through.'

Fair enough—the silent treatment because he won't sleep with her. Not now, Gallio wants to say, let's get this sorted and maybe then. You know I want to, only this is a difficult time, and she should remember he's married. Until now his marriage hasn't deterred her. She kept coming all the same, split up publicly with her boyfriend, a uniformed sergeant. I'm married, Gallio had said, but she sensed his weakness. She knows he doesn't believe that faithfulness matters, because like her he's ambitious, and what matters most is a promotion one day to chief of section Complex Casework Unit, Europe. As a minimum career requirement.

Their shared vision of the future can make 'now' feel a limited experience, and Jerusalem an insignificant posting. They earn a hardship allowance for serving in the field, but in these peaceful days the garrison feels more like a complacent army in camp. They can get frustrated, spies in a country where there's nothing to spy on. They have been bored. Then Lazarus. Lazarus changed everything. Now this.

'Thanks for your help,' Gallio says.

'You're welcome.'

Gallio submits a request to the Prefect of the Province of Judaea, in writing, to bring in a disciple from the leadership group. He doesn't care which one, probably Peter. The way Cassius Gallio sees it he can play Peter off against Judas: the two former colleagues in separate rooms, neither of them sure what the other may confess. Then in the same room, to wonder how much pain the other can bear. Not that the interviews need descend into violence. The anticipation of pain is often enough.

Pilate refuses Gallio's request, also in writing. He's covering his back. Pilate has seen no evidence to incriminate the disciples, and this is the Middle East. The zealots in the mountains are unpredictable, and in this particular region a riot could start a war. Cassius Gallio should avoid inflaming the situation, and an arrest would be a negative at this time.

Gallio barely goes home. He sleeps at his desk, arms as a pillow, woken by a.m. phone calls when his wife needs help with the baby. He tells her not now, he has a lot on his plate. She shouts down the phone, says if she'd known he'd be like this with his work then she'd have married one of her own.

'Like who?'

'Someone simple. A Jerusalem man without big ideas.'

'I don't do big ideas.'

'You do about yourself.'

In his office in the early hours of the morning, now that he's awake, Gallio wipes the sleep from his eyes and explores the angles: before, during, after, determined to work out how they did it. He reviews the coverage. Play, rewind, play. Pause. Break it down. Look for deviations from best practice. He finds so many they make him wince. He can't understand why this man Jesus was treated differently from everyone else.

The cameras pick Jesus up in the street outside Herod's Palace, and there's footage from there until the waste ground of Golgotha outside the city gates, where the execution takes place. The street-views on tape are cut from fourteen separate cameras, and the screen geeks have spliced the shots into a single sequence. From the beginning Jesus is not in good shape, weakened by flaying. He carries the crossbeam himself and often he falls. His mother breaks from the crowd to help him, a lapse in security. She should never have made it through the cordon.

Soon after that the uniformed escort forces a spectator, a youngish black man, to help with the crossbeam. Gallio freezes the face, but recognition software can't find a match. A little later a second unidentified individual, this time a woman, comes out of the crowd to wipe Jesus's face. No match, no criminal record or previous arrests. The first part of this death/resurrection scam is clean, Jesus and his disciples passing every test of criminal hygiene. Gallio uncovers no loose ends, no careless recruitment of accomplices with a history.

Jesus falls again. The third time he falls some more women, as a group, hold up the procession with their local weeping and wailing. They are suspects, and every face needs identifying before being cleared. Then Jesus falls again. Falling could be a signal, but this time nothing special happens, no one else arrives to help him, to deliver a message or receive instructions. The execution is back on track, though behind schedule due to the many delays. By the time the procession reaches Golgotha the soldiers have regained control. Beside the cross they strip the prisoner, following orders. Cassius Gallio's orders.

Gallio studies the images, even though he was there. On the cross Jesus is naked, to ensure he can't conceal some secret device to help him counterfeit death. If Gallio has learned anything in Jerusalem, it's that Jesus can't be trusted. He'd pretended to bring Lazarus back to life, and staged various medical illusions that he passed off as real. Gallio was wary of whatever he'd come up with next, and had vowed to be ready.

Naked, however, nailed to a cross, Jesus has been decisively outwitted. He dies. Gallio watches him die. Over and over again. Civilization is the winner.

The body needs to be down before sunset, out of respect for the Jewish Sabbath, but this next part of the tape makes Gallio's chest seize. The endgame is a lesson in bad practice. Either side of Jesus the two prisoners have their legs broken, as is standard procedure, to accelerate death. Jesus does not.

Why not? No one can tell him. The Prefect gave permission for a Judaean high priest and councillor, identified as Joseph of

Arimathea, to take down the body. Why would he do that? No one can say, but there are regulations, and the regulations have been flouted. The camera tracks Joseph, a known Jesus sympathizer, as he carries the body of Jesus to his tomb. His own tomb, private property. The body of Jesus disappears inside and the image blurs and whites out. Show over. The security geeks cut to a drug deal in a bus shelter, then a cat asleep on a bin.

The cameras see everything; understand nothing.

Rewind. Stop. Play, pause. Gallio stills the moment of death, watches Jesus die frame by frame in slo-mo, and Jesus has one of those faces. When the face is moving, it is him, recognizably a cult leader with a fanatical following. On pause, however, the stilled image never accurately captures the living individual Gallio would recognize. Forget the face and trust the body, bruised and defeated and bleeding—that part of it, the violence and the killing, is real from whichever angle Gallio chooses to look.

'Nothing? A total empty zero-shaped hole of nothing?'

Pilate slams his hand against the arm of his chair, against a marble pillar, and a third time against a window frame. He finds the hard edges of what is otherwise an office of soft furnishings, a big man running to fat since his posting to Jerusalem as Prefect. In the good old days, when he was a soldier, he had fewer crimson cushions in his life.

He paces. He points his rigid finger. 'All you had to do was guard a fucking corpse. You're a young man but you're also my regional Speculator, a member of the supposedly elite military police. What is going on here?'

'On the day of the execution there were irregularities.'

'Not good enough. This nonsense about resurrection has to stop. Now. Yesterday. The day *before* yesterday.'

Gallio feels a powerful urge to smack Pilate down. He's a Speculator, with authority to think more creatively than a senior administrator, stuck with his present tense chores. But after Lazarus, Cassius Gallio isn't so sure of himself, of what he can do or when he's right.

'The area searches are ongoing,' he says, calming himself with the facts. 'We have Judas in a safe house and the disciples under observation. I'm looking for the man who helped Jesus carry his crossbeam in the street. Also an unidentified woman who wiped his face when he fell. Messages may have been passed, we don't know.'

'Spare me the details. Get out there and put an end to it.'

'Can I bring in Peter?'

'No.'

Gallio is leaving when Pilate calls him back.

'The money, Gallio. I've heard whispers.'

Cassius Gallio doesn't know what Pilate is talking about, but Pilate has more to say.

'Don't let this story about money be true.'

'I have affidavits from the on-duty soldiers saying they received no unsanctioned payments.'

'For what?'

'For allowing unauthorized persons to remove a body from a tomb under guard.'

'So no chance they might be lying? And suspicion doesn't just fall on the grunts, does it?'

Pilate turns his fleshy head like a flightless bird. His nearer eye is sharp and alive, but the distant more dangerous eye is doing the looking. 'The Jerusalem high priests, including the Sanhedrin council, are suggesting we took money for relaxing our watch on the tomb. How else could a body go missing?'

'They made that up. The priests want to discredit any talk of resurrection. A man coming back to life is a stupid story, unbelievable, but some people are starting to believe it.'

'Find the body, Gallio. Please, for the sake of my sanity. And for yourself, for your future. Your time is running out.'

Valeria's ex-boyfriend is the sergeant in charge of executions. He has strong hands and a capable face made broad by early baldness. Lots of know-how, good with women. His eyes are moist, a little frightened. No one wants an interview with the Speculator.

'Why didn't you break his legs?'

The sergeant blinks. He recently lost his girlfriend, he doesn't want to lose his job. 'He was dead.'

'You ignored the procedure. You'll have heard the gossip that Jesus is alive and out there somewhere, free as you like on his unbroken legs. That's why we have a procedure.'

'We speared him, to make sure. He was dead.'

This enquiry is not personal, and Gallio hopes the sergeant appreciates that he's only doing his job. They are not competing to sleep with Valeria, and none of these problems are of his making. He will, however, find out the truth behind the execution and burial because everything has an explanation.

'Was he, though? Are you certain he was dead?'

The sergeant is a career soldier. He won't admit that he acted out of compassion, nor does Cassius Gallio want him to admit to it. He should be desensitized by now, because attending to executions is part of what he must do. The situation is different for Gallio. He took control of the Jesus execution as a chance to right the wrongs of his misadventure with Lazarus. He doesn't have the experience to be indifferent, or the necessary distance.

But nobody does, against an enemy like this. Gallio had called up soldiers to guard the tomb, and he acknowledges they were not the finest troops at his disposal. Whereas executions require precision, and a steadfast belief in the rightness of the civilizing project, to stand on duty outside a tomb requires an iron bladder. Gallio had picked the lowest soldiers they had, out of respect for the legion, men on charges for leaving live rounds in the chamber or wearing the wrong hat on parade. The hopeless cases.

Their mission was to guard a corpse, to ensure the dead stayed dead. He thought they might have managed a simple task without fucking up.

Gallio accesses the bank records of his idiot tomb guard detail, but none of them are that stupid. If the soldiers were paid off they've hidden the money, and sure enough Valeria finds a stack of used bills taped in a sandwich bag inside a mattress in the garrison block. Dumb enough.

'Who gave you the money?'

'What money?'

In the garrison jail no one can hear Cassius Gallio sigh. He upends the sandwich bag onto the floor, kicks through the bricks of paper money.

'That's not ours.'

Valeria picks up a solid packet of notes, and jabs the most stupid of them in the throat. The soldier is not forthcoming. She holds his nose and stuffs the money into his mouth until he retches.

He weeps. He blames a local man, named Baruch.

'He told us his name and offered to pay us. The body had already gone. The tomb was empty. What was the harm?'

'You should have refused the money.'

'He wouldn't take no for an answer. Swore he was an official of some sort, and the body was already missing. Not our fault, he said. He told us we wouldn't get into trouble.'

Or if they did, then this man Baruch would straighten it out. They were to say the disciples had stolen the body. The soldier has one hand over his Adam's apple, and he checks his teeth with his tongue. He sounds aggrieved.

'He told us the Jerusalem Speculator had approved what he was doing. He'd spoken to you.'

'Me? He mentioned me by name?'

'He did. Said you knew each other. We'd be fine.'

'He was wrong.'

Cassius Gallio lets his face rest, in all its misery. He has a downcast face, when at rest. When he's feeling nothing, and his face should look neutral, it relaxes into a picture of dejection. His wife has commented on this, after sex.

'So Baruch paid you to say the disciples stole the body. In this made-up version of events, that you couldn't even make up yourself, why didn't you stop them at the time? What lie did he give you to answer that? It's the obvious question.'

'They didn't steal the body.'

'How do you know?'

'We would have stopped them. We were awake the whole time.'

'But Baruch paid you to tell everyone the disciples did it. How would they have done it?'

'He said to say they were armed.'

'With what? Dangerous sandals? We've been through their hotel. No knives, no guns. Not a single offensive weapon. Not even a blunt object.'

Gallio has the sergeant and his execution squad complete the interrogation. The sergeant is not a bad man, and Cassius Gallio watches through a one-way mirror as he patiently asks the soldiers to take off their clothes. They have no scratching or bruising to suggest they fought for the body of Jesus.

'You fell asleep, didn't you?'

The sergeant is gentle with them, because every soldier learns on joining up that sleeping on duty is punishable by death. That's the tightness of the ship they run. Or rather, falling asleep on watch while active in the field is punishable by death. In camp, the guilty are punished with a beating.

'We're in camp!' the men shout. They come and bang their fists against the mirror, wanting to see who's behind it, seeing only themselves in reflection and their clenched terrified faces. They know Cassius Gallio is there, and he's watching. Cassius Gallio knows he's watching. It's up to him whether he chooses to intervene.

'We're in camp!' they shout, again and again.

Gallio presses the button for the loudspeaker, and the soldiers hear him as a disembodied voice. 'This is an occupied territory. We're in the field.'

By falling asleep on duty they endanger their fellow soldiers. They cast suspicion on their colleagues and superiors, especially their superiors, as if Speculator Cassius Gallio can't be trusted with a simple execution.

'We're in the field, gentlemen. You know the punishment.'

• • •

He revisits the crime scene, first at Golgotha and then the tomb. Beyond the police tape the tomb is a high-end Jerusalem unit, a cave sculpted to resemble a room. Inside, Jesus's burial clothes are folded neatly on a stone shelf, and more than two weeks have passed since Gallio was at another tomb, in Bethany, where Jesus called Lazarus out. Lazarus was bound up in his linen and Gallio with his own eyes had seen Lazarus fall flat on his face. His sisters Mary and Martha had to unwrap Lazarus and help him up, so in Jerusalem Jesus can't have acted alone. To make good his escape he needed accomplices.

On Gallio's orders, the stone door of the tomb had been sealed along the edges with household mortar. An extreme precaution, but after Lazarus Gallio was being thorough. Now his exceptional measures made the breaking and entering look twice as miraculous. The bastards had set him up. Calm, he thinks. The escape they engineered is clever, but not impossible. There is always an explanation.

Probably, allowing for the frailty of human nature, the idiot common soldiers had fallen asleep. Why stay awake? The corpse wasn't going anywhere. While the guard slept, the disciples removed the mortar and rolled back the stone and made off with the body of Jesus. Gallio has no idea why, but he intends to find out.

He increases the reward money. Judas could be bribed, so why not the others? None of the disciples comes forward. Days go by. Instead of a corpse the city throws up collaborator chaff greedy for a share of the reward.

'He was giving off a kind of brightness. Was he? A white kind. He had a beard. Who else could it be?'

Gallio feels like banging his head against the walls of Jerusalem, outside a one-chair barbershop, outside a launderette.

He realizes how happy he was with his ordinary problems, his wife and a baby he ignores for days on end. Judith accuses him of not loving her, not as a husband should, of neglecting his child, of sleeping with someone at work. He doesn't *deserve* a home, she says.

He stays longer in the office, as if complications can be solved by working harder, but no line of enquiry works out for him. It feels like a jinxed investigation. There's the woman in the street who wiped Jesus's face, but the image they have is grainy, and from above. There's no match on any of the likely databases.

Gallio issues the blurred picture to his people on the ground, and they move outward from the place where she broke from the crowd. 'Have you seen this woman?' Nobody admits that they have. While his agents persevere, Gallio plans a visit to Joseph, owner of a private tomb and a villa on the exclusive heights of Abu Tor. Only Joseph of Arimathea is an acquaintance of the Prefect, who refuses Gallio a warrant.

They do eventually track down the black man, the one on the tapes who carried the crossbeam. He's an African from Cyrene called Simon, caught trying to leave the country to the north of Jerusalem at the Haifa ferry terminal. This turns out, despite Gallio's high hopes, not to be the guilty escape it looks like. Simon is a tourist, first visit to Israel, visa in order, threatening to report his treatment as a hate crime. And no criminal record. He appears to be the last type of person a policeman believes in: a genuine bystander. Gallio has no choice but to let him go, watch him board the ferry. Simon turns from the deck and gives them the finger.

Gallio has yet to type up a statement from Judas, as part of the report he seems unable to write. He'd planned to file a full account *after* finding the body, a career saver framed as a success story for the values of civilization, as demonstrated by the victory of his powers of reasoning over entrenched local ignorance. Now he's mostly looking for someone to blame.

Pilate will feature in the report. Not even Pilate knows where he stands with the CCU, and the Prefect is responsible for a major anomaly. Once Jesus was dead, Pilate allowed a Jewish councillor to take the body from the cross. The Jewish priests, however amenable, are the enemy. The occupiers are friends with the enemy, but allowing them to interfere with executions is not, repeat not, good procedure. The crucified body goes into an uncovered pit for the overnight dogs. There is a reason for this. It precludes any doubt about the nature of the punishment.

Jesus died, fact. He was definitely dead, or Gallio who was there at the crucifixion would never have authorized the release of the body. Not to Joseph of Arimathea, not to anyone, but Jesus has been sighted alive so many times since his death that Gallio begins to doubt himself.

Briefly, he considers wording a request to reclassify the case as Missing Persons, but can't imagine how he'd argue for a change of emphasis. To investigate the resurrection of Jesus is in some sense to believe in it, and opening a new line of enquiry admits the possibility that a man nailed to a tree by expert infantrymen would not die. There are limits.

Cassius Gallio spends more nights at his desk, the office emptied, the case rooms locked. He calls Valeria. He hangs up. He calls Valeria and her phone switches to voicemail. He wants to say sorry, and please, but mostly he's saying he's there, and he needs her, or someone like her.

She calls back. He doesn't answer. He needs comfort, and the supernatural will not survive the warmth of Valeria's body, the reality of the backs of her knees. Whatever else is uncertain in this city, Gallio is certain he wants to sleep with Valeria, right or wrong.

She calls again. He picks up.

'That last message didn't sound like work,' she says. 'Got a job for me?'

'I want to see you.'

'You see me every day.'

'I'm in the office now, on my own.'

'Sorry, Cassius. Not coming.'

'Please, Val. You wanted us to spend some time together. Val?'

She's gone, or she's thinking. All she need say is yes, I will come to the office, I will hold you. Together they'll forget Jesus for an hour or so, remember what on this planet men and women who like each other are designed to do best.

'Cassius, you're in enough trouble. This will make it worse.'

'How so?'

'Losing dead prisoners, propositioning junior colleagues. None of it looks good, not from the outside. Trust me on this.'

Cassius Gallio visits Judas instead, and at the safe house Judas is grateful for friendship. Gallio feeds him and provides consoling wines, every sip the evidence that Judas has done no wrong and life on earth is fair. Judas eats and drinks and reddens in the face, he sweats and suffers while aiming to live happily ever after, to prove a point: I am enjoying myself, so there is no vengeful god.

When Judas is drunk, Gallio questions him about the miracles of Jesus.

'Saw them all.' His lips are black, and he squints at the level of wine in the bottle, rotates the base in tiny increments. 'Makes no difference. Who's going to believe us?'

Gallio organizes a press conference in which Judas sits in front of coloured microphones and denies witnessing miracles. He does not believe that Jesus has come back from the dead. He overturns his glass of water, then re-rights the glass but it's empty. The Speculator expenses account buys Judas new clothes to reassure him he's doing the right thing, and Gallio hopes other potential informers will notice and be impressed.

He bribes Judas onto the best table at Canela. This news will get out, get around. Among the Jerusalem high-achievers, the bankers and the journalists, the rich, the leaders, here is Judas reaping his rewards. He has cooperated with the occupying forces to enable the arrest of a terrorist. Good man. He is clapped on the back, an obvious success, an incentive to any right-minded citizen with information about the corpse of a convicted insurgent.

Come forward and all this can be yours. The restaurant, Gallio wants to say, the gossip. This is how winners have their story told. No one comes forward.

'Judas?'

The next morning at the safe house Gallio finds Judas slumped in the shower, sitting on the tiles as the water batters the bald spot on the back of his head. The disciples are up early again, declaiming in turns on the Temple steps, honing their version of events in which Jesus comes back from the dead. Judas, on the other hand, is in the black grip of a long night's wine. Gallio leans in and flips the water to cold. Judas wakes, panics, blows out his cheeks, tries to stand. Gallio holds him down.

'You've forgotten, haven't you? We have work to do.'

In the street Gallio tells Judas to stop worrying, he'll be fine. All Cassius Gallio wants him to do is to stand up for the truth, remind people there are contrary opinions about Jesus among his closest followers.

'Remember, even when you can't see us we'll be watching. You're totally safe. They can't hurt you, and they're cowards. They're not going to throw the first stone, you know that.'

'Can I have a drink?'

'No.'

They stop on the way for a stiffener, Judas in his fresh expensive clothes with his recently washed hair drinking two to Gallio's one. They leave with the bottle, Judas a public drunk, swigging as they approach the Temple. Gallio pushes him forward through the crowd gathered at the Temple steps.

One of the minor disciples, Simon or Jude, is promising the resurrection of the dead and the life of the world to come.

Judas objects, which is all Cassis Gallio has asked him to do. He shouts out his own name, fronts up to the idea of the living Jesus. He challenges Philip or Bartholomew to measure the size of their inheritance, and Gallio questions the wisdom of the drink. Judas holds up his wallet, richer than the other eleven disciples put together. He shoves a blind man across the back of a mobility scooter, sings chants for Beitar Jerusalem FC, proves his Jewishness categorically undimmed.

Then he loses interest, because he has more entertaining places to be. Does he? He has things to do. He's hungry, and he can eat what he wants. Can he? He remembers he can. He's hungry and he's thirsty. He doesn't have to stand here stating the obvious. No one has come back from the dead.

One month after the incident at the tomb Cassius Gallio

promises Judith, his wife, that when this is over he'll pay for a weekend in Rome. Just the two of them, for a whole week. The three of them. The baby can see a big-city specialist, they'll book her in. Ten days. A doctor for the baby and a family holiday, the three of them together, plenty of time to see the sights. He promises he'll take two weeks away from the office. He'll leave his phone.

'Cross my heart and hope to die.'

First, though, that body needs to come to light. Gallio writes a provisional report, explaining his strategy and his confidence that a breakthrough is imminent. He is using Judas to provoke the disciples into an act of retaliation, and when they crack he'll pick them up, one by one if necessary. Gallio has to go through Pilate but he attaches a second confidential copy of his report to Valeria. He wants her to feel included, and she'll see that everything's under control. He has behaved erratically, but he's had his reasons and he's on the way back, the same Speculator she once thought was amazing. He clicks Send.

'I've read your report,' Pilate says. There is a squared-off printout on the desk in front of him, old school. 'I'm not signing it off.'

'The disciples can't keep this farce going forever. No one comes back from the dead. We can break them apart, and I've set up a public debate with Judas head-to-head against Peter. Peter has a temper on him. Let's push him over the edge.'

'Can't risk it.' Pilate has aged, or needs more sleep. He seems to have lost weight. He pushes the heels of his hands into his eye sockets, then swipes the air beside his head, as if pestered by an insect. 'Judas will probably warn them in advance. They'll have some stunt ready.'

'Judas barely leaves the safe house. Or he's drunk. He's ours.'

'You increased the reward money. Ordered a new print run of posters.'

'Every disciple has his price. We know that from Judas.'

'*Dead or Alive*, that's what your posters say. *Wanted, Jesus, Dead or Alive*. You fatigue me, Gallio. You acted without my authority. You're supposed to be looking for a body, not a ghost.'

'I'm covering the angles. We're making progress.'

'You haven't found the body, which by now will be in a severely perished condition. It's in everyone's interests to sort this out. I want you to bring me Judas.'

'To the Antonia?'

'In the usual way.'

Pilate squares off the pages of the report, even though they're square. Gallio feels exposed, alone: the next time Judas enters the Antonia he won't be coming out.

'I promised him our protection,' Gallio says. 'He's essential to my strategy.'

'I promised him nothing. Certainly not the most visible table at Canela. He knows more than he's saying. He'll talk.'

'Will he?'

Torture hadn't worked with Jesus: overdo the pain and he'd confess to anything. I'm hurting, Jesus said, but they kept on until he swore he was the son of god, if that's what they wanted. Gallio is convinced he has a better approach: 'Your authorization for Joseph to take away the body is in my report. You may have noticed.'

'Is that a threat? I'll send you to Moldova where you'll dig latrines.'

'Where's Moldova?'

'Exactly. No fucking idea.'

Pilate shouldn't be speaking to him like this, not to a Speculator sent from Rome. 'Why did you let a senior Jew take charge of the body? This is material information.'

Pilate fends again at thin air, but can't brush away an imaginary insect. 'Politics. You wouldn't understand. Do a bad thing, send a man to his death. Then do a good thing, agree to a reasonable request from a senior member of the local priesthood. Keep a balance, keep the peace. Politics.'

'In that case, politically, let me have Judas for one more week.'

Pilate considers the balance, the this-way-and-that. Gallio adds weight to his side of the scales. 'I'll assume full responsibility.'

'One week. But don't let anything happen to him. Find the body in the next week or your career becomes my priority. And not in a good way.'

Day by day Gallio increases the pressure. He trains Judas to debate against Peter, providing every reasonable argument against life after death. Then in the afternoons he picks the weakest of the disciples, at least to his eyes, and follows them. By now it's them or him. The disciples travel in pairs, for security reasons or to keep their stories straight, and in East Jerusalem on a Tuesday afternoon Gallio wastes valuable time watching Bartholomew and Philip from an unmarked Antonia car. They're serving soup to the poor from the back of a van.

Cassius Gallio doesn't crack, he doesn't have a breakdown, despite what the army psychiatrist later claims on oath to the military tribunal. Cassius Gallio does nothing during this period that is irrational or unjustified. On this particular day he may have been guilty of impatience. He is frustrated. He wants to make something happen, and he tells his driver to move fast, brake hard behind the soup van. Doesn't bother with introductions, puts Bartholomew in an armlock and ducks him into the back of the Mercedes.

'Keep your hands off the leather.' Gallio dives in beside him. 'Drive.'

The car climbs the switchback up the Mount of Olives, until they pull in at a Panoramic Viewpoint, bumper to low steel barrier. Below is the walled city of Jerusalem, past and present merged in every stone. An Arab boy calls out from the ramparts. In the car park beside them the bin overflows with burger cartons. Bartholomew ignores the view.

'What do you want from me?'

'I thought you were Jesus.'

'I haven't done anything wrong.'

'My mistake. I can't tell any of you apart.'

Bartholomew is thinner, less solid than the others, but the resemblance is intact. He is thin-boned, breakable, like Jesus with a drug habit. Otherwise Gallio knows him from his file, which is flimsy: he was born in Cana, a Galilean like all of them except Judas. His father is a peasant farmer, but Bartholomew was training as a doctor when Philip recruited him to the cause. Bartholomew gave up his studies, seduced by the glamour of saving the world.

'Tell me about the Jesus appearances. In your professional opinion, as a medical student, would you say they're scientifically feasible?'

Bartholomew shrugs his thin shoulders. 'He appears to us. I wouldn't believe it except I've seen him with my own eyes.'

'Did you see inside the tomb?'

'Peter and John told us it was empty.'

'But you didn't see it? How can you believe it was empty if you didn't actually see it?'

'Jesus is alive. If that's what you're asking.'

Gallio smacks his hand into the headrest. Beside him Bartholomew flinches.

'Fine.' Gallio stares hard at the leather headrest as it pushes back the indent. Then at Bartholomew, at his alarmed brown eyes. 'You know this is not a story to be invented lightly?'

'None of us chose to be involved.'

'You want me to believe that Jesus can reverse the laws of nature? I want you,' and here Cassius Gallio pokes the top of Bartholomew's arm with his finger, to be sure he knows that 'you' means him, 'I want you to think of the consequences, for you, for everyone. I want you, properly, to engage with the responsibility for making up the resurrection of Jesus.'

In Barthomew's version of the world there is a god, but Gallio reminds him that evil has not ceased to exist, not in the last month in Jerusalem. This god of theirs watches over us, and can intervene in human affairs, but Bartholomew and others can be bundled at random into the back of official cars. Soon followed by the fortress and the sweatbox and the rest, with god reliably failing to intervene. Every atrocity, every tragedy, every accident is intended. Imagine the cruelty of this invented god, if that were so.

'Jesus is alive.'

'Sorry, can't be.'

Bartholomew rubs the side of his head. Gallio wants to tug on his beard, shake some sense into him, but in the rear-view mirror Bartholomew is making eye contact with the driver.

'Don't look at him. Look at me.' Gallio pinches Bartholomew's cheeks between his fingers and turns his head, squeezes a little until he can see the inside pink of Bartholomew's mouth. 'Look at me, Bartholomew, look.' Gallio could encourage him to be reasonable with the usual temptations, with girls or boys, with money. The disciples say they're not interested but they are. They must be, like everyone else, like Judas. 'Remember me, Bartholomew. One day I may be able to help you.'

Cassius Gallio watches for a reaction, studies this face so similar to the face of Jesus. Nothing. He pushes the face away. The side of Bartholomew's head cracks against the window. Gallio leans across and opens the door.

'How will I get back?'

'Walk. Like everyone else.'

The next day they murder Judas, and Gallio stops wanting to be the Speculator in charge. Not him, not any more. He doesn't want to have to explain to Pilate, to the CCU, to anyone.

Someone phones in, voice disguised, could have been a man or woman, any age. Cassius Gallio keeps the news to himself and reaches the field within the hour. The rope is lashed low to the trunk of an isolated tree, run up and over a high branch, with a single knot in the loop of the noose. At first glance Judas looks like a suicide.

Gallio is weary but he investigates. The details need attention, and he can't find a note, a decisive indicator if this is genuine. Judas didn't write a suicide note. At the tribunal, no one will be interested in the non-existent note.

He remembers cursing out loud. Fuck fuck you fuck you fuck. Cunt. Cassius Gallio had promised to protect Judas, had such brave plans for him. He slaps at the naked body, then remembers his training. Calm, breathe. Steady the body, flat hands, gentle, bring it to a slow dead stop. He checks the pale skin for abnormalities, marks, signs of a struggle. Breathe. The hands, the ragged tips of the fingers, look for blood beneath the nails. Judas has withered fingernails, self-inflicted by eating himself to death. His body stinks of sweat and alcohol.

At the base of the tree a folded pile of clothes and a wallet. His killers left the money. Clever. Make it look in every way, besides the absence of a note, like suicide. Time goes by while Cassius Gallio doesn't know what to do. He hears the whine of a petrol strimmer on a wind from the city. A plastic bag tumbles across the field, snags on a scrub-thorn. The rope creaks, heats in the midday sun while Judas turns, slowly, like a man afloat. His heavy body swells with gases, inflating with the hours of the day. Judas has been hanging three hours, maybe four, long enough for his skin to tighten and flies to breed on his tongue.

Here is a body, the wrong body. This isn't the body Cassius Gallio had wanted to find.

He might cry. Where are his people, his agents, his officers? Where is his Valeria, and his wife and the child? How did they let this happen to him? His frustration pushes from the inside out and distorts his face. He grimaces, his nostrils flare. He punches the body, and flesh envelops his knuckles. He punches Judas again, a left–right combination, punishment for needing protection. And again, with gritted teeth, for failing to be protected. A flat right to the belly.

The rope snaps.

The body thumps to the ground, the exploded rope whipping over the branch, following Judas down. His ripened belly heaves and here it comes, the bursting asunder, the innards and green-grey muck of Judas Iscariot sliding across stony ground.

A crow lands, cocks its mad-eyed head.

II

James

———

"BEHEADED"

Heat haze on the runway tarmac, petrol-blue C&A windcheater, sunglasses against the Jerusalem white light. Inside the terminal, blocking a long corridor between the gate and Immigration, a pair of officials ask for his papers. Just Cassius Gallio, not anyone else off the flight from Munich. The other passengers flow on past.

Terrorist prevention officers, one man, one woman. Security has tightened globally since the fire in Rome. They examine the name on his passport, check the photo against his face.

'Sunglasses. Take them off.'

His naked face against the photo. They get a good look at Gallio's blue eyes. Yes, he thinks, take your time. You know who

I am, the idiot who let a corpse escape, but much older and with a face creased like a veteran. Of something, of everything.

'Business?'

Gallio puts his glasses back on. 'Holiday.'

They laugh. 'Love to see that particular brochure.'

So they know he's here. Cassius Marcellus Gallio has landed in Jerusalem. All these years later and he's back, following orders, no idea what the Complex Casework Unit want from him. Presumably the Israelis are equally bemused, which explains their charade with the passport. They're watching. Everyone is watching. Now they know he knows they know.

The officials hand back Cassius Gallio's passport and wave him through.

Arrivals. He checks the limo name-cards, but no one has been sent to meet him. A local driver holds up a sign for Mr. Williams, and Gallio could borrow Mr. Williams's car as far as the old city centre. We all look alike to them, he thinks, pale-haired, blue-eyed, and in his case the cold-hearted north. However hard he has tried to assimilate.

Don't do anything foolish. Gallio tells himself he's been out of action a long time, and he's nervous. He's not the man he was, and should proceed with caution. As instructed, he buys a magazine—*Time* in English—Valeria's sense of irony. Then he follows the everyman signs for a disgraced Speculator without a waiting limo to *Exit*, to *Taxis*.

Cassius Gallio wades through the Israel heat, but the first cabbie won't take him, not at lunchtime: he has tomatoes and a flatbread on paper across his thighs. All Gallio needs to know. Next in line is a dented Mazda seven-seater and from the middle seat, through the Perspex screen, Gallio studies the driver's right ear. He makes an effort to imagine this man and his ear in the time of Jesus. Israel may have been brighter then, more optimistic, with a freshness to the lie of life after death. He can't remember, or needs more time to decide.

The driver's right ear has blackheads and a single unplucked hair.

'The Old City. In your own time.'

The driver activates the meter and the radio, rap music in Hebrew. He likes the song and turns it up, then heaves the Mazda in front of a delivery truck and swears forcefully, even though everyone in Jerusalem should now be good. That's what Jesus was supposedly for.

The meet is the Birman restaurant on Dorot Rishonim. Valeria's choice, and Gallio had checked out the place as best he could without resources, on TripAdvisor. *Great food but terrible service*, which didn't surprise him. Secret police love a place with terrible service. No eavesdroppers, and the staff barely notice the customers.

He wonders at the secrecy, and realizes that if he disappears no one will know.

On Jaffa Street Gallio taps his rolled-up *Time* against the screen. He pays, asks for a receipt, and steps out onto a relaid pavement. Car bomb, he thinks, sign of the times. The leaves are back on the trees so the blast happened at least a year ago, but in Jerusalem past and present coexist. Possibly the future too. Cassius reminds himself he doesn't know everything, so be careful, be so very careful.

He stands still for at least a minute, a rube, a tourist. He takes off his jacket and looks for heads in parked cars, for patterns in the traffic, for pedestrians who never quite manage to move along. He folds the jacket into his suitcase.

Nothing suspicious, or that he wouldn't expect to see. His wheeled suitcase is loud and innocent on the relaid pavement behind him, handle in one hand, rolled-up magazine swinging in the other. From half a block away he sees Valeria sitting at an outside table.

For years, ever since the tribunal went against him, Gallio has caught glimpses of women who remind him of Valeria. Valeria turns out not to be one of those women. Since the time of their youth her face has grown angular, stronger than he remembers. She is fuller in the waist, and with her sunglasses and sleeveless top she could pass, like Gallio, for a city-break believer.

He drops the *Time* magazine on an empty table, the signal to abort, and walks straight past.

Cassius Gallio can't arrive in Jerusalem and make the CCU his first point of contact—he has made a vow to be a better man than he was. The magazine stunt buys him perhaps an hour, while Valeria secures the B meet.

Within ten minutes Gallio is at the International School, and the gates are open: home time. Through the arched gateway he can see children of all colours running and shouting. One of these is his, and he ought to feel an emotion beyond the worry that his daughter won't be there, or that he won't recognize her. Then he sees her, he immediately knows which one she is, her movements less supple than the others. She's chasing a boy but one of her legs doesn't straighten. Sadness rises in him, to his throat.

He steps back, an outsider with his suitcase on wheels, a foreign salesman in windcheater and sunglasses, a lost obvious bomber. Fuck. He shouldn't draw attention to himself, or no more than he can help.

Alma has a caliper on one leg, a school rucksack over her shoulder. She's making her lopsided way to the gate, and Gallio imagines Judith will be picking her up. He panics. He retreats into a shop and watches from the shadow of an awning, half hidden by a stack of orange-crates. In her International School sweatshirt Alma looks like the others but the hitch in her step makes her somehow tough, unstoppable. Gallio might be wrong. He's her dad but knows nothing about her. He looks for Judith. Doesn't know much about his wife, either, not any more.

He's trying to force himself into making a decision, some definitive move either forward or back, when Alma looks straight at him. He's convinced she sees the half of him that's visible, though she won't recognize him, not after so long. He steps out from behind the crates, but then a silver Range Rover pulls up between them, the only car that dares park directly in front of the school gates. A man comes round from the driver's side and offers Alma his hand. She ignores his help and climbs in the back. The man picking her up is Baruch.

'Who was following you? We checked. There was nobody there. We made sure. Nothing.'

They're at the B meet—Gallio remembers the procedure—a Lebanese place in the Old City's Armenian quarter. Valeria is inside, at the back with an unobstructed view of the doorway, and Gallio sits beside her on a bench against the whitewashed wall. No eye contact. They watch the door instead, ready for surprises.

'Why all the secrecy?'

'We don't know who's watching.'

'Neither do I,' Gallio says, 'apart from your lot and the cops at the airport. Didn't like the look of the other place. Can't be too careful.'

Cassius Gallio had prepared for this meeting, had visualized it incessantly since her orders had found him in Germany. But now they're sitting beside each other he leaves his sunglasses on. From Valeria he gets: authority, curiosity, no perfume. A streak of silver in her hair.

She gets: he doesn't know what she gets, and wishes he didn't care.

A yellow drape over the entrance shifts in the late afternoon breeze, and at the other occupied table off-duty recruits rate the local women. They go through a range of criteria, count on their fingers, burst out laughing.

'You went to your daughter's school. That wasn't the plan.'

Of course she knew. Cassius Gallio is the junior now, the exile who should expect to be monitored.

'I haven't agreed to any plan.'

Gallio remembers this place, and the only change is a TV in a corner, halfway up the wall. The TV is off, or broken. He wants a beer, an Amstel, and probably a chaser if Valeria can claim expenses. His hands feel unsteady. He puts them under the table and orders a mineral water, gas. The bubbles may convince him there's more to the drink than the water.

'You look older,' she says. Her blonde eyes, turned on him for the first time, have a hard edge. A hard centre too. He wonders why she's putting on a stern face, auditioning for the role of an older woman. Then he realizes she is an older woman. She doesn't need to audition, because ageing has chosen them both.

'Thanks. Moldova, Germany. The ranks.'

'Must have made a big mistake.'

Cassius Gallio leans forward over his water, weight on his elbows, aware of Valeria at his shoulder. He does a thing he does. He taps the pad of each finger precisely against its opposite, pad after pad in sequence, thumb through to pinkie and back, proving his brain has absolute control over his ageing and sober body. He goes through the sequence several times. Finger to finger, back again. Never misses. 'So the judges of the tribunal decided. In their wisdom.'

They pinned him on two indictments: misplacing the corpse of an executed criminal and failing to protect a key witness, even from himself. They recorded Judas as a suicide, and Gallio didn't cover himself in glory by suggesting an alternative: the disciples had murdered Judas to avenge his betrayal of Jesus. Either way, the death of Judas was Cassius Gallio's fault, but he'd been confident of support from Valeria. As a Speculator, even a junior one, she should have insisted on approaching the evidence objectively. Judas was a civic hero who'd outwitted a leading terrorist. He had plenty of money, nothing to fear from the authorities, and he didn't leave a note.

The tribunal duly asked Valeria for her thoughts, and also a character reference for Gallio. She surrendered her notebook, empty apart from random geometric shapes which were of no help to him at all. As for his character she declined to comment, given their personal history.

Now, so many years later, Valeria is not Cassius Gallio's enemy. He won't have enemies, not at his age. She's a former colleague he knows not to trust. She sent him an El Al ticket, economy class from Munich, and he used it because he misses the man he was. He imagines she needs him. Her need makes her vulnerable.

Gallio takes off his sunglasses, some kind of defeat, and rubs at the side of his eye with a thumb.

'Why am I here?'

'I looked you up. The Jerusalem militia recently captured two of the original Jesus followers, which surprised us. We didn't think the disciples would dare come back, but these ones were found in the Lower City. We had the situation under control, and for a while the Israelis kept the two men safe in a lockup.'

'Don't tell me. The disciples of Jesus escaped. They were rescued by angels, and have a story to prove it.'

'You can help us.'

On the day Cassius Gallio had seen the body of Judas split apart, he'd texted Valeria. Later that evening, before they came to arrest him, he'd left a second message pleading with her to intercede on his behalf. He loved her, he said, and regretted not expressing himself earlier and more clearly. She understood the intricacies of Jerusalem, and should tell the tribunal that Judas wasn't the problem; Jesus was the mystery they needed to solve. When they found the body none of the other unknowns would seem so daunting.

Gallio sent the same message twice, to be sure it arrived and because he hadn't known who else to ask. He felt outmaneuvered by the Jesus faction, by Jesus as a personal opponent, so he'd persuaded himself he was special to Valeria beyond the call of duty. Between them they'd see that justice was done.

She hadn't replied, and after a year or two Gallio stopped feeling bitter. Valeria was an ambitious professional who valued her career. For her disloyalty, along with his shattered life, he shifted the blame onto Jesus.

Cassius Gallio applies pressure to the twitch near his eye. He is gentle with himself, pushes in with his thumb and then the heel of his hand. The nerve stops fluttering, it starts again. He gives it a tap. A harder double-tap.

'Cassius?'

'Here.'

'You know these people. You were closer to them than any-one else. We have a job for you.'

'You got married.'

'That's not why I called you in.'

'Someone important. Rome, obviously, for the right calibre of husband. Now you're the woman in charge.'

'You're well informed, but out of date. I'm divorced. I run the Complex Casework Unit, Middle East region. It's not the biggest job out there.'

'Nor the smallest.'

'We're reopening the Jesus case.'

Cassius Gallio fiddles with his sunglasses, uses a stem to spread ice melt into curves on the table. 'Hence the secrecy.' He makes alphabet shapes no one can read, not even himself. 'A bit embarrassing, investigating a dead man.'

'We don't know who was responsible for the fire in Rome. It was big. Thousands dead, damage still being repaired, and the CCU are ruling nothing out, not even provincial cults with a grievance. The Jesus belief is growing, even as far as Rome. We killed their leader.'

Valeria puts her hand on his, and Gallio doesn't know if she's forgiving him or asking for forgiveness. The case should never have been closed, not with so many questions left unanswered.

Cassius Gallio had been right, but being right was overrated. Being smart was safer.

Gallio registers the veins in Valeria's hands, and a grey liver spot. The years they've spent ignoring Jesus have aged them both, but she should have backed him at the time. He won't repeat his mistake, trusting her, projecting a life they never had, and he checks his heart and is glad he feels nothing. Or very little. He is immune to her so he pulls his hand away, makes the first misjudgement of his comeback.

'Why now? Why me?'

'We want you to identify a body.'

In camps and barracks beyond the soft reach of civilization, sweating or freezing, Cassius Gallio had tried to forget. The Jesus case was unlike any other he had handled. As was the Lazarus case, only weeks before it, but after the tribunal he had no incentive to unravel these enigmas.

Jesus stopped being his problem, and Gallio busied himself with the tedious life of common soldiering. Across the Empire, moving with his legion, he helped persuade the benighted and barbarian of the need for elected assemblies and stable leadership.

He tried not to feel nostalgic for a genuine interest in what he was doing. He followed orders, and acted as if the civilizing process was the inevitable end of history. The world could not go backward, not now. Those who swore by their gods would be persuaded that an imaginary friend was a less reliable leadership option than an educated governing class. A celestial city should not shine more brightly than a city built with planning controls over centuries. There was an order to the universe, and the first would be first. To suggest otherwise was to encourage false hopes, because observably the last will not be first. Not all of them. On the borders of civilization, wherever Gallio's legion was posted next, the last were poor and malnourished and oppressed. They were firmly last, and none of the local superstitions had ever changed that fact.

Yet still at night he lay awake, letting the darkness do its worst. How had the disciples vanished the body of Jesus? From Tripoli to Colchis he collected variations on a theme—mineshafts, quicklime, the furnace. None of the tested methods for disappearing a body applied to Jerusalem, not in this particular case. Gallio had investigated every possibility, and kept returning to a story his stepfather used to tell from the birth of civilization, or soon after.

Romulus, the founder of Rome, enters an underground room in the Forum. He is old, his pulse weak, his service to the city complete. His senators in their purple-striped togas follow him into the room, which has no windows and only one door. What follows is a classic sealed room mystery: Romulus is never seen again.

He vanishes.

'So then.' His stepfather liked to unstrap his sword and rest it across the arm of his chair. 'Tell me what happened. Work out the crime, and how they made him disappear.'

In popular legend Romulus had rejoined the gods. A story spread that instead of dying Romulus had ascended to heaven, which explained his missing body. This was not the answer Cassius Gallio's stepfather wanted. When Gallio first suggested the ascension of Romulus as a solution, his stepfather had unsheathed his sword and whacked him across the thighs.

Eventually Gallio's stepfather spelled out the lesson he

wanted the boy to learn: a rational explanation is available. Romulus was murdered by the senators. Of course he was. Always suspect those closest to the victim.

The senators had closed the door and stabbed old Romulus in silence, alerting none of the Forum's hyper-alert slaves. Then they knelt to dissect the body. Each senator concealed a small section of flesh or bone beneath his toga, and they carried Romulus away from the sealed room in pieces. The cuts of meat they dispersed through the city, flushed into cisterns or tossed to scavenging dogs. No trace of Romulus was ever found.

True story.

'We thought the Israelis were going to finish off the cult on our behalf. They made a decent start.'

Valeria walks quickly, wearing trainers with her skirt and sleeveless top, a tourist like any other. She has her familiar fast stride, and Cassius Gallio admires the vigour that comes from a lifetime of civil service health insurance and not making mistakes.

She stops and points out a street where the locals stoned a Jesus follower to death, a short while after Gallio's disgrace. An Israeli agent called Saul set up the hit to showcase his talents, but the street has reverted to what it was and always will be: shopfronts filled with toiletries and battery-powered fans. Gallio checks they're not being followed. Jerusalem puts him on edge.

'Ruthless, ambitious, highly capable. We liked the look of him. Saul was the kind of driven local agent who didn't need our help.'

Valeria walks on. Gallio lets her go, watches her hips sway

left and right, her buttocks, then catches up. 'Saul targeted Peter in Damascus,' she says. 'A trained international agent against a lake fisherman in a major world city. Should have been a mismatch.'

'Peter turned him. Saul became one of them.'

'Well done. I'm glad not everything passed you by, but the truth is we didn't have a back-up plan. We kept to our civilized policy of not intervening in religious affairs. Saul was converted, but even then we expected the Jesus cult to fold.'

'But it didn't. It hasn't.'

'It hasn't followed the usual pattern of Judaean self-hatred and implosion, no. Every year the number of Jesus believers increases, and across a wider geographical spread. We underestimated them.'

'You don't say.'

The disciples of Jesus had negated a crucifixion and rigged a burial. They could break in and out of a sealed and guarded tomb, leaving no trace, and managed to hide a body in a city under martial law. Simple upcountry peasants? Cassius Gallio didn't think so.

'They could organize a fire,' he says.

'Possibly. What's certain is the disciples have a history. Whatever they've become will depend on what happened in the past. We need people who were there at the beginning and who appreciate the specific difficulties.'

They walk into a cavalry exercise ground, separated from the housing scheme behind it by a high link fence. On the far side of the fence, the public side, about fifteen to twenty gawpers—including children, an Asian family—cling to each other and cry out. Yellow crime-scene tape flutters across the door of a stable, the centre stall in a block of five.

Gallio is first to duck under the tape. Old habits.

Inside, a free-standing aluminum spotlamp heats up the base note of rotting straw and horseshit. Two objects on the ground. The first looks like a hessian sack, but closer up the lump is beige clothing silted with blood. Gallio holds his hand across his nose. Get closer, right up close, because closeness comes with the job, and a nub of tendon glistens in the half-light, where the head should be. Blackflies rise from the severed neck, settle on the top of the spine.

Above the lamp, Gallio notices, looking away and up, and further up, anywhere but down, afternoon sunshine pierces the knotholes in the roof slats, light coming through in pinpoint beams. He looks back down. The second object is the head. Valeria finds a riding crop on a nail in the wall. She asks Gallio for a handkerchief. She takes his handkerchief and uses it to handle the whip, which she unhooks and pokes at the severed head. It lies stubbornly on one side on a patch of straw. She levers the head upright, it pauses, seems for a moment to be the head of Jesus (long brown hair, beard) then topples back onto a blood-caked ear.

'You were there. You saw the twelve of them together. Is this Jesus?'

In Benghazi, staring at a pathway of moonlight across the water of the bay, Gallio had allowed the killers of Romulus a change of clothing and rolls of plastic bags. He could speculate about their actions but couldn't unmake the world he knew: with minor improvements their murderous scheme looked plausible. The senators would need odorless floor-cleaning materials, concealable in a toga. He gave them some water, or sand. A brush, a mop.

49

Gallio spent night after night picturing eleven Galileans in a sealed tomb lit by flickering lamp-flames. Busy, each and every one of them, as they carved away flesh from the bones of Jesus. The disciples sawed through ligaments and tendons, then broke the skeleton, bone by bone. The tomb belonged to Joseph of Arimathea, private property, and he could have stored cleavers and a hacksaw in advance, along with other useful supplies: fresh clothing, rolls of plastic bags, cleaning materials (water, sand, brush, mop). On an earlier visit Joseph could have left a commercial pestle and mortar. The disciples, most of them with a background in manual labour, silently grind the skull of Jesus into powder, non-stop in shifts for seventy-two hours. Three days and the labour of eleven men to annihilate a human body.

These were the same men who hanged Judas and made it look like suicide. The disciples could have made Jesus disappear, and Gallio knows there are people who can do such things to others they once fully loved. He reads the newspapers. He keeps up to date with human atrocity.

Logistically, eleven adults (one with basic medical training) could have dismantled the body of Jesus in three days. The disciples were absent from the crucifixion, but not because they were scared of being arrested. While the authorities were distracted by the death of Jesus the disciples hid inside the tomb. When Jesus was carried in they were already concealed inside, waiting with their knives and buckets, their plastic aprons and gloves.

The tomb was sealed, which would have muffled any noise, and the soldiers on watch heard nothing. To be fair, they weren't making an effort to listen, even though Gallio had ordered them to guard the dead man as if alive. He used those exact words and signed the order himself, and at the military tribunal his signature was used against him. 'Unhinged,' they said, because dead men don't need a guard. 'Not in his right mind,' because tombs remain closed without a seal.

Night after night, as the months and years of his exile passed, Cassius Gallio would lie awake denying the resurrection. Life after death meant the end of the world as he knew it, but if Jesus were a fraud and never actually died then his later appearances weren't the end of the world.

Gallio would put his head beneath his army-issue blanket and concentrate on his breathing. In, out. Feel the biological processes of being alive, oxygen in his lungs, blood in his veins and his brain. Make the bad supernatural thoughts go away.

He regretted not staying at the burial site, in person, for all three days. But at the time he'd made his point and he was the winner: Jesus was dead. The Lazarus story became instantly irrelevant, and Gallio worried that Valeria would despise him for watching a corpse so closely. He didn't want to appear tentative about life after death, and by killing Jesus he had solved that problem. Whatever the story with Lazarus, Jesus now was dead.

In any case, he couldn't have known the disciples were planning a breakout on the Sunday. How long should he have stayed? A week, a month, until the end of time? Gallio would still be there now, and no one would understand why, not even the army psychiatrists.

Cassius Gallio saw his first statue of a disciple on a transit through Belgium: a life-size piece in white marble, Simon leaning casually on a two-handled saw outside the Church of our Lady in Bruges. On the same trip he was surprised by a painted Jude in a roadside shrine near Avignon.

The cult was growing, and Cassius sometimes felt nostalgic for Jerusalem and his one big idea. He'd wanted to control the Jesus movement by setting up Lazarus as a client Messiah. Together he and Lazarus, taking the place of Jesus, would have preached a god of compromise amenable to the values of civilization. Pay taxes, respect the rule of law, be reasonable.

His plan hadn't worked, which left the disciples with their unreasonable lies that encouraged the poor and feckless. Cassius Gallio was occasionally angry, but the military life inhibited sustained feeling. Thankfully. His legion was posted east, where he supervised building works and assembled collections of coins. For months on end he'd forget to wonder what the story of Jesus could mean, obsessed with blisters and his next appointment with the booze. He consciously refused to look for Jesus, in the bottle and once in the arms of a shop girl. And soon after that, Gallio didn't look for Jesus in the waiting room of a sexual health clinic. He didn't look for him and he wasn't there.

While a doctor swabbed him and asked how much he drank, Gallio did think briefly about Jesus and how to get his life back on track. He wasn't without virtue: he refused to pay for sex and every month his wages were deducted at source and half sent to his wife and child in Jerusalem. Not that he had much choice. He was a grunt in the civilized army from the civilized world, and obligations were expected to be honored.

If he was ever homesick, and he thinks he sometimes was, it wasn't a sickness for Judith and Alma or for any of the homes he could remember. He longed for a kind of unnamed absence, with a tearfulness he found unsettling. Sentiment, self-pity: he wiped his eyes and dismissed these useless emotions that brought him no relief. He was not the person he'd wanted to be. The world was not decipherable as promised, with a reason for everything if only he could see what it was.

An unamused nurse burned off his genital warts, smoke rebounding from the ceiling. Gallio remembered Valeria, but whatever his problem Valeria wasn't the solution, and antibiotics with beer and loneliness felt like a punishment that had finally arrived. Only he didn't believe in cosmic justice, so he preferred not to think at all.

'How can you tell it isn't Jesus?'

'I just know.'

The dismembered head belongs to a disciple, though Cassius Gallio can't say for sure which one. He has been a long time away, and the eleven survivors always looked similar to him: they look like Jesus. Ten. Judas gone, now this one too. Ten survivors left, and anyway Jesus is dead. Why had Valeria asked if the dead man in the stable was Jesus?

Observation, reason. The dark horseshit in the stable contains pieces of yellow straw. No, beyond that. The shit is lightly cracked, days old.

'How could it be Jesus when Jesus is dead?'

'You tell me. I asked the Israelis to wait for our experts, meaning you. As the representative of a global power I made an official recommendation to a tiny security service. Hopeless. They couldn't follow a simple instruction.'

'Who couldn't?'

'Baruch. Not an easy man, but on their side he deals with everything Jesus. Always has.'

Gallio knows who Baruch is. He tried to kill Lazarus after the incomprehensible events at Bethany, when Lazarus appeared to come back to life. He killed the son of the widow of Nain, a teenage boy who Jesus also allegedly resurrected. A military patrol found the boy in a wood outside his pathetic little village, his throat cut from ear to ear. That's Baruch, who picked Cassius Gallio's daughter up from school. The involvement of Baruch feels like further punishment, but Gallio doesn't know for what.

'I think this head belongs to a James.'

Gallio squats down and looks closely at the half a dead face he can see. Memories flood back, and he warms to the idea of becoming an expert, of knowing what few other people can know. 'I'm fairly sure. Who was the other one they captured?'

'They say it was Peter. Unconfirmed. He escaped.'

James and Peter, but Valeria has let herself speculate that one of the captives was Jesus. This is the more interesting information that Gallio now has in his possession. If the CCU are prepared to reconsider, and conclude that Jesus may be alive, it would explain their decision to reopen the case.

Some kind of commotion starts up outside, which gives Cassius Gallio an excuse to stop speculating and stoop under the tape and out into the fresher air. The sun is hot and the flies loud. A woman in a POLICE anti-stab jacket is photographing faces through the fence. Beside her, pointing out anyone she misses, is an unshaven man in a dark suit. He turns round, open-neck white shirt, sees Cassius Gallio and taps the photographer's shoulder. Gallio watches the zoom lengthen as she takes her shot. Baruch, hands on hips like the man in charge, laughs at his funny joke.

Baruch is Gallio's age, a little older, but he moves better. He shoots his cuffs and dances over, soft leather shoes avoiding small rocks and the obvious piles of horse dung.

'Cassius Gallio! You should have phoned from the airport! We'd have sent a car.'

They're about the same height. Baruch offers his hand at a slight downward angle. To take it, Gallio would have to expose his palm like a white belly, like a dog rolling over. He offers his hand at the same angle, palm facing down. Their fingers barely touch.

'Yet somehow you knew I was here.'

'Boys,' Valeria says. She swishes the riding crop at a couple of flies.

'Congratulations on killing an unarmed disciple,' Gallio says. 'Keeping yourself busy, I see.'

'Not guilty. I'm helping to clean up the mess, and making sure the press stay away. Let the press in on something like this and it's pictures, words and before you know it they've written the opera and everyone's crying. Completely misrepresent the facts.'

'Try me with the facts.'

Baruch smiles. 'My men were overenthusiastic, which isn't the end of the world. And no need to look so miserable—ten more where this one came from. The disciples of Jesus come to Jerusalem at their own risk. The founder of their cult is a convicted terrorist, so what kind of welcome do they expect?'

Baruch bends under the police tape and Gallio follows him into the stable. Police work develops muscular thighs.

'Say hello to James,' Baruch says, poking the head upright with the toe of his shoe. This time it doesn't fall over. 'The other one was Peter.'

Gallio can't see why Baruch would lie about this, though clearly Valeria doesn't trust him. She'd wanted to check with an expert from her own side, so she called in Cassius Gallio even after the prisoner was dead. Gallio had been in Jerusalem with Jesus, and there aren't many of the original players left.

'Where's Peter now? Is he in the city?'

'Probably,' Baruch says. 'We lost him, but it's only a matter of time.'

A chain of errors, but each link toward the death of James has its own logic. Baruch's excitable jailers had the bright idea of taunting the captured disciples with a salami. An Italian salami, imported from Milan, and clearly labelled as a percent pork product. James ate several slices with apparent pleasure, because he was hungry. His captors decided to take offence and felt compelled, on behalf of their god, to be appalled at James for eating an unclean food.

James refused to repent. The argument escalated, to the point where James eating the salami was a contemptuous attack on Jewish law in general and the beliefs of their parents in particular. Their mothers. James was laughing at how their beloved mothers had brought them up. He was spitting in the faces of innocent women. He was striking them to the ground.

Before the salami, neither of the disciples had been questioned in a methodical way. No demands were made: Tell us the truth about Jesus and we'll let you live. Tell us where the body is buried and we'll feed you. These were the same questions Cassius Gallio had once asked of Judas, but the Israelis had squandered an opportunity to acquire significant new information. A primary Jesus witness was dead and another had been allowed to escape.

'You've forgotten how the world turns,' Baruch says. 'Especially here in Jerusalem. Plan ahead if you like, but accidents will happen.'

Gallio remembers Baruch at Alma's school, offering to hand

his daughter into the Range Rover. He's had a big day for remembering how the world turns.

'The guards dragged James onto the exercise ground,' Baruch says. 'They haven't seen a beheading for months, and none of them wanted to miss the action. While they enjoyed the spectacle Peter walked away.'

'He walked away.'

Cassius Gallio requests an interview with the two militiamen responsible for the salami and hastening the execution. One of them is short, the other tall and they haven't washed in a week. But what's done is done, and for Gallio these men represent an opportunity. He treats them like intelligent human beings.

'How did the two disciples behave, while you had them locked up? I want to hear what you made of them. As people, what were they like?'

The guards look at each other. 'Not very funny.'

The shorter one nods, crushes his hands into his armpits. 'Neither of them had much of a sense of humour. No real banter.'

'Two older brothers in a room,' the tall one says, pleased with his observation. He excavates an ear with his little finger, assesses the gunge that comes out. 'Serious types.'

'Did you hear specific conversations?'

'Death.' The guards nod at each other, agreed. 'The Galileans talked about death, their favourite subject. Both of them said they were happy to die, but neither wanted to go first.'

'Naturally.' Baruch straightens the crease in his trouser, insists on being present at the interview, but he's leaning against a wall and he's bored. 'Who in their right mind would want to die first?'

'They both did. It was weird. Both the disciples volunteered. They argued about it.'

'You said the opposite, that neither of them wanted to go first.'

'That's how it started. They both wanted to go first, which meant going first was unkind to the other, because that's what the other one wanted.'

'So it was kinder to go second,' the taller one says, scratching his head. He leaves the residue from his ear in his hair. 'They both wanted to die after the other. Out of kindness.'

They look puzzled. 'If that makes sense.'

'Which ends up being completely normal,' Cassius Gallio says. 'I'd want to go second too, if it were me.'

Their brains continue to grind as Baruch hovers behind them. 'Who actually did the deed, took his head off?'

The men don't want to say, in case there's a punishment. But they do want to say, in case there's a reward. Gallio pities them their inner struggle so he speaks up—with Baruch in the room he can save them from a fatal mistake. 'If you remember anything else, you let us know.'

'Via the usual channels,' Baruch adds.

Cassius Gallio yawns. 'Jet lag. I'm sure you have an Attempt To Locate out for Peter. I'm going back to the hotel. This isn't my case.'

'I know,' Baruch says. 'I let you talk to the guards as a favour, for old times' sake. Reckon they're telling the truth?'

'No idea. I don't have the clearance to risk an opinion.' A thin-shouldered man in a blue tracksuit follows Cassius Gallio through Jerusalem, settles himself in the hotel lobby while Gallio checks in and drops his bag with the concierge. Gallio takes the lift to his floor, walks past his room, finds the stairwell and leaves through the basement parking garage.

Behind, in front, left, right. Gallio looks up, sometimes down, making sure he's alone. Baruch knew Gallio had arrived at the airport, and Valeria would have known that too. Yet still they went through the routines for a secret meetup. She must be worried that someone, other than Baruch and his people, is watching. Whoever it is, they must be good.

Gallio takes random lefts and rights through the evening city, and he's amazed at the number of tourists. Jerusalem wasn't like this in the old days, and without making a decision he ends up not at his apartment, where Judith and Alma still live, but at another street he recognizes. It has a new name, the Via Dolorosa. Cassius Gallio follows in Jesus's footsteps, like so many others, and tries to get a feel for what once happened here. Much has changed, yet somehow the place is the same. An atmosphere, an indent. No event is ever entirely lost.

At Golgotha, where the execution itself took place, little of the original site remains. Since Gallio was last here the developers have moved in—construction work and safety barriers erasing what he remembers as a crime scene. The tourist board are building some kind of memorial, and a falafel stall sells canned drinks to a queue of visitors when they're not being pestered by beggars.

For Gallio's purposes, and Valeria has reminded Cassius Gallio of his purpose in life, any usable evidence from the scene has long been removed or corrupted. He briefly wonders who made it their business to tidy the truth away, though he can understand how that happened. Easier to pretend that nothing out of the ordinary took place here, at least before the tourists started insisting that it did. And now they keep on coming, even without any evidence. The new Golgotha is teeming with souvenir hunters, women, believers, unbelievers. There's a handcart selling crucifixes, authentic rubble, icons.

Cassius Gallio thinks he sees Peter.

A beard, beige clothing, long brown hair. If the man is Peter, he immediately has luck on his side. A group of teenage boys blocks Cassius Gallio. They jostle him, wanting to know if he's Inglese or Arab. He doesn't know which answer is safest, so he guesses Arab, and they throw a Coke bottle at his head.

By the time Gallio scatters them, Peter the disciple has gone.

Valeria drinks mint tea from a glass cup that she replaces with care on a glass saucer. At this time of the evening Cassius Gallio fancies a vodka and tonic, a blister pack of ephedrine sulphate, showgirls. Not to touch, because he'd expect to be punished, but nothing wrong with looking. He orders the same tea as Valeria, giving her nothing of himself, not even his menu preferences. I'll have what she's having. Easy on the mint.

They drink tea on the terrace of the American Colony Hotel, where Allenby and Blair take rooms whenever they're mediating the region. Both are on holiday. The two men are famous for being on holiday, leaving the region forever unmediated. A diplomat's son swims laps in the pool. He has a hard and fast body, worth watching.

'No trace of Peter,' Valeria says. 'Nothing apart from your possible sighting at Golgotha. They're smart.'

'Always were. I told you that years ago. Nobody listened.'

'We're listening now.' Valeria is making an effort: five-star hotel, terrace, drinks on the section tab. 'The case has been passed to Complex Casework mainly because the cult survives and is growing. No one understands why. We've gone over the events that led to your tribunal, and considering the various loose ends we've decided to reopen the investigation. I've recommended your involvement.'

'You have other Speculators. Most of them undemoted and undisgraced.'

'No one with experience is volunteering to investigate provincial cults.'

'Ah, I see. What do you want from me, apart from assuming I'm available and desperate to get back in?'

Valeria watches the long-armed backstroke of the boy in the pool, examines her nails, acts like someone who could change her mind. 'I wouldn't ask you to do this if I didn't think you were capable. I fished out the psychiatric assessment from the tribunal.'

'Get to the point.'

'If it's any consolation, I don't think you're unstable. Didn't think it at the time and don't now. We all missed something, way back then. Let's not make the same mistakes again.'

'Please tell me what you want. In plain language.'

'We can offer you a viaticum. Double pay for every day on the road. In euros.'

'I want my rank back, the right to call myself a Speculator.'

'It's not the title that counts, but the state of mind. This is a tiny job in an obscure region.'

'So why should I take it?'

'The money and a fresh start. I'm guessing that's enough. That and your pride, which had you running for the plane in Munich.'

She knows him too well. Gallio feels the long waste of sleepless nights under army blankets, sifting through memories for the piece he missed, the clue as to how they tricked him. Cassius Gallio is convinced he'd have found the answer, if only Judas hadn't been killed. The disciples had cut off his enquiry just as he was getting close.

'You were a witness,' Valeria says. 'You saw the death of Jesus, and how the disciples acted after the event. We've respected official policy, tolerated this cult, waited for their beliefs to fade. Except in this instance their beliefs aren't fading. Something strange is going on, and I've decided that bringing you back is worth the risk to my reputation. You were there. That counts for something, and I'm giving you a chance to clear your name.'

'I have nothing to prove.'

'I think you do, Cassius. You were publicly humiliated. Hard for anyone, let alone a Speculator. You did your work but reason did not triumph, which is what in training they taught us would happen. But reason will triumph, in the long run. That's why we rule the world and in Israel they have goats.'

'Do I get a team? I'll need researchers, analysts, forensics. Maybe some feet on the ground.'

'You'll work with Baruch. Politics. They're backward but we need to keep them sweet, for the sake of stability. Also the Israelis are as keen to wrap this up as we are.'

Cassius Gallio bites the skin at the side of his thumbnail, watches the swimmer splash back and forth. Backstroke, the full twenty-five meters, tumble turn, crawl. Gallio peels off a thumbnail with his teeth, spits it from his lower lip. It sticks. He blows it off.

'Baruch is a contract killer. A nobody.'

'We all used to be something. You'll need to control him, but if there's trouble you're deniable. It's important you understand that, Cassius. As far as our reasonable and non-believing superiors are concerned, this operation does not exist.'

'So where am I expected to start?'

Valeria looks away. This mission is rotten with absurdities that stick in her throat, but they have to start somewhere.

'I've seen the pictorial evidence of the crucifixion, every angle, the different styles,' she says. 'I know how dead Jesus looks in the images, but I want you to search for him as if he's alive. You're to find out if Jesus survived, if somewhere out there he's among us.'

III

Jude

———

"SHOT WITH ARROWS"

Baruch doesn't like the car. Cassius Gallio insists on following Valeria's briefing, to the letter, which means they stay inconspicuous. At the Hertz concession he turns down models that proclaim either the wonder or the futility of existence. He needs the camouflage of the middle ground, where people learn to cope, less splendid than a 3-liter BMW 6 Series but not as miserable as an entry-level Chevy Aveo.

They end up driving north out of Jerusalem in a family class Toyota Corolla. Gallio respects the speed limit and keeps his distance from the vehicle in front. He slows for camels, for carts pulled by donkeys. Mirror, signal, maneuver.

'For fuck's sake,' Baruch says, one foot on the dash. He can't even smoke, because those days are gone. 'You know, Cassius, happy as I am to be working with you again, I'm surprised Valeria called you back.'

Baruch blows his nose, disposes of the tissue out of the open window. Checks the palms of his hands. 'I'm thinking maybe it wasn't only your soldiers who were under suspicion. I mean if I'm looking for a reasonable explanation for how the body left the tomb, after all this time. If Jesus is alive, someone patched him up and let him out. You were the man in charge.'

'I was cleared at the tribunal.'

'Of that particular act. Not of much else. The sentencing document is a classic, and I like the paragraph that declares you unstable and incompetent. I believe those are the words they used.' Cassius Gallio keeps his eyes on the road. 'Incompetent. Strong stuff.'

'But not guilty of receiving illegitimate payments to allow the removal of the body. The tribunal had no evidence of that, no witnesses.'

'They fired you once, they could do it again. That must worry you. Dereliction of Duty. Professional Negligence. And one other, I think, yes, I remember now, suspended Gross Misconduct for sexual harassment of a junior colleague. I looked up the charge sheet.'

'It wasn't harassment. Nothing happened.'

Baruch is joshing, and he is not. Gallio can't blame him, because anyone who wanted to steal the body would think first of corrupting the senior officer. That would be a logical approach to take, so the question needs to be asked.

'All we know for sure is the body was gone,' Gallio says. 'Why are you picking my daughter up from school?'

Baruch flips his foot off the dash, and as the city thins he gazes at the street-side storefronts. Driving out the slow way, dentists and driving schools give way to car dealerships and furniture outlets.

'Where'd you hide the money, Cassius?'

'How's my wife? Been seeing her long?'

'Intelligent man like you. Offshore, I guess. Your family—I mean the wife and child you abandoned—they could use some extra income.'

'I never intended to abandon them. First, I don't have money because no one bribed me. Second, if I'd let the disciples steal the body I'd know too much. I could undermine their resurrection story at any time, and they'd shut me up like they shut up Judas.'

Baruch turns in his seat, sizes up Cassius Gallio as if for a coffin. 'Does that prospect frighten you?'

'No, because I don't know too much.'

'They didn't kill Judas. Suicide. Investigated thoroughly, with official stamps on the verdict. You were getting a lot wrong back then, weren't you, Cassius? I've heard the details from Judith, your ex-wife. You were wrong at work and wrong at home. Someone had to repair the damage and it wasn't going to be you.'

'It could have been me, except they sent me to fucking Moldova.'

'You're deluded. Says so in the tribunal report. Stubborn, isolated, unreasonable, prone to fantasy. You could no longer function professionally, not even at procedural tasks like locating a corpse. Or keeping a marriage alive. She'd never take you back now, not after what you did. And poor little Alma with her leg, she's grateful for a real-life father figure.'

Gallio stamps on the accelerator. Not much happens, the car's a Toyota Corolla. He backs off, calms down. His family is someone else's business, and he can hide in the here and now, in the mission that Valeria has given him. He's driving to Beirut, to find a man who looks like Jesus.

At first, after hearing Valeria's proposal, Cassius Gallio had said no. Valeria didn't accept his decision, told him he should think it over.

'No, really no. Jesus is dead. I'm not going to look for him.'

'Sleep on it. I think you'll take this on, because what else would you be doing?'

Barracks near Stuttgart, barbarians at the gates, a single bunk, long sleepless nights and a routine designed to use up the time before he dies. At best, Cassius Gallio will look for his socks in the morning. He will look for the cheapest item on the canteen menu, and for an almost entertaining program on evening TV. Otherwise he'll look for nothing.

In Jerusalem, with or without his rank as Speculator, Valeria was offering him a goose chase he could drag out for months. Jesus was dead. He was killed years ago, and the trail was cold. If Valeria and the CCU had decided to speculate otherwise, then truly this was a complex case. One they wanted to pursue, and if so then who was Cassius Gallio to object?

'We'll give you a desk in the Antonia,' Valeria said. 'Security clearance for the files and archives. That's the most we can offer. We're going on a hunch as it is.'

The next day Cassius Gallio sat at his allocated computer on an upper floor of the Antonia Fortress, swinging in a swivel chair pinched from Human Resources. It felt good to be back, and the open-plan Antonia operations room was in a familiar state of distress. Desks pushed together, files everywhere, computer screens glowing the colour of bad rice. Someone had polished their football boots and left them in a corner, stuffed with newspaper, on a plastic bag from Hamashbir.

For the first hour or so Gallio watched the junior intelligence officers of an occupying army, who kept themselves busy by sifting standard police reports for incidents of obscure significance. Stolen official cars, ABH against a minor civil servant, graffiti at the TV station. Usually these crimes were not significant, not even obscurely so. The youngsters in the office avoided Gallio because he was attached to the CCU. Also because his sole and slightly shameful responsibility was to hunt a man who was dead. For the second hour he mulled over his mission, steepled his fingers to his chin, swivelled his chair this way and that.

The story was baffling, from beginning to end, but Gallio was in no special hurry to return to barracks. He decided on an approach: not optimistic but conscientious. Either he would solve the Jesus mystery or he would not, and when he eventually set to work he started with the events the disciples claimed to have seen: Jesus, so they said, had risen into a cloud above the Mount of Olives. Gallio found this hard to believe. He'd kept the disciples under surveillance, yet they claimed to have seen this ascension with their own eyes, the same eyes that once witnessed Jesus walking on water.

People passed by Gallio's desk. He looked busy, wrote himself a memo: *Miracles/hallucinations. Galilee connection? Check lake for cadmium/mercury trace. Industrial pollution/poisoning? Would explain a lot.*

He found a report Valeria had commissioned in the previous month. On the relevant dates there had been no heavy industry operational near Lake Galilee, no processes at work to leak toxins into the water supply.

Cassius Gallio binned his memo and started again from the only fact they knew for certain: someone was dead. Between then and now Gallio had seen hundreds of pictures of Jesus on the cross, because he was interested and provincial museums and churches were full of them. Paintings, carvings, sculptures. No other death in history had been so exhaustively recorded. Jesus was dead.

At the same time, and Gallio finally confronted the truth of this, he had never stopped experimenting with the idea that Jesus had survived. Jesus only appeared to be dead on the cross, and had entered some kind of trance. Gallio's soldiers (what happened to that sergeant?) neglected to break the bones in Jesus's legs, meaning that severe physical trauma was confined to feet and hands, giving him a shot at survival.

Gallio called up files from the archive and stacked them beside his desk. He went through the dossiers one by one, relived the familiar story. From the newer material he learned that Valeria had investigated lung capacity. Jesus had form as a public speaker, and for three years he projected his voice to large crowds in open-air spaces without amplification. If orators developed abnormal lung efficiency, then Jesus's oversized lungs might have delayed asphyxiation, a common cause of death when chest muscles and lungs were hyper-expanded. Even then, considering his other injuries, Gallio didn't see how Jesus could have survived for more than a few weeks afterward. A month at the outside, with expert medical attention.

There was always another file to open. Gallio respected the assignment, such as it was. He treated Jesus as a missing person and pulled relevant information from Valeria's Complex Casework networks. He reviewed every theory. The rational approach was to keep an open mind until the evidence convinced one way or another, and the Speculator protocols came back to Gallio like riding a bike. He contacted Israeli banks and had them search for an account in the name of Jesus of Nazareth. He was meticulous, accessing the benefits register to see if any likely Jesus was claiming, and if so how he collected his money. Neither initiative generated a result.

Cassius Gallio swung on his chair, this way, that way. He chewed the end of his propelling pencil. Why not? If you've lost something, as his stepfather liked to say, look again in the obvious place. He spent a morning checking police and hospital records for unidentified bodies. He respected the assignment but he was a realist. If Jesus didn't die on the cross he might have died since, and the alleged resurrection hadn't put a stop to violent assaults in Jerusalem, nor vagrants dying alone. The worst of life continued, here and now as everywhere and always, and the official records contained a separate category for unclaimed corpses.

Some of the dead bodies, not many, had mutilated fingers where prints had been removed by sanding or slicing. Gang crimes, scores settled and souls lost. Not one of the unclaimed corpses had extremity damage compatible with crucifixion. And even if a likely candidate did emerge, Gallio didn't have a DNA profile to confirm the match with Jesus.

The burial clothes, those left behind at the tomb, had long gone missing. There were no body fluids to sequence or physical remains to analyze. The cross, pretty much any remnant of it, would provide blood spots for a DNA sample, but no one could locate the cross. Valeria had tracked down fragments across the ancient world, but the provenance was never certain. And in any case, so many hands had touched these suspect relics that the DNA was unusable. The contemporary evidence was lost.

Gallio looked again in an obvious place: the family. Valeria had labelled a dossier 'Nazareth,' and repeated searches of the house where Jesus grew up were routinely logged in the weeks after his body vanished. Gallio now sees from photocopies that he signed the original warrants himself, back in the day, but Valeria had raided the house more recently. Empty, mother gone, father long dead, neighbours adamant that Joseph and Mary had seemed a normal couple who kept themselves to themselves. Yes, they remembered Jesus. Always had time for everyone.

None of these enquiries revealed a hidden twin who could have died in his place. Valeria made sure her people asked, checking back through school yearbooks and birth certificates. No secret twin or brother of about the same age. Only Jesus, from Nazareth, and his circle of Galilean friends.

His friends. The original twelve disciples, with the violent exceptions of Judas and James, were alive. No reported deaths from natural causes, as yet, but not one of the disciples was resident in Israel. The beheading of James was unlikely to tempt them home.

Gallio thought some more about the disciples, and how they looked so similar. He dug out the tape of the crucifixion and watched it again, and again. He stayed in the office after everyone had left, and gradually he remembered how to speculate. Cassius Gallio felt meaningful for the first time in years, and reacquainted himself with his youthful desire for glory, like a lost friend he was surprised to recognize.

Then he suppressed his ambition as best he could. There was no glorious return to Rome in this, consuls rising to acclaim him. The CCU did not call for its finest minds to track down a missing Jewish mystic who was anyway probably dead. Valeria had assigned the case to a washed-up ex-Speculator. Cassius Gallio knew that, but this was also his second chance. He knew that too.

Find Jesus and take him alive. Parade him in a cage before a glut of academicians who will explain his escape from the tomb. Either that or prove once and for all that Jesus is dead. The most ridiculous illusion in history will unravel, for the entertainment of the rational classes.

Cassius Gallio watched the tapes, remembered his vocation, and a possible solution began to emerge.

'There's more to life than Jesus.'

Baruch is a restless passenger. The road climbs through the glitter of sunlit olive trees and he fiddles with his phone, with the buttons of his suit, with the radio. He can't find a decent station, too much news not enough music. 'I have plenty to be doing in Damascus.'

'Like what?'

'Hunches. Seeing a man about a dog.'

Cassius Gallio sets the satnav for Damascus, but there's only one road over the mountains, a ribbon of tarmac through the summit passes. Before long they leave the horse-drawn traffic behind, and near the highest point on the road Gallio pulls into a lay-by, comfort break. Though not straight away. Before getting out of the car they wait, as a precaution. No other vehicles but the Toyota Corolla out on the ancient highway.

'Safe,' Baruch says, and they both climb out of the car.

Up in the mountains a wind blows through, and a rush of clouds hustles across the peaks, blocking and unblocking the sun. The hills and the road go dark then light, and in the dry bush to the side of the Damascus road, on rusting poles, triangular signs warn of landmines.

Baruch ignores them, steps through some flowering thorns toward a solitary scrub oak. He survives, pisses, shakes, zips. He strolls back and survives again. Either he's lucky or he has access to privileged information.

At the car Cassius Gallio leans with his hands on the bonnet, straight-armed, stretching his calf muscles. Baruch sits on the front wing and lights a cigarette, inhales.

'I tell her I don't smoke.' He sighs out the smoke, a long relief, at last. 'Figure she's heard worse lies in her time.'

Gallio swigs from a water bottle, watches a pair of eagles glide high in the blue above the summits. Like a bird of prey, Gallio can rise above Baruch's goading. He can be patient. Baruch points up at the eagles with his cigarette hand. 'Vultures. A rich and varied life.' He takes another drag. 'The misfortunes of others will provide.'

'Eagles.'

'Whatever. She's a lovely woman. No side to her.'

'Shut up, Baruch.' Gallio points the water bottle at him, and Baruch points back. Bottle versus cigarette, water against fire, but in this form neither much good as a weapon. 'Shut up or we'll have to fight.'

'She is, though. You must be interested.'

'OK, tell me about Judith. How is she?'

Gallio drinks the water, Baruch smokes the cigarette.

'To be honest, she bores me. She doesn't bother me. That's why I like her.'

Gallio raises his face to the sunshine, breathes. Baruch flicks his cigarette into the bush, then stands and sweeps his arm over the rocky hills. 'Here, or somewhere near here, Jesus intercepted Paul.'

'Allegedly.'

'That was after the ascension.' Baruch puts his hands on his hips, looking, thinking. 'Of all the appearances, Paul was the last person to see Jesus alive.'

The wind dies, leaving in its place a complicated silence. Gallio stretches and makes the moves to show he's starting the car, very soon now, as soon as his brain can find a story that's more reasonable than a dead Jesus appearing to Paul on the road to Damascus.

'I'd take my chances with Jesus if I met him.' Baruch cracks his knuckles, and Gallio checks but Baruch isn't joking. His face is set. 'Don't believe in hell. And if I decide to go easy on him don't believe in heaven either.'

Baruch is not sorry for the enemies of Israel he has killed. Perhaps he regrets the son of the widow of Nain, a little, who may have had valuable information about the afterlife. And also he was only a child.

'Paul is an ongoing investigation of ours,' he adds. He walks back to the car. 'No organization likes their best employees to defect.'

'Not many witnesses.' Cassius Gallio slaps Damascus road dust from his hands. 'Not in a place like this. Anything could have happened here.'

'Not anything. Neither of us believe that.'

'Time to make a move.'

They used a substitute. Another man died on the cross in the place of Jesus. Cassius Gallio analyzed the record that remained, and each time Jesus fell on the way to Golgotha strangers broke from the crowd. It was chaos, the soldiers pushing back, not knowing which way to turn. As soon as they restored order there came another fall, another interruption, three times in all.

The disciples needed three attempts at manufacturing the incident—the heat, the pain, the mayhem—to exchange a stranger who looked not dissimilar to Jesus. The substitute, his features disguised by blood and bruising, then died on the cross while the real Jesus slipped away through the crowds, hidden and supported by his disciples. At that point in the proceedings his injuries were skin deep, and he could later reappear uninjured.

This switch theory called for meticulous planning, and a follower (probably from Galilee, for the looks) willing to make the ultimate sacrifice. Such a gesture wasn't unthinkable, because belief in eternal life could inspire drastic errors of judgement, and on the day of the crucifixion there were twelve men in Jerusalem who were known to look similar to Jesus.

Back to the office, to the files. One of the few fresh pieces of information was an updated image of the young woman who had left the crowd to wipe Jesus's face. Now this was interesting. Cassius Gallio could speculate that 'wiping his face' was a cover, a misinterpretation. She was preparing his face, or checking his wounds so that the substitute Jesus could look as similar as possible when they enacted the exchange the next time he fell.

Compared to resurrection, Gallio reminded himself, no other version of this particular story was ridiculous. In that sense, every possibility was a possibility.

The new picture was higher definition than the freeze-frame Gallio had extracted at the time: oil paints brought out the paleness of her skin and a strand of reddish-brown hair escaping a headscarf. The image captured the moment the woman leaned in toward Jesus, but with improved technology she could be identified from mortgage records as an Old City householder named Veronica. The file had her address on the Suq Khan el-Zeit.

As Gallio counted down the numbers he noted that the street was residential with occasional independent retail. A convenience store, a hairdresser, and then he found it. He checked the numbers on either side and he was in the right place: the residential address from the file had been converted into St. Veronica's Gift Shop. The shop was open. Gallio pushed through a bead curtain and as the beads settled he browsed through stacks of tea towels imprinted with the face of Jesus. The likeness wasn't quite right; it wasn't how Gallio had Jesus in his mind—close, but not the man himself. Or the image was an idea of Jesus but not Cassius Gallio's idea.

A girl behind the counter, school-leaver by age and attitude. Sullen, pretty, and she looked Gallio over as if wondering whether they'd ever had sex. Bad sex.

'I'm looking for Veronica.'

The girl's tongue pulled bubblegum back behind her teeth. She chewed once, raised a drawn-on eyebrow.

'I'm asking if a woman named Veronica lives here?'

A man bustled through from the back. He could be the girl's father, a broken blood vessel in his cheek, his belt missing a loop of his trousers. He registered Gallio's miserable face, decided he was probably harmless.

'Last week someone else was asking, same as you,' he said. 'All we know is she's gone.'

'Leave anything behind?'

'No, just like the last time I was asked. She sold her possessions and made a donation to the School for the Blind. Then she sold me the empty house. Couldn't its potential. Her loss. She gave the money from the house to the Daughters of Charity.'

'No forwarding address?'

'None. Last I heard she went abroad somewhere. France? One of those places.'

Gallio reached for the beads in the doorway, then turned back. 'The other person asking after Veronica. What did he look like?'

'Could have been a woman.' This from the girl, who popped a bubble as a follow-up.

'Your father came in because of my voice.'

'He's not my father.'

'Forget it,' Gallio said. 'It doesn't matter.'

The Swiss passports provided by Valeria keep Gallio and Baruch out of trouble. Cassius Gallio is travelling as a pharmaceutical salesman from Basle. He had wondered, briefly, why Valeria needed him undercover.

'Jesus disguised himself as a gardener, and an angel,' Valeria had reminded him. 'He went undercover as a *carpenter*. To catch him out we can learn those lessons.'

With Jesus, the trickery is without end. If he feigned his death he was extending a pattern that started with the miracles because what you see, with Jesus, is rarely what you get. He turned the death of Lazarus to his advantage, and then his own crucifixion. Jesus is not a problem that can be approached head-on. Jesus has skills, fieldcraft, and at a purely professional level is a worthy opponent for a disgraced Speculator with a point to prove.

Cassius Gallio tells lies to cross the border into Syria and the lies don't matter, are part of how once he'd decided to live. His only regret is being out of practice. The good news is that they reach the Al Kadam station in south Damascus without incident, where Baruch is scheduled to leave him. No trains are running, so Baruch walks away into the bombed suburbs without looking back. Not many cars on the roads, but a yellow Cherokee is in the Toyota's mirror when Gallio pulls away.

His stepfather the Roman general, who knew what he wanted in life, had expected Cassius Gallio to join the uniformed army. He'd planned to ease Gallio along, using his experience and connections to nudge his stepson ahead of contemporaries and competitors. He wasn't a great believer in colleagues, or friends. Not in the army. Gallio's main refuge from his stepfather's ambition was the chess club, and one evening after he'd checkmated a civil servant their casual conversation shaded into recruitment. We don't call it spying, the man said, because that's not exactly what it is. We're looking for bright people like yourself to police civilization, and to shape everyone's future for the best.

A successful Speculator, as Gallio would soon learn in training, must be rational, deceptive if necessary, then ruthless. Powerful, invisible, but never a killer beyond the rule of law, or at least not without a transparent objective. No one should be certain he existed. And remember, his instructors said, knowledge is power. Knowledge is always power.

His stepfather was furious but Cassius Gallio escaped overseas, and on his first posting to Jerusalem he was greedy to learn as much as possible as quickly as he could. Initially this meant the language and the women, the easiest available territories. He met Judith, who was direct and uncomplicated. Gallio had lived in a villa with his stepfather's third wife, and was cynical about communication between the sexes. It was therefore a relief to spend time with a woman and not expect immediately to understand her.

Or Cassius Gallio was lonely, and Judith in Jerusalem was kind. He'd been aiming to conquer, in a small way, but at the same time he'd needed comfort, and to be comfortable. He can't remember. They'd met a long time ago, but the early marriage became convincingly part of his cover, his legend. His photo ID said military attaché, with full immunity, but his more effective disguise was Judith. Spies and secret police shouldn't marry, everyone knows that. They should keep the hours and the secrets and the dangers to themselves, which is such obvious common sense that a single diplomat immediately rouses suspicion. Meaning that all serious spies are married, but ideally not for love.

The trouble, as with the Jesus fiasco, was that Gallio never knew enough. He didn't know that Valeria was on her way, young and culturally compatible and willing. He couldn't see the future, only his lonely past, and if he had his time again he'd allow the past no more influence than it deserved. That's what he's doing now, in Damascus. He's ignoring his earlier failures and taking his second chance.

The dead-drop is the Travelex exchange in the lobby of the Damascus Sheraton. Gallio picks up an envelope of dollars, and exchanges half with the concierge for a room key. Then checks into his room where in the wardrobe he finds a grey Strellson suit, as favoured by Swiss sales reps. On the hanger beside it a purple shirt and tie set completes the look, and on the floor of the wardrobe a white cardboard box, stamped with the same pharmaceutical company name as his business cards.

He lies down on the double bed, closes his eyes and sleeps. He wakes up and showers, the water as hot as he can bear. He turns off the shower and sits on the floor of the wet room and breathes. In, out, as deeply and slowly as he can. Occasionally, according to no discernible pattern (but there is one, there must be one, and the pattern can be represented as a mathematical formula) a solitary drip from the shower lands on top of his head. Cassius Gallio and Jesus have unfinished business, but if Gallio solves this case then he can become, for the first time, the man he'd wanted to be.

When he drives away from the hotel there's no sign of the yellow Cherokee, and at the Lebanese border, a salesman from Basle in a grey lightweight suit, Gallio passes without incident between allied Arab states. He stops for petrol between the border and Beirut city, but before moving off he pulls the cardboard box onto his lap and opens it up. A truck appears in the distance, takes a long time to arrive, then rushes past. The Toyota rocks on its suspension.

Gallio rummages through the box for antibiotics. He knows the samples are in there somewhere. He flips out a blister pack of doxycycline, thumbs himself a capsule, swallows it without water. Reads the list of side effects, thumbs out another, throws his head back and swallows that one too for luck. Even with a double dose in his system Gallio won't be a hundred per cent safe, but nobody ever is.

He brought bags of pistachios into the office at the Antonia, then forgot them in a desk drawer as he went through the logged post-death appearances of Jesus. For about a month after Jesus vanished he was everywhere and nowhere at once. He was seen by Peter, by the disciples together (behind locked doors, avoiding surveillance), by more than five hundred followers, by James, and then again by the disciples.

During each appearance Jesus walked, spoke, ate. He had to

conclude that Jesus wasn't severely handicapped, despite his extreme ordeal. More reasonably, if his death could be faked then so could his injuries. But Cassius had witnessed at close quarters the wounds of Jesus when he was nailed to the cross. He could pull up comprehensive pictorial evidence to confirm the event. Someone had been severely injured and had died, even if it wasn't Jesus, meaning the switch theory looked increasingly plausible. Though not yet convincing enough to present with confidence to Valeria.

Cassius Gallio pursued the logic of his speculation. If Jesus had arranged a switch, then Joseph of Arimathea was implicated. In the absence of the disciples (who, minus Judas, were hiding the real Jesus somewhere in the city) Joseph had taken responsibility for hauling the body off the cross before sunset, hiding the evidence in his private tomb before standard post-mortem checks could be made.

Joseph had a security file, like every high priest in Jerusalem: his address, his voting patterns, and a record of his sympathy for the Jesus cult. To fill in the gaps Gallio tried out his new phone, CCU issue, and googled Joseph of Arimathea. No network coverage, not behind the historic walls of the Antonia, so Gallio made do with his desktop. The Internet turned out to be as vague as the dossier: Joseph was originally from Arimathea, but may have fled to Europe, a thin-lipped man with a chin-end wispy beard. According to the pictures, he had a taste for ornate headscarves.

Gallio concluded that if he wanted unique off-the-record information, of the type that would unlock secrets, he'd have to put in the legwork.

Outside Joseph's former villa, on the wealthy upslope of Abu Tor, the roadside shrubs were overgrown and a landscape services van was parked in front of a chained sign saying *Gate in Constant Use*. Next door to Joseph's address, a gardener was trimming the base of the boundary wall. Gallio waved his arms until the man turned off the machine, flipped ear defenders off one ear.

'Is this your van?'

'Not blocking anyone. No one's lived there for years. Who are you?'

'Estate agent. Lost the keys. Might have interested a buyer.'

'Well, try and sell it.' The gardener snapped his defenders back into place, which made him shout even louder. 'It's an eyesore!'

Gallio knew from experience that the secret of life—anywhere, at any time—is to act like you belong. He squeezed past the van, stepped over the rusted chain and brushed through the weeds in the gravel driveway. The windows at the front of the large house were boarded up, but those round the side were intact. A shop-bought kennel and a green plastic water butt. Gallio stood on a metal dustbin and tried the top of what looked from the outside like a toilet window. Secured.

He jumped down, steadied himself, pushed with one finger at the back door. Locked.

Gallio looked more closely. The locks had been changed and replaced with imitation Yales. He ran his finger over fake brass. Leave now, said the voice of reason. Take a breath, step back and call Valeria. Get a warrant. Respect the procedure, as a lesson learned from the botched execution. But a warrant would take forever.

Cassius Gallio was a Speculator, even if Valeria refused him the title. He'd excelled in training, where he'd picked up a range of skills they told him he'd never forget. He glanced over his shoulder. No one was watching. He was inside the house within thirty seconds.

The back hallway looked a mess. The plasterwork was patchy and a ray of sunlight picked out a wall scorched by a pallet fire. Squatters. The air inside the house had settled, colder than outside, stale. Some scrabbling noises, mice making themselves scarce, possibly a bird trapped in the roof.

No one home, and hadn't been for years. Cassius Gallio called out, a courtesy to the unknown. No reply. To the right of the hallway was the kitchen, cupboards stripped, floor tiles cracked in several places. Gallio went past the kitchen and opened the next door on the left. In this room the mirror above the fireplace was smashed. Gallio felt behind the frame, then up into the chimney. He sifted through ashes in the grate, but he was aeons behind the curve. Every room was the same: empty and open drawers, rotting skirting boards, mice briefly interrupted from generations of digesting the evidence.

Gallio left the way he came in, securing the door behind him. He was about to walk away when he considered the metal dustbin beneath the window. He'd intended to put it back in its place, but instead he lifted the corrugated lid, peered inside. At the top was a pretzel bag that dated from earlier that year. He checked both ways—still no one watching—then upturned the bin. The contents slumped in a heavy mess across the paving stones. A rusted tuna can with an ancient sell-by date—more or less what he was hoping to see. Older than the tin can was a grey layer of biodegraded sludge, and in the sludge some shards of glass.

He took out his handkerchief, last used by Valeria to avoid fingerprints on the crop in the stable. Gallio retrieved two pieces of glass and knotted them inside the handkerchief. All was not lost.

'I'm not going to trouble the lab,' Valeria said. 'Not yet.'

'These could be significant pieces of evidence.'

'Which you acquired without a warrant. You haven't formally launched your operation and already you're breaking rules. First things first, you know that.'

First, Valeria suggested Cassius Gallio should work out as precisely as possible the nature of the man he wanted to find. What would Jesus look like now? Gallio had read second-hand accounts of the time the disciple Thomas put his fingers in Jesus's wounds. So Jesus wasn't injured, in the sense of being handicapped, but the records suggested he was visibly scarred.

Gallio added this conclusion to a provisional Missing Persons description, but regretted not having paid closer attention at the time. The CCU had coached him to be observant, and in the line of duty he'd witnessed the arrest and death of Jesus. He was therefore surprised that he had no stable image of Jesus fixed in his memory. Jesus would be older now, but Gallio struggled even on basic descriptors like height, the shade of his hair, the colour of his eyes. Identification 101.

He hadn't considered Jesus worth memorizing, not back then, when as a rookie Speculator he'd been more intent on recruiting Judas. Gallio had made no special effort to settle the physical Jesus in his mind. The secondary sources of information, which could have supplemented his memory, were unreliable.

Valeria stopped by his desk to tell him to hurry up.

'Nearly there. One final detail.'

Gallio had to decide on an image of Jesus for his official

Missing Persons bulletin, and although Valeria had commissioned various artists' impressions the results were variable. In the pictures Jesus ranged from angelic rabbi (fair, slender) to swarthy warrior (determined, muscular), by way of the occasional portrayal as an unearthly cosmic light. They'd never find him if they searched for cosmic light.

The disciples. Cassius Gallio had the disciples on his mind. By all accounts the disciples strove every day to be as much like Jesus as possible. They had dark hair and were bearded. They wore clothes of a beige or cream colour, and sandals. Their eyes were brown. This was the Galilee model of a disciple, with variations. Peter was broader in the shoulder, while John sometimes shaved, but every disciple had the basic likeness to Jesus, which was unsurprising. All ten surviving disciples were from the same region of Israel. Four of them were brothers, some were cousins, and each could pass for any of the others. The head of James, as Valeria had demonstrated, could be mistaken for the head of Jesus.

Gallio decided to settle for a physical approximation. Jesus would look something like his disciples, so he attached an image for distribution based on the severed head of James. At least the picture was recent. He then summarized his findings about Jesus into a Missing Persons template, and saved it to the central computerized register. The protocol gave him two options before going live: Jesus could be Missing, or he could be Wanted. Gallio clicked Missing, then Done.

At various stages in the city's history there have been pleasant parts of Beirut, especially close to the seafront. That's where Cassius Gallio parks the Toyota. Then he hails a cab for the other Beirut, the southern suburbs, where there's no sea view and parking is at the owner's risk.

He walks the last couple of blocks, white cardboard box of pharmaceutical supplies wedged under his arm. The scarred low-rise buildings smell of river weed, and women in veils burn rubbish beside the unmade road.

Men stand around and watch. A dog the colour of cement takes Gallio seriously and a motorbike chugs by, low on its axle through the potholes, metal milk churns rattling in the place of panniers. As a friend of the poor, if he were genuine, Jesus could hide in a place like this.

For some time, however, Gallio has known he's on the trail of Jude. He found Jude's name in the Lebanon *Daily Star*, where the classified ads are full of messages of thanks. *Thank you Jude, for your Intercession*. That is, unless Jude was the disciple who'd changed places with Jesus for the crucifixion, and this disciple in Beirut is secretly Jesus. It would fit. Jude is a minor disciple, less likely to have been missed in the aftermath.

From early responses to the Missing Persons bulletin, and Jude's name in the newspaper, Gallio has tracked this alleged disciple to a community hospital in the centre of one of Beirut's southern city camps. Beirut shelters refugees from conflicts dating back to Assyrian wars and Canaanite rebellions, but no one gives up hope of a better life even now. Taped to the door of Jude's hospital is a sign in black marker pen: *No Guns Beyond This Point*.

Inside the entrance, sitting behind a table, is a squat man in camouflage trousers and a Christian Surfers T-shirt. Jags of scar tissue interrupt the growth of his two-day stubble, and on his side of the X-ray scanner there's a black steel crossbow. He picks it up in a good-natured way.

'Bolt can go through a horse. Your ID, please.'

He nods at the Swiss identity card, hands it back. 'Are you ill?'

Gallio holds up the box. 'Drugs. I'm here to help.'

Security in a Beirut hospital comes with dreadful teeth. 'Ha! We prayed for medicines. We must be expecting you. Come on in.'

Gallio walks around the metal detector. The man holds up his hand.

'Through the gate, please.'

Gallio beeps once, backs out, takes off his belt and tries again.

'Arms out, we can't be too careful.'

He frisks Gallio, armpit to hip, takes his phone and wallet from the Strellson jacket. Waistband. Inner leg. 'You'll get your stuff back when you leave.'

Gallio feels nervy without his phone, suddenly back in a more vulnerable era when backup was in the hands of the gods. A small boy slides out from a corridor. He's carrying a bow fashioned from a car aerial, and aims a homemade arrow at Gallio's eye. The man cuffs the boy across the head.

'Don't frighten people you don't know.'

The lift doesn't work. The boy covers them across every angle of the stairwell as they climb and turn, bow poised, arrow in the slot. The hospital seems deserted.

'Contagious,' the doorkeeper says. 'Everyone else had to leave. Jude keeps the infected patients on the top floor because the air is better.'

On the understanding that knowledge is power, Speculators value small talk for the information it can yield. As they climb the stairs Cassius Gallio gets the man to talk about how Jude cured him, and also his son. Like the patients at the top of the hospital, father and son had the plague.

'Which is what, exactly?'

'Some long medical name. We all call it the plague.'

Out of gratitude to Jude the man takes care of security, and besides, jobs in Beirut are scarce.

'Why does Jude need protection?'

The man hauls himself up by the stair rail. He may be cured but he's not in good shape. 'You wouldn't believe the nutters in this city. Some of them think we've enough gods as it is. Others think we have too many. A god strong enough to heal the sick looks to some people like a bad omen.'

The citizens of Beirut have a historical instinct for the damage religion can do. Gallio understands that, because he too has suffered. 'I thought the worst was over? I heard Beirut was getting safer.'

'It is.' The man holds up his crossbow, balancing it on his meaty trigger finger. 'No guns in this sector of the camp. Not even in the hospital. Believe me, that counts as progress.'

He turns, flips the crossbow upright, and fires at the *Push* panel on a door about thirty yards away. The bolt punches two-thirds of the way through the door. Gallio and the boy admire his work. The man has sent the bolt from A to B, a straight cause and effect between him and his target, the reassurance of connecting what he intended to happen with what then visibly happens. Bullseye. It's practically all anyone wants.

On the top floor they push through another set of doors into a ward. High ceilings, a double row of beds. For a heart-stopping moment Gallio sees Jesus—the long hair, the beard. The fluorescent light, possibly, quivering on washed-out linen. The eyes, the pitiful brown eyes.

• • •

After sending out the Missing Persons bulletin, Gallio had waited to see what would happen, which was pretty much the essence of police work as he remembered it. The waiting, and the hope that he wasn't entirely wrong. Some bright Antonia IT spark had written code for a drop-down tab that displayed a map of the known world. As soon as a station or associate bureau responded to the bulletin, a small star would light up in that place on the map. One sighting was all Gallio needed to justify his existence, and to make his first progress report to Valeria. A star, a light, a reason to begin.

Within minutes, a star lit up in southern Turkey. The city of Hierapolis. Gallio paged Valeria. Another light in Ephesus, then a star above Athens, and another in central France. Lights started blinking across the screen, in Beirut, north into Russia. A star appeared above Whithorn in southwest Scotland, over Cyprus, across into Turkmenistan.

Gallio could barely keep up.

'What's going on?' Valeria leaned over his shoulder, her head close to his. 'How can he be in all of these places at once?'

Gallio rolled the cursor over each light in turn but the text box never guaranteed the identification. Not a hundred per cent certain. These were sightings that fitted the description on the bulletin, but none positively confirmed a location and lock for Jesus.

'The disciples, it must be.' Cassius Gallio pushed his chair back from the screen. 'They look like Jesus, act in his name. Wherever they go the disciples are mistaken for Jesus.'

'Or Jesus is mistaken for them.' Valeria took over the mouse, rolled over each of the lights one more time. She stopped, read the text that appeared over each star, moved on. 'He can pose as a disciple just as his disciples pretend to be him. Clever way to hide.'

'It would be, if that's how he's hiding.'

'Call Baruch.'

Valeria chaired the meeting in a disused case room. Apart from the reopened Jesus puzzle, Israel was quiet, and the room was currently the military police storeroom for military mops and buckets. Valeria sat Gallio down and invited him to talk them through his switch theory. She let Baruch guffaw and draw a penis in the dust of a storaged whiteboard.

'One of the disciples stood in for Jesus on the day of the crucifixion,' Gallio said. 'It wasn't Jesus who died. That explains how he could reappear after the crucifixion.'

'We'd have noticed at the time.'

'Would we? If there were ten disciples instead of eleven, who really would have noticed? That's why he had Judas killed. Judas would have worked it out, eventually, because he knew the disciples up close. Nobody else can tell them apart, except their families who were safely out of the way in Galilee. The disciple who changed places with Jesus would have been one of the lesser ones. Collateral damage.'

'I always forget their names,' Baruch said. 'I mean apart from Peter and a couple of the others.' Suddenly this seemed relevant, as if the junior disciples were deliberately forgettable.

With the point of his index finger Baruch dotted semen spurting from the penis. Made one of the dots into the eye of a circled happy face. Then he pulled up a chair and sat on it backward. 'Simon, Philip, one of those. No idea what they're for, if not for this.'

'Jude,' Gallio said. 'None of the minor disciples would be missed, would they?'

'So how do you suggest we act on this?' Valeria was always looking forward, to a future where the confusions of the past could be straightened out, definitively.

'We confront them,' Baruch said. 'We might get lucky. Track down Simon and he turns out to be Jesus. Hit the jackpot.'

Valeria checked the screen on her laptop. 'According to this, the sighting in England may be Simon. The back of beyond is a long way to go on the off-chance that Simon is actually Jesus.'

'So you're saying no to England?'

'We don't have the budget. Times have changed.' Valeria decided she might as well tell them the truth. 'This isn't a high-priority mission, not these days, or not yet. We can start somewhere nearer.'

Gallio hadn't been gone so long he'd forgotten the bad weather of budgets and cost analyses. Work within the possible, one of the mottoes of the Speculator cadre. 'Let's start in Beirut,' Gallio suggested. 'Put some pressure on them close to home.'

'If it's Jesus, how will you know?'

'We'll know,' Baruch said. 'We saw him when he was alive.'

Cassius Gallio wasn't so confident. Would he recognize Jesus? Jesus might be the gentle son of god spreading the wealth and healing the sick. Or he could be an intolerant fucker, good with a knife. Gallio would be happier with a scientific method for confirming the identification.

'We should send the glass from Joseph's bin to forensics. I brought it in as potential evidence. We might get some DNA we could match against the disciples, or against Jesus.'

'After all this time? Don't worry, I have your pieces of glass. I'll keep them safe.'

Valeria looked from Gallio to Baruch, then back at Gallio.

At this stage they were all she had. 'Beirut it is. You both knew Jesus and I'd trust your positive identification. Start with Jude in Beirut.'

A city that within budgetary restraints they could reach in a hire car from Jerusalem. And even that wasn't so simple. The special needs of the region meant that traffic from Israel into Lebanon had to pass through the demilitarized zone with document inspections at every checkpoint. Valeria didn't want diplomatic hotlines demanding why exactly her CCU agents were moving across these particular borders.

'Damascus,' Baruch said. 'Let's go via Damascus. Cassius can pursue your fool's errand in Beirut and I'll deal with the living. Let's find out what in Damascus they remember about the conversion of Paul.'

In the Beirut hospital ward the smell hits, but thankfully Gallio's collar is loose and he can pull his purple shirt and tie up over his nose. Jude the disciple of Jesus, patron saint of hopeless causes, steps toward him. He distrusts nobody! Cassius Gallio looks at Jude's hands, no scarring, and up close Jude's face is heavily lined and nothing like the face of Jesus, or Jesus in Jerusalem as Gallio remembers him. Jude eyes the cardboard box held in the crook of Gallio's elbow.

'Welcome. Come and see the work that Jesus has been able to do.'

Gallio lets his collar drop and bears the smell, glad he swallowed a double dose of antibiotics. In the beds along the ward Jude's patients wring their sweating hands, or lunge sideways to vomit into plastic bowls. Some are seized with cramps, others have drops of blood beading in their ears.

'No room left at the UN clinics, but there's a limit to what I can do without medicines.'

The most extreme cases reach out, desperate to touch the hand that has touched the hand of Jesus. Even at a distance, they believe that Jesus through Jude has the power to heal.

'I can't save them, not all of them.' Jude touches everyone, no exceptions. Every hand that reaches, he holds. 'The nurses we have are wonderful, but some of our patients die, some don't. It makes us sad.'

'I brought antibiotics.'

'We can use antibiotics.'

Jude has not offered Cassius Gallio his hand. He suggests Gallio distribute some of the sample pills, which is hardly fair, as Gallio is neither a medical professional nor even very caring. He can do this. Gallio holds his breath and picks out those who look the furthest gone, with neck glands so swollen they can barely breathe. He expects some kind of approval or gratitude, but is disappointed.

'How many boxes like this can you get me?'

The whites of Jude's eyes, Gallio now sees, are yellow and veined. He notices how Jude licks his dry lips, and how his frail hands tremble when he attends to the sick. Jude's method of healthcare combines basic hygiene with prayer, but together they're not enough.

Gallio reminds himself why he's here. The disciples can be harried into mistakes, like the story they invented about the ascension. Without being immodest, the sudden absurdity of the ascension reflected well on Gallio's earlier efforts. The ascension of Jesus reeked of panic, as if the pressure were beginning to tell. For forty days Gallio had crowded the disciples, crawling all over them until finally they had to add to their story. It couldn't be a coincidence that only the closest followers saw Jesus ascend, the men who'd be punished most severely if he or his body were discovered.

The ascension story meant no body, no physical remains to unearth, dead or alive. Investigation over. Or so they hoped.

Cassius Gallio had rattled Jesus, though he hadn't recognized his victory at the time. The ascension was an interference strategy, designed to confuse and divert resources from the search for a physical body. Unfortunately for Gallio, when he should have been reacting to this new development he was halfway to Odessa on a troopship. Now he finds the ascension a reassuringly ludicrous event, proof that Jesus and/or the disciples can lose their discipline. They will contrive implausible fictions and excuses. This is a weakness to exploit.

'Can we go somewhere quieter?' Gallio means away from the smell, from the sick.

Jude leads him out of the ward to sit on the stairs, midway between the top floor and the landing for the empty wards below. From the stairwell they hear the zing of makeshift arrows as they scrape off walls and into doors. Jude rests the box of pharmaceuticals across his knees, and sorts through the various packets and tubes.

'Feel free,' Gallio says.

Along with doxycycline Jude turns up eye ointments containing azithromycin for restoring sight to the blind. He reads the advice leaflets for samples of anticonvulsants to use against demons, and the dosage of antidepressants for milder cases of possession. Gallio has brought him divine intervention in easy-to-use blister packs, miracles from the civilized world.

There are no drugs in this or any other box that will bring a patient back to life.

'You've delivered almost exactly what we prayed for. Thank you.'

'We need to discuss terms.'

Jude looks blank. Perhaps he doesn't understand how business works, whereas Gallio has arrived with a range of possible deals. He'll send for more drugs in exchange for information leading to the arrest of Jesus. If Jude wants to do this nicely. If he doesn't, Gallio can harass him on suspicion of the murder of Judas. Gallio is ready to invoke Interpol, confiscate Jude's papers, close his beloved hospital, make his life a misery, but sitting beside him on the stairs Gallio doesn't believe that Jude is the murderer of Judas. Nor is he Jesus in disguise.

Jude places his hand on Cassius Gallio's hand. At last Jude touches him, flesh to flesh, and looks him squarely in the eye. Gallio wonders what he wants.

'You're not a pharmaceutical salesman, are you?'

The stairwell lights clunk out. Beirut power outage. The two men sit in the darkness, holding hands. A not unpleasant experience, Gallio thinks. In fact he finds himself strangely comforted.

'I can organize a delivery of medicines,' he says. 'But you have to tell me about Jesus. Is he still alive?'

'He is.' Jude squeezes Gallio's hand. His palm is dry, waxy. 'I am the least of the disciples but this much I know. Jesus is alive. Very much so.'

'Where can I find him?'

'At the right hand of the father.'

'He's not in Nazareth. We checked. Do you have proof, some evidence you could show me?'

'In my heart I do.'

As his eyesight adjusts, Cassius Gallio thinks he sees Jude smile. He withdraws his hand, and wonders if Jude is mocking him. The stairwell is too dark to be sure.

'Wherever we spread the message we gain new converts,' Jude says. 'Take that as the proof. We tell people the good news that Jesus is alive, and they believe us because it's true.'

'Your former associate James is dead. I don't know if bad news ever gets through to you, but he was publicly beheaded in Jerusalem.'

'I remember you now.' Jude leans away, as if in the almost dark he'll see Gallio better from a distance. 'You're coming back to me. You used to dress differently, and you were younger, but you led the original search for the body of Jesus, didn't you? You used to hang around in the lobby of our hotel.'

'Are you in touch with the others?'

'I pray for them. I'm confident they also pray for me.'

'I mean in the real world.'

'I did hear about James. He was beheaded in Jerusalem in front of a crowd, but was so courageous he never flinched. His executioner was deeply moved, and he converted to Jesus instantly.'

'That's what you heard about James?'

'We have more followers now than ever.'

Cassius Gallio would like to be gentle, as he would with any-one who isn't all there. He feels for his phone to show Jude some images of Jesus, to confirm the most accurate likeness. Gallio doesn't have his phone.

'Jude. I know certain things about you.'

He reminds himself that along with eleven others Jude is implicated in theft, murder, terrorism and a lifetime of religious deception.

'You've used at least three alias names at border controls, including Jude Thaddeus, Judas Thaddaeus and Lebbaeus. You've created a bureaucratic mess for Customs that on its own could get you deported. You also have a murky past in Jerusalem as an associate of a convicted criminal.'

'He was innocent.'

'They always are.'

'My turn to ask a question. Are you truly looking for Jesus?'

Jude sounds tetchy, which is good. Gallio wants to harry him, to push him to his breaking point, ascension level.

'Jesus is dead,' Gallio says.

'Jesus is coming back.'

Cassius Gallio sits forward in the dark, elbows on his knees, and does the thing with his fingers. In the dark he can't get the pads of the little fingers to line up properly, or not as neatly as he'd like. Now he can. He is fully in control.

'What does that actually *mean?*'

'He's coming back to judge the quick and the dead.'

Gallio's fingers slip. 'Where should I go to see this?'

'He didn't mention a place.' The tone of Jude's voice is difficult to gauge, and Gallio can't tell if he's disappointed or evasive. He's a very practiced liar. 'Jesus will come down from the clouds, and the world will end.'

In a nearby street an Arab wedding bursts with music then stops as suddenly. A sound-test for the amplifiers.

'Show some pity for the sick and dying upstairs,' Gallio says. 'Be more precise, and I'll give you every drug you need. You can save every patient in your care.'

The twitch near Gallio's eye is back. He lets it hammer, and the nerve doesn't tire until he pinches the skin between his fingers, squeezes until his face hurts. 'When is the second coming due to happen? When you last saw Jesus, how much detail did he give you?'

Jude inhales deeply through his nose, extra oxygen pulled into his brain for a big decision. He holds his breath. The drugs will alleviate suffering, and whatever Jesus is planning no one can stop him, not if Jesus is the person Jude believes he is. He exhales.

'He'll come back while at least one of us is alive. That's what he said.'

'One of who?'

'His disciples. He made that promise quite clearly.'

'Which one?'

'The one he loved.'

Gallio rocks back and whistles through his teeth. Now he has something, a clue, a first sense of how long Jesus plans to stay in hiding. It's a start, and yet he worries that progress like this is too good to be true. 'I thought he loved you disciples equally, loved everybody?'

'He does,' Jude says, 'even you, if you give him a chance. Give him a chance to love you. Otherwise I doubt you're going to find him.'

'Don't change the subject. He loves one of you more than the others. Is that right?'

'If you want to find him, be serious about looking for him.'

Cassius Gallio can't place Jude in a category. He knows from the files about Jude's rural upbringing in a family of Galilean farmers, and Gallio respects him for the distance travelled between Nazareth and here. Jude wasn't born with the same advantages as Gallio, but Gallio is prepared to believe that a former peasant from upcountry Israel should have information worth procuring. What he can't understand, if god doesn't exist, is what kind of person believes he's called by god.

'Why are you doing this?' Gallio asks. 'What do you expect to gain?'

Jude gave up a steady living to tell anyone who'd listen that the last would be first and the first last. He is confident that the meek and the peacemakers will be blessed, along with those who accept they're spiritually weak. The humble will be rewarded, as will the merciful and the pure of heart.

'None of your wish list is going to happen, Jude. Believe me. I've seen the world, and you're asking too much.'

'Jesus will be back within a lifetime. He promised.'

'Is that a threat?'

Cassius Gallio wants to make a stand, as he had the first time round in Jerusalem by insisting on the human truth that somewhere in the city the disciples had hidden a body. He could kill Jude now, here in the dark, in the stairwell of a quarantined hospital. Except the CCU are not assassins. This enquiry, entrusted to him by Valeria of the Complex Casework Unit, will proceed on a civilized and rational basis. Jude can pass on a warning about this meeting. Let the surviving disciples know that Cassius Gallio the former Speculator is back, and he's seriously looking for Jesus.

The electricity clunks back on, and they shield their eyes from the light. Jude's hands tremble, and his face is pale and bloodless. He's dying, but Gallio will not be distracted. Jesus is alive or Jesus is dead. Only one of these statements can be true.

'Is Jesus injured? How will I recognize him?'

'I've told you what I know.'

'The drugs, Jude. I'm thinking you want to save the little children.'

Jude rests his hand on Gallio's shoulder, then pushes himself back to his feet. He has work to do. 'You're talking to the wrong disciple, my friend. Try Thomas. Take your doubts to doubting Thomas. He can tell you the truth.'

IV

Thomas

————

"STONED AND SPEARED"

The Babylon morgue is on the far side of the Euphrates bridge, next to police headquarters, a long hour's drive from the airport. Baruch is silent, recovering from his second flight in two days, this time deep into the saddle of land between the Mediterranean and the Persian Gulf. Not a good flyer, Baruch. Gallio looks the other way, out of the reinforced window of the commandeered UN Land Cruiser.

Babylon never stops. The streets are crammed with bicycles weaving through cows and goats, the animals grazing at middens of household waste. Everyone in this city has something to do, somewhere to go, and if they could get there faster they would, to the exchange and markets, to the roadside traders with nimble hands who sort through car parts and electrical innards. There are so many people here, so many Babylonians, that Cassius Gallio finds it hard to believe in the sanctity of every life. Millions have come before him and millions will come after.

In his own way Cassius Gallio is a believer, not in divine oversight but in medical investment and the rule of law. The work of civilization is rarely spontaneous, like a miracle, but it is solid and worth pursuing. The disciples with their superstitions threaten the status of civilized progress, because reason and observation insist that death is death. If the CCU let the Jesus mystery slide, along with the myth of his continued existence, they're committing cultural suicide. Gallio feels he's providing a genuine service by tracking down the truth about Jesus.

The Babylon police chief was at the airport to meet them, and on this occasion Cassius presented genuine CCU ID, issued to him by Valeria to establish his authority in Babylon. The embossed eagle to the side of his photo is a guarantee that he comes from the arrowhead of human evolution. Not just now but always. He has access to education and information that the citizens of Babylon can barely imagine.

The chief has pitch-dark eyebrows and sad green eyes. He knows the reality of international politics, where every lesser power owes allegiance to the dominant culture. He sighs, and from the front of the car he asks where first. 'Morgue is closer than the crime scene. As instructed, we've sealed his apartment.'

'Idiots,' Baruch says. In the back seat of the Land Cruiser he fails to click his seat belt, tries again, fails again, lets the belt recoil across his shoulder. 'They've already moved him.'

Up front the chief shrugs, an elegant and foreign gesture. He doesn't expect the advanced West to understand every nuance of the Old World. 'We wanted to avoid hysteria. Thomas has built up quite a following.'

'Morgue,' Gallio decides. His instinct with the Jesus followers is to check they're really dead. 'Let's see what's left of the body.'

The morgue is underground to hide from temperatures that in summer can reach 40 degrees Celsius. The broad lift is reserved for the dead (going down), but for the living the attendants burn incense in the spiral iron stairwell. Not quite enough of it. In the main underground autopsy room the overhead fan is stuck on slow, and stains watermark the ceiling above the walk-in fridges. In the centre of the room, a corpse on a steel trolley is covered in a green sheet. The sheet is too narrow and a male arm, naked, pale, sparsely haired, sticks out to the side.

Cassius Gallio approaches the trolley, while Baruch hangs back. They can't be sure, not yet, that this isn't a case of mistaken identity. It seems a grim coincidence for a second disciple to die so soon after James, and as at the Veronica souvenir shop Gallio senses other forces taking an interest. He hopes this isn't so.

He stares at the thin exposed fingers. Thomas is the disciple who doubted the resurrection, which meant he helped convince the others it was true. According to Jude, Thomas put one or all of these fingers into the various wounds suffered by Jesus, who was crucified and came back from the dead.

Jude was probably lying.

Nevertheless, Gallio uses his imagination. Thomas would most likely have used his index finger, one of the fingers Gallio can see, and he supposedly placed it inside a five-day-old wound. Thomas would have had to go deep, to be sure of the severity of the injury, as far as the second knuckle at least, curving his finger past bones, inside the flesh. Waggle it from side to side, to make absolutely certain. Dead, alive. Dead and alive.

'I could have made the bastard talk.' With his feet back on solid ground, the memory of the aeroplane fading, Baruch is livening up. Poor Thomas, who for Baruch has let himself down by getting himself killed. Careless of him. Instead of lying here in the morgue he should have waited for Baruch, and been tortured before he died.

'You're seconded to CCU,' Gallio reminds him. 'We can't be having any torture.'

'Too real for you?'

'Something like that.'

The murder of Thomas isn't ideal. This is the disciple who persuaded the others that Jesus had come back to life. He was heavily complicit in the original lie. Peter and John were first into the tomb, but Thomas authenticated the wounds. Three or four disciples in this story were dominant, and they could have been used by Jesus to bully the others into believing, Thomas acting as a kind of insurance for anyone outside the loop who had doubts: Jesus died, Thomas assured them, and Jesus returned from the dead. For those disciples who weren't in on the switch, and maybe not all of them were trusted, no one but Jesus had been crucified. No one but Jesus came back.

If Thomas was telling the truth, that is. Cassius Gallio will never know for sure, not now, not from the man himself. He takes the top seam of the sheet, stamped *Babylon City Morgue*, between his finger and thumb. Gallio is gentle with it, as if the green polyester were itself a living thing. He peels back the sheet.

It is him. It is Thomas. Gallio has no doubt about it, even though he looks like Jesus.

• • •

They could have arrived earlier, and Cassius Gallio could have saved the life of doubting Thomas, only Baruch had won the battle of the Jude debrief.

Back in Jerusalem their case room had been cleared of mops and buckets. An electrician was shooed away so they could talk, sitting on folding chairs round a trestle table. Pictures of Jesus had been pinned to the walls. Gallio squinted: images of Jesus, of disciples, hard at a glance to tell one from the other. Between two long windows a map of the ancient world was dotted with plastic pins for each confirmed sighting: eight so far.

Gallio opened the meeting by reporting on the intelligence he'd gained from Beirut. Essentially, though without being able to say when or how, Jude was convinced that Jesus was coming back.

'What does that *mean*?' Valeria had her hands flat on the table, a signal everywhere in the world of straightforward honesty.

'Don't know,' Gallio had to admit, 'but it sounds dramatic. Jude told me Jesus is coming back while at least one of his disciples is alive, so that's our best idea of the timescale. Also that Thomas is operating out of Babylon. Our next step should be a visit to Thomas, interview him about the switch theory. Thomas has privileged information about the health status of Jesus in the period after the crucifixion.'

'Any other way he's special?'

'He was allowed to doubt the resurrection. Then he confirmed it, so Thomas was picked out to spread the significant lie. True or false, he knows more than some of the others.'

Cassius Gallio was pleased with the progress he'd made, but Baruch had not been idle in Damascus. While Gallio was questioning Jude in Beirut, Baruch had convened meetings of his own in Damascus about Paul. Not all his encounters had been consensual, and occasionally he sucked at the grazed lower knuckles of his scuffed right hand.

According to Baruch, there were features of Paul's story relevant to this investigation that failed to compute. Many years ago Paul had set off on an Israeli-sponsored mission to infiltrate and assassinate the disciples. On the Damascus road, up in the mountain passes, some unexplained event had interrupted his journey and he arrived in Damascus blind and incapacitated. The Jesus sect knew who he was, after earlier persecutions in Jerusalem. They should have taken advantage and killed their most vicious public oppressor. At the very least they should have fled from him. Instead they stayed and cared for him and made him welcome in the city.

Baruch still couldn't understand, even after his ruthless day and night in Damascus, how the disciples had turned Paul from oppressor to believer. At first—and Baruch accepted some of the responsibility for this—the Israeli home security forces had refused to believe in Paul's dramatic conversion. Stand back, Baruch had advised them, wait for the pay-off. He'd assumed that Paul was running his own interference, an ingenious solo mission of his own devising. Paul was a high-flyer capable of coldly orchestrating the fatal stoning of a Christian called Stephen in a public Jerusalem street. He'd have worked out a plan for Damascus.

'I remember that time like yesterday,' Baruch said. 'We sent Paul into Syria with instructions to find and eliminate Peter, who was leading the spread of the lie about the resurrection of Jesus. But Paul, Paul was always ambitious. We could imagine him lining up all twelve disciples, and he'd have thought deeply about how to do it. He'd have worried that by starting with Peter he'd scare the others into hiding, and have to spend the rest of his life finding them one by one.'

Baruch had admired Paul's talent, his energy, so he wasn't fooled by the first emergency encryption from the Damascus bureau. *Paul ambushed in mountains.* In the following days the bureau stopped bothering with encryption. Paul's plight was more shocking than that, arriving in the city blind, delirious, not the cool and ruthless agent they'd been briefed to expect.

His sight returned first, if not his sense of reality.

'Claimed to have been struck by lightning,' Baruch said. 'Also to have spoken with Jesus. This last time in Damascus I had to remind several people that Paul was a liar, because by then Jesus was dead or in heaven. Either way, he wasn't on the road through the mountains.'

'They only had Paul's word for it,' Valeria said. 'He must have been convincing.'

'Something else I checked out in Damascus. In a full and frank exchange with a witness who was there at the time. He confirmed that when Paul arrived in the city he was in bits.'

The first time Baruch heard Paul's version of events he'd burst out laughing. Lightning, a speaking appearance by Jesus, the whole bold performance was transparently a wonderfully conceived plan. Paul's instant enlightenment was a brazen invention, a faked event perfectly targeted at believers in the miracles of Jesus. In his own life Baruch had never experienced revelation, and it seemed reasonable to assume that neither had anyone else, including Saul of Tarsus. Paul had set out to infiltrate the disciple network in Syria, and his first move, in an isolated spot on the Damascus road, was to strike himself down in a storm. He comes out the other side a Jesus believer, changes his name, the full defector's charade.

Baruch had remained convinced for years that Saul as Paul was faking it. It would be only a matter of time before Paul filed the inside line on every mystery and miracle, trapping the disciples and rolling up the network. But so far, right up until now, there had been no pay-off and no big reveal. Baruch and the Israeli hierarchy were still waiting, and in Damascus Baruch had failed to uncover any telling inconsistencies. Paul might truly have gone over to the other side.

'This has gone on too long,' Baruch said. 'We need to talk to Paul himself, find out what really happened on the Damascus road. If Paul was confronted by Jesus, as he claims, then Jesus must have made some kind of offer he couldn't refuse. That's also the most recent sighting, the freshest lead we have. On the road to Damascus Paul was the last person to see Jesus alive. He's the only member of the cult to have seen Jesus *after* the ascension, by which time Jesus was supposed to have disappeared. This fact has to be significant. Paul made Jesus break cover, and he deserves our attention.'

'Paul is unrelated to the immediate investigation,' Gallio said. He remembered his hours of work on the dossiers, the risks he took in Beirut. 'We're looking into the switch theory, a plot the experienced disciples were hatching while Saul was a boy tentmaker in Tarsus. Paul had no personal connection with Jesus. And don't forget that he's one of us.'

'He is,' Valeria said. 'He has the full protection of the law.'

'That's something else that needs clearing up,' Baruch said. 'Once Paul went over to Jesus, why didn't Rome revoke his citizenship?'

'He's one of your lot too,' Valeria said. 'A Jew.'

Baruch pulled a finger across his throat. 'He's in this up to his neck.'

Gallio had heard enough. As far as he was concerned Paul was a latecomer, a hanger-on who'd missed the main event. 'My recommendation is that we follow the lead from Jude that points us toward Thomas.'

'We should lean on Paul.' Baruch sucked at a knuckle, made some progress on a scab with his teeth. 'Jude threw us a few scraps, no more than that. We're not any closer to Jesus after talking to him, so why should Thomas be different?'

'You didn't even bring Jude in,' Valeria said. 'You can't think the disciples have every answer or you'd have brought Jude in.'

'I doubt he'd have lasted the journey. He's not in the best of health. I got some solid information, more than we'd hoped for.'

'Paul,' Baruch said. 'Paul's the man.'

'Thomas.' Cassius Gallio hated to see his speculations go to waste. From Jude's suggestion he'd projected a specific and important role for Thomas in the creation of the Jesus legend. They should follow the path as indicated. 'Thomas. It has to be Thomas. We should pay a visit to Babylon.'

Valeria held up her hands. 'We can't go after both, not at the same time.' She stood up and looked at the map with its scattered pinheads, then more closely at the headshots on the walls.

'If the switch theory is correct,' Gallio said, 'one of those disciples out there is Jesus.'

'Paul was the last person to see him alive,' Baruch said. 'That has to count for something.'

Valeria sat down and clasped her hands together on the tabletop, a sign of decisiveness not yet matched by a decision. 'We need to make some progress, see if it's worth allocating staff to the casework. Not everyone takes Jesus seriously, but you two saw him in action and that's why we need you involved. You know better than anyone that the weekend of his crucifixion leaves certain questions unresolved. So we have to decide: Thomas or Paul. I'm the boss. My decision.'

Gallio and Baruch spoke over each other but Valeria held up her hands for silence. 'Look. We've been asked, discreetly through diplomatic channels, to move Thomas on from Babylon. He's upsetting the wrong type of people, and he's an incident waiting to happen.'

'Thomas is a peasant a long way from home,' Baruch said.

Valeria closed her eyes until he stopped. She waited. Opened her eyes on the silence.

'On the other hand, Paul draws crowds wherever he goes. He gets invited to speak at conventions. Last week Athens, this week Antioch. It's Paul. That's my decision. Talk to Paul, but a word of warning. Remember he's not a disciple. He may be more dangerous than that.'

Valeria and Cassius Gallio sat opposite each other in the Antonia canteen, Gallio toying with a tubbed salad he didn't really want. Valeria had her green tea, the square tag hanging outside the takeaway cup.

'Why did you listen to Baruch?'

Gallio had asked Valeria for a quiet word, just the two of them, alone. She agreed, but this time she didn't propose the American Colony Hotel. 'You brought me back to lead this investigation, and I gave you sound reasons for going after Thomas.'

'Don't take it personally,' Valeria said. 'I have to keep Baruch sweet, as if we're equal partners. Politics.'

Gallio remembered hearing this evasion somewhere before. 'My call was Thomas. You went with Baruch.'

'Stop being childish. This isn't about you. In case you missed it we had a fire in Rome that lasted six days and devastated ten out of fourteen districts. Thousands were killed or made homeless. Jesus may have been involved, and I haven't sent you to find him on a whim. I hired lexicographers to study transcripts of his speeches, and those of his followers. The word "fire" comes up big and bold in every word map.'

Gallio had seen the printouts, and it was true the Jesus followers were obsessed with fire. The unquenchable fire, the hell of fire, the eternal fire; cast, thrown, fallen into fire; tested and refined and scorched by fire; fire in tongues and pillars and lakes. The fury of fire and revealed by fire. Fire will be coming down.

'If we discover they're connected to the fire of Rome,' Valeria said, 'they will be punished.'

Cassius Gallio should have been pleased. Valeria had changed her mind about the disciples, and about Jesus. Their talent for deception was at last being taken seriously, and he almost sensed an apology—as he alone had insisted at the time, the disciples weren't as blunt as they seemed. Gallio felt a momentary nerve spasm in his jaw, but quelled it by biting his cheek. 'You haven't answered my question.'

'Listen. Thomas may be about as useful as Jude, another earnest man in sandals who's self-righteous about the poor.'

'There's no reason all twelve of them should know everything. A subgroup of disciples may have stolen the body, and only a favoured few are in on the details, like where Jesus is hiding. That would be standard procedure in a terrorist cell.'

'Jude is surviving Beirut, so Thomas can be left to his own devices for a while longer in Babylon. At the very least we eliminate Paul from our enquiries, and if on reflection Paul denies meeting Jesus on the road to Damascus then we make progress. We can ignore an awkward sighting. Look, let's not fall out over this. I've been impressed by your work so far.'

Valeria pulled the teabag from her cup, let it swing like a pendulum, then dropped it into Gallio's salad. It leaked tea across his lettuce, which they both knew he wasn't eating. Not now, anyway.

'I think it's personal,' Gallio said, 'because you once thought we had a future together.'

'We did. Here we are. I don't want to revisit that.'

'A future with a different past.'

'No such thing.'

'I told you from the beginning I'd never leave my family.'

'And I hope you enjoyed your reward. You didn't go to heaven, and you're not going to heaven. You went to Moldova, and all points east.'

'We can't turn back the clock.'

'It's ancient history, forget it. Your problem was you didn't know how to change your mind. That's a weakness, Cassius. They called you on it at the tribunal.'

'No one stood up for me, or believed the disciples were highly trained. Remember the tomb. These people plan in advance, and their following keeps growing, so their long-term strategy must be working. That's why we need to question Thomas right now.'

'You lost a corpse, Cassius.' Valeria zipped her bag and stood up, looked down her nose at him. 'I expect you and Baruch to work together, which means having a chat with Paul. Cooperate, and you'll be fine. You two have more in common than you think.'

She could say the words but that didn't make them true. Gallio didn't reply. She was wrong and her error didn't deserve a response, as wrong as that.

'You don't believe Jesus is alive, do you?' he said. 'You're pretending.'

'I'm doing the job that Complex Casework asked me to do.'

Gallio had spent his first viaticum pay cheque on a shipment of medicines for Beirut. Jude could save himself, and his patients shouldn't have to suffer because their hospital was run by a man who believed in Jesus.

Valeria put the bag over her shoulder, checked her watch. 'You lost a corpse and you should have left your wife. You lost her anyway. Your judgement is fallible, Cassius. That's why it's Paul, not Thomas.'

At the Babylon crime scene Gallio keeps his ID open for his own benefit, to remind himself he knows what he's doing. The plastic wallet hangs limp in his hand. Thomas was murdered at a construction site, on a concrete slab foundation about ten meters by ten, with two plastic utility pipes raised at one corner.

'Speared,' the police chief says, not looking so dapper since the passing of midnight, since the detailed examination of the body in the morgue, since this journey into the Babylon badlands. The dawn is not a sight he usually sees. 'You've been over the body with the coroner. Thomas was stoned first, then finished off with a length of iron foundation rod. Through the heart.'

The sun breaks over a building. Gallio folds away his ID, puts on his sunglasses, and the Polaroid lenses turn blood on concrete into rust. He hunkers down on his heels. Must have picked up some tinnitus from the air travel, or the hum of fridges in the morgue, sound in his ears at a frequency his brain can't decipher.

'Time of death?'

'Hard to say. Three in the morning, maybe four. One of those holes in the night where we're unlikely to find a witness.

He used to work late, hold his meetings late, make his speeches. Not usually this late.'

'Suspects?'

Gallio is growing tired of the police chief's eloquent shoulders. They rise, they hold the position, they fall. In foreign lands, especially those with a history, people are born to not care less. 'Anyone with respect for common sense. Or it could be a political killing. In Babylon we have a fragile economy, and the deputy minister of finance was a conversion risk, or his wife was. A big fan of Thomas, the minister's wife, when any top-level defection to the cult of Jesus would likely slow the figures for economic growth.'

'How's that?'

'He did insist on social justice.'

'Which is not right now a priority, here or anywhere else.'

The police chief holds out his hands. Sadly, it is so. Thomas had failed to understand the capitalist priorities of the age. He was a disruptive influence.

'Stoning suggests a group.' Baruch is back from exploring the wider area while Gallio is yet to move from where the body came to rest. Hands on his hips, he gazes at the surrounding high-rises. Not Babylonian architecture at its finest.

'At least two or three decent stone-throwers,' Baruch says. 'Otherwise a stoning can take forever.'

The footprints on the slab foundation tell no single story. Too many shoes, in too many directions. Cassius Gallio picks up a stone the size of a bread roll, common enough in modern Babylon. He extends his arm, feels the weight in his hand, lets it go. The stone cracks off the concrete.

'We bagged some bloodied stones and took them to the station. We don't expect them to tell us anything. Toward the end someone took pity, and speared him through the heart. Not that Thomas was an innocent.'

'I need to talk to someone who knew him.'

The deputy finance minister lives in a Babylonian villa with a partial view of one corner of the Hanging Gardens. Inside his walled compound he has an Abyssinian greyhound and caged canaries, the best of everything. The minister is out, but Gallio wants to interview his wife. She is in tears, desolate across a Moroccan sofa in an upstairs sitting room, a crucifix and a forty-two-inch television on opposite walls. She wants nothing more than to talk about Thomas.

'He was a wonderful man.' She dries her eyes, but the streaked mascara tells a story.

'Maybe,' Gallio says, 'but he was also running a property scam.' He won't try to break this to her gently. 'In our part of the world Thomas was a major player in a criminal fraud. Did you know that?'

'He was not.' She's a handsome woman who hasn't been pretty or thin for as long as her husband can remember.

'Thomas was a serial confidence trickster,' Baruch says. 'He was known to the Jerusalem police and wanted for questioning in connection with a fraud involving the faked resurrection of a felon.'

Gallio sighs as if the truth is routinely sad, but, given his criminal profile, Thomas in Babylon had behaved as expected. The wife of the deputy finance minister should not be surprised that Thomas took investments large and small on a development he never intended to build, using grandiose language to mask a misleading dream.

'We made donations.'

'You gave him public money.'

'For a good cause. He wanted to build a heaven on earth.'

'Does your husband, the minister, know the extent of your donations?'

Cassius Gallio doubted a government minister could be shocked. Housing scams were not unusual, especially in Babylon. However significant the sums of money, an experienced minister would expect Thomas to ensure generous returns for the rich from substandard housing that exploited the poor. Business as usual.

'Laundering?' Baruch presents the suggestion like a gift. Thomas had received cash donations. The city leaders can make his murder look like a gangland hit for a laundering scheme gone wrong. If they so please, if such an explanation keeps the politicians happy.

'That's not what he was doing.' The woman sits up straight and swallows the last of her tears. She adjusts the chain round her neck to settle the medal of Thomas flat between her breasts. 'He was a good man. He donated money to the Friends of the Vulnerable of Babylon.'

Gallio makes a visual inventory of the room, checking off the mementos of opulence earned from a lifetime's graft by a successful political official. He sees many objects with no obvious function made from precious metals. The woman sobs, can't help herself, holds her hand to her mouth.

'I'm sorry for your loss,' Cassius Gallio says. 'A few more questions and we're finished. Did you ever see Thomas with Jesus? You'd know because they look similar, like brothers.'

'Thomas said Jesus was often with us.'

'But did you ever actually see him? I need you to be clear on this point.'

We can cut through their delicacy, Gallio thinks, through

their carefully confusing wording. 'We know that Thomas claimed to be acting in the name of Jesus. Did you ever see Jesus or know how Thomas received his orders?'

'It wasn't like that.'

'So you didn't see him?'

'No.'

'Who do you think killed Thomas?'

'Satan,' she says, no hesitation. 'Satan carries away the servants of Jesus. He is a savage wolf, and he is among us.'

Cassius Gallio tries again. 'Calm down, please, no need to exaggerate. Now tell me, did Thomas have any enemies?'

He'd still be alive if they hadn't flown first to Antioch, on Turkey's eastern Mediterranean coast, to interrogate Paul who wasn't even one of the original twelve. Paul wasn't there when Jesus threatened to pull down the Temple or turn the world on its head. He was a hanger-on, an afterthought. He never spoke to Jesus and never met him, but in their wisdom Baruch and Valeria had decided to target Paul.

Baruch made a fuss about flying, which he claimed was unnatural. He had pills to take, and then he didn't take his pills. He slept most of the connecting flight of the journey, KLM to Amsterdam, and for the next leg while the Boeing taxied across the Schiphol runway he put a mask over his eyes. He pulled it off. When they were airborne he couldn't believe the plane stayed up.

'The last one did.'

'Flying is presumptuous. One day we'll have to pay.'

'Go back to sleep, caveman.'

Baruch preferred the aisle seat, to be closer to the emergency exit when the plane crashed into mountains. He unclipped his seat belt, clipped it again. Gallio refused to give up his half of the armrest.

'You're in a plane. The world is not about to end.'

'But if it were, though. If the world were about to end, what would you do differently?'

Gallio ignored him and looked out of the window at the heavenly weather of air travel, sunlight rebounding from the white upsides of clouds. He felt lucky ever to have seen this.

'Would you abandon Judith like you did the first time?'

'I wouldn't have this conversation.'

'Maybe you would. Faced with the end of the world.'

'But we're not facing the end of the world, are we?' Gallio gave up looking for heaven in favour of shutting Baruch up. 'Listen, we're on a flight from Jerusalem to Antioch with a change at Schiphol. Whatever the destination, there's always a change at Schiphol. The world as it is keeps turning.'

Gallio remembered Jude, sick and hopeful in Beirut, waiting for the return of Jesus. 'You don't really believe the world is ending, do you?'

Baruch snorted. 'Of course not.' The stress lines beside his eyes deepened. 'Just the important part of the world that's conscious in this plane as me. Do you believe Jesus is alive?'

The return question felt like a test, but Cassius Gallio had been employed by Valeria on behalf of the CCU. His personal beliefs were irrelevant, and the correct answer would be to claim he was doing his job. Instead, he told Baruch the truth. Baruch was his partner, and one day Gallio might need him to cover his back.

'I saw Jesus die. We both did. I'm ninety-nine per cent sure it was him.'

'So why are you pushing this switch theory?'

'It's the explanation that remains when others have been eliminated. What about you? Think Paul knows something?'

Baruch managed a grim smile, an Old Testament curse in his eyes. He wanted revenge. Paul had made a fool of everyone who initially believed in him.

'And Jesus?'

Baruch repaid Gallio's favour of honesty, and his honest opinion was hardly surprising. 'Dead. Gone forever. Don't believe in miracles.'

Paul was giving the keynote lecture at a Faculty of Theology conference at Mustafa Kemal University in Antioch. His subject was the death, resurrection and lordship of Jesus Christ. The title didn't suggest nostalgia for his earlier rational self.

'He's staying at the Ottoman Palace.' Baruch had been on the phone since Customs, and he was connected to someone now as he joined Gallio in the queue for conference accreditation. He covered the mouthpiece with his thumb. 'The man has a retinue. A secretary and a bodyguard. Hold on a sec.'

He checked the phone but had lost the signal. One bar, none, like living in the past. He dropped the phone into his jacket pocket. 'A bodyguard. Think about that. A bodyguard and the Ottoman Palace Hotel. Jude in ruined Beirut this is not.'

The lobby of the conference hall was filled with academics on a junket to the sun, and they were clueless about security. A graduate student checked bags at the door, his mind on a dissertation about the nature of grace.

'We'll pick Paul up after the lecture,' Cassius Gallio said. 'Shake the tree. He sold you out, so you can lead the questioning.'

'Really? Valeria wanted us to be careful.'

'Valeria isn't here.'

Gallio wore clothes to blend in with the occasion—jeans, a soft-collared shirt, a cotton jacket. Brown shoes. It was a brown-shoes academic event, with flip-flops at the hotel for the pool. Baruch was sticking with his suit, no tie, in line with the more self-regarding associate professors.

'Are you carrying a weapon?

Baruch swept back the side panels of his jacket, sank his hands into his trouser pockets, as if that proved he was clean. 'No.'

'Don't do anything stupid. Not here.'

In the lecture hall, deliberately early, they memorized the cameras, their angles, the rows in the auditorium the cameras didn't reach. Gallio staked out the entrance, pretended to make notes in the program, drew shapes instead.

The first delegates arrived and Gallio looked for familiar faces, maybe a surprise disciple. Like everyone else he had his name on a lanyard, his area of interest recorded as *Jesus Studies*, and he was in the lobby when Paul swept through, dressed like the disciples but in a darker colour. In close attendance he had his bodyguard, a slab of a man who stared at collars for comms equipment. He was good, an experienced professional, but Gallio gave nothing away. He gazed at Paul like every other star-struck theologian.

At the lectern, Paul cleared his throat and assessed the audience. He was short and bald, the grey curls at the sides and back of his head cropped tight to his skull. The stage lights reflected from his pate, and cast a shadow from the boxer's snub nose in his middle-aged face. He was clean-shaven, not from Galilee, not a disciple.

He shuffled his notes, lifted one foot then the other from

the floor, by habit a walker more than a speaker. He slapped a strong hand onto his forehead and ran it down his face, over his eyes, flattening his nose, dragging down his jaw. He blinked, recovered himself. Then he smiled.

'Thanks for coming,' he said, his voice unexpectedly high, but confident and clear. 'You know who I am, and most of you know what I do. Like it or not, you're going to hear about Jesus.'

He spoke fluently, perhaps a little fast, as if he was overfamiliar with his material. Cassius Gallio struggled to recognize Jesus in Paul's description of an all-conquering Christ who would come again bringing fire and destruction. Crucifixion and death would change anyone. But not this much, not from a Nazareth carpenter to the lord of heaven and earth. The Jesus described by Paul sounded like an idea, a useful projection, as if in Paul's version the cult had moved beyond a living Jesus.

In that sense, Paul made the second coming sound like a code, and Gallio sat in the auditorium speculating a new official leader. Whoever emerged strongest from among the surviving disciples would lead as if Jesus had returned. Then again the second coming could be literally what Paul said it was: Jesus reappearing from beneath whichever rock had been hiding him. Or not a rock, but a cloud. Jesus would arrive by air, descending from the clouds. In Paul's world of international conferences this was not so outlandish a notion. Paul reminded the audience that he had been the last person to see Jesus alive, which validated his every opinion: Jesus would come again.

He winced and straightened at the microphone, his back killing him. Paul's view was that yes, Jesus had communicated directly with the disciples, but alas they'd failed to appreciate his message. The disciples could be theologically naïve, trusting Jesus to deliver them from evil, just as James had trusted, poor

James, recently beheaded in a public place in Jerusalem. Paul's thoughts and prayers were with the family and friends of James at this difficult time.

Paul ended his lecture with a reminder that death was not itself an ending, not since Jesus had come back to life. So be of good heart. The troubles of now will fade before the glory of the great not-yet.

Everyone clapped. During the Q&A Cassius Gallio raised his hand. He waited his turn, then tried a question about an intriguing conflict he'd read about in the files.

'You don't always agree with the disciple Peter, do you? What exactly is the nature of your quarrel?'

Paul stared evenly at Gallio, but with a hint of pity, as if Gallio had forgotten to turn off his phone. An easy mistake, but he'd still managed to embarrass himself. 'I have opposed Peter to his face, that's true,' Paul said. 'But only on minor points, and when he was clearly in the wrong.'

On circumcision, for example, and food purity. But Paul didn't want to dwell on their differences, which had been taken out of context.

'You preached specifically against John.' Cassius Gallio tried again. 'You said you didn't want to meet him on your travels. Do you have a problem with the disciples?'

'I love the disciples, every last one of them.'

At the end everyone clapped, as loudly as they had the first time. Paul clapped them back, arms above his head, hands barely coming together. He did not look at Cassius Gallio. He did not go to the bar.

Outside the lecture hall Gallio turned his phone back on. He had three messages from Valeria. He ignored them. She wanted Paul, and he was getting Paul.

'Come *on*.' He made sure Baruch was out of the hall, and following. 'We'll lose him.'

Baruch caught up with Gallio before they reached the taxi rank, where they barged the queue and had the cab tailgate Paul's limo to the Ottoman Palace Hotel. Paul and his retinue crossed the marble and chandelier lobby without stopping. They waited for a lift, the bodyguard facing back into the lobby, then into the lift and up. Sixth floor.

In Beirut, Jude the disciple of Jesus was helping those in need, while dying quietly from a preventable illness. In Antioch Paul had a hotel with spa and a personal staff and official platforms from which to spread his views.

'He's a jumped-up coat-holder,' Baruch said. 'He's got answers for us, I'm sure of it.'

A change had come over Baruch. The chairs in the lobby were designed for lounging, but he sat forward and turned an invisible ring on the thumb of his left hand. He was a former killer, and it seemed his past remained available to him. He could access a primitive state of mind beyond the reasonable boundaries that Gallio tried to respect. Baruch was entering his special zone, which wasn't where Gallio wanted him to be right now.

'Paul is a citizen,' Gallio said, 'we have to respect his rights.'

'Or what?'

'There'll be repercussions. Valeria won't forget, and she's not good at forgiving. I'd say that's one of her weaknesses.'

Baruch bribed the concierge in dollars: there were two rooms booked in Paul's name. Another softened greenback and he had the number of the larger room, a suite. They waited. A lot of what Cassius Gallio did, when he wasn't speculating, was waiting. He didn't ask again if Baruch was armed.

'I reckon the secretary has the smaller room.' Baruch was

winding himself up. 'The bodyguard sleeps in the suite with Paul. That's how I'd arrange the beds, if I was worried about security. The bodyguard may be carrying. I looked but couldn't be sure.'

'What about Paul?'

'You must be joking. If the bodyguard's clean, it's two against two.'

'You don't believe that. It's two against one.'

Paul didn't count as a genuine opponent, not at close-combat fighting.

The lift to the sixth floor opened onto a peach-coloured carpet. Along the corridor a straight-backed chair obstructed the door to Paul's suite. Baruch lifted it to one side. Gallio placed his thumb over the peephole and rapped on the door. No answer.

'Paul,' he kept his voice low, speaking close to the door, thumb down over the peephole as if condemning a gladiator to death. 'Paul, I have news about Jesus. Open up. Something you should know.'

He rapped again. Nothing. He stood back and let Baruch pull a magnetic key card from his pocket. The card had a USB lead connected to a flash disc, and Baruch slipped the card into the slot. The light went green and the door clunked open. Gallio worried about Baruch, about his particular skill set from this point on, so he pushed into the suite ahead of him.

The double bed was undisturbed, and in the bathroom fresh towels were warming on the rail. Paul and his retinue had gone, but Gallio would not be outwitted, not again. He fumbled with his phone, saw another voicemail from Valeria, pressed Call and before she could speak he told her Paul had disappeared from his hotel. He needed CCU backup for an Antioch area locate and lift. Immediately.

'Slow down,' Valeria said. 'I've been trying to get hold of you.'

'He can't have gone far. He must have been tipped off by someone. He knew we were coming.'

'Something's happened,' Valeria said. 'In Babylon. You'll need to change your plans.'

Thomas won't be needing his rented apartment, not any more. The studio is in a five-storey block made primarily from asbestos, and however much money he'd collected in 'donations' he'd spent none of the profits on himself.

In the kitchen area his cooker looks unused. In the main living space Baruch turns over the mattress on the single bed, peers behind the TV. He holds up the power lead—the plug has been removed and rewired to a lamp on the bedside table, where there's a line drawing made on a white paper napkin. Boxes, rectangles. Shapes.

Baruch considers the diagram with his head to one side. 'Floor plan.' He points with his finger—'kitchen, bathroom.' With his forefinger he cuts an imaginary window in one of the imaginary walls. 'Needs more light.'

'And maybe more actual building.'

Cassius Gallio asks the police chief if Thomas ever invested funds in tangible, real-world construction. The police chief shakes his head. 'His blueprints existed in the upper air. Illusions, delusions. Never laid a single brick.'

They check behind the curtains, explore the bathroom, but it soon feels as if they're done. Gallio speculates that someone has been in the flat before them, because no one lives as simply as this. Thomas doesn't own a phone or a computer, so he can't have kept in touch with the others, or not from here.

He has a wardrobe but no clothes to fill it, and a kitchen cupboard empty of kitchen implements. Gallio would normally sift through Thomas's possessions, looking for clues, but Thomas has no possessions.

His personality is absent from the Babylon studio, and assuming no one else was here before them, the fieldcraft shown by Thomas is close to perfect. The Jesus disciples were handpicked and have been impeccably trained in the business, in Cassius Gallio's business, to make a difference but leave no personal footprint. The flat doesn't hold out much promise for traces of DNA. Gallio makes a final tour of the sanitized single room, and feels a dull feeling of infinite sadness.

'How did he settle his rent?' Baruch like Gallio feels they must be able to learn something here.

'Cash,' the police chief says. 'Promptly on the first of every month. We looked into it.'

'Pay any taxes?'

'You're joking.'

Thomas lived outside the world of telephone books, credit cards, medical insurance, voters' rolls and utility bills. He didn't leave forwarding addresses for deliveries, or passport details with money changers.

'People gave him stuff. Food, his rent money. Probably shoes and clothes too, for free. Hard to believe, but true.'

'The cash economy, dependent on handouts.'

Baruch is a government employee with a mortgaged house and a pension and at least one adopted family. He lives in the borrow-and-spend economy, never depending on handouts. 'How do they get away with it?'

'It's a strategy,' Gallio says, 'all mapped out.' He rubs his finger across the kitchen counter, not a trace of dust. 'This simple lifestyle, dependent on the will of god and human fellow feeling, is supposed to express a philosophy. It also allowed Thomas to avoid detection until now. That's not a coincidence.'

Baruch gives Gallio a quizzical look. 'Everything all right, Cassius? Holding it together?'

'Never better.'

Gallio's heart rate is a little fast, and he leans over the counter and makes the ends of his fingers fit together, back and forth, until he gets it right. In Germany and beyond he'd worried about losing his skills as a Speculator, but he can still put a story together that doesn't involve Jesus as a supreme being.

'Think of James in Jerusalem,' he says, straightening up. He can do this. 'Think of Jude in Beirut. The disciples favour cities, classic fugitive behaviour, and immediately after Judas died they split up and dispersed. They took evasive action and committed to the cash economy. Jesus even picked two men called James. He wanted to confuse, keep us from catching up with them, which he'd need to do if he was alive, making his appearances, telling them what to do. Sometimes maybe pretending to be one of his own disciples.'

'We should investigate every donor who supported Thomas.' Baruch hates the idea of the disciples getting something for nothing. 'You can't explain his survival in a dog-eat city by kindness. Jesus has to be channeling food and supplies through intermediaries.'

'The donors check out,' the police chief says. 'Mostly the poor, with no obvious connecting factor except a belief system that includes Jesus coming back from the dead. Their motives seem entirely selfish. They helped out Thomas to be rewarded in heaven.'

'The wife of the deputy finance minister said Thomas didn't have enemies.'

The police chief laughs at that.

'Imagine I'm a god,' he says. 'I'm going to be thrilled if you tell me I don't exist. Thomas told the Babylonians their gods were worthless. So excuse me, if I'm the god, and my faithful believers decide to take revenge, as a furious god I reckon I'd give them a hand.'

Baruch looks under the pillow. 'Who doesn't exist now, Thomas?'

Gallio keeps his thoughts to himself. There may be a feud within the group of original disciples, and this killing is part of a power struggle. Jesus, presumably, would be on the winning side, and Thomas in the morgue wasn't an obvious winner. It's only a theory, Gallio reminds himself. Don't let the speculation get out of control. The murderer is more likely an outside antagonist.

'You're right,' Gallio says. 'The disciples are not universally popular.'

He is preoccupied with the thought that if the disciples can live like this, off the grid, then presumably so can Jesus.

Can he? Gallio checks and checks again that he's making a thoroughly professional deduction—no one found a corpse, so reason dictates that Jesus may well be alive. That's a reasonable conclusion, and one an objective Speculator needs to accommodate. If Jesus survived, by means Cassius Gallio doesn't presently understand, he can be re-apprehended for significant rewards: an honorary doctorate, lecture tours, hotel room with spa for the visiting keynote speaker. Acclaim, forgiveness, a kind of heaven.

The glory awaiting Cassius Gallio will be greater if he finds Jesus and Jesus is alive. Eating food, sleeping in beds, hurting when he realizes how many lives he has ruined. Looking round the emptied Babylon studio-room Gallio is suddenly convinced

that Jesus is involved in this murder. This realization is un-
comfortable, almost unthinkable, but he follows his speculation
through and checks once more in the obvious place, under the
bed. Lies there on his stomach, his cheek against the grain of the
floorboards. Lies there some more. The secret is knowing how
to look.

V

Philip

———

"INVERTED HANGING"

Antioch, Schiphol, Babylon, Schiphol, Jerusalem.

They feel like seasoned travellers, hand baggage only. At Ben Gurion Cassius Gallio deactivates flight mode, and as soon as his CCU phone picks up a signal, between the gate and Passport Control, there's a text from Valeria. Code Yellow, it says. Code Yellow requires immediate attendance at the Antonia Fortress. All the same, this is Israel, now as always. Baruch with his Israeli passport is waved through Customs. As a foreigner Gallio waits in line, and has to explain his lack of baggage.

The Antonia case room, when Gallio eventually gets there, has evolved in the short time they've been away. More computers, more desks pushed together, exploded dossiers, cold take-out coffee and an empty pastries box. Several of the screens have switched to their savers—free-form shapes that bounce from edge to edge, waiting out the hole caused by Valeria's displeasure.

'What?' Gallio is unnerved by the silence, and also by the five or six officers he hasn't seen before. Crossed arms, all of them, never a good sign in a case room. 'I'm sorry I'm late. It wasn't my fault.'

Philip the disciple of Jesus is dead. Code Yellow. James, then Thomas in Babylon, now Philip. Three disciples down, and Gallio with his feet not yet safe beneath the desk. He feels like it's next to no time since Valeria called him back.

'We were investigating the murder of Thomas in Babylon,' Gallio says. 'Philip wasn't on our radar. Which one's Philip?'

'You should have assessed the risk,' Valeria says. 'You could have identified the pattern before we had it confirmed. Someone out there is killing disciples.'

'Is it a pattern, though?'

'You must have missed something.'

Changes are under way in the case room. A man from the works department power-drills the wall, making it ready for a big whiteboard fresh from cardboard packaging. A graduate trainee rearranges pins on the wall-map. In Jerusalem and in Babylon, she replaces the pins with an adhesive black disc, one each for the dead disciples James and Thomas. For Philip, at the southwest corner of Turkey, the disc is brown until Philip's identity can be confirmed by Baruch and Cassius Gallio, the only two operatives on station with personal knowledge of Jesus.

At a new desk in the corner, a young woman in an Italian sweater wears a landline headset, nods at whatever she's hearing and types rapid notes into her computer.

'Everyone should calm down,' Baruch says. 'Whoever killed Philip can't be the same perp who stoned and speared Thomas.'

Baruch has recovered from the flying, though lack of sleep makes him irritable, a man back from a long journey with a home to go to. At the same time, assassination and killing is his business, so he's not planning on leaving this discussion to amateurs.

'We need the details,' he says. 'How did they kill him?'

'Nastily. So no reason it couldn't be the same killer.' Valeria is captain of crossed arms, of hands on hips, not in a sunny mood. 'We call it the miracle of flight. If you can catch a plane from Babylon to here, an assassin could fly from Babylon to Hierapolis in Turkey in the same time period. We've checked the timetables, and don't forget the killer had a head start. Thomas was dead when you arrived.'

'Could be a coincidence, like Baruch says.' Gallio makes eye contact with his surprise ally, his partner. 'We need more to go on than possibility.'

On the plane Gallio had slept like a baby, thousands of feet above the earth, and he feels calm and reasonable because Code Yellow is not so high a security level. Code Yellow: Elevated. Two clear stages below Severe. 'The disciples of Jesus make themselves unpopular pretty much wherever they go. James, Thomas, Philip. Common sense catches up with them and they're due a losing streak, which happens to have started now.'

Gallio helps himself to the last of the filter coffee, avoiding Valeria's glare. In Speculator training, coincidence is a forbidden word, and his fearlessness surprises them both. Unstable, she'll think. Not all there, as befits a career that began with a view of the Colosseum and was finishing in Germanic Lowlands.

'Coincidences do happen.' Gallio swallows some coffee, and wishes he hadn't. 'Luck, bad luck, inexplicable sequences of events. We'd make sensational mistakes if we assumed everything had to be connected.'

Too much. Valeria points her finger, like Pilate once had, then changes her mind about putting him right. He knows, and doesn't need to be told. A Speculator is tasked with making connections, exactly that, with finding the pattern and meaning in disparate events. Jesus has defeated their attempt once, by faking his death then claiming to come back to life. This time Valeria will not be deterred from being too clever. Every connection has to be made, to stop Jesus from outsmarting them again.

'Cassius is right,' Baruch says. 'There don't have to be connections between these deaths. The beheading of James was an accident. I was involved with locking James up and we didn't mean him to die, but it happened.' He frowns, hoping someone was punished, and if he ever gets a moment he'll check. 'Then Cassius tracks down a couple of Galilean immigrants in cities far apart, first Jude in Beirut, next Thomas in Babylon. You've seen how the disciples dress, making no attempt to assimilate. They exist outside the mainstream, with no record of gainful employment, which suggests they're involved in unlawful activity. That's enough probable cause to explain why Thomas and Philip can get unlucky in similar ways, thousands of miles apart.'

Valeria paces. 'The case has been upgraded,' she says. 'We've moved to Elevated, Yellow. The bad news is you shouldn't plan any days off. The good news is we can access more resources. I've sent those glass samples to forensics, for example, and the two of you are getting some help.'

The young woman in the corner is back on the phone and has a pad and pencil in her hands. She looks clever, Gallio thinks. Attractive, but mostly clever. Cassius Gallio wanders toward her desk and looks over her shoulder. She manages a grimace and a raised finger, then listens hard while shading abstract shapes in her pad. A hexagon, almost perfect; could mean anything.

• • •

What will be will be. Valeria has made up her mind and on one of the days that follows, whether they like it or not, Cassius and Baruch will fly on an early-hours charter to Denizli Cardak airport in western Turkey. As their cover, they will be carrying advance tickets for a Bible Lands coach tour to Hierapolis and Pamukkale. Gallio will dress to blend in: hybrid walking shoes, cargo-style trousers, a fleece. Baruch makes fewer concessions, and will be what he is in his suit.

On the coach Baruch will refuse to sit with Gallio because during their flight Gallio said 'for god's sake, no' when asked to demonstrate the brace position for the fifth time. But in some ways that's a good thing, because on a Bible holiday journeying alone is not unusual. Cassius will take a seat toward the back, and as the coach moves away the airport streetlights will strobe the faces of their fellow travellers. If Jesus were alive, he might rely on a secret network of helpers like these, single women from church groups and couples who hold hands against the darkness. Two black teenage girls, wearing knitted maroon bobble hats, smile so broadly they must never have heard of sex before marriage.

A red sun will climb above the horizon, and Cassius Gallio will attune to the holiday excitement. The black girls tell a nun that at his Antioch conference Paul shared the platform with a disciple, it said so in their parish newsletter. The Jesus passengers are enthusiastic but ill informed. A man in a fleece winks, a punchline coming up, and says it's nice to take the bus because on his last church trip he had to walk. Santiago de Compostela. Two hundred miles on foot to touch the bones of James.

The bones. Only now will Cassius Gallio spare a thought for bones. The disciples continue to exist as relics after they die, but however long he lives Gallio will never understand how the bones of James travelled from the city of Jerusalem to the coast of northwest Spain. The when and how rarely matter to pilgrims: every Christian tripper has walked all or part of the Camino, and the once-in-a-lifetime adventure provides a lifetime's subject of conversation. James the disciple of Jesus will and will not end his days in Jerusalem, and even though the authenticity of the Compostela bones remains unproven, future believers will forever keep on walking.

In the second hour of the coach trip the conversation fades, and Gallio rests his head against the window. He will sleep lightly, meaning not well. He will dream of his head pattering the glass of the emergency exit, of the stutter of his past and fragments from his life yet to come.

'Hi, I'm Claudia.'

They know. Valeria has just introduced her. She's Claudia the highly rated analyst, arrived from Rome this morning. 'I'm joining you on background research.'

She has a face that makes Gallio think of the future, of what his life would be like with Claudia as part of it. That's his Speculator first impression, he tells himself. After further objective assessment, of her dark eyes and angled jaw, he decides that she's not unreasonably pretty but she is an impeccable shape, slim at the waist, broad-hipped. Probably not that useful in a scrap, to be honest, no bone weight.

'You two can't do everything.' Valeria sucks her teeth, as if to dislodge the taste of the little they've done. 'I've asked Claudia to give you a briefing.'

Claudia walks over to the new incident board, now in place

and dominating the far wall of the case room. At the top in the centre is an artist's impression of Jesus, which only Gallio knows is the image based on James. The incident board looks like a family tree, with lines of connection branching from Jesus at the top down to the more prominent disciples: Peter, Thomas, John, Andrew. Then more lines connecting to a bottom row of disciples who are less well known. The hard bald face of Paul is the odd man out. His image is pinned mid-row in a gap between John and Philip.

Cassius Gallio, as a professional, evaluates Claudia as she talks, and he's careful not to miss anything: grey sweater, black trousers, highish black heels. Quite tall, good hips. He remembers he already noticed the hips. Unprofessional. To the heels and back again. He doesn't think anyone notices.

First presentation, unfamiliar surroundings, so as a young woman she brings her business voice.

'I'm up to speed with the context,' she says, 'and my job is to work out why Thomas and Philip are dead, and whether these murders connect either to each other or to your recently launched enquiry into a certain missing person. James may also be relevant, if we pick up obvious echoes.'

Claudia is efficient, but also vulnerable, because there must be more to her than efficiency. Whatever she's hiding, Gallio thinks, she can be found out.

'What type of connections?' Baruch asks. 'I presume you mean whether they were killed by the same person.'

Gallio suspects Baruch knows the answer but wants Claudia's attention. So transparent. Claudia takes a red marker pen from Baruch's desk and turns to the incident board. She taps on the images for James, Thomas and Philip, the three dead disciples. Gallio hasn't seen this picture of James before, kneeling in prayer while an angel with a broadsword waits to behead him. That can't be how it happened, not in that equestrian backyard in Jerusalem. Claudia uncaps the pen and draws a cross through James's face.

She moves on, crosses out Thomas and then Philip, recaps the pen and taps it against each of the images. Tap, tap, tap. She lets the pen rest on Thomas. In this picture a muscular infidel wearing a leather helmet is driving a spear into his chest. It's all speculation.

'We need to establish whether any of the connections are material. So far Thomas and Philip are linked as disciples of Jesus and as victims of violent crime. One was stoned and speared. Unusual. Philip, hundreds of miles away in Hierapolis, had a rope worked through his hamstrings. He was then hauled up on the rope, head down, feet in the air. He was left to hang and bleed until he died.'

Claudia lets them consider the fate of Philip, and the process of passing a rope through a chunk of living resistant muscle. Gallio's legs feel flimsy, insubstantial. He pushes his thighs into the edge of the chair and imagines the specialist tools, the necessary hardware. He's in awe of the implacable will of whoever decided to sew a rope through the flesh of another human being.

'Both disciples died curious and violent deaths,' Claudia says. 'Agreed? In that case, we have the beginning of a pattern.'

Hierapolis is the end city in an earthquake belt that stretches from southwest Turkey round the northeastern Mediterranean as far as Israel. The coast is not rock solid here, never was or will be, and the planet can crack and shift seventy miles out to sea and six miles down. At Pamukkale, near Hierapolis, the earth's core has thrown up terraces of travertine rock where hot springs deposit calcium carbonate that hardens into an impermeable crust. The whiteness of the mountainside pools turns the water a bright crystal blue.

The matching blue sky is scarred by vapour trails. An occasional seagull will drift left, drift right, looking for food or other seagulls to love. At the postcard stand, at the van selling Pepsi. Tourists without a guide probably won't know either about the geology of the region nor that up the hill behind Pamukkale, beyond barefoot vacation snaps in the white-blue water, the ruined martyrium of Philip is waiting. Philip the one-time disciple of Jesus.

Claudia carried out her analysis and from that point onward Cassius Gallio and Baruch were destined to start up this hill, the sun lunchtime high and the path at a serious angle. They will persevere, hands on knees as they struggle with the gradient, a challenging hike even in sensible shoes. They will overtake some stragglers and Gallio will recognize passengers from the coach tour. Who will soon overtake them back again, because unlike Gallio and Baruch they've trained on the rigors of the Camino.

'What do we *care* if the disciples get killed?' Baruch will stop to rest, doubled over, breathing heavily.

'We don't care. Not really.' Gallio will also suffer, but he has recently returned from active duty. He will recover his breath more quickly. 'The disciples are important because of what they tell us about Jesus. Three of them are dead. Something is happening, as if we've shaken their nest.'

Baruch will look up through the trees and groan.

'We should have gone for Thomas before Paul,' Gallio will say, 'which I recommended. Then we might have learned something. If Jesus is with us, and if he can be found, we'll trace him through his disciples. That's my informed professional opinion.'

'Not through Philip, though. Can't wind up much more dead than Philip.'

'No, but if they made a switch on the cross we'll gradually get closer. Stands to reason. One of these disciples isn't what he seems, and I have the feeling someone wants to stop us from closing in on Jesus.'

The next section of climbing means it will be easier for Baruch to agree than to argue. First, though, to delay the pain, he'll find he has more to say. 'We struck at the shepherd, now someone is rounding up the sheep. But if Jesus is alive we'll find him, retry him, and kill him again. That's nobody's job but ours.'

As a former killer Baruch will forever insist on his right to be an expert about death. Death has been his life, and he's confident that he can't be surprised by any aspect of killing or dying. Jesus is dead, with no resurrection possible, and Jesus will remain dead because some surprises are impossible and all is well with the world. Or Jesus is alive because he never died, which is an utter scandal. Whoever is responsible will be punished, and if that means the disciples then so be it.

Cassius Gallio will ask Baruch whether he believes in an afterlife. If he asks on the uphill trek to Philip's martyrium, Baruch will struggle both to walk and answer at the same time.

'Unlikely.' He has to stop to make his point. 'If there's an afterlife I'd never have dared kill anybody. Too many unknown factors involved, including the threat of retribution after the event. A whole world of trouble.'

'Good.' Cassius Gallio will squint into the sunshine and assess what's left of the hill. Same as there ever was. 'One last push. Come on, my friend, not far now.'

•   •   •

'So who's killing them?' Baruch makes himself the centre of attention in the incident room because murder is his specialist subject, and everything else is garnish.

'Someone who's willing and able to travel,' Claudia says, 'if the killings are connected.'

'How many people involved?'

Claudia glances at Valeria, and gets a nod so she carries on while Valeria looks inside a coffee cup: dregs but old and cold. Don't read too much into it, Gallio thinks. The good stuff is not always in the past.

'Maybe more than one person,' Claudia says, 'but not too many, because the killings are clean. With Thomas and now Philip they did a tidy job, leaving nothing behind we can use to construct a forensic link.'

'In Babylon the crime scene was compromised,' Valeria says. 'They moved the body before you arrived. In Hierapolis we've managed to intervene in time, and they agreed not to cut Philip down, especially as for the moment he's not putting off the tourists. The delay isn't ideal. Might have been different if we had had our own people on the ground.'

'Or there may be no pattern at all. That's also a possibility.' Claudia is comfortable double-teaming with Valeria, as if they've worked together before. 'Despite comparable levels of violence, Philip and Thomas were murdered in obviously different ways. Serial killers usually fall into habits that betray them, but not here, or not that I can see.'

'So it wasn't the same killer. That would explain the differences in the method.'

'I've dug up some grudges,' Claudia says, 'motives. Philip's killing may be a local quarrel, specific to the Hierapolis region, and again it may not.'

She projects a PowerPoint slide onto a blank white space on the far wall. Baruch sighs dismissively and pulls out a chair, his body language announcing that everything was better in the old days, before Claudia was born. She reads her list of Hierapolis suspects off the screen, clicking through a roster of potential assailants that the disciples of Jesus risk provoking wherever they stop to preach. Same for Philip as for Thomas—so connected, but also coincidental.

Along with local priests opposed to atheist upstarts, every ancient city has its share of rationalists, of undertakers, of embittered materialists who insist on tooth-and-claw mortality. In Hierapolis Philip had offended pimps and landowners, businessmen and local moneylenders who wanted no enlightenment beyond the laws of supply. He had truly aggrieved the parents of dead children, enraged by chatter about resurrection.

'Stop talking,' Baruch says. 'Yak yak yak. You're being too clever.'

Claudia ignores him. 'And we shouldn't forget that in both cases the disciples were survived by people on their own side who blamed Satan.'

Cassius Gallio coughs gently, throat dry from the flying, and finds he enjoys the way Claudia turns her young, pretty face toward him. Attractive, clever, both ways round. He holds up a plastic evidence bag. Inside is a splinter of wood about six inches long.

'I found this in the flat Thomas was renting in Babylon. If we now have access to the labs I'd like it analyzed.'

'From here it looks like a piece of wood,' Baruch says. 'Hardwood. The floorboards in Babylon were pine. Indulge me.'

Claudia glances once more at Valeria. Valeria nods, interested in every lead. Gallio places the baggie on Claudia's keyboard, where she won't be able to ignore it, but Claudia hasn't finished speaking. He studies her lips, her chin, the indent of her waist, her long hips. Cassius Gallio is not a good man. Really, he is not.

'There's another connection we need to consider,' she says. 'The murders of Thomas and Philip took place after the two of you started looking for Jesus.'

Baruch sees the implication an instant before Gallio, but Baruch had spent his early life constructing alibis, even when he was innocent. 'Are we suspects for murder?'

'I don't know.' Claudia has the same hard edge as Valeria. Gallio took this long to notice it. 'Are you?'

'Of course they're not,' Valeria says. 'They were flying back from Babylon when the news came through about Philip in Hierapolis. The point is not that you're suspects. It's that the search for Jesus may be connected to the killings. Maybe you're right about the switch theory, and you're closing in. We should keep pushing. Go to Hierapolis. Identify the body and learn what you can.'

'Got anything else for us?' Baruch is imagining the plane, the brace position, the landing on water—how is that even possible without a miracle? 'We're not going to find Jesus. He's dead.'

'We've told you what we know,' Valeria says. 'Though there's one more thing. Philip has his own martyrium, to commemorate his selfless death. That's where he was killed, so you'll need to get your head round that.'

Beyond the crest of the hill the path levels out, and directly ahead on a flat area of ground is Philip's martyrium. Baruch will be infinitely grateful for the flattening out, and after a breather he and

Cassius Gallio will approach the ruined building. The ancient stones are scratched with graffiti: the sign of the cross, the sign of the fish, and in black permanent marker *Gaston makes girls come.*

Pilgrims who make the effort tend to linger, setting down their kagouls to sit with a view of the ruin. They will aim to take some quiet time of their own to meditate on the death of Philip the disciple of Jesus. Gallio will recognize the radiant black girls from the Bible Lands coach, in duffel coats and their matching maroon bobble hats. They will sit on plastic bags, taking turns to bite an apple. Even they will look a little sad, because it's too late now to intervene. Philip is dead. Philip was dead. He will always from now on be dead.

Gallio will step through a damaged gateway into what was once the centre of the octagonal martyrium, and from the moment Philip was called by Jesus in Galilee this is where he would die. This is where he died. Cassius Gallio will see him clearly—from a crumbling stone arch, just pillars and a span, a man hanging upside down. Philip is naked like an angel, arms extended, mouth open, forever falling from heaven. It will seem unlikely that Philip is the disciple Jesus loved. A rope has been forced through the meat of his thighs, behind the bones. On the cracked flagstones beneath his head, sparrows peck at a stain of blood or dried rust. Could be either now that time has passed.

Violence is Baruch's territory, his background. He will approach the body, make his experienced assessments.

'Naked,' he says. 'Makes sense. Safety measure.'

The assassin or assassins will have checked for concealed devices, drugs, amulets, looking to remove any protective padding or breathing apparatus that could keep Philip alive and later be misinterpreted as divine intervention.

'Thorough,' Cassius Gallio will say. 'Whoever did this

wanted to avoid another Jesus, a resurrection. No way Philip's coming back, not after this. It's a professional hit.'

The rope, Phoenician hemp designed for inland boats, will creak as the fibres stretch, as Philip's inverted body catches the breeze. The complaint of rope is a warning signal, a sign of the times saying that whatever the man-made world has lashed together, either with effort and ingenuity or in haste without care, threatens to break apart.

For Cassius Gallio, the creaking rope will be a reminder of Judas in a field long ago, the beginning of the end of his career. 'Still think Paul did this? He has alibis. He was nowhere near the killings of either Thomas or Philip. He'll have witnesses.'

'He disappeared from Antioch,' Baruch says. 'We had no idea where he went, and look at his record. When he killed Stephen he kept his own hands clean, but from that period of his life he knows plenty of capable people, and they can follow instructions. You've seen his bodyguard. Cassius, you have to admit Paul has form. He does, doesn't he?'

This, Gallio will later think, is the first time since they started working as partners that Baruch has asked for an opinion. Cassius Gallio will look at the hanging naked body of Philip the disciple of Jesus and he will try to establish what this particular death changes. A Galilean eyewitness to the miracles of Jesus is dead, and a V of migrating ducks passes overhead. This year, next year. Sparrows in the ruins hop two-footed in search of packed-lunch crumbs, different sparrows but the same basic patterns, century after century. Nothing will obviously have changed.

'Cut him down, for Christ's sake.'

Tourists don't bring the right kind of knife. The walkers and pilgrims have penknives for their cheese and apples, but nothing with the blade for Phoenician hemp. Baruch will have a knife.

'What did you expect?' he says. 'I carry a knife. I've always carried a knife.'

He will pull a Sicarii killing dagger from the sheath inside the back of his belt, but as he approaches Philip he is distracted by a flash of reflected light from a laminated board.

'Wait a minute,' he says. 'We missed something. Take a look at this.'

A weathered information board that occupies an angle of the octagon in Philip's martyrium. The text boxes are for the benefit of unprepared visitors, who may be interested to know that in most legends the disciple Philip was hanged upside down alongside a second disciple, his close friend Bartholomew. Bartholomew, at the decisive moment, was saved.

'So where is this Barthomolew?' Baruch will resheathe his knife. 'Philip is dead. Nothing we can do for him now. Let's pick up the other one.'

In southwest Turkey only the Divriği hospital has the facilities to accept a foreign national in a critical condition after a brutal assault at Pamukkale.

'I'm sending Claudia to join you,' Valeria says by telephone. 'Wait for her. She'll make sure you ask the right questions, but work together. Try to get some sense out of this Bartholomew.'

The Divriği, in the hills the other side of Hierapolis, bears no resemblance to Jude's hospital in Beirut. The springs of Pamukkale have been a place of healing for centuries, and the city of Hierapolis has traditionally welcomed the latest developments in medicine. Bartholomew's private room has a waxed linoleum floor, and an Insect-O-Cutor fixed to the ceiling. The machine buzzes from time to time, killing indiscriminately, doing its work.

Cassius Gallio has used the authority of Security Code Yellow to relocate Bartholomew from the public ward. The disciple is unconscious, with IV drips in his arms and a catheter in his bladder, his body a filter for morphine and high-grade dextrose-saline. Gallio invites Baruch and Claudia to join him at the bedside, but Bartholomew won't be answering questions.

'Lucky bastard,' Baruch says. 'I'd have made him talk.'

Unlike his friend Philip, Bartholomew the disciple of Jesus hasn't had half-inch Phoenician hemp sewn through the muscles of his thighs. The assassins tied rope around his ankles and hauled him aloft beside Philip, and Bartholomew is suffering an aneurism caused by a surfeit of blood to the brain. He also has lung damage, and skull trauma from when passers-by cut him down but failed to protect his head. Each of these injuries alone could have sent him into a coma.

'Why did the killers treat them differently?'

'Time constraints?'

Gallio is trying to be realistic. The murder of Philip could have taken longer than expected, with the sewing involved. Bartholomew would have died, in any case, if he hadn't been unexpectedly rescued. Luck. Too late for Philip, but Bartholomew with luck on his side was saved.

Though unluckily not soon enough to save him from a coma. The three investigators take turns in the two chairs, and as they consider what to do next they remember hospitals they've visited in the past. The injured, the dying, their incomplete emotions as witnesses to the misfortune of other people. Cassius Gallio has a clear picture of his stepdad waving away a nurse to show off the shiny stump of his amputated leg, admiring the elevation he could get and expecting Gallio to admire it too. The legion's doctors had taken decisive action and Gallio's stepfather was delighted. Their intervention would give him ten added years of life and this was the reason, he said, this was the reason that anyone of sane mind owed allegiance to the march of progress.

A trolley crashes in the corridor.

Claudia sits beside the ECG monitor and flips up the leather cover of her iPad, googles 'coma.' Gallio has a side view of her face, her forceful nose, the upper lip tight across strong white teeth. Braces, probably, at just the right stage of teenage development. One day there will be no imperfections.

'What would you have asked him?' Claudia prepares to write notes, to take the positives from a frustrating situation.

'How about—who tried to kill you?'

'Would be a good place to start,' Baruch says. One more journey by plane and his reserves of patience will be empty.

'Is Jesus still alive?' Gallio suggests. He's interested in the killers only in so far as they can lead him to Jesus.

'Don't you hate Paul?' Baruch says. 'That's what I'd ask him. What the fuck are we doing here?'

Claudia closes her iPad. 'We're wasting our time.'

Cassius Gallio wonders who she is. Analysts sit behind their desks, and that's where they stay, compiling bar charts. Claudia is smarter than that, pretty, about the age Gallio was on his first tour of Jerusalem, and now Valeria has assigned her to Gallio's case. Claudia had somehow been entrusted to him, or he to her, and Gallio suspects she may be a test sent by Valeria, a revenge across time. He admires her collarbone and feels the full, sad stupidity of unrequited lust.

Claudia flicks her wedding band with her thumbnail, making her ring finger jump. All the way from Rome for this.

'You'll be missed at home, I should think.'

Gallio tries out small talk, a Speculator instinct, never

knowing what he'll find until he finds it. He's feeling for cracks that may later widen to let a less guarded Claudia out, let Cassius Gallio maneuvre in. 'Your husband must miss you.'

He won't make the same mistake twice, foolish, lovesick, spying on a life he can never have.

'Comes with the job,' she says.

'We could torture him,' Baruch says. 'Even though he's unconscious. Why not?'

Baruch would love to make his trip by air worthwhile. He is angered by obstacles, by Bartholomew in a coma, and for Baruch hesitation is a type of failure. In his experience clarity is achieved with decisive action. Specifically, he wants to torture Bartholomew into giving up secrets, and torture could plausibly wake the dead.

'Or not,' Gallio says. 'If he doesn't wake up, then how can he beg for mercy? You'd kill him.'

'The coma is a problem,' Claudia agrees, whatever Baruch might think. She has shadows beneath her eyes, and a vertical line in the centre of her forehead that will deepen for the rest of her life.

'What do you think now,' Gallio asks her, 'do you believe Philip's murder was random?'

'It doesn't matter what I believe. Either it is or it isn't. Our job is to find out what's true.'

She thinks and talks like a Speculator. If Claudia is a humble analyst, then Cassius Gallio is a Swiss drugs salesman.

'We should keep him with us,' Gallio decides. 'Make sure he's out of danger, at least from the assassins. We'll put him on a military flight to Jerusalem.'

Claudia nods, all three of Valeria's team now assembled at the bedside like family mourners with a recent corpse. Bartholomew is laid out in his hospital gown, a thin-boned Jesus—eyes closed, pale inner arms bared to the strip lights and IV feeds, a smile at the corner of his mouth. A nurse puts her head round the door. Baruch gives her a targeted stare and a two-fingered point. She leaves.

'What about Paul?' he says. 'We can't discount his involvement.'

'Can't rule him out, you're right.' That frown-line again cuts through Claudia's forehead—so young, and the thinker of such difficult thoughts. 'Paul used to be an Israeli operative, and years ago the priests sent him to assassinate disciples. He could be a double agent, and Jerusalem continues to run him.'

'But Baruch would know if that were true,' Gallio says, emboldened by the serenity of Bartholomew and his deep, easy breathing. 'You'd know if Jerusalem was running Paul, wouldn't you Baruch? Senior man like you?'

Cassius Gallio is not alone in having suffered for Jesus. Baruch had once been the top Israeli fixer in Jerusalem. Back in the day, whenever the priests had a Jesus problem, Baruch was the man to solve it—the son of the widow of Nain, Lazarus after he was brought back to life. Following the insolence of the crucifixion weekend, his superiors lost confidence in his powers.

'Maybe I wouldn't know.' It hurts Baruch to say it. 'Not these days. They could run Paul without keeping me in the loop. I have to accept that.'

'Not as vital to the cause as you thought you were.'

'Who is?'

'Let's stick to the information we have,' Claudia says. 'Thomas and Philip were targeted, we can agree on that, and these hits are professional. The incident sites are clean, and the killers know what they're doing. That doesn't mean Paul is involved.'

'Paul knows what he's doing. Remember Stephen.'

'Remember Judas,' Gallio says.

No suicide note, when Jesus and his disciples had an obvious motive for killing the man who'd betrayed them, but for Baruch the disciples are short of practical ability. They can talk and they're kind; none of them are killers. Cassius Gallio isn't so sure. He remembers Judas hanged, alone on his blood-money property, swinging from the neck for hours in the morning sun. Judas was a lesson, a vengeance killing. His death was public and violent, a classic gangland memorandum: Jesus and the disciples sweep clean. Jesus was human and he wanted revenge on Judas, as would Cassius Gallio, if Judas ever happened to him.

The murder of Philip fell into a similar category. An inverted hanging had the same vengeful showiness, the theatre.

'In Babylon, Thomas was stoned and he didn't run,' Gallio says. 'Philip had a rope pulled through his thighs but not a single bruise on his face. Look at Bartholomew. He's had a disturbing experience, but I can't see any evidence he fought back. There's not a scratch on him.'

They dutifully examine Bartholomew's unblemished face and hands, pale as alabaster. With a single finger Claudia moves a strand of hair away from Bartholomew's eye. His brow is unmarked, and in his sleep unlined.

Gallio says: 'It looks like they knew the killer.'

'They know Jesus,' Claudia says.

'They know *Paul!*' Baruch shouts. He calms down, chastened by the room's hygienic echo. 'Jesus isn't a killer. He doesn't have the record.'

'He escaped his own execution,' Gallio says. He brushes a fly from his face. It veers upward and is zapped with a single buzz. 'A man who dies and doesn't die could easily set up a stoning and a hanging. I'd say it's within his capabilities to wipe a crime scene.'

'Paul used to kill for a living, and he's completely alive and traceable. Everything fits to incriminate Paul. For fuck's sake, let's find Paul and bring him in.'

Gallio is alarmed by the tension in Baruch, who can't see beyond Paul the defector. His fingers twitch, words beginning to fail him, but their disagreement is cut short by Claudia's phone. She answers deadpan, 'yes' and 'go on.' She turns to the window and listens, ends the call with a nod. 'Thank you, I understand.'

She looks at the screen, disconnects, composes herself. She turns round and shares the news.

'It's Jude in Beirut,' she says. 'Shot by arrows. He's dead.'

VI

James

"BLUDGEONED TO DEATH"

Cassius Gallio finds the red marker pen, and at the incident board he considers the latest magnified image of Jude. The print dates from before Jude fell ill. He is younger, unyielding, holding some kind of framed picture. Gallio strikes a red cross through his face.

The CCU operations room has double-checked the encryption codes, and can now confirm the reports from Beirut have more than a single source. The news remains consistent: *Missionary dead in Beirut. Israeli national, more than one alias. Stock of international prescription drugs, no receipts.*

Verifiable data about how exactly Jude was killed is less forthcoming, and so far no Lebanese militia group has claimed responsibility. Jude was shot with an arrow or arrows, a setback to supporters of Beirut's gun-free zones. The death is currently being treated as an accident.

Gallio tosses the permanent marker onto a desk and leaves the incident room, walks up two flights of stairs to the Prefect's office. He hasn't been here since Pilate's day, and after the mishandling of the Jesus episode the status of Prefect has declined to the point where Valeria can commandeer these rooms at will. These days no one knows the Prefect's name, or needs to know it. CCU runs the show.

Valeria lets him in, and they sit in high-backed chairs in a reception room with one wall open over the city roofs of Jerusalem. 'Thanks for coming up,' Valeria says. 'I wanted to see you alone, without Baruch, and up here we'll get some privacy.'

'Baruch and I are supposed to be partners.'

'We worry about him. Gives off a definite tension. Is he all right?'

'He doesn't like flying.'

'What about you? You seem to be bearing up.'

At the balustrade Gallio leans on his elbows and looks at roof tiles and satellite dishes. Is he bearing up? He thinks he is. A decent amount of time has passed since he last had to crush a rogue nerve in his face, and his search for Jesus feels successfully purged of emotion. He is thinking again like a Speculator, following procedures, pursuing an achievable objective. He feels back on track, a somebody. Down below, in the streets of Jerusalem, the people are so indistinct they could be historical figures.

Valeria joins him at the balustrade. 'I'm not convinced Baruch can see the bigger picture. He takes everything so personally, and doesn't always appreciate that we have everyone's best interests at heart. That's not surprising, of course. We have so much power in the world that he loves to chip away at us, as if everything is our fault.' She peeks over the balustrade. 'Without our civilizing influence they'd still be sacrificing children.'

'What's this about?'

Valeria smells the warm air, looks at the figures scurrying and stopping below. 'Who do you think killed Jude?'

Gallio has been asking himself the same question, and keeps coming back to the same conclusions.

'Someone who knows what they're doing,' he says. 'They're good, whoever it is, very good. In Beirut the killers adapted to a weapons ban, after moving unobserved in and out of Babylon. At Pamukkale the killer carried rope and tools through a World Heritage Site and not one terrorist-aware tourist identified suspicious behaviour and called it in. Jesus should be on our suspects list. No one can vanish and reappear as effectively as Jesus.'

'Give me his motive,' Valeria says.

'He had a motive for killing Judas. As for the others, I don't know.'

'Come on, speculate.'

'OK. This is what I've got. After years of doing nothing we reopen the case on Jesus. We start looking for him as if he's alive, and if anyone knows where he's hiding it's the disciples. Thomas dies, Philip dies. Bartholomew is in a coma. Jude dies. Jesus doesn't want to be found, or not by us.'

Gallio can do this. He hasn't forgotten how to speculate. 'Every time a disciple dies there's less of a path to the leader, the kingpin, the king of the Jews. The disciples have done everything he asked of them. They've cooperated with the switch move, spread the false story about resurrection, grown his following. Now Jesus is telling them something else.'

'Fuck off before you mess up,' Valeria says. 'Better dead than betray his whereabouts. Not much of a thank-you. Who else is a suspect?'

'One or more of the disciples.'

'Motive?'

'Internal feud. Probably a power struggle to decide a new leader. Might be connected to the second coming, and jostling for position before that happens.'

'What is that, exactly, the second coming?'

'If it's not Jesus emerging from hiding, it could be one of the disciples standing in for him, and picking up where Jesus left off. Another switch play. They'd each be anxious to be number one.'

'Good. Convincing. Anyone else?'

'Jesus and some of the disciples together. Same reason. Judas is proof they're prepared to take action against anyone who threatens their plans, and maybe Jude in Beirut shouldn't have told me about the beloved disciple. An arrow to the heart, and he won't slip up again. Then there's Paul. He's easier to classify than the others. He enjoys influence, and five-star hotels. The Jesus movement grows in every city he visits, and in every community that receives his letters. Most converts see him as an equal to the disciples, but the disciples are also his competition. They're rivals in spreading the message.'

'I thought he wanted to join them?'

'Except they didn't let him join, did they? Even if he's not being run by Jerusalem he has a motive. The disciples rejected him. He owes them. If he eliminates them from the story then his version of Jesus wins out.'

'How is his version different?'

'The disciples aren't so important in it.'

Valeria sits in one of the chairs, and Gallio turns to face her, the top of the terrace balustrade sharp in the small of his back.

'Come and sit down, Cassius. Baruch isn't here because there's information I want only you to have. It's about Paul. He's a public figure and he can be useful to us. In fact the CCU encourages Paul. We don't disapprove of the work he does.'

Throughout the known world, Rome had always supported client kings. Valeria's concept of Paul was as a client apostle, because his version of the faith suited the requirements of an advanced nation state. Paul believed in marriage and social stability and paying taxes, solid civilized virtues.

'That's my idea,' Gallio stays by the balustrade, wishes Valeria had shared this information before now. 'In Jerusalem I had that idea with Lazarus, and wanted to recruit him as a client Messiah.'

'It was a good idea. That's why I've reused it. If we empty Paul's story of the elements that make Jesus dangerous then we'll disarm their religion, and since your trip to Hierapolis Claudia has made a new discovery. She has a lead on the second coming.'

Gallio moves from the balustrade to the chair. He sits down, leans forward with his elbows on his knees, fingertips planted together. He senses that at last this is the real reason Valeria called him to the Prefect's office, alone.

'The second coming is disciple code for the next big event, and for some time I've suspected Jesus and the disciples of working up to a major new incident. Claudia has analyzed the documents. We think they're planning a terrorist attack.'

Gallio listens to Valeria as she presents the evidence. According to Claudia's analysis, every Jesus story starts with health care and spreading the wealth but ends in fire and di-saster. The Temple is destroyed, or the Antichrist or Satan is destroyed. The way the disciples tell the story something big finishes up in the bin, the world effectively at an end. The disciples use the rhetoric of terrorism to promote violent fantasies of a catastrophe that involves the fall of civilization. Cities will burn, walls come tumbling down, and a deliverer will lead his followers to a final, crushing victory followed by a general resurrection of the righteous. CCU can't ignore that, not in today's climate.

'The clues are there in the language they use,' Valeria says, 'and we'd be foolish not to pay attention, the way the world is now. I have a bad feeling about an attack on Jerusalem. Jesus spoke openly about taking out the Temple.'

'Or Rome.' Cassius Gallio will not be out-catastrophized, because his story should be the big story. The ambitious Speculator he once was has survived exile and sleepless nights and shattered nerves. The bigger the story the more significant a figure Cassius Gallio will be. 'Don't underestimate the disciples. They're highly capable people.'

'They are, I think.'

Valeria had been sorting evidence, assembling the pieces. She had spent the days of Gallio's absence in Hierapolis full-time speculating, and can now foresee a level of danger that Gallio finds thrilling. His story is the big story. This time round Cassius Gallio will get his chance.

'I'm changing the status of the Jesus search,' Valeria says. 'The security code increases from Elevated to High.'

'That's a terrorist level.'

'It is.'

One obstinate doubt nags away at Gallio. 'And the murders?'

'If the disciples are eliminated, every truth and secret they know dies alongside them. Jesus would benefit.'

'I don't understand. How does that implicate Jesus?'

'He can't risk his crucifixion being revealed as a fake, not now, when the next phase is imminent. He needs the death and resurrection story to hold together, especially now before the second coming.'

But there's more that Gallio needs to know. For Cassius Gallio this story is his story, or he'd have no reason to care. 'You brought me in to lead a Missing Persons enquiry. That investigation became a murder case and now we're policing a terrorist alert. Am I still the principal on this?'

Valeria smiles at him, her first gift since she put her hand on his in the Lebanese restaurant. 'You are. We're treating Jesus and the seven survivor disciples as a terrorist threat. An outside chance, admittedly, and a long way from the centre of civilization, but CCU doesn't gamble with people's lives.'

The Complex Casework Unit defines itself through internal security issues, and is always taken seriously for funding because the imagined consequences of doing nothing are extreme and distressing. The CCU speculates, more often than not, on the end of civilization, playing to a reliable terror of decline and fall. The conspiracies and threats identified by the Unit tend to be clever, they have to be, because Rome is not at risk militarily.

'Not such an outside chance,' Gallio says, enjoying his new importance, 'or as the section chief you wouldn't be personally involved.'

'We need to know what the disciples are planning, and how big this second coming thing is. What, when, where and who's involved. I want to know whether Jesus is alive, controlling every move, or if a smaller group of disciples is acting alone.'

'How much does Baruch know?'

'Baruch is our liaison partner for the Jerusalem security services.'

Which means not very much, Gallio thinks. Valeria acts like a god in her localized CCU region; she has knowledge, and can intervene, but she chooses to do so selectively.

'I'll find out what they're planning,' Gallio says. 'And then stop it.'

'That's the general idea. Nobody gets hurt.'

In the fully furnished major incident room at the Antonia Fortress Cassius Gallio is in charge, and he relishes the responsibility. He feels he always knew instinctively that the story would end in Jerusalem. The membrane between god and man is thin here, between the living and the dead, madness and sanity.

He embraces Valeria's theory about Jesus as a potential terrorist threat, as it supports his reasonable instinct that Jesus is alive. And if Jesus is as powerful as his disciples claim, then the Temple in central Jerusalem is an appropriately spectacular target. He'd once threatened to pull down the city's landmark building, so for Jesus the Temple is unfinished business. At the same time, a Jesus capable of such miracles should have been able to protect his disciples from violent death. Either way, the second coming will find Jesus out; he's involved and immensely powerful, or he's not and he's a fraud.

Cassius Gallio develops a strategy, approved by Valeria. He'll intensify the search for Jesus, which has caused the death of four disciples. Searching for Jesus is the key to making progress.

First Gallio ensures that Bartholomew is safe. From Hierapolis with an escort of nurses Bartholomew transfers on a military Hercules to the Shaare Zedek Medical Center in Jerusalem. The journey by air, above the clouds, fails to wake him from his coma, though in Jerusalem a disciple in a coma needs guarding like a corpse. This time Gallio does not assign the most stupid conscripts.

Next he chases up forensics about the glass fragments retrieved from Joseph of Arimathea's bin. The results show the glass comes from two separate vials. The smaller piece shows traces of a saline solution. The lab needs more time for further tests. The larger curved piece of glass once contained a liquid solution of opium and belladonna, traditionally used as an anesthetic.

Forensics confirm that the glass dates to the correct period, and at last Cassius Gallio has credible evidence of a sabotaged, stage-managed crucifixion. From the picture archive he knows that on the afternoon of the execution, when Jesus or a substitute was nailed to the cross, a sponge was touched to his lips. Soon after this event the man, whoever he was, lost consciousness. Until now the sponge was thought to have been soaked in vinegar, to wake Jesus up, though the sponge is missing so the liquid substance can't be verified.

In which case, the sponge could instead have been soaked in a sedative prepared in advance. Sponges are traditional carriers for anesthetic, with the active ingredient released by a touch of water. So the crucified man received pain relief.

Gallio decides to put every scrap of information into the public domain, to make Jesus sweat. Over the next twenty-four hours he goes through the documents and collates every descriptor of Jesus. Jesus is Jesus, and Gallio assembles the physical images that exist, mostly sculptures and a great many paintings, and also the imprint on a shroud. But according to his closest followers Jesus is simultaneously not Jesus. He is also the door, the light, the way, the bread, the water, the life, the resurrection, the refreshment, the pearl, the treasure, the seed, the abundance, the grain of mustard, the vine, the plough, the grace, the faith and the word.

Any one of these definitions could generate a positive response. Gallio includes them all, looks up from the screen of his computer, and he's alone in the case room. Everyone else has gone home, even Claudia. He has no one to tell that the material is nearly ready.

Instead he has an unwanted flashback to his posting the last time round. He's working too hard, making the same mistake. How can Jesus be a door? he wonders. How can Jesus be a plough? He reaches for the telephone, and his home number is there in his head and he dials it. His ex-wife, Judith, picks up.

'Hello,' she says. Gallio doesn't know what to say to her. In the silence he might as well not have bothered. 'Hello, hello,' she says again, 'is there anyone there?'

The silence stretches out. Gallio wants her to know he exists, and that he doesn't mean any harm, but he doesn't know where to start, not after so much time and so many errors. His silence and his unknowness end up frightening her.

'Whoever you are, stop it. Don't call again.'

And then it's too late to make himself known, and anyway, Judith hands the phone to another person in the room wherever she is. It's Baruch.

'Fuck off,' he says. 'Whoever you are. Do this again and I'll trace the number and hunt you down and kill you. Understand?'

Cassius Gallio puts down the phone, but gently, so they might think he never put it down, and that in fact he is always there, should she want him. He reactivates his computer screen, his list of hopeful words alongside pictures of a man either dying or dead on the cross. Jesus is the pearl. He is the grace. Gallio can't see the connection: for him, Jesus is harsh and without compassion. The soldiers who guarded the tomb were sentenced to death, their wives and little children tormented by shame and grief. And not just the guards, Gallio thinks, what about me? I was a decent human being before Jesus.

At least he thinks he was, or could have been, but Jesus ignores the damage he causes. He comes back from the dead but his disciples still die, horribly and for no apparent reason.

Cassius Gallio concentrates on the here and now, on uploading his data. At the final screen, before going live, he once again has the choice of Missing or Wanted. He considers calling Valeria for guidance, but decides the responsibility is his. He taps Wanted. And Done. This is now a manhunt, and the live alert activates an immediate fugitive warrant across every civilized territory. The priority of a file marked Wanted brings back a reply within minutes.

They have a man answering the published description of Jesus. He is in Jerusalem.

The sighting is recent, the evening of the day before, and Gallio is still in the office and shocked by the time. It's the morning of the next day already. He checks the Wanted response. An individual fitting the description of Jesus was issued with a verbal warning by the Jerusalem traffic police at 18:12 the previous evening. The suspect was helping an elderly lady across the road, but was reprimanded for not using a designated crossing, which is hardly surprising. Jesus is an outlaw, a potential terrorist and a suspect for at least three murders. He's not going to wait for the man to go green.

Cassius Gallio gets the traffic cops out of bed.

'Why only a warning?'

'He was very polite.'

'You took an address?'

'We did.'

Gallio calls in Code Orange, and signs out an unmarked Lexus from the motor pool. He hesitates, then calls Baruch on his mobile. If Jesus is dangerous, Gallio needs backup.

Twenty minutes later they're sitting in the Lexus, no siren, parked with a view of Veronica's Gift Shop.

'Networks within networks,' Baruch says. 'How the Jesus cult survives. One in all in.'

The shop has a *Closed* sign in the window. No evidence of the owner or his daughter, but the man who looks like Jesus gave his address as the flat above the shop. Gallio watches the second-floor window. A shadow, moving one way then the other. Baruch fixes a long lens to a camera, puts the window down and aims at the Juliet balcony.

'You want to make the big announcement we're here?'

'I think he knows.'

A figure appears at the window. Jesus. That's Cassius Gallio's honest first impression. Jesus has a telephone in one hand and pushes it between his ear and his shoulder as he opens the double window. He stands there talking, enjoying the fresh air, sometimes listening and smiling. Baruch reels off a set of automatic shots. Then he sits back in his seat.

'Shit,' he says. He looks at a series of digital screen zooms. 'It's not him, is it?'

'Run the photos against the database.'

They look at each other, two middle-aged security operatives on a stake-out with no idea how to use the technology. They phone Claudia, wake her up. She talks them through it. They have the camera leads? Yes. Camera to phone, JPEGs to her office email. She'll activate the program. Once the photos are in the database a match will come up within minutes.

'We knew that,' Gallio says. 'But thanks.'

While they wait for the results they tell each other they never expected this Jesus to be Jesus. Statistically, with seven disciples at large, a Jesus sighting now in Jerusalem always looked unlikely.

'I'm tired.' Gallio rubs the base of his thumb into an eye. 'I've been up all night. I'm seeing things.'

Claudia texts the results back to the car, and Baruch says in the old days they'd never have believed it: he'd still be unloading film from the camera. Gallio holds his phone toward the centre of the dash where they can both read the screen. The jaywalker staying in the flat above the Veronica shop turns out to be James, the second James, a disciple but not the man himself. Seconds later Claudia texts across the Wikipedia page.

'Could be worse,' Gallio says. 'He's an original disciple, not a nobody or an impostor.'

'Are we going to pick him up?'

'No, I don't think we are.'

They wait. If James knows they're watching he doesn't let that stop him from leaving the building. Early evening, plenty of people on the street. Gallio decides James doesn't know, and they follow him on foot. He stops a few times to touch this hand or that, well wishers who recognize his face. Baruch wishes he'd brought his camera, but James is moving again, and he goes into a church in the Armenian quarter. A new church, built since the first James died and dedicated to his memory. Death has not deterred the Armenians.

'Let's pick him up,' Baruch says. 'What are we waiting for?'

'We're not after James. He's a means to an end.'

In the St. James Armenian Cathedral the disciple has a full congregation, and in their rapt attention Gallio sees they couldn't care less which of the disciples James is, or even which James. For the churchgoers he is an early adopter who has touched the hand of Jesus, and that direct connection is enough. Or more than that, Gallio thinks. In James they see the face of Jesus, and are made glad.

From the pulpit James repeats the stories his listeners mostly know: what Jesus said, what he did. He acts as if the disciples, possibly in Jerusalem after the disappearance of Jesus, held a strategy meeting and decided that a popular story would be enough to keep their movement alive. Good triumphs and evil is vanquished. Why not? Gallio too would like to believe in this.

Like the other disciples James has told and retold the story: a manual worker grows up in a provincial backwater of Israel. I know, Gallio thinks, I know this, I've heard it before. Also, the information is in the file. Around the age of thirty Jesus reveals extraordinary powers, including a flair for public speaking that he uses to promote a notion of social justice. He argues for the existence of a single god, a supreme being attentive to individuals, who will reward the virtuous with joyful everlasting life. But only after they die.

There is nothing that James will not do for Jesus, no heartening story he will not tell. James finishes his sermon with the second coming, when Jesus will return from the clouds along with tongues of fire. He will judge the living and the dead.

'Oh for fuck's sake,' Baruch whispers from the back of the church. Heads turn, frowns in place. 'Let's pick the fucker up.'

'No,' Gallio says. 'We wait.'

For the first time they have not one but two disciples under observation, James in central Jerusalem and Bartholomew in the Shaare Zedek Medical Center. Cassius Gallio's strategy is to make Jesus come to them: Jesus didn't like Gallio interviewing Jude or closing in on Thomas. Now James and Bartholomew in Jerusalem will lure Jesus in. If Valeria is right, and disciples are being killed because they know too much, the killer needs to act before Gallio picks James up, which is what he'd expect Gallio to do.

'We wait,' Gallio says, 'and we watch. James is bait. If Jesus is the killer we trap him when he makes his move. If he isn't, we catch who we catch. If no one comes for him, then we find out how the disciples keep in touch. We'll learn more from surveillance than from locking James up in the Antonia.'

'I can't just *watch* people all the time,' Baruch says.

Now he gets a definite shushing from the churchgoers. Cassius Gallio receives an audible alert on his phone, and the two of them are instantly the least popular atheists in the St. James Armenian Cathedral. Gallio reads the message, and places a hand on Baruch's sleeve.

'You're in luck,' he says, dropping the phone into his pocket and standing up. 'Because we have a new arrival in Jerusalem. Paul is in town. The believers are coming together. This is the gathering.'

It takes twenty-four hours for Cassius Gallio to coordinate surveillance. At Terrorist Threat High, Code Orange, Valeria gives him the resources he needs.

'Including Claudia?'

'Whenever you need her.'

Each night after his sermon in the Armenian Cathedral James the disciple of Jesus, also known as James the Less, presses the flesh. But always by ten o'clock he's back in the second-floor flat above Veronica's Gift Shop. Often, his landline rings, because the phone number is advertised on flyers at the cathedral. *Any problem*, the flyers say, *any time*. Cassius Gallio watches James through binoculars as Claudia phones him just after eleven. Gallio has decided the call sounds more innocent coming from a woman.

'I'm a nurse,' Claudia says. 'At the Shaare Zedek Medical Center. It's about Bartholomew.'

She draws it out, acting a part, thinking James should know that Bartholomew is utterly alone, which is surprising for an original disciple. Only recently arrived, she confirms, yes, from Hierapolis in Turkey, not in good shape, no, but receiving first-class hospital treatment as if in answer to prayer.

'Visiting opens every day at nine,' Claudia says. 'He never has any visitors.'

The next morning Gallio shadows James as far as the hospital, where he witnesses a touching scene. The guards let James through and he prays at the bedside while Bartholomew fails to wake. While James is at the hospital, Baruch enters the flat above the gift shop to install CCU eyes and ears. In these old city buildings the electrics are prehistoric so another engineer with a toolbox barely raises an eyebrow. From now on, Gallio will see and hear everything. He expects answers.

In the surveillance hub, which is an Ideal Flooring van across the street from Veronica's, Claudia switches on the monitors. When Gallio arrives back from the hospital he's impressed by Baruch's placing of the bugs and cameras. In the black-and-white images they can see a single bed, tightly made with a blanket and sheet, an upright chair, a wall-mounted crucifix, and on a low table the landline telephone handset. The room looks like a statement of simplicity, or like expert fieldcraft—if anything is disturbed James will know. Only Baruch has more experience than that.

Baruch calls in. 'All working?'

'You know it is. Great job.'

'Then I'll stay where I am.'

Baruch has volunteered for the surveillance shift on Paul, who is booked into a garden suite at the five-star King David Hotel. Paul knows Baruch from when they worked as colleagues, but Baruch insists they've changed since then, both of them.

'Anyway, he won't see me, so he can't recognize me. He didn't see me in Antioch. I didn't ask rash questions from the floor, unlike some people.'

For Baruch, keeping an eye on Paul is synonymous with protecting the two disciples currently in Jerusalem. Paul is involved in the killings, Baruch is convinced. This leaves Claudia and Gallio to work as partners in the van. They sit and watch and wait for signs of the second coming.

The inside of the Ideal Flooring van is laid out lengthways, one side taken up by a narrow bench seat with a black plastic cover. Everything inside the van is either black or silver, and opposite the bench there are screens, amplifiers, equalizers, levellers. Gallio and Claudia share the bench, wait with pens and notebooks to make black-and-white notes about the beginning of the end of time.

They wait some more.

'What will you do if they're right?'

Three days go by, and they're living another slow morning in the van. The first takeout coffee of the day is halfway drunk, and Claudia would rather talk than not. 'Say the world is going to end at lunchtime. What would you do?"

Gallio would kiss Claudia. At least ask her if a kiss might be acceptable, at some point between her question and the end of the world.

'I'd have my lunch now,' Gallio says, so as not to lose out on everything.

'Coward. If you don't risk saying what you want you'll never get it.'

'And then the world will end.'

'On a day like any other, full of disappointments. Monitor One.'

They watch Jesus supporters drawn to the street where a genuine disciple is known to be staying. Claudia manipulates the streetcams to freeze close-up headshots, then on her laptop she runs face-checking software on everyone who enters and leaves the building. As believers these people are used to feeling watched, but none of them are red-flagged insurgents. None of these people are Jesus. They're men and women from different classes and professions, with no distinctive hairstyle or clothing. As a means of identification they're supposed to act kindly, though the confessions phoned through to James at night are not unfailingly kind.

Whereas Cassius Gallio, who is not a believer, makes a point of acting kindly toward Claudia, a young recruit new in the field. She has a husband and possibly children in Rome, and he tells himself he would not be so unkind as to try to seduce her.

Still nothing happens, day after day. Baruch reports that Paul stays within the compound of the King David Hotel, mostly in the business centre where he writes his letters. Cassius Gallio gets nervous. With Claudia he speculates that the presence in Jerusalem of two former disciples, and also Paul, is a strategic decoy. While Bartholomew and James make Jerusalem the centre of the Jesus world, for now, the man himself is stalking the other survivors. Matthew has been traced to Egypt, and is in danger there. Andrew is in Scotland, probably, and there are stories of John along the Black Sea coast and Simon in Southern England. Gallio keeps the disciple map open on his laptop, but the lights stay on. The disciples far from Jerusalem are alive and well.

Cassius Gallio holds his nerve. This is Jerusalem, where Jesus made his name. He is expected at all times.

More pressure is required. When darkness falls, Valeria sends in the riot police, she stations an armoured Land Rover outside the Veronica shop, and twelve paramilitaries on eight-hour shifts. The black-clad police officers are a challenge, a provocation: Come on Jesus, kill James now. The riot police raise the visors on their helmets and do what riot police do. They lean on barriers and watch women go by. They fiddle with their chin-straps, and their fingers brush the clubs at their belts.

James keeps to his nightly routine. He is back at the flat before ten and between phone calls asking for help, whenever a pause develops, he kneels to pray. Gallio gives the prayers of James a chance to work. Nothing immediate ever happens, either inside or outside the room. No change in the van, where the latest technology fails to identify how this series of actions in this order keeps James in touch with Jesus.

Again before sleeping James prays like a champion, on and on, eyes closed, head bowed, lips moving. He prays as if he knows he's being watched and will be judged on prayer and simplicity. He sleeps on top of the grey blanket, hands visible on his chest.

Gallio passes Claudia the bag of pretzels, but just now she's cutting an apple into slices. On reflection she leaves the apple on a paper plate, takes a pretzel and pops it into her mouth.

James's phone is busy tonight. He hears from Judith whose marriage is over. She wants to kill herself. He hears from Joseph whose son is dead and his life therefore meaningless. He wants to kill himself. James listens patiently then reassures each desperate caller with the story of Jesus. Don't worry, he says, because the world is about to end. Jesus is alive, and he will return. Whatever the problem, even if you want to kill yourself, make yourself ready for the Day of Judgement.

At the end of each call James prays, eyes closed, lips moving across patterns of words. Gallio asks Claudia how she became what she is. 'How did you get involved?'

'I'm somebody's daughter.'

'Ambitious?'

Her mouth angles down at the edges. 'Do what I'm told.'

'You're well placed, at your age. Married young. That's serious ambition, in our business.'

'I suppose, by some measures. I have two kids. Girls.'

'Excellent,' Gallio says. 'Get it over with. Efficient.'

'Something like that.'

Claudia swipes through her phone and shows Gallio a picture of her daughters. White background, a studio session that betrays no details of her home. The girls are lying down, chins on hands, grinning at the camera.

'They're very pretty.'

'Thank you.'

She puts her phone away, lifting one buttock off the bench to free her pocket.

'What does your husband do?'

'Architect. Good time to be an architect, after the fire. The place won't be rebuilt in a day.'

Claudia doesn't want to talk about her husband, so Gallio asks about the fire. 'How bad was it?'

For years, in the ditches of the Empire, Cassius Gallio imagined Rome as the eternal, shining city. Pillars gleamed white, and high-browed senators applied the law with justice. Rome was the past and future, a model of organization that made outlying superstitions look feeble. If nothing else, he never stopped believing in Rome.

Claudia tells him the fire made tens of thousands homeless. The city housing authority had set up a tent city with running water on the Campus Martius, but the crowded conditions bred wild speculation about who'd started the fire.

'Human nature to speculate,' Gallio says.

'Right. But not many people are experts.'

A grease fire, the amateurs agreed. For as long as anyone could remember, carts selling street food had traded from beneath the wooden arches of the Circus Maximus. Fry up some veal brains or dough balls, fat catches fire, immigrant chef panics, chucks on a bucket of water.

'People wanted someone to blame,' Claudia says. 'Persecute the short-order cooks to teach them some health and safety. And if it wasn't them it was probably the Jesus followers, who had a motive.'

'How's that?'

'Jesus is a carpenter. Paul is a tentmaker. Plenty of work in Rome for their sort now.'

Claudia must have realized that Gallio has guessed she's not a lowly analyst. She's a Speculator. But he doubts she knows he prays. What Cassius Gallio does is this: he closes his eyes and lets his hands go loose, as James does, and he makes a conscious effort to visualize Claudia. In the darkness behind his eyes he builds a clear picture of her pretty, clever face. There she is, inside his head, her corrected teeth, her tight upper lip, her distinctive nose. Then he pours himself into her brown imagined eyes (the eyes in the image he's made) and takes up the space inside her imagined head (inside his head), from where he looks back out to a clear mental picture of himself.

Gallio is amazed, sometimes, by what the human brain can do. His mental effort is a kind of prayer, a way of projecting an ideal Claudia who thinks about him as much as he must think about her, to construct that image in the first place. His intense imagining feels like a mind game powerful enough to deserve results, but he doesn't know if his system works. The prayers may never have reached her.

'This mission could get you noticed,' Cassius says, though that isn't what's on his mind. Apart from the prayer thing, which can be intense, he could tell her he feels calmer when she's around. 'We find Jesus and it's medals for both of us.'

On the central monitor James kneels, sits on his heels, rests his hands loose on his thighs. On a side monitor the streetcam shows riot officers leaning in a doorway. They burst out laughing, and for one of them the laugh becomes a cough. He's wearing too much equipment, and when he doubles over his baton and webbing make him stumble.

'Who would win in a fight,' Claudia takes another pretzel, fingers in the bag. 'Achilles or Samson?'

Gallio has spent hundreds of nights alone and has previously considered this question. 'Depends.'

'On what?'

He scratches his ear. 'On Samson's haircut.'

'Wrong. Depends who discovers the secret weakness of the other.'

'You mean who discovers it first.'

'Correct. Which means the hero with the stronger god, who can identify weakness and is powerful enough to get the message across quickly and clearly.'

'Or whichever man is luckier.'

Gallio wonders if she can hear his heart.

'Cassius?'

'Yes.'

They're sitting close together on the bench seat—his feet on a toolbox, hers on a backup monitor—and Gallio worries about his breathing. He doesn't breathe properly, not like her husband breathes. Claudia will register the fact that he's not a normal breather, or that he's doing it wrong. He hasn't felt like this for a very long time.

'The night at the tomb.'

'Don't want to talk about that.'

'When you were demoted. What did they charge you with?'

'Failing to prevent the theft of a body.'

Claudia pulls her legs underneath herself and turns toward him. She wants more. Despite the narrow bench she's making the van intimate by acting out an idea of comfort, suggesting Cassius Gallio can comfortably tell her the truth. Not some tired tribunal truth, but the truth.

'You think I'm trying to use you in some way,' Claudia says.

He wasn't thinking that, but now he does.

'You can check me for a wire, if you want. I'm clean. I'm interested in what happened back then, and what that means for now.'

Finally, in the privacy of a surveillance van (with the latest recording equipment, the hidden cameras) Cassius Gallio will tell a sympathetic colleague (her photos of her children, her sharing of the pretzels) whatever secrets he failed to confess in the past. Claudia is good at this, very good.

'After the shock of Lazarus I was keen for Jesus to stay dead. That's why I put guards on the tomb, but the tribunal didn't believe me. They couldn't understand why I ordered a watch over a dead man, and they preferred a more rational explanation. They decided I was involved in the escape. I either drugged the soldiers, or hypnotized them, I fabricated an errand so they were absent at the critical moment and then made them the scapegoats. The accusation was ludicrous, or I wouldn't be alive today.'

'So what happened to Jesus? You must have some idea.'

'I don't know. We never found the body.'

'Valeria told me you used to be the best. You were the Speculator with the brightest future.'

'I was young, and believed in reason and the burden of proof. I had a lot to learn.'

'I know that feeling.'

She touches his arm, and Gallio pushes a button to change a view from the streetcam. 'Go to sleep.' He stands, crouched into the van, looks for a place to sit on the floor. 'Overnight shifts start now. I'll wake you in four hours.'

Claudia stretches out on the bench seat, arms behind her head. After a while Gallio thinks she's asleep.

'I love my daughters,' she says and shifts onto her side, cheek on hands. 'In case you were wondering. I love them more than anything or anyone I can think of.'

• • •

The next morning they feel claustrophobic, as if neither has slept off the closeness of the night before. In his morning break, Cassius Gallio collects the paper cups and the empty pretzel packet, decides to stretch his legs. He takes an innocent stroll, not far, to a rubbish bin and then round the corner to the International School. If the world is about to end, as James keeps promising his callers, Gallio would like to see his daughter one more time.

He loiters in the gateway of the school, and predicts the immediate future. If he hangs around long enough they'll call the police, so he changes the future by pushing the button on the intercom.

'I'd like to speak to one of your students, Alma Marcella Gallio.'

If the world has until lunchtime, that's what Gallio chooses to do.

'She's in school. In school hours. Are you her parent?'

'I have a message for Alma from Baruch.' The ruse works, as Gallio gambled it would. He hears the hesitation at Baruch's name. They'll see what they can do, and Gallio's absent father's heart gives an unexpected flutter. He'll ask about Alma's leg. How's the leg? Maybe not. He'll skip the small talk, tell her that whether the world ends at lunchtime or not a happy life is possible if she's prepared to renounce ambition. Don't waste the time that remains, he'll tell her, don't chase empty shadows.

The gate swings open, and Alma limps forward followed by a teacher, who will not be leaving a schoolgirl unattended with a strange man at the school gates. Good. This is exactly the kind of sheltered environment Gallio wants his alimony to pay for.

'Thanks for coming out.'

She doesn't recognize him. Why should she? The family was broken up by Jesus when Alma was a baby, and Gallio doesn't know the stories her mother tells to explain how and why that happened. Instead of a genuine emotion, he feels he ought to feel more than he does.

'You had a message?'

The teacher wants to be somewhere else, but she can't shake off her habit of encouragement, even with grown men.

'I'm sorry,' Gallio says. 'Yes, I do.'

He is aware of staring, of seeing a new human being who is neither himself nor her mother, and of not being able to get his message across. One day I'll die, he'd like to say, though obviously that's not the place to start. What he means is Alma should spend his military pension on a sunny villa in a civilized territory where people are safe and well. Take love where you find it, he wants to tell her, because if not for that what can life be for? Succeed where I have failed.

Alma smiles and the miserable look doesn't run in the family. She wants to put him at his ease, whoever he may be, but he's not a competent dad full of wise advice. The teacher looks at her watch.

'Don't worry,' Gallio manages.

'Why not?'

A reasonable question, and if he answered he'd sound like a dad: because in the long or short time that remains to us there will be good moments as well as bad. Gallio doesn't know if this is true, but it seems the end of the world makes him hope for the best. He says: 'The message. I've forgotten to give you the message.'

The teacher has to prompt him. 'It's from Baruch. We need to be getting back into lessons.'

Alma's face changes. The miserable look does run in the family after all. 'Is he angry? Again?'

'He's not angry. He'll be a few minutes late.'

'But it's not his day,' she says. 'He hasn't fetched me for weeks.'

'Well that's what he said.'

Gallio is saved by his phone. As it rings he makes a show of fumbling it out of his pocket, and then he's walking away, pointing at the phone and at his ear to explain what he's doing. He waves and answers at the same time, making his escape, a solid lump of emotion in his chest. He doesn't know what the emotion is, but to feel it coming is feeling enough, and he regrets calling his daughter out of school. He doesn't know what he was thinking.

The call is from Claudia: 'For once. You have your phone turned on and you answered it.'

'What happened? Is James on the move?'

'Not James. Paul. We forgot he's a trained operative. He picked up on Baruch and identified him from the old days. He sent his bodyguard over for a chat. Paul wants our protection.'

They schedule a meeting for 15:45 in the Israel Museum. Claudia stays in the van, eyes on James, while Cassius Gallio dresses up. Unlike the disciples, Paul likes to mix with men in suits, and in the designated room—Feasts and Miracles—Gallio greets Paul with a handshake. The file says he was once a tentmaker, but not recently, and Gallio holds Paul's soft preacher's hand for longer than he should.

'You already know Baruch,' Gallio says. 'What can we do for you?'

'Not here,' Paul says.

He's a professional. Never talk in a room where the oppo-

sition arranged the meet. Paul turns and sets a discreet brows-
ing pace from Dawn of Civilization through to Land of Canaan.
Despite the air conditioning Israel is heavy with history, and
remnants of the old days always break through into now. Brand-
new building, ancient objects.

Whether Paul turns left or right, walks straight on or doubles back, the bodyguard stands close enough to make a difference, and Paul is complicated in ways that Gallio admires. He
doesn't have the simplicity of the disciples, and has been surprised by Jesus, blinded by him. Paul has experienced the hurt
that Jesus can cause, and he and Gallio have this knowledge in
common. Paul surely has his reasons for employing a bodyguard.

'First of all,' Paul says. 'I had nothing to do with the murders
of Jude, Thomas or Philip. I have solid alibis and witnesses.'

He chooses to talk while walking, into Illuminating the
Script and out through Costume and Jeweler. Baruch sometimes
gets ahead of him, walks backward, fails to blink his Old Testament eyes. Baruch's mind is stuck on a single thought, and out it
comes in The Cycle of the Jewish Year. 'I remember when you
were Saul. You killed Stephen in the street.'

'I changed my name, like Peter did. Simon to Peter. Saul to
Paul. Saul is long dead.'

'You kill him too?'

'In a manner of speaking.'

'Nothing changes, then.'

Gallio registers the intensity between Baruch and Paul, neither man prepared to compromise on his version of the past. He
searches for common ground. 'No one else needs to die,' he says.
'The situation is bad enough already.'

'Seven disciples left.' Baruch wants only to provoke. 'The
others gone under.'

'Which is why we need to talk,' Paul says.

'Barbarous deaths,' Baruch says, 'in outlandish places. Not pleasant at all.'

'I need protecting from these assassins.'

'You have a bodyguard.'

'One man is not enough.'

'You have your god.'

'Philip had god on his side,' Paul says. 'I'm sure of that. He also had a skewer through the back of his legs.'

Paul decides they've walked enough, and in Modern Art he takes a rest on a leather bench facing Salvador Dali's *Immaculate Conception*. He is as inattentive to surrealism as to seventeenth-century bridal caskets, and acts in all these galleries as if he is the dominant attraction. Gallio sits down next to him. He places a foot on his knee and holds his bony ankle. Straightens out his sock. He's about to speak but again Baruch is quicker.

'You're one of us,' Baruch says. He does not sit down, or betray an interest in abstract art. 'When they killed Stephen you held the coats of the murderers. You can look after yourself.'

'I've been forgiven my past,' Paul says. 'Though obviously not by you.'

'We do not forgive defectors, nor do we forget them.'

'No fighting, please,' Gallio says. He revolves his black shoe and thinks it could do with a polish. 'Not in a public gallery of the Israel Museum. We can protect you, Paul, but you have to give us something in return. Politics. You'll understand the politics. Where can we find Peter?'

'I don't know. We're not in regular contact.'

'Maybe you should be, if you want us to offer you protection.'

'Honestly, I know everything and everyone, but I haven't

heard from Peter in a long time. He's disappeared off the face of the earth.'

'Liar,' Baruch says. 'Always was, always will be. The Jerusalem security services pick out the finest liars at a very young age.'

Paul's secretary scuttles in from Oceanic Art with a pile of letters on a silver tray. Paul waves them away, then calls the man back, looks more closely at the letter on top (address, back of envelope, front) then drops it and waves the man away again. 'Peter may have died, of course. The disciples of Jesus are not immune from natural causes.'

'Or unnatural ones.' Gallio pulls his ankle higher up his thigh, doubtful that natural death is an event the disciples are likely to experience. 'But you're not in the same danger, are you, Paul? You should be happy. You're not a disciple so you're probably safe.'

'I met Jesus like they did.'

'But you didn't, did you? Not properly in Galilee. The disciples were chosen when Jesus was alive, and they worked and travelled as a group. You're a latecomer, not in the same category, so you'll probably be fine.'

Paul slaps Gallio on the knee, indulging him, acknowledging Gallio's boldness in teasing the mighty Paul of Tarsus. Except his hand stops on Gallio's knee, grips, and Gallio understands that the Saul from a darker lifetime hasn't been entirely banished. Paul does not take kindly to suggestions he's second best, especially when the lesser disciples can barely explain the Trinity.

'What's your deal with Peter?' Baruch approaches a painting of geometric shapes, looks at it without looking, hands on his hips, jacket wings pushed out behind him. Gallio sees the hilt of his knife, and then it's hidden again as Baruch turns back to Paul.

'Who's second in command to Jesus? You or Peter?'

'We don't have a deal.' Paul looks pained, because Baruch is seriously unenlightened. 'We once reached a loose agreement.'

'You convert the Gentiles, Peter sticks to the Jews. That's what they told me in Damascus. But Peter is the beloved disciple, isn't he? He's witless, but Jesus loves him.'

'He's a fisherman,' Gallio says. 'Not that bright. He can tell a story but couldn't unpack it in a keynote speech.'

Gallio decides to refine Baruch's attack, though he's probing the same weakness, Paul's obvious pride. Good cop, he remembers. The nice guy used to be one of his roles. 'Why deny your differences? Jesus appeared to you on the road to Damascus because the disciples needed help. The Galileans couldn't communicate his message, not on their own, they didn't have the brains. They heard the stories and saw his miracles but never knew what they meant. That's what you do so well, interpret the stories and bring meaning to Jesus. Personally I like meaning, and I appreciate nuance because I'm an educated man, Paul, as are you.'

'Whereas Peter,' Baruch says, double-teaming, 'knows how to thread the bait for flatfish. An underrated skill, I feel. The hook goes in at the eye then down the gut and out through the anus.'

'The disciples aren't a big help, are they? Can't write a decent letter between them.'

'It's not that.' Paul stands up and walks away from what he's about to say, looking for an exit, but his doubt keeps pace with him and he says it anyway. 'Twelve was the wrong number from the start.'

He exits to Impressionism and bustles through Orientalism. Everyone follows him—the bodyguard, Gallio, Baruch. Paul stops at a Meromi sculpture, then an Aboriginal dream painting, but none of the art on display can distract him. 'Jesus had too many original disciples. No one can have that many friends around him, or advisers. He lost track, and the result was Judas.'

Gallio feels that at last they're making progress, with Paul trying to communicate some sense of the difficulty of being Paul.

'Twelve is a very trusting number,' Gallio says. 'You're right about that. Perhaps overly trusting.'

In Archaeology, Baruch stops at a display of Sicarii killing knives through history, and his unexpected fascination with this single exhibit draws everyone over to the cabinet. They stand round the glass sides of a free-standing box, glinting daggers between them in the refracted light.

'Someone is hunting us down,' Paul says, the curved blades holding his attention.

'They're targeting the disciples,' Gallio corrects him. 'No one apart from the disciples has yet been hurt.'

'I'm their equal. Believe me. If the disciples are in danger then so am I. I need official protection. Are you going to protect a citizen or are you not?'

Paul appeals to Gallio through the glass, across the vicious ancient weaponry. Baruch's hand moves under his jacket toward the small of his back, and it may be Gallio's imagination but the bodyguard takes a step. Not toward Paul, as Gallio expects, but away from him. Baruch scratches himself, his hand reappears.

'None of the murdered disciples tried to run away,' Cassius Gallio says.

He checks his phone, as a sign their interview is over, and no news is good news. James is fine, undeviating in his monastic routine. Claudia is bored in the van. Bartholomew is comatose in the medical centre. In short, everyone at risk is alive and well.

'The disciples are not scared of dying. You are. That's one reason you're not a disciple. You're not in the same category. Also you have a bodyguard. Request for protection denied.'

About one o'clock the next morning a phone rings. Cassius Gallio blinks his eyes open, realizes he's asleep on duty, then that the sound is coming from the landline in James's flat, broadcast across the central monitor. Gallio grabs headphones, plants one cushioned speaker to his ear. Then with his free hand he zooms the camera in the flat, watches as James stops praying, answers the phone, listens.

James doesn't say anything and neither does the caller. Gallio frowns at the static, a bad line, nothing coming through. No, he hears something. Breathing. He can hear the caller breathing. He pushes a button to activate a trace. James hangs up. Damn. On the monitor James stands up and dusts himself off, though he's no more dusty than before. He leaves the room.

This is new. Usually the phone calls stop and after his prayers James sleeps the sleep of the just. Gallio shakes Claudia's shoulder, moves to the bench when she swings her legs off, switches to the interior corridor cam. Lost him. Streetcam, manual operation. On to the house, to the window. No sign of him, then yes, James is up on the building's flat roof. He's up on the roof. Why? Claudia yawns and stretches, stomps her feet one two to the floor.

'Something's happening.'

She rubs her eyes, leans forward.

'The street,' Gallio says. 'Get me a camera on the street.'

She fumbles a dial and the shopfront blinks up. No public or passers-by at this time of night, just the riot police in the doorway with thumbs in their belts.

'Call Valeria,' Gallio says. 'Get her down here.'

Gallio pushes open the back of the van and jumps into the road. Claudia is behind him. 'No. Keep the cameras on James. Don't lose him. Stay in the fucking van.'

He runs. The riot police see him and suddenly they're alert, walking to intercept him hands free, shoulders squared. Gallio flashes his card, and throws himself at the door of the shop. It's locked. So is the door to the stairs for the flat. The fire escape. Gallio runs round the side of the building and jumps onto a metal staircase that zigzags up the brickwork as far as the roof. He shouts up to James and tells him to get back in, because on the roof he's exposed and anyone could be watching.

'Go back inside! You're not safe!'

Through the lattice of the ironwork Gallio checks on the street as he climbs. No Claudia, that's good. The riot police are out in the road, pointing upward. Five or six of them now. They draw their batons, spooked by Gallio's urgency. He makes it to the roof, in time to see James step toward the edge.

Gallio stops. He doesn't want to startle him, but James is oblivious. He lifts his hands, palms upward. A signal. From Gallio's angle James looks like Jesus. He knows the shape he's making.

'James. Step back from the edge. Come down with me. You'll be safer inside.'

James stands on the edge of the flat rooftop, hands out, speaking to himself, praying. Cassius Gallio hears roughly one word in three: Jesus, glory, living, dead. Kingdom no end. Gallio recognizes what's about to happen, but even as he starts forward he's already too late.

Across the city, in the Shaare Zedek Medical Center, Bartholomew opens his eyes.

VII

Simon

———

In retrospect, the task had been easier at the beginning, with Jesus and his disciples collectively active in Jerusalem. Cassius Gallio had been able to organize a textbook infiltration, an exemplary piece of fieldwork in the Passover season while the city heaved. He'd followed the disciples of Jesus through the holiday crowds and worked out that Judas, as treasurer, was entrusted once every day to make a solo trip to buy supplies.

The next morning, in the covered market, Judas found an unexceptional foreigner (linen trousers, short-sleeved shirt) close against his shoulder. A moment of your time, sir, no need to look around. An investment, a guaranteed return. Not today, not now, but alas if the mission of Jesus were to fail, if his plans for a righteous uprising should end in disappointment.

And the next day again: Judas, friend, it's hardly my place to judge, but if Jesus has influence with the almighty shouldn't his project have moved forward more rapidly?

And the next: forty pieces of silver, think it through, no rush, a generous offer to a fringe member of a minor cult.

'A terrorist cell,' Judas eventually replied. He would not be undervalued. 'That's what you fear we are.'

Terrorists were worth more, and fifty pieces of silver bought a plot of unimproved land not far from the city walls. A little patience, some prudent management, and the land becomes a field. Keep some money aside for livestock. Sell premium lambs to the Temple, Judas his own boss in a seller's market.

Fifty-three, final offer. Don't be greedy, Judas, I could ask one of the others. Fifty-five pieces of silver. Absolute tops. You're breaking me here.

Judas had a head for numbers so he could do the maths. Fifty-five as capital outlay for the field, then he'd borrow against future tenant revenue from grazing. With loans he'd buy a pilgrimage inn that overcharged during festivals, and then he'd borrow again against the capital value of the property. He'd have nothing and he'd have everything. He'd have the big fifty-five, and by these calculations betraying the son of god should work out fine.

Judas walked away, not glancing behind, not looking back.

You're being ridiculous. Cassius followed him, stayed close on his shoulder.

The devil, Judas said, tapping his handsome head, I can hear demons whispering in my ear.

Thirty now, thirty on completion. Final offer. Think it over.

Cassius Gallio had designed and implemented an impeccable covert operation, for which he never received full credit.

And until they killed Judas nobody died, not even Jesus.

At Ben Gurion airport the flight is delayed, held because of ice at Luton. Bartholomew has slowed their progress. The medical centre had to discharge him, and then on the road to the airport their unmarked car was trumped by the lights and sirens of Paul's military escort out of Jerusalem. Come on. Cassius Gallio was in a hurry. He touched the crusted row of fresh butterfly stitches pinching the skin above his eyebrow. Motorcycles, a Mercedes and a Mercedes backup, an armoured vehicle, all for Paul and at public expense. Baruch would have been enraged. Even more enraged, wherever he is now.

Their flight is diverted to Heathrow, and when they land the sky is pink with snow about to fall. At Nothing to Declare Cassius Gallio lets Claudia go through first. He hangs back beside Bartholomew and senses they're being watched, a presence at the edge of his vision. He blames Bartholomew, whose familiar features and clothes attract attention. Gallio hurries him past the one-way mirrors and waits for a disembodied voice to call them back, but they make it through. Probably nobody watching, or watching but not caring.

Luton would have been a better airport from which to start. They now have a three-hour taxi drive to the town of Caistor, on the edge of the Lincolnshire Wolds. Baruch is somewhere in England, ahead of them, but despite his head start they can catch him if they make good time around the M25, M1, A46. These roads are like the weather, clear now but threatening to turn for the worse, and the traffic eventually closes in on the A near Historic Lincoln. Gallio resents the jam. Why queue here? What in British Lincolnshire could be so worth seeing?

Except, of course, another sighting of Jesus.

In England a man answering the description was first seen at Glastonbury, then Westminster, now he's further north at Caistor in Lincolnshire. Here in the outlands they've never known anything like it, and early unconfirmed accounts rival the miracles of Jesus. A man who fits Gallio's Wanted profile has performed incredible exploits, healing the sick and thwarting demons. Voices speak from the clouds and animals talk.

Gallio gazes out of the taxi window. This is such a backwards fringe of the Empire, but if Jesus plans to descend from clouds he's come to the right place. The car battles against snow, then hail, as if their journey opposes the planet's direction of travel. When the hail stops, as abruptly as it started, the sky breaks open and lets through a cold cosmic light. It is hard to believe that people live here.

The taxi crawls forward, and Gallio uses this crawl time to start the questioning. In the back seat beside him Bartholomew is as lightweight as when Gallio first picked him up in Jerusalem, years ago, though the coma hasn't helped. He looks like Jesus after a month in the desert. Claudia sits up front, and she'll struggle to hear the conversation but Gallio expects she'll make the effort.

'I don't like to be the bringer of bad news,' Gallio says. Claudia slides her seat back a notch. 'But did you hear what happened to James in Jerusalem?'

'He had his head cut off.'

'The other James, this week, also in Jerusalem. I want to show you something, so you'll understand why it's in your interests to cooperate. You don't want to die like your friends. We wouldn't wish that on anyone.'

Cassius Gallio lights up his phone. Another disciple down, and because these deaths are real they're available on YouTube. Gallio scrolls through the Google search results for *James Bludgeoned to Death*. The YouTube listings include *Mexican Immigrant Beaten to Death by US Border Patrol Agents*, *Baby Beaten to Death by Her Nanny* and *Gay Rights Activist Beaten to Death*.

'It's not coming up,' Gallio says. 'Don't know why, but this one's close enough. You'll get the idea. And by the way, welcome back to the world. Take a good look at what's been happening in your absence.'

The footage of *Mexican Immigrant Beaten to Death* is ill-lit but visible, filmed on a cell phone and available at a click anywhere in the civilized world. The microphone picks up '*Por favor*,' and 'Señores, help me.' At this point, Anastasio Hernandez Rojas is surrounded by US Border Control agents, but he is lying on the ground and not resisting when tasered at least five times. The agents then kick and club him.

The Border Patrol claims self-defense. Methamphetamine was found in the victim's bloodstream, and the police reaction was a measured response to extreme antisocial behaviour. The exact moment of death, on YouTube, is unclear.

'Why did James and the other disciples suffer unbearable deaths?'

'I don't know,' Bartholomew says.

'Want me to play the clip again? There must be a reason.'

Bartholomew can't say what that reason is.

'No one came to save James from the riot police. Philip was the same. No one intervened when he was hanging upside down from his legs, and no one stood up to help Thomas or Jude. You were in a coma for weeks. If Jesus is alive, he's indifferent to your suffering.'

'But I'm still alive. I'm here.'

'Thanks to me.'

'Jesus may have sent you.'

'Jesus didn't send me.'

'Without you knowing. You wouldn't have to know.'

'I would know.'

'Would you?'

The hail is back, vicious fistfuls on the car windows, deafening on the roof. Claudia thumbs a text, her face lit up by the screen. The sky darkens and the car is barely moving so they stop in the services at Thorpe. Cassius Gallio buys everyone a flapjack, including the driver. Bartholomew likes coffee, so Gallio fetches him a cappuccino from the Costa, and Bartholomew makes a big effort to leave intact the heart shape in the chocolate on the milk. That is not a heart, Gallio wants to say, it's a coffee bean. You are protecting a bean shape that looks like a heart.

Bartholomew says: 'Ouch. That eye of yours looks like it must have hurt.'

The night before, Gallio had organized the removal of the body of James from the pavement. Then the formal suspension of seven members of Valeria's riot squad. After that, he'd sat with Claudia in the van. They reviewed on the monitors the last moments on earth of James the Less, the sixth disciple of Jesus to die.

James looked old, Gallio thought, realizing he too must be old. They had grown old together.

'One more time,' Gallio said, and Claudia pointed the remote control.

One more time for the very end, a rooftop wind fluttering the Galilean clothes that James and the other disciples chose to wear. James ignores the whistling and jeering from the riot police below, and focuses entirely on his will. He prays, lips moving. He steps forward. Into a pure drop of silence he pronounces the name of Jesus.

He jumps.

'We need that trace on the phone call.'

'It's coming.' Claudia says. 'Be patient.'

'James received a phone call. He listened, but whoever was at the other end of the phone had nothing to say. James ended the call. He left the flat and went up to the roof. He held out his arms like Jesus. He jumped.'

'Maybe he heard something on the phone we didn't. Or the silence had a different meaning to him than it does to us.'

Cassius Gallio had reached the roof edge a second after James stepped off, in time to see that the road surface below had done most of the damage. The riot police finished the job, attacking James as if he were deranged and dangerous, a surprise assailant from above that they had to subdue. He'd launched himself unprovoked at officers of the law. They had no choice.

In the van Gallio felt they were missing a piece of the puzzle. James ended the silent phone call, stood up and went to the roof. His immediate reaction suggested an agreed sequence, and explained why he prayed so much—prayer kept him close to the phone and in a heightened spiritual state, ready for the call, in the mood to jump.

Gallio found it hard to rewatch what happened next. The

riot police should not have responded in the way they did, even though Cassius Gallio was increasingly convinced the disciples were shielding a secret. They denied it: everything pointed to it. They'd rather die than be disloyal, and if James was prepared to jump then Bartholomew's initial silence in the taxi to Caistor came as no surprise. Unlike Baruch, however, Gallio didn't believe in coercion. Six disciples had died horribly, and no new information had surfaced.

Claudia did eventually get a trace on the call, that same night. When the results were phoned through she listened closely then clicked off her phone. 'Landline,' she said. 'Via a switchboard. Internal phone at the King David Hotel. We have a room number.'

'Paul,' Gallio said. 'I'm guessing the room number matches up.'

'It does. Surprise, and yet not.'

Cassius Gallio whistled. 'No, you're right. Paul. I'm more surprised than not.'

The two Speculators made eye contact, but in the van everything was too close and they quickly looked away. Neither of them were convinced that Paul was responsible, even though he had motive. He wanted to be a disciple but they wouldn't let him join. He also had the experience, a killer from the beginning of his career.

'In the Israel Museum Paul was genuinely frightened,' Gallio said. 'I don't believe he's the killer.'

'But the call came from his suite. Somehow he made this happen, or that's what it looks like. What do we do?'

'Paul is all we've got,' Gallio said. 'We have no option. We pick him up at the hotel, and make Baruch a happy bunny.'

When they arrived at the King David, Baruch volunteered to make the arrest. 'My reward,' he said, 'seeing as I'm the only one who suspected him from the start.'

Baruch wasn't interested in the how or why. Paul had made the phone call, which was evidently a signal. James had jumped. Paul was involved up to his neck, and he'd devised a way of killing James without even having to speak.

'So explain how that works.'

'Don't know,' Baruch said. 'But give me a few days with Paul in custody and I can assure you details will emerge.'

In the breakfast room of the King David Hotel, while Paul was shaking out his napkin and dabbing at the corner of his mouth, Baruch gave him the right to remain silent. Gallio gauged Paul's reaction, but this wasn't his first arrest and he calmly rearranged the tableware, made sure the cutlery was aligned at a correct distance from the plate.

'You're arresting me on what charge? Making a phone call?'

Paul adjusted his spoon, then volubly and coherently he waived his right to silence. He'd need to hear a legally valid charge. He intended to make an official appeal, which he was entitled to do as a citizen like any other. He demanded a secure escort to Rome, where he'd be happy to defend himself in person at the appeal hearing. He'd expect to retain his personal bodyguard because he was innocent until proven guilty.

'Why did you telephone James?' Gallio asked. He didn't believe Paul was the assassin, who could kill with a phone call, but he couldn't be sure.

'We traced the call,' Claudia said. 'You made it. James jumped.'

'No one could prove that connection. I'm sad that James died, and I'll miss him, but his death has nothing to do with me.'

'You deny phoning him?'

'I do not. I had an issue I wanted to discuss. A private matter, of a theological nature.'

'So why didn't you speak?'

'At the last minute I changed my mind. I decided not to share.'

'James jumped from the roof of his building after you put through a call. Have you been blackmailing him?'

'I don't have to answer. You're obliged to allow me an appeal in Rome.'

'You're enjoying this, aren't you?' Baruch studied Paul's face, and he was right. Paul was enjoying himself. 'You end up with exactly what you wanted when we met up yesterday. Protection. Look at you. You don't give a flying fuck about James. You get what you requested in the museum, as if you'd planned this death for your own benefit.'

Cassius Gallio recognized Baruch's sense of being used, and it made both of them uneasy. Gallio felt the mysterious hand of Jesus deploying the pieces, devising outcomes that favoured his followers. A death was not a death, any more than this arrest of Paul was a punishment. Jesus had worked out the moves in advance.

'This isn't right,' Baruch said. 'Something here is wrong.'

Paul laughed. He couldn't help himself. He beckoned the waiter, but no waiter dared approach, not while Gallio and Baruch were ruining Paul's breakfast. Paul knew differently, that not everything was as it seemed.

'Congratulations,' he said, 'there's hope for you yet. Something is wrong. Everyone senses it, and from this feeling religion begins. There are features of our existence that feel wrong. Jesus offers an explanation.'

'This is a set-up,' Baruch said.

His phone rang. A second later so did Cassius Gallio's. News from the medical centre; Bartholomew was out of his coma.

'I'll go,' Baruch said.

'We'll both go.'

'I'll drive.'

No one forgets Judas, and his betrayal of Jesus is proof the disciples can be weak.

Bartholomew has a weakness for cappuccino. Back from his coma he's in love with life and surrounded by god's miracles, including Italian frothed coffee and slot-machine lights at the A46 services near Thorpe.

Cassius Gallio hopes to turn Bartholomew as he once turned Judas, but even on his second Costa he's yet to be bought. Gallio leans across the laminated table. 'You don't remember me, do you? Many years ago we had a chat in the back of a car. I said that one day I'd help you, and seventy pieces of silver is a lot of money. However you choose to look at it.'

'I'm looking down on it,' Bartholomew says. 'What would I do with so much silver?'

'I'll buy you some catalogues. You don't need to be short of ideas, not these days.'

'Jesus will provide.'

Yet Bartholomew declines to explain how Jesus will arrange a dead-drop or other fieldcraft details, on these mysterious future occasions when Jesus will deign to provide. They're soon back in the taxi, Bartholomew fascinated by the spaces that divide one town from the next. Strip villages, obese children, and marshes where wheat refuses to grow. Rivers. England is a developing region, the kind of backward territory where gibberish can flourish among the uneducated, but sometimes Gallio just looks, and forgets he's looking for Jesus.

'I sense you're troubled,' Bartholomew says. 'What can I do for you?'

Gallio compliments him on his sensitivity, and says that to be honest he's troubled by the latest forensic reports. 'I doubt you can help.'

'That isn't what I meant. You're avoiding the question.'

And Gallio continues to do so because this is his taxi, his story. He will ask the questions and sift the answers. He will speculate, because that's why he was put on god's good earth. 'We've found evidence of high-strength anesthetic stocked in Joseph of Arimathea's house during the period of the crucifixion.'

Perhaps Bartholomew can be useful after all. Gallio runs through one of his Jesus survival theories, not the switch but the sedative on the sponge. What does Bartholomew make of that?

'It's possible.'

Bartholomew trained as a doctor so he should know. He also wants to be kind, allowing Gallio to speculate, and surprised by Bartholomew's meek response Gallio sees for the first time how tired he is. As a Speculator he should take advantage.

'In the sense that anything is possible? Or that the sedative made it easier for whoever took Jesus's place? A minor disciple. Like Simon, for example, crucified in the place of Jesus but mercifully spared the worst of the pain.'

'I don't know. I can't say whether your theories are true or untrue. They're not unreasonable.'

'Tell me how Jesus stays hidden.'

'He's not hidden,' Bartholomew says. 'He is everywhere.'

'Yes, but where exactly, right now? Is Jesus here in England? Is he standing in for the disciple who's been located in Caistor?

Tell me and put an end to this. We won't hurt anyone and you can relax. Seventy-five pieces of silver would set you up, even in this day and age.'

Cassius Gallio offers himself up as a saviour, and as soon as Bartholomew allows reason to prevail then Gallio will have saved him. But Bartholomew stares out the side window, captivated by the forecourt of a BP garage, the first one he's seen, another everyday miracle. He wipes a hole in the condensation to let in the green and yellow glow of prices and pumps. For the moment the secret entrusted to the disciples is safe with Bartholomew.

'How well do you know Paul?'

'Not at all. We've never met.'

'I arrested him in Jerusalem. We think he's involved in the death of James.'

After the BP garage a superstore, a Real Ale pub, a slow length of road following a vintage Morris Traveller. Bartholomew is easily distracted from explaining how a god can appear on earth. 'Who do you prefer, Peter's Jesus or Paul's Jesus? I think I can predict the answer.'

'What's the difference?'

'The Jesus according to Peter is a Nazareth carpenter who champions the disadvantaged. Paul thinks Jesus has a direct line to god and can take over the world. Peacefully, as long as everyone believes in him.'

'I don't prefer either version. Both can be true.'

'Paul's Jesus is winning.'

'He makes skilful use of the postal service.'

'Paul is not the person you think he is.'

'I try to remember Jesus as he was to me.'

Gallio tries another angle, flattery. Bartholomew escaped

the carnage of Philip's martyrium. He was spared a terrible death, meaning he might be the chosen one, as described by Jude. Bartholomew could be the disciple Jesus loves. 'Couldn't you? That would explain why you're alive.'

No disciple with a human heart could fail to warm to this idea, the glory of the disciple beloved above all others.

'I think that's Peter,' Bartholomew says. 'Jesus called him the rock.'

'Do you know where Peter is now?'

'I don't. I'm sorry.'

Of course he doesn't. None of them know a thing. The disciples claim encounters with divine omniscience through Jesus, but can't keep in touch with each other.

'Really, I'm the least of all the disciples.'

They do love to brag, each disciple more humble than the next.

The traffic congestion eases at a section of dual carriageway, and the taxi eases out past double-trucks carrying hay bales, then makes way for a full-beam fish van hurtling back to Grimsby. Claudia is asleep in the front seat of the taxi, head lolled forward.

'We can give Peter twenty-four-hour global response protection.'

This is a genuine proposal. If an assassin or team of assassins is targeting the disciples then the CCU has a civilized duty to protect them. At the same time, Valeria could monitor Peter night and day to reduce the chances of a terror attack. Bartholomew, the least of the disciples, closes his eyes.

Cassius Gallio is doing his best: good cop, carrot, the agreeable side of life. So far he has spared Bartholomew the bad cop and the beatings, but both methods carry more weight in the

Antonia. Fewer contemporary distractions, but Valeria has sent him to England. She wants him to get ahead of Baruch and restore a sense of control, because Baruch gone rogue threatens the outcome of their mission.

'You should have fitted him with a tracer.' Valeria hated not knowing where everyone was, and what they were doing. 'You had plenty of opportunity in Hierapolis.'

'We're supposed to be partners.'

'But you fell out. You should have seen it coming.' For the first time since Gallio came back Valeria was flustered, but she too had her career to consider, and the CCU was obsessed with results. Welcome to Jerusalem, Valeria, welcome to the complex case of Jesus.

Gallio wonders what damage Baruch can do in England. Unless, and this is not impossible, the disciple identified in Caistor as Simon is Jesus. Jesus has been hiding away on barbarian shores as a minor disciple, biding his time in an obscure and forgotten territory. Simon in Caistor, England, matches these requirements. Gallio urges the taxi onward, because Baruch mustn't get there first.

Even with a knife flat-bladed across his forehead Gallio had been optimistic that he was not in a proper fight with Baruch. A proper fight, with Baruch, was to the death, but they seemed to have reached a moment in the Shaare Zedek Medical center where the fighting could reasonably stop. At least, Gallio was hoping they had.

'You don't want to die, do you, Gallio? You're frightened of death. I can smell your little man fear.'

Baruch turned the blade, the cutting edge honed to the idea

of slicing off an eyebrow, whole. In fact only Gallio had stopped fighting, and he waited for his life to flash before his eyes. It did not, which was encouraging, though as he'd noticed in other moments of extreme stress, most of them connected to Jesus, time did change shape. Time swelled, slowed, or everything happened at once. Time became unreliable, in the open moments between life and death.

Baruch's knife stayed flat against Gallio's forehead for several seconds, or for several years. He forgets.

'You are pathetic,' Baruch's knife-face wavered. 'You are old and ineffectual.'

Warm, wet, dripping into Gallio's eye. The bastard, Gallio thought, he cut me. Gallio put his hand to his face and it came away wet and red, and not even a proper fight because he sensed the worst was over. He pressed his fingers hard against the wound, like a clumsy salute. Baruch had cut him, but he dared go no further because behind Cassius Gallio was Valeria, and behind her the CCU, and the legions, all the way back to Rome.

The two men had arrived at the medical centre to find Bartholomew sitting up in bed with a bowl of chicken soup. He was pale, but he managed a smile of welcome. Baruch sat down on the end of the bed, eyes greedy like an ancient prophet, sizing Bartholomew up, no suffering too extreme to imagine. Bartholomew steadied his bowl. He had no idea.

'Leave him alone,' Gallio said. Paul's smug acceptance of his arrest, turning it to his advantage, did not sit well with Baruch. On the journey from the hotel he'd driven like a man possessed, his anger fierce enough to deter every possible accident. Now Gallio wanted to intervene before the anger from the road found a way to settle on Bartholomew. 'He's been unconscious since Hierapolis. What can he tell us?'

'He has information about his attackers. Maybe an identification.'

'We arrested Paul,' Gallio said. 'You wanted Paul. Leave Bartholomew to me.'

'Why should I? Paul will get his escort, the works. Cushy house arrest in some middle-class district of Rome, and now we can't touch him. They're pulling us out of shape, like last time, leaving too many questions unanswered.'

'Baruch, we're on the same side. We're partners.'

Bartholomew sipped at a spoonful of soup, licked his lips, re-discovered entry-level distinctions between alive and dead. Eating was one of them. Baruch stood up and Bartholomew spilled soup on his sheets. Advantages, disadvantages.

'Who was trailing me in Damascus?'

Gallio took a step back from Baruch's undivided attention, but at least he was distracted from his prey.

'You were followed?'

'You know I was. And who tipped off Paul in Antioch?'

'Why are you asking me? Ask Bartholomew, he's more likely to know than I am. But do ask nicely, please.'

'That's exactly what I plan to do.'

Bartholomew had moved his bowl to the safety of the bed-side table. Baruch sat closer this time, the disciple's eyes, nose and throat within his reach. 'Start at Hierapolis,' he said. 'This better be good.'

'Nicely.'

Bartholomew opened his mouth, but at first no words came out. He coughed into his hand and tried again. His voice was weak, feeling a way back into speaking. 'I remember the beginning of the attack.' Another cough, more forceful this time. 'If that's what you want to know. They were quick. They put a sack on my head. I didn't see any faces.'

'How many of them?'

Bartholomew shook his head; the memory simply wasn't there for him.

'What about voices?'

'One voice, I think. Maybe more. It was difficult to hear, because of the sack.'

'Try to place the voice,' Gallio said, and compared to Baruch he sounded like a saint. 'A man or a woman? What language were they speaking?'

Bartholomew smiled thinly, tired now. 'At the time,' he said, 'I thought that's how the devil would sound.'

'Like the devil,' Baruch said. 'Thank you hugely for your help.'

For a full half minute of silence, Cassius Gallio considered Satan as a suspect. Satan had been accused twice, in Babylon by the wife of the deputy finance minister and now by Bartholomew. Gallio resisted coincidence as an explanation, but could hardly bring in Satan for questioning. Instead he reasoned their latest suspect away: from inside a kidnapper's sack voices will sound satanic.

'Another question for you,' Gallio said. 'If you feel up to it. Why did James jump from the roof?'

Bartholomew looked confused. 'Did he do that? I didn't know.'

'What do you know?'

'Leave him alone, Baruch.'

'Or what?'

Baruch reached around and pulled out his knife, laid the blade across his thigh.

'He's doing his best. He's telling you what he remembers.'

'He's lying. Disciples lie. That's their defining characteristic, to lie about what they've lived and seen. They're keeping a secret, and Bartholomew is going to hand it over.'

'The knife isn't the way.'

'So what is the way? Look at you, with your reasonable questions and your miserable face. I don't know what the truth is with Paul, but I do know he goaded Jesus into an appearance. He stung the living Jesus by setting up the murder of Stephen on the street in Jerusalem, then Jesus ambushed him on the Damascus road. The two events are connected. Hurting a disciple can incite Jesus to intervene.'

'That may be a correlation, not a cause.'

'So let's find out. Let's taunt Jesus and see what happens.'

Baruch picked up his knife and Gallio reached for his arm. Baruch was up and on Gallio with the speed and expertise of a killer. He hissed like a snake. He pressed the blade flat against Gallio's forehead, and cut him. He cut him above the eyebrow. He drew blood.

Then he pushed Gallio away, and with him everything Gallio stood for, the CCU, the legions, civilization. With practiced ease the knife found the sheath in the small of his back. 'I'll have answers,' Baruch said. 'If not here then from one of the others, and without your help.' He made for the doorway, as if Jerusalem were full of disciples and he was in a hurry to find them, and to damage them. 'I'll deal with the disciples my way. You and your procedures are holding us back.'

Baruch slammed the door on his way out, making the liquids in the IV bags tremble.

'It's all right,' Gallio said. He stood there with his fingers clamped to the cut above his eye. Blood found its way through to his knuckles, across the back of his hand as far as his wrist. 'I won't let anyone hurt you. I'm one of the good guys.'

Caistor is on the edge of the Lincolnshire Wolds, away from nearby towns, away from significant transmitters, and the broadband is patchy at best. The town has under three thousand inhabitants, and the spire of the Church of St. Peter and St. Paul is a central feature, though in English market towns every building has history, or will have. The fire station on the hill is closed down or not yet operational. It's difficult to find anyone to ask, because cold and late the market square is roadblocked by squad cars. Blue lights flash in the darkness, sliding across the slick black numbers on the white car roofs. A helicopter hammers above, searchlight strobing the narrow streets.

Cassius Gallio spits into the gutter, and his spit freezes on double yellow lines. A hostage situation. Not what he needs right now, but as likely in Caistor as anywhere else, as the big city, as an isolated farmhouse—wherever the human brain decides that action needs to be taken, that destinies can be changed by force.

In Caistor, hubris requires the presence of emergency police from Hull, who have surrounded a large Georgian house just off the market square. To the side of the driveway are three lock-up garages, the far one subject to a breaking and entering. The two men inside the garage refuse to leave peacefully, hands in the air, as requested by a thirty-watt police loudhailer. The authorities will do the rest. The intruders are foreigners. No one understands a word they say.

Cassius Gallio of the Complex Casework Unit, specializing in sightings of disciples, arrives from over the sea. He has his ID with the embossed eagle. He has the face in its misery, and an overcoat and scarf and leather gloves for the wind that blows in from the Humber. He expects, and receives, a respectful welcome at the crime scene.

The press are in attendance with their lenses and recorders. They film Cassius Gallio shaking hands with the local police commissioner, and shout out for a comment. Gallio grips the commissioner by the elbow and guides him across to the safer side of the police line, nearer the criminals than the press. He shows him two pictures of Jesus from a selection on his phone, a Rubens and a Tissot. The local policeman shakes his head.

'Similar, but that's not the man.'

Gallio swipes through the disciple images and stops at Simon. He has a photo of the sculpture he once saw in Brussels, Simon in white marble leaning on a two-handled saw. The commissioner studies the face.

'That's him, that's the hostage.'

'And the kidnapper?'

'We don't have a description. He's armed. He has a knife.'

Gallio updates Claudia—the disciple Simon is the hostage—and suggests she makes Bartholomew safe. 'That's why we brought him, after all. We can't trust anyone else. Find him a room, somewhere warm. And don't let him out of your sight.'

A kidnap negotiator offers Gallio his loudhailer. He waves it away. He phones Baruch's number, and after a lengthy rerouting via Israel and back to England, the phone rings and Baruch answers. Gallio has to shout, because the background noise sounds like a sawmill.

'What's going on? Never mind. Stop whatever you're doing. I'm coming in.'

The uniformed police are impressed. A WPC in a stab vest, crouching and keeping her eye on the corrugated door, accompanies Gallio to the third garage along. Cassius Gallio walks upright, wishing he'd brought a hat, holding the phone to his ear. 'Open it enough for me to get in.'

Camera flash whitens the winter gloom. Baruch leaves the door as low as possible so the press can't get pictures, and Gallio drops to a press-up position and slides in underneath. They'll get front-page shots of a Speculator in action, a special agent's fearless first contact with the hostage taker.

Cassius Gallio pulls the door closed behind him and stands up inside the garage. Christ. He kills the phone. He doesn't want to see what he's seeing but this is what has happened in Caistor. The event can't be undone. Simon is naked and hanging from chains, head down, the weight of his shoulders slumped on a workbench.

Gallio holds vomit into his mouth with his hand. Christ. Christ alive, this will make Jesus pay attention, surely it will. Every act of evil is an appeal. An atrocity is a provocation, always has been: gods, if you exist and have any shame then show yourselves. When they choose not to show themselves—and according to modern historians this is usually their choice— the horror has failed to shame them. More horror is needed. What about this atrocity, and this? What about this act of evil now? Jesus, what about this here now? Baruch has accepted the challenge.

He has chained each of Simon's ankles, and hauled him up by a pulley attached to a steel roof beam. Simon's legs are spread and in the air, his exposed white vertebrae curled into the bench.

Baruch has taken an electric chainsaw and split Simon from the groin, starting in the hinge between his legs. How could Jesus not come back at the sight of this? If not now, then when? Come Jesus if you're coming, come on. Baruch is sawing your disciple Simon in half.

Civilization cannot tolerate acts like this. It sends for the police and civilization is the police. Civilization intervenes, says with divine certainty that this must never happen, though it does happen. Cassius Gallio defies Jesus to explain Simon, and what he thinks the torture of Simon means. None of the recorded parables illuminate a fate such as this in a provincial English garage.

The garage has a brushed concrete floor, and on hooks in the breeze-block wall tools are ordered according to size. The fourteen-inch electric chainsaw is missing from its outline next to the cordless hammer drill. The saw is plugged into an orange flexed extension socket and has been used to slice through Simon as far as his lower stomach. There is a gallon of blood on the concrete floor, as if an engine block's been emptied of oil.

Cassius Gallio's mind turns away, saving itself, just as his eyes know never to stare at the sun. He couldn't chainsaw a man in half, he thinks, but Baruch can. Gallio is a negotiator, a finder of the best way forward. He feels the pressure of conscience, of knowing that Simon shouldn't have to suffer like this, and conscience feels suddenly like the presence of Jesus. Does it? Cassius Gallio could probably shoot someone with a gun. He's no saint.

He doesn't have a gun.

Simon is alive. Gallio sees his fingers twitch.

'Bastard might as well die.' Baruch sweats heavily into his white shirt, jacket off, buttons undone even though the garage is cold. He is exhausted, deflated. 'I couldn't break him.'

Baruch has moved beyond reasonable decision-making. If

anything, reason contributes to the problem because lies are a reasoned attempt to mislead. Pain is necessary to destroy Simon's ability to reason, and therefore to lie, and Simon has certainly felt pain. He should have told the truth about Jesus by now. Before now. A long time before.

'He talked, but came out with the same old stuff. Jesus walking on water, and making blind men see. Jesus back from the dead, Jesus to come again.'

'Baruch, what are you doing? What have you done here?'

Baruch starts crying, sobbing up huge gulps of grief. Gallio risks a glance at Simon. There, again, a flicker of movement right at the end of a fingertip.

'I wanted to call Jesus out.' Tears run down Baruch's face, both cheeks, the corner of his mouth. 'Paul managed it, so why can't I? How can Jesus bear to put up with this? He should be here, but he knows I won't roll over like Paul. I could take him. I know I could, because he's a coward. If he had anything about him I wouldn't get away with this.'

And then he has no sobbing left inside him. He wipes his eyes, and anger returns as a reliable emotion, the one he knows and uses best. Anger rises and revives him, and with a new sense of purpose he puts down the saw. One more time he wipes the back of his hand over his eyes. He pulls out his knife.

'Put down the knife, Baruch.'

Cassius Gallio is unarmed. He feels colossally stupid and arrogant for shutting the door of the garage. Baruch sniffs back the last of his tears then points his knife at Gallio's throat, like an essential step in his reasoning.

'I've been killing Simon for hours, trying to taunt Jesus out of hiding. I was expecting him to appear to me.'

'Obviously it doesn't work like that. Your analysis is flawed.'

'I know how Jesus works.'

'Do you? I thought Simon didn't talk.'

'Didn't need to. He betrayed himself in the way he acted. The torture was necessary to find that out, but now I know their secret.'

Gallio is distracted by Simon's fingers, watching them until they're no longer closing, however faintly, as a sign that his brain is reaching for grains of life. Simon is breathing, hearing. Something outside himself is understood, and then it is not. His fingers are still. The soul goes out of Simon, and Cassius Gallio waits for a profound insight or thought. None comes.

The seventh disciple is dead, but Jesus stays away. He does not have a human heart.

'Let me tell you what I did with the bones of James,' Baruch says. 'This is important. Not the last James, the one they beat to death. The first James, the disciple my men beheaded in Jerusalem. I was pleased he was dead. Didn't bother me in the slightest, but I felt we had a point to prove with his body. I wasn't going to risk a second Jesus, or Lazarus, so James had to stay dead. I boiled his corpse in a horse cauldron. Left it in there for hours, until the meat floated off. Beige in colour, I remember, like boiled pork. I chucked the meat to a dog. Other dogs turned up and fought for the scraps, no manners at all. I emptied the soup of James from the cauldron, watched it soak into the dried earth. The bones I collected into a sack, wrapped it in duct tape, and I personally signed off the package with UPS to Spain. It was the furthest place I could think of. James the disciple of Jesus was dead and he would not be coming back. That's what I thought: this time when they die they're dead.'

'James gets visitors.'

'I know. Hundreds of thousands of pilgrims, trekking miles to touch his bones. They talked about it on the coach to Pamukkale, and this is the secret the disciples want to keep from us. Whatever we do, they've planned ahead. Every decision we make works in their favour, if only we could see into the future. We were wrong about Philip and Thomas, they didn't have to recognize their killer. The disciples don't fight back because they're happy to die. That explains why they don't run, because the future is secure. Death is irrelevant to them. They have an insight into life after death that we should take more seriously.'

Baruch's eyes are alight with a brightness Gallio fears: shimmering, brittle, sick.

'Baruch, the British police are outside this garage in numbers. They're not unreasonable people, and they'll look after you. Give yourself up.'

'Simon knew where he was going, and he wanted to get there. He suffered, but without the level of suffering I expected him to show. He had an absolute certainty about what was going to happen next.'

'Jealous?'

The word slips out before Cassius Gallio can stop himself, a thought so evident that to think it is to say it. Baruch isn't angry, he's jealous, this is the most reliable of his emotions. He is the expert on death, but the disciples have information about the afterlife that he does not.

'I am jealous, yes. I want to know where they go, and why it doesn't scare them.'

Baruch places his killer's knife in the looseness of his left hand. He fixes Gallio eye-to-eye and blows into the palm of his right, flexing then clenching his fingers.

'Tell it to the police,' Gallio says. 'Don't do anything you'll regret.'

'I know what I'm doing. Have a little faith.'

He rolls his shoulders, preparing himself. Tosses the knife back into his right hand, grips hard. Baruch stabs himself deep in the windpipe.

VIII

Bartholomew

———

"SKINNED ALIVE"

Shit. This kind of mess won't clean up itself.

The next morning Gallio keeps Claudia involved, and that line in her forehead will not be softening any time soon. Her coping mechanisms involve pointing and tutting and snapping at Caistor locals who are too quick, too slow, too *clumsy*. Is it really so difficult, her body language asks, to get a pair of bodies bagged for airfreight to Israel?

The heavy lifting they leave to John W. Varlow and his son, undertakers from Chapel Street, while Gallio feeds a diversionary story to the press about foreign gangs and ancient grudges and the chronic use of Humberside Airport by international drug mules. He mentions Albania. The ladies and gentlemen of the press suck their teeth. Naturally, Albania. He provides a prime-time story they recognize, along with its familiar ending. The kidnapper killed the hostage then turned his weapon on himself. That will be all, thank you.

For the people of Caistor, from that night onward, the horror is safe in the past. The murder of Simon was a freak event, however grisly, but no one need think too deeply about what has happened here, not far from the market square. The case of the sawn-in-half disciple becomes a curiosity for out-of-towners, and a leaflet is available in the Heritage Centre.

Gallio has a report to write for Valeria, to close off the episode, but for him the incident lives on. He supervises the police as they decontaminate the crime scene, and reassures the commissioner that no other disciples of Jesus are expected in the region. The police commissioner glances at an upstairs window, above the long blue sign for *White Hart Free House and Accommodation*. Bartholomew is occasionally seen in silhouette, and he's always conspicuous at the post office.

'Except him,' Claudia says. 'But he's harmless. He's helping us with our enquiries, and we'll take him with us when we go.'

They stay in Caistor. Speculators aren't machines, despite their best efforts, and temporarily, while the double killing seems random and senseless, Gallio loses the urge to look for Jesus. He misses Baruch. He didn't think he would, but he does. Baruch has been a part of his life as far back as Lazarus, and Gallio grieves for another story lost that connects the past to the present.

Keep it together, he tells himself, but his ambitions feel undermined by so much death and so little Jesus. He remembers Thomas on the morgue trolley in Babylon, Philip swinging from his thighs in Hierapolis, and now in Caistor Simon with legs splayed sawn almost in half. These murders are unforgettable, deliberately so, but what kind of death does Jesus need to see before objecting? What has to happen before he intervenes and makes his presence felt?

If Jesus is alive, and as powerful as Bartholomew believes, then he is everywhere and the answer to every question. He may even care. But if he doesn't intercede he might as well not exist—the Jesus who abandons his followers to the saw and the rope and the stone is not worth seeking out.

Gallio asks the younger John Varlow, in a break from bagging up the corpses, to recommend a tea shop in Caistor. In fact there's only one, the Tea Cosy Café over the model railway shop, with a view of the market square. This is where every morning Gallio and Claudia debrief, comparing notes where Bartholomew can't overhear. There is often not much to say, so they watch the time go by.

'Stop looking at your phone,' Gallio says. 'Life is also here.'

They take the table in the window, though if life is here in Caistor life is once again slow. Claudia holds out her phone, screen facing Gallio. A text from Valeria, not the first. 'Read it. She says good things about you.'

Gallio sees the length of the message, sighs, pushes his cup and saucer to one side and holds the phone in both hands. Valeria is full of praise. She commends Cassius Gallio for containing what sounds like an appalling situation. Baruch was a loose cannon (she always thought so) but now they can push on against Jesus free from Baruch's obsession with Paul. Valeria advises Gallio, frankly, to keep his phone turned on. They're not living in the Dark Ages. Next, she has new intelligence that the disciple Matthew is in Cairo.

'According to our sources he's writing a book,' Claudia says. 'Valeria reckons he's their archivist. If so, he may have privileged information about a terror attack.

'And he may not.' Gallio hands back the phone. 'She wants me to fly to Cairo.'

'I know. Caistor, Cairo. International man of action.'

'I can't do this any more.'

Claudia looks up from her phone, sees he's serious and makes a show of powering the phone off. She has to study the edges and the top to remember how to do it, the line has to appear in her forehead, then she places the dead phone face down on the table and slides it to one side. She leans forward over her hands. 'You can't give up now. We're making progress. It can't get worse than Simon.'

'No?'

'Baruch was a confused individual.'

'He was deranged, but I liked him.'

'He started taking the afterlife seriously. We made a mistake letting him get ahead of us but he's done us a favour. Simon's killer isn't Jesus and it isn't Paul, who's under observation and house arrest in Rome. It looks like no single assassin is responsible. Baruch killed Simon. We know he didn't kill the others. The riot police killed James. The murders are random.'

'In which case there's no point searching for Jesus. He's not a controlling genius with a secret plan, and he doesn't have conclusive answers.'

Claudia reaches across the table and places her hand on Gallio's hand, her movement a textbook copy of Valeria in the restaurant when he first arrived back in Jerusalem. Claudia's wedding band is hard against Gallio's knuckle, but he doesn't mind. He leaves his hand where it is, under hers, never making the same mistake twice.

'You look miserable.'

'I live in a randomly brutish universe.'

'We've done our job. Nothing more we could do.'

'I wonder. Where do you think Baruch is now?'

'In a bag in cold storage at John W. Varlow and Son.'

'He changed his mind about death being of the end. Baruch couldn't stand the idea that Simon knew more about death than he did. He came to believe that the disciples had made a decisive discovery, that changed everything.'

'So now Baruch is chasing dead disciples in the afterlife?' Claudia withdraws her hand. She can allow Gallio a day or two of vulnerability, considering the bloodbath he witnessed, but he shouldn't fall apart. 'This isn't easy for me, either. I didn't sign up to strap a man's hips back together before he'd fit into a body bag. If you're not thinking straight give the reason a name. Shock. Symptoms are confusion and energy deficit. First week of Speculator training.'

Cassius Gallio adds sugar to his tea and stirs, even though the tea is cold. One day he might even get around to drinking it.

'Where's Bartholomew?'

'At the church. Where he usually is.'

'Not a committed mourner, Bartholomew. You probably noticed. Hardly overcome with grief, is he?'

'Let's go back. We should pack.'

They have a twin room upstairs at the White Hart. Bartholomew has the next room along, a double. Claudia booked them in on the evening they arrived, when the pub's other two rooms were taken by married ramblers and an agricultural products salesman. All three left Caistor first thing the next morning, after a blue-lit night disturbed by mayhem and murder. Two days later Gallio and Claudia are still in the twin. Gallio blames confusion and energy deficit. Claudia cites Valeria's budget, and worries that Gallio might be scared of the dark. Between them they can easily justify the twin beds, and they confirm that this is a strictly professional arrangement by showing the utmost respect for each other's privacy.

Gallio flops onto his single bed, lies on his back. Stomach, side. Back. He kicks off his shoes in the middle of the afternoon, pulls a pillow over his face.

'We're supposed to be packing. Cairo, remember? Matthew is doing whatever he does in Cairo. He's at risk.'

'I have this picture stuck in my head,' Gallio says.

'What?'

Gallio lifts up the pillow. 'Baruch before he killed himself. The determined look in his eyes.'

On the table separating the beds is a novel Claudia pretends to read before sleeping. Gallio picks up the book, reads the premise on the back. Young Americans adrift in Spain, deft, very very funny. He wonders how she can relate to that, when here in England a disciple of Jesus was sawn in half.

'I'm going to shower,' she says.

'Again?'

'Then we should make a move. We can't stay here forever.'

She locks herself in the bathroom, though Gallio would like her to lie down next to him on his narrow single bed. He'd like that very much, though he wouldn't know how to ask. He has spent a long time living with men, making sure to avoid sex except for that one misjudgement in Hamburg. He went back to the shoe shop the next afternoon, to apologize and to offer the girl money. She refused, said she liked him. He never saw her again.

Of course he's shaken up, and he understands his reaction. He has seen death and he wants sex, suddenly alert to the only clock that matters, death then sex then death then sex then death sex death, one thing after another. He needs to fuck Claudia. He wants, needs, whatever, to push her head down into the sheets and to be in her. Not just now. He wanted it already last night and the night before and every night but he stayed where he was in his bed. He's suffering from an instinctive reaction, an equalling out, and he recognizes his impulse for what it is. Sex as a compensation, a consolation. Sex as the opposite of death.

He is, all the same, slightly ashamed of himself for wanting Claudia so fiercely. It reminds him that before he was civilized he was not. His people long ago and seemingly forever lived in forests in Germany, until they were massacred in battle by an army with superior technology. Civilization had arrived. Gallio's stepfather, the general in charge, had offered to adopt the orphaned children of slaughtered enemy chieftains. He was full of human decency, after the battle was won.

But however young those children, the slate was never wiped entirely clean. Cassius Gallio can dream of matted blonde hair and double-edged hatchets. In his past, somewhere in the history that made him, a blue-eyed shaman pierces a chain through his tongue, and for years on end he drags a clutter of human skulls behind him. In days gone by, a long time ago, this must have seemed important. The shaman and the papery skulls and the firelight chant to Odin for victory in the upcoming battle.

They lost.

As an adult, a modern civilized man, Gallio almost believes that reason will prevail. Sometimes, though, the instinctive equations reassert themselves, and no rational argument will deny them. We should pray for victory in the battle. Sex is the opposite of death.

Claudia sits at the end of her bed wrapped in a hotel bath towel. A smaller towel is around her hair like a turban.

'You haven't moved.'

His eyes settle on her damp neck like fingers, then move across her reddened ears and along her jawline to her chin. This is so inconvenient for him, if he wants to be good.

'I need to wash my hands.'

'Again?'

Cassius Gallio goes to the bathroom and washes his hands. He comes back out, and in the last half hour between them they have used three of the four guest-room towels provided, thus hastening the end of the world. Gallio can't bring himself to care, not after the last few days. He lies on his side, watches Claudia inspect her toenails.

'One more day,' she says, 'then we move on.'

She bumps herself up the bed and sits back against the head-board, picks up her book and puts on her reading glasses. Reads for a bit, looks across at him over the frames. 'I was thinking. If you ever come to Rome there are places I'd like to show you.'

'I know Rome pretty well.'

'Take your mind off the disciples.' Claudia has given up on packing. If Gallio isn't leaving today, neither is she. 'The city changes. Changes all the time.'

'But also stays the same.'

Gallio could fuck her now. Reach for her, exploit his instinct that life wins out over death. He'll have to deceive her a little, pretend he likes her more than he does, that he's always liked her, suggest that sex between them is therefore inevitable, and it is right and good. His feelings for her have a past and a future, that's the message to convey, even though he's not sure what those feelings are.

He wonders if he ever loved his wife, or Valeria. If he did he loved them and he lost them, but he was young, and the earlier love is lost the less serious it is, like chickenpox. He moved on and he was lucky because losing love later, as a grown-up, can scar the victim for life. People can actually die.

He'd be a fool to fall in love now. Wanting Claudia is probably connected with Valeria, and with his younger self. He wishes he didn't think so much.

Still, Gallio could fuck her now. He swings off the bed and waits until he's sure his feet are making solid contact with the floor. Then he stands up. He locks his hands behind his neck and pushes his head back against them.

'To work!' he says. He flings out his arms. The disciples of Jesus have no monopoly on virtue.

They're in Caistor the next day, and still they haven't packed. Cassius Gallio has a pain in his left shoulder from the single bed, and at some point in his sleep he pulled out the stitches above his eye. He checks in the bathroom mirror, tugs out the one remaining stitch, and disinfects the seeping wound with aftershave. He is not entirely indifferent to the future.

Claudia spends time on the phone to Valeria, excusing the delay, proposing fresh explanations for Baruch's excessive behaviour. Stress disorder, exhausted in the line of duty. Also, they need another day or so because two Jewish corpses on the same night in Caistor, one of them a disciple of Jesus, is not routine police work. There are loose ends.

'Yes, yes,' Claudia promises, 'as soon as we can. We can't leave any sooner than that.'

Valeria phones back. What the hell are they playing at, really?

We're not playing, Claudia thinks, we're being sensitive to each other's needs at a difficult time. Not what Valeria will want to hear. 'We're questioning Bartholomew. He lacks the physical strength for another journey.'

She could go on, and does. Bartholomew is frail from his coma, and without careful handling could suffer a relapse—a lie Claudia tells beautifully, because most of the time they can't even find him. Bartholomew is out, he's about, doing the work that disciples do.

Meanwhile, his protectors discover that in the slowness of Caistor a Speculator can avoid the headache of Jesus and global terrorism and Valeria's complex casework. The displaced Romans enjoy bright English afternoons, savoring this time between horrors when children can walk home from the grammar school. In the market square a parish councillor raffles tickets for Caistor in Bloom. Under striped tarpaulins, on Wednesdays and Saturdays, the market has tables of vegetables, meat, pet food, and Cassius Gallio honestly can't see that the world is going to end, not soon, not here in provincial England. Simon the disciple of Jesus may as well not have been sawn in half here. Life continues as if he never existed.

At the church on Sunday Bartholomew speaks from the pulpit, unaffected by Simon's death. He is confident that what will be will be, which seems to include his return to health and a renewed commitment to Jesus. Cassius Gallio slides into a pew near the back, and feels a twinge of metaphysical envy: to feel a sense of destiny would be a blessed relief. He thinks about his frailties and his failures and corrects himself—but only if that destiny were favourable.

He listens to Bartholomew advising the older churchgoers not to be scared of dying. Then Bartholomew reassures the middle-aged who are frightened of the death of the old, and, in smaller numbers, he consoles the young frightened by the fear of the middle-aged. Bartholomew the preacher promises to honor the strongest and most urgent human wish: that we should never die. In exchange, the parishioners of Caistor bake cakes and sort jumble at the town hall on a Thursday. Simon is dead, yet their belief in Jesus and eternal life remains alive.

Caistor already has a stipendiary vicar, a bearded graduate of Sunday schools, who repeats stories he knows from Simon. Bartholomew stands aside with clasped hands and hears about the miracles of Jesus, the sayings of Jesus, the death and resurrection and ascension of Jesus. James, Jude, Thomas, Philip, James, now Simon himself. All eyewitnesses, all dead, but the stories live on. The parishioners of Caistor sing 'Thine is the Glory.'

In the high-ceilinged Church of St. Peter and St. Paul the hymn resonates with longing fulfilled, and in a moment of weakness Cassius Gallio wants everything they believe to be true. Jesus promises justice and love and eternal life. That would be a lovely and perfect solution to injustice and hate and death, thank you, but from experience he has his doubts.

After the preaching and the singing, Bartholomew visits the misfortunate of Caistor. Gallio watches and learns, loyal to his vocation as a Speculator, as does Claudia. They tell Valeria this is what they're doing, and this is what they do. Bartholomew picks up where Simon left off. He performs his small repertoire of country doctor tricks, easing the ailments of the rural poor. Cassius Gallio hands him bandages and presses him for a medical opinion on Jesus.

'Up on the cross the point of a spear went into his side. That's right, isn't it? If Jesus bled from the wound then at that stage of the execution his heart must still have been beating, correct?'

Bartholomew is dressing an ulcer on the leg of an immigrant farm laborer. 'Could have been. I'd need more information to confirm a diagnosis.'

'So clinically he was still alive?'

Bartholomew shines a penlight into the milky eyes of an ancient woman who as a child was blessed by a retired naval chaplain who'd opened a gate for Queen Victoria. Everyone tells him a story.

'At that point yes. Probably.'

'Thank you. I appreciate your honesty. Where were you during the crucifixion? Where did the disciples go?'

'I'm sorry,' Bartholomew says, 'I'm busy.'

The people of Lincolnshire keep on coming, and Gallio feigns an interest. With Claudia's help he hands out hot meals and financial advice to people who believe in Jesus instead of understanding the macroeconomic pressures of a global civilization. He makes crutches for the lame, and forces himself to be patient with children, because if Bartholomew trusts him he's more likely to confide his secrets. Gallio shows him the photos of Jesus on his phone—he's a late starter, but he's committed to finding Jesus. 'Is that him?'

Bartholomew should know—Jesus sad but tough, with a crown of thorns, by Antonello da Messina.

'Yes, that's him.'

Jesus muscular but wary, again with thorns, by Peter Paul Rubens. 'What about this one?'

'I'd say so. The likeness is certainly apparent.'

Gallio swipes again: Jesus frail and wide-eyed, bent-backed beneath the weight of the cross, by El Greco. 'Jesus?'

'What a fantastic picture. Yes.'

Jesus angry but in control, under the weight of the cross again, by Titian. 'Is this one Jesus?'

'Oh, very good. Maybe my favourite. See how he captures the mouth.'

And so on. Bartholomew asks to see more, and for once Gallio has an Internet connection so the pictures keep on coming, and Bartholomew swears that every image is recognizably Jesus. Gallio starts to protest, they can't all be Jesus, but the slide show is interrupted by a boy from a travellers' camp near Market Rasen. He has an open sore on his forehead, like red stained glass. His mother is carrying a baby with maggots in its eye.

That's enough compassion for Cassius Gallio, for one day. Bartholomew can manage on his own.

It is raining. Outside the window of the White Hart pub the cone of rain lit by a streetlight changes the orange beam into a showerhead. Gallio and Claudia sit on the twin beds, notebooks in hand. They have a report to draft, but neither is confident about where to start. Simon, Baruch, Bartholomew. Line or curve. Circle or square. Stay or go.

In an effort to hurry them up, Valeria has forwarded the latest forensic results. She insists that the death of Simon doesn't negate the threat of an attack by Jesus or his surviving disciples. The security level remains Orange, High. And even though Baruch killed Simon, with a witness present, the assassins who murdered the other disciples haven't ceased to exist because of Baruch's lapse into madness.

Bad Luck. Cassius Gallio writes the heading in his notebook, underlines the two words twice. Joins up the underlines to make a long thin rectangle. Valeria can worry away at Jesus and his disciples all she likes, but the Complex Casework Unit can't deter a random universe. They're wasting their time. This is what the report should say, and it explains why Gallio doesn't know where to begin. His adult life has been wasted, if the universe turns out to be random.

According to Valeria's lab results, the saline solution on the glass from Joseph's bin conforms to the salt composition of human tears. The DNA extracted from this trace matches blood on the piece of wood from Babylon, found by Gallio beneath Thomas's bed. Mementos. Someone collected the tears of Jesus; Thomas kept a splinter of the True Cross as a reminder of the man he agreed to follow. They have scientific confirmation that Jesus existed and that he suffered, but even with modern forensic techniques no more information than that. Jesus existed. That doesn't mean he exists. There is no obligation to go looking for him, or to believe that he's coming again.

Claudia makes some dots on her empty page, joins a few of them at random. Gallio sketches a cartoon Roman nose. She leans over to look at his drawing. He moves across the bed making room for her, and she shifts across the space and sits beside him, puts her hand on his knee. That's new. Cassius Gallio should offer a gift in return. 'Thanks for staying in Caistor. Was worried you'd leave me to it.'

'Operational reasons. Bartholomew will trip up sooner or later.'

'Or he might potter about until the end of time. Be honest. I only half believed Jesus survived the cross, either by my switch theory or through carefully administered pain relief. He probably died.'

'We may never know.'

'There's no devious plot here, the product of a brilliant mind.'

'You mean no god.'

'I suppose I do.'

They hear the murmur of Bartholomew's voice in the neighbouring room. Prayers, always the praying, but like his fellow disciples he's trapped. Basic psychology. If Jesus is dead, and therefore an ordinary human being, Bartholomew left home for no good reason. To justify the arc of his life Bartholomew has to keep Jesus alive, and the more logically anyone protests the more forcefully he and the disciples resist. Jesus is alive, they say, and this fact explains their unemployment, their unfashionable taste in clothes, their hard exile from Galilee. Jesus is the son of god, so no devotion is excessive.

Bartholomew mumbles on. Gallio could pop next door and kill him. Bartholomew, disciple of Jesus, smothered with a pillow. Baruch, if he's looking down, would be disappointed: a pillow over the airway can't compete with a chainsaw, so Jesus will remain unmoved. Gallio doesn't bother. He guesses Bartholomew won't fight and he won't run, a stupid combination invented by the followers of Jesus.

'Let's talk about something else.'

Which can work, for a while. Talk about something other than god for the next two thousand years. Try. Gallio tests Claudia on the labours of Hercules, and she can remember seven or eight, and as they're doing this they make each other laugh. Gallio turns more toward her. He doesn't love her. Maybe her husband back in Rome loves her, and surely she is loved by her children. She turns more toward him, and smiles often enough that he's impressed by her perfect teeth. He can touch her, if he wants, on her hip. He will start at the hip, on the iliac crest. There. Bartholomew continues to pray. His god does not warn Gallio off.

So there's the sex. But also Gallio can imagine the framed

photograph he'll place on his desk. The two of them smile against a pure white background, in the studio of a parallel universe.

'I think I'm falling in love with you.'

Lies are good; lies make it worse. Is this how he started with Valeria? He can't remember. Claudia touches his cheek, and her fingers on his skin could mean anything, though he never stopped his version of praying, projecting his desires inside her mind, imagining her projecting desire back out at him. He expended effort in making that connection, and brainwaves of such purpose can't simply dissipate. Besides, they're a long way from home. No one will ever know. They are lonely, and life is preferable to death.

At the White Hart in Caistor Live Music Night starts now, and the 4/4 beat of classic rock thumps through the floor. Hits from the ages drown out Bartholomew's prayers, fill up another evening in Caistor of not looking for Jesus, as does Gallio's hand on Claudia's hip, and from her hip into the dramatic indent of her waist. This is one of the loveliest available shapes, Cassius Gallio thinks, in an empty random universe.

Try not to lie, be kind to people, live forever. Gallio concedes that Bartholomew has tempting ideas, but he resists temptation.

When the music stops, hours later, some time after midnight, Claudia insists she has no regrets. She's glad it happened. But please, she says, let's not do this again.

By now there's no visible police presence in Caistor. The town is a Co-Op, a Spar, and a timeless sense that nothing significant either good or bad will take place here ever again. The people of Caistor carry on doing what they've always done, overpaying for the lottery and looking for love. It is complacent to live like this, but life at least is bearable.

Gallio and Claudia have questioned Bartholomew endlessly, without great success.

'What's your opinion of Paul?'

'I like Paul.'

'You said that as if there's a but.'

'Paul always wants to *explain*. Sometimes Jesus just is.'

Valeria runs out of patience and orders them by phone and email and text to give up on Bartholomew. Once, twice, three times. She wants Cassius Gallio in Cairo, because even her researchers struggle to remember Bartholomew's name—as a disciple he must be unimportant. Gallio suggests Bartholomew is about to crack, while after-images of Claudia from the night before mean he couldn't care less.

'Leave Bartholomew alone,' Valeria says, 'before I have to send someone to fetch you.'

Claudia tells Gallio their time is up. The reality they have to face is that no one can live in Caistor indefinitely. She invites Bartholomew to join their daily meeting in the Tea Cosy Café, and over a disappointing cappuccino she convinces him he's done everything he can in Caistor. The hour has come, she says, for him to turn his thoughts to more benighted corners of the earth.

'We'll pay your fare,' Claudia says, and Gallio wishes she wasn't in such a hurry. He assumes that for her the twin room in the White Hart pub has been an interlude, a brief fantasy, and now she wants home with her children. She's young, she'll recover.

'Wherever you feel called to go,' she tells Bartholomew, 'as thanks from Rome for your help.'

Caistor has no travel agent, which gives Cassius Gallio fresh hope of a new delay, but Claudia discovers Internet terminals at the Heritage Centre. Claudia is keener than he realized, past the café inside the entrance, the three of them loud on the stripped floorboards, up the stairs beyond the library to the computers on the second floor.

Claudia sits Bartholomew in front of a computer screen and shows him pictures of Greece, gorgeous and blue. Greece needs love and medicine and social justice. She leans across him and searches for a flight, departing Humberside Airport, and the earliest available is a last-minute package leaving later in the week to the northern Peloponnese, west of Athens. Not an established tourist destination but the new-build hotel has sea views. Looks promising. Fly into a city called Patras.

Bartholomew holds up his hands, shakes his head. Not Greece. He's less interested in gorgeous and blue and more in overrun by idolatry. Claudia clicks to Ibiza, but Bartholomew points further along the alphabet to Iran. Iran. Claudia will struggle to find Tehran four-star specials with pool and buzzing nightlife.

But Bartholomew insists, so Claudia puts together a route leaving the next day that involves three transfers to the airport at Bashkale in Armenia, which is the closest she can get him to the border. She downloads for Bartholomew an Armenian visa for an Israeli citizen available on the Internet for immediate travel. The final stage, the short trip into Iran itself, he'll have to arrange by himself. She fills out his booking details.

'How many bags?'

No bags. One-way.

The next afternoon they share Bartholomew's taxi for the short ride to the airport, leaving plenty of time before his first leg to Amsterdam (Schiphol, inevitably). Gallio buys him a cappuccino at the café in the airport, and there's a smiley face in the chocolate on the milk.

'About the cross, and Golgotha,' Bartholomew says. He has milk froth on his moustache, and Gallio hopes for a last-minute confession, a decisive offering before Departures. Instead Bartholomew asks a question. 'At the very end, when Jesus died, was there light?'

Hopeless. The disciples give nothing away, but they're happy to take from others. 'You had to be there.'

Gallio immediately regrets his unkindness. Bartholomew missed the crucifixion because he was scared, or preparing an escape for Jesus, but at Humberside Airport Gallio has no further use for him. A bit of kindness won't hurt either of them.

'Yes, now you mention it. I'm trying to remember. I think there was light.'

Bartholomew is joyful like a child. He wants the same story at every bedtime, even when in daylight there are more convincing versions available. He ignores the implications of an anesthetic-infused sponge, even after Gallio has brought it to his attention. Jesus looked dead but in fact was sedated, which connects into a new plausible story: Joseph's tomb was prestocked with medicines and dressings. Even so, given his injuries, Jesus needed three days to gain strength before his accomplices could move him.

A gate number appears on the flight information screens.

'Better make a move,' Bartholomew says, hands flat on the table, but Gallio can feel the levelling of those Galilee brown eyes, saying talk to me one last time, while you still can. You may never see me again, and I am a disciple of Jesus. 'You'll not stop looking for him. You know that, don't you?'

'The investigation is ongoing, and for the time being the Wanted bulletin remains valid. I'll be looking for Jesus while that continues to be my job.'

'I feel I've neglected you. Somehow I got very busy, even in Caistor, but we should have spent more time together. I sense I could help.'

'Where's Jesus?'

'Everywhere.' Bartholomew drains the last of his coffee, a regular dark-skinned guy with a beard wearing pale Middle Eastern robes. 'When you find him you'll know, but maybe he's not the one who's hiding.'

Since identifying the body of James, weeks ago in Jerusalem, Cassius Gallio has worn the disguise of a Swiss pharma rep, a religious tourist, an academic, and most recently in Caistor a normal human being muddling through while giving his time to the Church. None of these pretend people are him. If the quest were the other way round, and Jesus were to look for Cassius Gallio, he wouldn't know where to start.

'Maybe I should stay,' Bartholomew says. 'Point you in the right direction. I'd like to help you feel his love.'

Bartholomew's flight is called. Boarding. Claudia suddenly remembers he hasn't checked in but she rushes his e-ticket details to a self-service terminal. His destiny is not to stay in England, and when confronted by automated check-in Claudia is the answer to his prayers.

'Open yourself up to him,' Bartholomew says, as Gallio ushers him in the direction of the gate. 'He knows who you are.'

'Me? By name?'

Cassius Gallio stops on the concourse, and Bartholomew does too. A flight crew has to dodge to avoid them.

'You were there at the crucifixion. He never forgets a face.'

'You should go through,' Claudia says, but Cassius Gallio gives Bartholomew a last opportunity to tell the truth.

'Nobody comes back from the dead, my friend. That's common knowledge. Tell me what really happened.'

Bartholomew does not take this opportunity at Departures to change his mind. 'I'll pray for you,' he says, 'that you find what you're looking for.'

'You need to go through Security,' Claudia says. 'Go now.'

'Jesus did not come back from the dead,' Gallio says. 'I hope you can live with yourself.'

'Don't worry about that. Worry about the fire that's coming, when Jesus returns and has dominion over the earth.'

'But if he doesn't?'

'He is coming, along with the cleansing fire.'

'Go,' Claudia says. 'And good luck.'

He embraces them both, whether they like it or not, but Cassius Gallio has one final question. He whispers into Bartholomew's ear. 'Who is the disciple Jesus loved?'

But Bartholomew has already gone, showing his boarding card, joining the queue for the scanners, and he never answers the question. Gallio watches him through Security, though he can't think of anyone less likely to set off the alarms. Bartholomew has no hand luggage. He has no pockets.

Back at the White Hart Gallio and Claudia rut like animals. Cassius Gallio sometimes opens his eyes on her, or changes positions for the benefit of Jesus, should he condescend to be watching. See? See what you're making us do? If god exists we have no privacy. There is no time on our own, up to our secret devices.

Gallio finishes. He starts again. After the second bout he comes back from the bathroom and Claudia is on the phone. To Valeria, Gallio thinks. He doesn't know why he can tell, but he can.

'Who are you talking to?'

Claudia disconnects her call, checks the screen for Call Ended.

'I have a family. Any objections?'

Her cover, her legend. Every ambitious spy is married, and lonely, because the secret of the secret police is that they search for connections they never find. They face a lifetime of detection to discover that life has no detectable meaning.

Gallio speculates a scenario in which Valeria suggests to Claudia the idea that she should sleep with him. He takes Claudia's phone from the unused second bed and puts it screen-up on the windowsill. They rut like animals. Coming back from the bathroom, Gallio sees she's asleep. He checks her call log. Deleted.

When Claudia wakes beside him Gallio holds her, skin to skin, treasuring the touch of her while he can. He moves his lips close to the softness of her ear. 'We could move here,' he says, 'leave our problems behind.'

'Don't be ridiculous.'

She twists to look at the other bed, then at the windowsill.

'You don't need your phone.'

Gallio feels how much she longs to reach for it, to confirm her existence in the world outside this room at the White Hart free house in Lincolnshire. Through the wall, from Bartholomew's former room, they can hear chat TV, bursts of studio laughter. There's nothing to keep them in Caistor. Even their made-up reason has left.

'You could bring your girls over. We'll enrol them at the grammar school. They say it's one of the best in the country.'

'Want me to check its rating?'

'Leave the phone. I'm serious. We could build a new life here. Just the two of us, and your two girls.'

The dilemma of Jesus is a complex case best left to Valeria, while Claudia and Cassius Gallio stay out of harm's way, cultivating a mild version of heaven in provincial England. They don't need much: a service pension and retirement villa, occasional sunny spells as they love each other to death in a territory that's safe and sound. Caistor will be eternal life, or feel like it.

Claudia's phone vibrates on the windowsill. They look at the white light from the lit-up screen, doubled in reflection on the window. The phone stops vibrating—voicemail, or the caller hung up.

'I'm sorry,' Gallio says. He touches her stomach, her hip, pulls her into him. 'We shouldn't have done this.'

Easy to say. Most words are easy to say. He doesn't know what he's saying.

The phone vibrates again, moving across the gloss paint of the sill with each new shudder. It stops. It starts again, and unless the caller gives up soon the phone will reach the edge and fall. Claudia gives Gallio his hands back and gets out of bed. She answers the phone, turns away until the far side of her face and her underarm reflect in the black of the window. She snibs her hair behind her ear. Her buttocks contract.

'Totally,' she says.

She disconnects, tosses the phone on the bed, looks for a towel. Can't find one, pulls on her pants instead. Then jeans from her suitcase. She clicks on the bedside lamp, and Gallio shields his eyes.

'Bartholomew is dead.'
'That can't be true.'
'In Bashkale, not long after his plane landed.'
'Jesus.'
'He was skinned alive.'

IX

Andrew

"X CRUCIFIXION"

Cassius Gallio sits naked, head in hands, in the upstairs room of a pub in an English market town. The stress of chasing after Jesus has cut lines through his cheeks. He has grey in his days-old stubble, like cobwebs in foliage, and a diagonal pillow scar above the wound near his eyebrow. Knife-fighting in his sleep. He scratches his chin. Apart from the blue eyes he could pass, from a distance, as an apprentice disciple of Jesus.

Claudia is filling her suitcase. Like disciples, spies have limited belongings, and Gallio watches Claudia roll her anonymous tops, bag her sensible shoes.

'Stay in Caistor with me,' he says. 'Live happily ever after.'

'Bartholomew is dead. Skinned alive.'

'That's in the past already. It'll be forgotten today or tomorrow, what difference does it make? Doesn't change anything, and the world keeps turning.'

Claudia looks frightened, and older. Married. 'We've been ordered to report to Valeria, in Rome. The case has moved forward. She increased the security code to Severe, as a response to Bartholomew's killing. Code Red, unlimited budget.'

Skinned alive. Sawn in half, bludgeoned to death, hung upside down, stoned, shot by arrows, beheaded, hanged and now this. How random was a skinning, an eighth violent murder of a disciple? Each was more dead than the last, like a demonstration that no loving god could protect them.

Gallio imagines the inner Bartholomew, and without his skin his delicate body is tubes and fibres and feathered blood vessels that branch and branch again into nothing. His anatomy is full of gaps, with empty space between vein and muscle, between muscle and bone. His vital organs are barely acquainted.

'We should have kept him with us,' Claudia says. 'At the end he almost stayed.'

'Why does Valeria want us in Rome? What about Cairo?'

'She said Rome. Those are her orders.'

Rome, after all this time. When they were cleaning Simon's body out of the garage Gallio had thought it was over. He had failed, again, and Baruch was a sad dead example to anyone sincerely attempting to understand Jesus. For a short while Gallio had preferred the delusion of life in Caistor, where the planet could tilt and the raffle would still be called. The absence of significance in provincial England had seduced him.

'She suspects the disciples Peter and John of being in Rome,'

Claudia says. 'Trying to trace both of them, so far unsuccess-
fully. This isn't finished.'

Gallio puts his hand on her shoulder. She zips her suitcase.
He wants to slow her down, to establish that the value of now is
equal to then and next. Caistor, in the present, can compete with
the lure of future glory or the flight from past mistakes—even
with Rome. Claudia should give him a sign that she takes this
present moment seriously, as he does.

'Stop, Claudia. Stand up and look at me.'

He wraps her in his arms and holds her, her eyelashes on
his neck, blinking, brushing his skin, so her eyes must be open.
She's waiting this out, arms at her sides. Her elbow moves and
Gallio suspects, behind his back, that Claudia is checking her
watch. Time to let her go. He lets go. She picks up her book from
the bedside table, gathers brushes and pots from the bathroom.
Gallio follows her like a lost dog.

'You don't have to jump as soon as Valeria whistles. She's
chasing shadows.'

'I have to follow orders. We both do. That's how the CCU
works.'

'We could just not go. Exercise our free will.'

'You mean disobey a clear instruction. We've pushed her as
far as I dare. Stay and that's desertion, for which the penalty is
death, but it's up to you.'

'We're in the back of beyond. What's she going to do? Simon
is dead, forgotten, and nothing else of importance will happen
here. I feel the safety of this place in my bones.'

'What about Bartholomew? In the wider world disciples are
being slaughtered and civilization is threatened. This isn't all
about us.'

Claudia turns side-on to move past him without touching,

checks one last time she's left nothing behind, looks under the bed and reaches for a pair of knickers. She stuffs them into the pocket of her case. She's ready.

'The summons to Rome feels like a set-up,' Gallio says.

'You're not dressed.'

'No, listen. Valeria suspects Jesus of starting the fire in Rome. Now maybe of planning something worse, but the CCU is neurotic about terror threats, always has been. I'm not above suspicion, all things considered, not when contact with terrorists is a convictable offence. I've had contact with Jesus followers, right back to the beginning in Jerusalem. I've been actively searching Jesus out, which looks bad. I sent drugs to Jude's hospital. Should have told you that. Then we let Bartholomew wander off unattended.'

'The CCU brought you back from Germany to do a job. Valeria wouldn't abandon you now.'

'I'm not convinced she's that interested in Jesus. Sooner or later she's going to take her revenge.'

'You exaggerate. Why would she want revenge?'

'History. Something that happened between us. Please, Claudia, sit down and think it over. At least try to imagine living happily ever after in Caistor.'

Gallio tries to hold her again, but she's always moving and is made of elbows.

'It's not that simple,' Claudia says. 'She knows my house, my family. You have no idea what she's like. Now put some clothes on. Valeria wants us in Rome and we've stalled here as long as we can. She isn't joking about sending someone to fetch us. We don't want that, believe me.'

'Valeria can make mistakes. She doesn't believe Rome can ever be outwitted, or go backward. She thinks all she needs is a reasonable plan of action and with logic and strategy she'll control the future.'

'Why is that so wrong? Reason will prevail. Don't waver, Cassius.'

'The future is under control only as far ahead as she can see. Which isn't very far, in the scheme of things.'

Cassius Gallio trusts in his previous experience of Jesus, which makes him question every change of direction. He remembers the feeling of helplessness that overwhelmed him in Jerusalem, in the week of Passover, all those years ago. Jesus had plans of his own for Cassius Gallio. Gallio had made everything happen—the arrest, the trial, the sentencing. But everything he made happen corresponded to preparations Jesus and his disciples had made in advance. Now Gallio has a similar anxiety about Rome, a doubt like a shadow in his mind since Antioch. He and Baruch had travelled to Antioch to question Paul, on a convenient detour while Thomas was stoned and speared in Babylon. They had been maneuvered, and should have learned a lesson. Again.

Gallio reaches out for Claudia but she's at the doorway, suitcase in hand.

'Not now, Cassius. Come on, we have a plane to catch.'

'Bartholomew's death isn't our fault, and like Simon he may have wanted to die. Baruch said Simon wanted to die. We don't know. There's another disciple in Scotland, Andrew. That's not far from here. We could take the sleeper train, finish what we started, save the CCU some money.'

'Where we go and what we do is not your call to make.'

'I don't trust Jesus. He's playing us.'

At last, the angle of Claudia's head suggests she feels for Gallio, maybe pity, but better than no emotion at all. 'Are you staying,' she says, 'or coming with me? Make up your mind.'

Cassius Gallio needs more time to speculate. He is convinced that he's of no use to Jesus's master plan, whatever it is, in Caistor. He therefore wins a victory by staying in England. Rome, on the other hand, is not Gallio's choice, and to change the world in Rome Jesus will be needing all the help he can get. Gallio will not be duped into helping, not again.

'You do what you feel is right,' Claudia says, 'but I won't go down in flames because you want to waste your life in Caistor. Phone Valeria. She'll tell you straight: Rome. That's why they issue us phones.'

'To keep us in line.'

'I can't cover for you. What should I tell her?'

Claudia genuinely intends to leave. Gallio rushes on his trousers, a T-shirt, follows her down the stairs and into the public bar, which barely makes sense in the predawn light, out of its usual time. Beer mats and carpets and chairs upturned on tables, waiting to come to life.

'Claudia.'

She's outside. Gallio pleads on the pavement in his bare feet, slaps his arms for warmth. 'We don't have the complete picture,' he says, and the words leave his mouth as steam. 'Tell Valeria I'm on my way, but I'm researching the bigger picture.'

A minicab pulls up, and while the engine runs Claudia holds out her hand. After everything they've done she wants to shake on the end of the deal. It is finished. He refuses, and she says fuck off then and climbs into the back of the cab, pulling in her case behind her. In his bare feet, cold, alone, Gallio holds up a flat Roman palm to say goodbye, watches the car cross the square and away past the Georgian house. The truth is he has no concept of the bigger picture. It feels too big. He should have settled for the smaller picture, himself in the back of a minicab with Claudia. Wearing his shoes.

Upstairs at the White Hart he packs his small bag, waits for daylight, decides against a final English breakfast. He walks down the hill to the Heritage Centre, where he sits on a wall until it opens. Not much to see, a dog, some vans, litter in the wind. He bangs the heels of his shoes against the bricks. Caistor is a perfect place to lose himself, he is sure of this, and to be lost to Jesus. He'll click onto a property site and find himself a one-bedroom flat. Job first, then flat. With his experience he should be able to pick up something in security, at the industrial estate or a superstore on a bus route.

And from then on working and sleeping and hiding away in provincial England will eat up his time. He cannot look, not love, not live, be as good as he likes. Rome burned once without him and Rome can burn again, will always have burned whether he's in the city or not.

Finally the Heritage Centre opens its doors. At a computer screen he logs in and for the last time, out of habit, he uses his Speculator ID to access the restricted Missing Persons pages. He clicks through to the locator map, and at first he thinks there's a glitch, or that he opened the wrong program. Eight of the disciples are dead, he knows this for a fact. Gallio had expected a maximum of four lights for the surviving disciples—Andrew, Matthew and, in or near Rome, John and Peter. But the map is signalling multiple sightings, many more lights than twelve, double that number in locations all across the screen. A light comes on at Ephesus in Turkey even as Gallio watches. The disciples seem to have divided, and divided again, and from limited beginnings can now be everywhere at once.

The nearest sighting to Caistor is a light on the southeast coast of Scotland. The drop-down box, unconfirmed, names the disciple as Andrew, last seen in a town called Whitehorn. Gallio magnifies Scotland's North Sea Coast, activating a refinement that plots Andrew's movements from the page history. In the last few days Andrew has been moving steadily southward. Gallio sits back and considers the light, thinks about Andrew coming closer. He's heading in the general direction of Caistor.

Cassius Gallio blinks twice and the third time he keeps his eyes clenched shut, mouth stretched tight, showcasing the wreck of his face. He grimaces and dips his chin into his collarbone. He can resist them. He can run away from Jesus, like in the old days in Germany.

The light representing Andrew moves a measure south, reaching the border with England. Gallio wants this over. He rocks forward and links through to the travel websites accessed by Claudia the day before. The northern Peloponnese, to the west of Athens. Not the most popular of Greek holiday destinations, but a world away from Lincolnshire and from Andrew, and in Patras Jesus has no obvious use for him. Cassius Gallio puts the holiday package on his credit card, taxes included, flying from Humberside Airport later that day.

Patras is a medium to large southern European city, rich with history but made present by urban planning and prestressed concrete. The season is Carnival. Through the window of the airport shuttle bus, on a city-centre route to his designated hotel, Cassius Gallio sees Argonauts blowing saxophones and Socrates on a Jamaican steel drum. Nothing is sacred, everything is allowed, and in Patras at this time of year at this time of night Bacchus the god of revels is god.

His bus brakes at traffic lights and Gallio reads a wall of flyposts for the Black Pussy club, first sixty-nine ladies in for free.

He doubts Jesus would linger here, but if Jesus is watching, if he's interested, he'll see that Cassius Gallio has disengaged. He has given up looking for good.

Gallio makes an arbitrary decision to get off the bus at a stop near the Roman Odeon. The heat of the Greek night rises from the pedestrian asphalt, a welcome change of temperature from Caistor, and in among the sailors and angels, hearing the timeless music, Gallio enjoys being no one. He does not represent Complex Casework. He attempts none of the difficult answers.

He retreats, blots himself into the corner of a streetside bar. In the warmth and the flamelight, Cassius Gallio convinces himself that the disciples are of as little concern to him as they are to the revellers of Patras. Also he is indifferent to Claudia, reunited in Rome with her family. The point is, he reminds himself, nothing matters. There is no god, no love, no plan. He raises his arm to the waiter for another drink. One more, and then he'll justify Patras to Valeria. He turns on his phone, off since the plane, to show his positive intent.

For this second failure of his they'll probably skip the tribunal. Gallio has bungled his search for Jesus as completely as he did the crucifixion. He overcomplicates, he thinks, or complications happen around him. Should have killed Lazarus while he had the chance. Should have closed Jesus down in Jerusalem before he went to trial.

He drinks half his Mythos beer then texts Valeria his resignation. *Hereby,* he texts—not a word recognized by autocorrect— *Hereby I end my connection with the Jesus case.* He could thank Valeria for giving him a second opportunity to fail, but settles for *Best wishes* and a reminder of his full family name, *Cassius Marcellus Gallio.* Repeat any name often enough and it sounds absurd.

He sips his beer, adds an X, and sends the text. Then he

sends another with a single word: *Sorry*. He sits and drinks and waits for a reply that doesn't come. The penalty for desertion is death. He does not want to die.

He sits and drinks, but alcohol hadn't helped in Moldova. He sits. He sends back a double ouzo from a man alone at the bar. He doesn't want to care and he doesn't want to die. Or to kill. For his sanity as well as his safety he needs to engineer a disappearance. In training a Speculator learns procedures for most patterns of behaviour, including the urge to vanish off the face of the earth, and it occurs to Gallio that Jesus and CCU Speculators have similar skills. Though Gallio can think of more discreet ways to disappear than starting with a faked crucifixion. Show-off.

Gallio will wipe himself out. Caistor wasn't disappearance enough, and drinking himself into oblivion in Greece is too predictable a refuge. Valeria would find him in no time, visibly helpless in the gutter.

He pays up and hails a cab. At the hotel Gallio signs the register, agreeing to the many unread terms and conditions applicable to a seven-day package at the Patras Porto Rio. This is the first step in his textbook disappearance. There will be a final sighting, so he might as well make his last known movements more enjoyable than dying on a cross. He sleeps soundly between the fresh sheets of a hotel bed.

In the morning Cassius Gallio fills up on buffet breakfast at a table within range of the restaurant's single security camera. One more slice of cheese before dropping his napkin on the table and pushing out his chair. The trail has to end somewhere, and the procedure requires Gallio to be traceable on the grid. He knows what he's doing. He walks to the cashpoint machine in the hotel lobby and withdraws 3,900 euros, the limit. There is an extortionate charge, which in the circumstances doesn't bother him.

So far he has risked nothing. The credit card transaction for the holiday package already links him to the charter flight and the Patras hotel. He might as well withdraw the money while he's here. In his room he packs his bag with essentials, toothbrush and underwear and a hat, and his last recorded act in the hotel is to pay cash in the gift shop for another hat, a conspicuous straw panama. The sun is already high and hot so he puts the panama hat on his head and leaves the hotel on foot, steps serenely into an unexceptional city that most people have never heard of.

One more thing: ten minutes later, in a local bar without CCTV, he downs an espresso and crumples his hat into a sanitary bin in the toilets. Wearing a plain black baseball cap, he leaves the bar. He disappears.

Gallio ought to feel safe, lost, confident of an invisible journey from the Patras ferry terminal to Corfu and from there to any of a hundred Greek islands. Instead, in a city he doesn't know and where nobody knows him, he is convinced he's being watched. He can't explain it. He has followed the approved procedure but in his inner ear, and in his heart, he senses that he's not alone.

Stay undercover. He doesn't know how, but it must be either the disciples or Valeria, and instinctively Gallio feels the surveillance is coming from above. The CCU have satellite, so Gallio ducks under the parasols of pavement cafés, excusing himself between the tables. As the streets fill with people he slips into a one-room bookshop, and browses a Lonely Planet while checking the street for anyone walking too slowly or too fast, but Carnival cancels out normal. A teenage girl dressed as a Pierrot does nothing much but smoke a pipe. A giant head bobs past, an Uncle Sam in papier mâché. Men are women and the last are first. Half the people in the street are wearing masks, others walk with heads down, hands in pockets, kicking the overnight cartons.

Cassius Gallio works his way toward the centre of Patras, wary of mime artists and the occasional surge of revellers. He passes the Catholic Church of St. Andreas, and shelters for a moment in the shaded courtyard of the Protestant Church of St. Andrew, where a curate is brushing the flagstones. He detours along Andrew's Avenue and ignores the woman in the St. Andrew's Juice Van who shouts at him to cheer up, it might never happen. He hurries past the general hospital, the Patras Agios Andreas, and for a sick moment thinks a nurse is following him. In his paranoia the world is suddenly all about Cassius Gallio, and if only they weren't watching him so closely he could settle on a plan, shape the immediate future.

A tracer. He stands still. Of course, what a fool he is, that's how they're keeping track of him. Gallio remembered Valeria snapping at him for not planting a tracer on Baruch while he had the chance—as a precautionary measure that would have warned them he was leaving for England. For Valeria, tracers were standard CCU procedure, and in Caistor Claudia had had all the time in the world to fix up Gallio. The shared room, the sex: he was not being vigilant. Gallio pats his clothes. No, she was a Speculator, and the tracer would be expertly hidden.

Gallio is not breathing well. He's panting like a dog, sweating. The hard drive in the computer at the Heritage Centre, credit card records, the hotel register in Patras. He'd been so pleased with his procedures, but if CCU were tracking him then Valeria would find him regardless. She sees everything and knows everything. He needs a concealed place where he can locate and destroy the tracer.

The facade of the Greek Orthodox Agios Andreas church looks like a train station. Inside, every wall and archway glitters with mosaic, and Gallio's footsteps on the marble floor echo back from the central dome, decorated with Jesus in the centre surrounded 360 degrees by his disciples. The twelve of them twinkle brightly down on him, watch as he searches for a confessional box, any place of privacy.

But today Cassius Gallio is out of luck. The ornate interior of the huge church is mostly open space. Gallio negotiates thousands of seats set out for a church performance that coincides with Carnival, not just this year but every year. At the end of one of the rows a nun is kneeling at prayer, black headscarf wrapped squarely across her forehead. No confessionals. There's a screen at the front of the church and Cassius Gallio acts as if he belongs, steps behind it into the space reserved for priests and for god. He's in a hurry. In the private half darkness he puts his bag on the ground and kneels to rummage through the contents. So many mistakes. He spreads out a T-shirt and pats it down, feeling for a foreign object the size of a watch battery. He squeezes toothpaste out of the tube, and breaks soap onto his T-shirt. No sign of a tracer.

He takes off his clothes, all of them, fingers the seams of his trousers and the collar of his shirt. Naked, he checks the waistbands of his underpants.

His phone rings.

Shit. In church the ringtone sounds out like a blasphemy. *Unknown number*, which he rejects. The phone, of course. He dresses clumsily, but fast. Claudia couldn't leave phones alone, whereas Gallio is from an older generation and leaves his unattended. Now he feels old as well as foolish but the tracer is inside the phone, it has to be. He goes down on one knee, takes aim and

slides the phone across the marble floor and under the altar. Bullseye. Then his ID, spins his ID under there too. He becomes no
one, absent without leave. He disconnects himself, because nothing matters. There is no god, and no CCU, and Cassius Gallio is
disinclined to look for Jesus.

He tucks in his shirt, inhales deeply, picks up his bag and
emerges from behind the Orthodox screen a free man. He bumps
into Jesus. In front of the holy screen of the Agios Andreas, in
the city of Patras in the Greek Peloponnese, Jesus appears exclu-
sively to Cassius Germanicus Gallio.

'Surprise,' Jesus says. He holds out his hands.

Gallio drops his bag, clutches his heart.

'Sister Hilda told me which way you went.'

It is Andrew. Gallio peers at the face and Andrew is a wiry,
toughened version of Jesus, up close not as young as he used to
be. His gaunt face has dried out with the years. He is pale, papery, illuminated.

'You can relax,' Andrew says. He has the eyes, the beard, the
sandals. 'I found you.'

Gallio does not relax. He looks beyond Andrew into the
body of the church, the thousand waiting seats. Left, right, up to
the dome, down to the floor. Where else is there?

'Calm down,' Andrew says. 'You're like a man possessed.'

He lays his hands on Gallio's shoulders, leans heavily on
him as once Cassius Gallio had weighed himself down on Judas.
'Trust me. I'm here for you. I can drive out your demon.'

'What do you want from me?'

'Jude told me you were looking for Jesus. I can help.'

Very kind, Gallio thinks, but not now. From the beginning,
way back in Jerusalem, the disciples had led him on, luring him
into traps he mistook for his own intentions. He's had enough

of their prayers, their blessings. Andrew makes the sign of the cross.

'How did you know I was here?'

'Jesus has a special place in his heart for you. For all of us.'

'It was a tracking device, wasn't it?'

Gallio had instantly blamed Claudia, but it could just as easily have been Bartholomew. In between the bandaging and the handouts, with Gallio distracted by social inequality, Bartholomew could have accessed his phone and planted the bug. 'The tracking device was yours. I should have guessed. I am god's biggest idiot.'

'You're in a basilica, Cassius, in a cloudless country open to the eye of god. How did you expect to hide from Jesus in a big open church? He can see you everywhere, that's true, but in here you come to us.'

Andrew's implacability is exhausting. He must have tracked Gallio first to Caistor, asked questions, sorted through Search History on the computers in the Heritage Centre, then out to Patras on the next chartered flight. Gallio sits down on a front row seat, defeated. Andrew sits next to him. On the screen of the sanctuary they admire the visual focus for every eye turned toward god in the Agios Andreas, which is an oversized icon of Andrew the disciple of Jesus in cobalt and gold. Andrew is roped to an X-shaped cross, a shimmering image on which to meditate a spiritual truth, and Andrew's iconic expression is inscrutable, as he gazes directly back at Gallio.

'Jesus remembers you from Jerusalem,' Andrew says. 'And from that fantastic day with Lazarus. You've seen and shared so much with us. You could tell people what you know, what you've witnessed with your own eyes. You'd be welcome to join us.'

Cassius Gallio could give himself up, especially his ambition and pride. He could discard his former self, and this knowledge shines like light—to become a believer he need only be weak. That's why Jesus has so many followers. But surrender feels like possession, like being inhabited by a person who isn't him. The meek shall not inherit the earth, not while Valeria is regional director of the CCU, and anyway Gallio isn't confident of what he's witnessed or how much he knows. He doesn't have the facts.

'Approach Jesus with humility,' Andrew says. 'Not as a Speculator, hunting him down, but opening yourself up to him.'

'Speculators have open minds. That's one of the requirements, written into the job description.'

'Not your mind, your heart. That's how we the disciples came to Jesus. We felt something was wrong, and we believed Jesus could put the wrongness right. After you find him with an open heart the rest is easy. Then he's always there.'

A ray of sunshine beams through a window high in the dome, whitens a rectangle of marbled floor. 'Think how much you have to give.'

'Nothing,' Gallio says. 'I've resigned from the case, and I'm looking for no one. You should leave me in peace.'

Cassius Gallio rejects Andrew's idea of Jesus and tears brim in his eyes. He hates that. He has several thousand euros in his pocket, and he's in a Greek ferry port where he can buy travel tickets without question for cash. He should be looking forward to a quiet and comfortable retirement, but the disciples of Jesus want more than his ruined career. Not once, but now twice. Still they refuse to let him be.

'Are you scared of dying?' Andrew asks.

'Yes, like everyone else. Aren't you?'

'No. That's the difference between us.'

Gallio believes him. Andrew projects the same certainty

253

Gallio had envied in Jude and Bartholomew—Jesus died and came back to life, which to a sincere believer constitutes proof that something or somewhere exists on the far side of death. Andrew can die horribly, and at the same time he can succeed. This is the story retold in mosaic on the walls of the basilica, and Gallio remembers the ruined martyrium where Philip hung from his thighs. It was a beautiful spot, high above the blue pools of Pamukkale, impeccably picturesque. The story had been plotted in advance, because Jesus is always a step ahead.

'Persecutions have started in Rome,' Andrew says. 'They're blaming Peter for starting the fire.'

'I didn't know, I threw away my phone.'

'You need to be careful. Nice beard, but you're beginning to look like one of us.'

In the Agios Andreas Gallio's eyes sweep across images and icons but he blocks them into manageable shapes. Andrew is talking but Gallio isn't listening. His heart is calloused, and Andrew says the dead in Jesus are not dead, Gallio hearing the words but not understanding. He refuses to be tempted into weakness. He'd rather kill himself, confronting death with courage, knowing that death is the end. Cassius Gallio sees no virtue in dying for the selfish reward of a perfect life in heaven.

When he finds his voice he is cruel. 'Your brother Peter shouldn't have gone to Rome, which isn't the wisest place to be, for a disciple of Jesus. He makes himself easy to blame.'

Gallio's statement becomes a question, a default process for a Speculator. 'CCU know Peter is in the city. Is he coordinating some kind of attack?'

'We have high hopes for Rome,' Andrew says, 'if everything goes to plan. Is Peter imprisoned in the Mamertine dungeon? Or not yet? He's going to be a great comfort to the other prisoners, even though the jailers will make him suffer. My own fate is kinder. I'm a lesser man than my brother, the least of the disciples, but I expect to arrive earlier into the kingdom.'

'You mean you're going to die?'

'Thanks to you, Cassius Gallio, yes. I'm grateful to you for bringing me to Patras.'

Cassius Gallio adapts his strategy, takes control of his destiny. He refuses to make himself vulnerable on a boat, where they could trap him with no place to run. Either the disciples or the CCU, whoever catches up with him first. Out in the country he'd be equally exposed, so he needs to stay hidden in the city.

He decides that paranoia is preferable to being burst asunder or skinned alive. Everyone wants their share of him, and in the centre of Patras Gallio searches out unforgiving faces, hard-skinned palms that can handle ropes and stones. He catches a drunken Greek god looking his way, and is spooked when a boy bangs a drum. He does not want to die.

'You'll be back,' Andrew had said, calling out to him over the rows of seats, walking fast to keep up as Gallio headed for the door. But Andrew was wrong. Gallio wasn't going to join them, not now. He'd slept with Claudia in Caistor, to make Jesus pay attention. Look Jesus, with a married woman I don't love. A married woman with two baby girls, and I don't love any of them. No response. Andrew wouldn't let him go, followed him through the doors and out of the basilica into the sunlight. Gallio stumbled through solid heat, collided with a topless man in britches and a wolf-mask. He spun, lost his balance, righted himself. He ran, pursued by the howls of the wolfman.

In the streets of Patras Andrew had been busy, presumably

on his way to the basilica. He'd made an exhibition of himself, preaching against the sins of Carnival and taking public exception to the Bourbilia, a popular rite where women danced lasciviously for men. Andrew had dared question the supremacy of Bacchus, he'd criticized the local football team and the morals of the mayor's son. Since the last time Gallio walked these streets, Andrew had been asking for trouble, and as an endangered disciple he ought to shut his mouth. He has offended everyone, making all of Patras a potential assassin.

Cassius Gallio needs cover, and the Botanical Gardens contain copses of mature broadleaf trees. He weaves through the tree trunks, finding the centre where up above a canopy of leaves greenly deflects the sunlight. Mustn't be visible from the air. A noise slides from his mouth, a whine of animal fear, and Gallio lies down and covers himself in leaf mold and litter. He crawls into the soil, hiding from the eye of god. He plants himself, and is still.

He'll wait this out. With one eye open he spies on joggers running off the edge of the path to save their knees. He spies on mothers with pushchairs. Cassius Gallio is buried alive, and he pisses where he lies. A madman, a timeless vagrant without papers, he shall ripen in the warm until he rots.

His visible world is cigarette butts, a used plastic water bottle and a pair of torn Patras cinema tickets. However hard he tries, he finds it impossible to do nothing. He dehydrates, and as his brain dries out he hears voices, ghost versions of Jesus. James and Bartholomew, Jude and Thomas, Philip and James and Simon. They say: 'I am the least of all the disciples.'

Time passes. Cassius Gallio doesn't know how long. He may have slept but however many centuries he missed, when he wakes the problem of Jesus remains unsolved. He blinks. He raises his face from the forest floor, and bark flakes from his cheek. He spits a seed off his tongue.

A revelation is making itself known. One of the voices has something to say, and Gallio tries to isolate what is important from what is not. Eight disciples dead, he thinks, but their message continues to spread. Gallio bites the inside of his cheek, tastes blood and soil. Whoever is responsible for killing the disciples, for whatever reason, is not fully informed. Killing them is counterproductive, because every martyrdom is a fresh story that nourishes the original lie: life after death. He remembers the icon of Andrew in the basilica, and realizes the disciples continue their work when they're gone.

He pushes himself up onto his elbows. He's a Speculator, and should question everything. That's why Valeria hired him, and at last Gallio sees a truth emerging: they have had everything the wrong way round. In Caistor Simon could have escaped from Baruch, if an escape had suited Jesus. James in Jerusalem had jumped from the roof, with no more encouragement than a silent phone call. Jude could have arranged professional security in Beirut, and Thomas had chosen to live in Babylon, a city of famous jeopardy.

Now Andrew has followed Gallio to Patras, where every year on this day the Carnival celebrates the death of Andrew the disciple of Jesus. The disciples want to die, which means this story is not like other stories. Gallio sits up, brushes leaf scraps from his hair and shoulders. Lazarus went first, then Jesus at the crucifixion, until these subsequent killings look like entries in a competition: Which disciple of Jesus can die most horrifically, to prove he has no fear? The assassins, whoever they are, say yes you may want to die but not like this, surely, you must surely be frightened by this? Or this, Bartholomew, no one chooses to be skinned alive.

Finally, Cassius Gallio begins to understand. The disciples don't feel pain, not like he feels pain, because their eyes have seen the glory of the coming of the lord. They believe in a better place, so why linger here? Beheaded, shot with arrows, stoned, speared, hung upside down clubbed, sawn in half, skinned alive—to the disciples death is a happy ending. Heaven is real, and they love their enemies who send them there.

Jesus is a ruthless opponent and he calls death, time and again, down upon the disciples he claimed to love. His will is done. Jesus coordinates every move his disciples make, as one after the other they die hideously and happily.

Cassius Gallio rises up from the forest, the truth revealed to him. Jesus *wants* his disciples to die, and knowing their secret Gallio has to act, as Baruch did, with Simon. Except Baruch took the wrong type of action. The answer is not to make the disciples suffer, hoping to taunt Jesus into an appearance, but to refuse the idea of a Jesus in control of whatever happens next. Andrew will not die in Patras. The future is not shaped in advance, but can be changed by willed human action. This is a core principle of civilization, as Gallio has been taught to defend it.

By the time Gallio reaches the Agios Andreas the basilica is filled to capacity, with three thousand worshippers in the tight rows of chairs. They have come to see Andrew die, as they do every year. The wolfmen and the drunken police and the Greek gods of Patras lash Andrew to an X-shaped cross, the flesh of his wrists and ankles swelling round the liturgical belts that bind him. The heavy rhythmic chanting of Andrew's killers is part of the Carnival entertainment, and will remain so for years to come, the old familiar song as Andrew the disciple of Jesus is lifted up. The spectators join in. They clap their hands to the rhythm of the singing as his cross rises high on wires, up and above the holy screen, halfway to the dome and heaven.

Every death is planned, and Andrew the disciple of Jesus is ecstatic, triumphantly not dying of old age or exhaustion. He has avoided those desperate fates, and is intent on joining the eight who have gone before. The bindings cut into his wrists, into his ankles on the X of the cross, and Andrew is the ninth atrocity.

Gallio struggles through the standing-room-only at the back, bursts into the central aisle but for Andrew he's already too late. Civilization will not save Andrew now, because what's done is done, from Andrew's collapsing lungs to the blood in lines between his teeth. Gallio knows about the blood, and the bloodstained teeth, because when Andrew catches sight of him he smiles.

X

Matthew

"BURNED ALIVE"

Jesus is the connection. Nine times Jesus, but Cassius Gallio does not accept defeat. He knows the secret of the disciples, their love of death and dying, and two of the three survivors have been sighted alive in Rome. Gallio will save them. Whatever Peter and John have planned, they will not die on Gallio's watch. Jesus and the disciples have manipulated death to their advantage for long enough.

On his covert journey from Patras to Rome, in the seafront chapels and quayside shrines of southern Europe, Gallio sees memorials to the crucifixion of Jesus. Every crucifix reminds him that the disciples are capable and cunning. Peter survived Baruch in Jerusalem, even though he was captured. He has avoided every assassin as far as Rome, the heart of civilization.

Which is why, some time after the death of Andrew in Patras, Cassius Gallio finds himself sitting in a Roman bus shelter. He stares at primary colours advertising hair products and free-delivery bathroom suites. Also and always posters for the Circus, here and at every Roman kiosk: the latest films, plays, albums, the next Circus in line. This coming Saturday, in the first major performance since the fire of Rome, the Circus posters promise wild dogs, chariot-racing, and the public execution of Peter the disciple of Jesus.

Gallio groans. Valeria has no idea what she's doing. The death of Peter is exactly what Jesus wants, and Gallio is determined to stop it happening. He hasn't shaved since Caistor, barely washed since his meltdown in the Botanical Gardens in Patras. From Patras to Brindisi, to Venice, to Rome. He loses track of time. Andrew died weeks ago, or it could have been longer, and since then Gallio has been jumping ship, travelling in the cash economy, a deserter without papers in ragged clothes with unkempt hair and the look of a criminal Jesus.

Strangers help him along the way, and yet he distrusts them. People are kind, offering food and shelter, which makes Gallio suspect the Jesus network of encouraging him, urging him toward Rome for purposes not his own. Know your enemy, he thinks, and he learns the sign of the fish, an increasingly familiar shape on his undercover journey from Greece. Two lines curve from a point and intersect to make the tail, a simple but recognizable symbol of the fish for fishermen, for the disciples.

With the aid of fellow travellers, many of them believers in Jesus, Gallio arrives in the eternal city. He has formulated a plan of action that starts with Paul, who is under house arrest in a district called the Fourth Regidor. However, Gallio's most direct route from the port is blocked by police on the Fabricius bridge. The officers are stopping and searching, security level Code Red: Severe. Gallio turns back, looks for a safer route, tags onto pedestrian tours and pretends to take an interest in SPQR bracelets and letters whittled from Lazio wood. Pick out R O M A and take the letters home. Pick out the name of your favourite saint while keeping an eye on the patrols on the Via Palermo and the Viminal Hill.

Every main thoroughfare is blocked, until Gallio ends up in the bus shelter. He wants a meeting with Paul, but forces beyond his control don't want him getting through. Interesting, but as a deserter he can't risk the backstreets and a patrol picking him up. Lost for ideas, he makes the sign of the fish with his finger on the dusty Perspex of the bus shelter. A middle-aged woman with plastic shopping bags asks him if she can help, and Gallio is no longer surprised by the reach of their network.

'I was hoping to see Paul,' he says, 'in the Fourth Regidor. Jesus would rather I didn't.'

'Nonsense,' she says, 'your information is out of date, that's all. Paul moves about freely and was last seen outside the city at the Abbey of the Three Fountains. You can take a bus.'

It could be a trap. On the other hand not even Jesus could brief all his followers, every single one, on the off-chance they'd meet Cassius Gallio at a Roman bus stop. Gallio is using them; they're not using him.

He crosses the road and waits for a bus heading in the opposite direction, away from the heightened security in the city centre. For a long time there's no sign of a bus, just carts full of sand and building materials. Rome is a permanent work-in-progress, chisels on marble, shouting, the bang of hammers getting things done. Gallio sees free-standing columns where life thrived before the fire, he sees roofless temples and doubts if the city will ever be fully restored.

He doesn't believe that Peter and John are responsible for the ruins, not all of them, yet Peter is the entertainment at this Saturday's Circus. *Saturday 2–5*, says the poster in this and every bus stop, *The Greatest Show on Earth*. It looks like exactly the kind of extreme result a disciple would welcome.

At last, after about a million years, a bus arrives. The driver knows the abbey, and tells Gallio to watch out for the Three Fountains bus stop, near the Siemens Italy offices, can't miss it. The driver is right, and the Siemens headquarters is at a busy out-of-town junction beside a flyover. Gallio walks down the hill, cuts across a park, and picks up signs to the abbey.

From the entrance, when he arrives, Gallio can see a long garden bisected by a tree-lined path leading to the abbey itself, which from a distance looks like many of the old church buildings in Rome. A baby cries, his mother one of a handful of believers compelled to see the site where an apostle died. Mum and pushchair are leaving, and at this time of day the café at the lodge is closed.

Just before the main abbey building, next to a bubbling water source set into the green bricks of a wall, a man and two women are standing in close conversation. Fieldcraft, Gallio thinks, they're using the running water to counteract listening devices, but fortunately he knows how to join them. He stands nearby and with the toe of his shoe he makes the shape of the fish in the gravel at his feet. They recognize the sign, and welcome him in as a fellow believer.

Yes, they say, Paul is known in this place but he hasn't been here recently. They're more interested in Peter in the Mamertine Prison—he's in the underground dungeon, and they were just saying that apparently he baptizes fellow prisoners with the damp from the fetid walls.

'Amazing. As if the water presented itself there for just that purpose.'

'Only three left,' Gallio reminds them, before they get carried away. 'It's too late for Peter but thank god for John, and for Matthew. At least in Cairo he's safe. Have you heard from John? He ought to get out while he can.'

They correct him: sorry, but Matthew is dead. Assassins tracked him to a two-room house in the Entoto suburb of Addis Ababa. They broke down the door. In his study they found a simple chair and table and a roll of blank papyrus imported from Egypt.

'He died horribly.'

The assassins chopped off Matthew's hands, and in the yard of the house they wrapped him in his papyrus then soaked the paper in dolphin oil. They poured brimstone over his head, and asphalt, and pitch, then piled up tow and scrubwood beneath him. They invited local dignitaries to come along and watch what happened next. Bring your friends, bring golden images of your gods. See if Matthew the disciple of Jesus will burn.

When everyone was assembled and sitting comfortably, the gods and the men, someone struck a match.

The Christians at the abbey outside Rome take grim pleasure in the details of Matthew's death, which evidently hasn't worked as a deterrent. In one sense Matthew is as thoroughly dead as the nine disciples before him, but he is also a light in the darkness. Faith is rewarded by persecution and death, but a brighter day is coming.

'What is the brighter day?' Gallio asks. 'When can it be expected to arrive?'

He realizes his mistake: he ought to know, or as an honest follower believe without facts and details. Jesus is coming back, an article of faith for true believers.

'Who are you, exactly?' they ask. 'What do you want? Can we help you?'

This is their response to every quandary, and to every challenge Gallio has tried to devise: they think they can help him.

'I need to see Paul,' Gallio says. 'Wherever he is now I have important news for him. I was with Andrew when he died.'

Early the next day Cassius Gallio is climbing over rubble in Rome's shattered back alleys, avoiding the main street patrols that encircle the Fourth Regidor. The Christians at the abbey told him about a safe route through to Paul's house, and along this or that interrupted vista Gallio sees new buildings squeezed next to old, satellite dishes fading up to ancient domes, a lone seagull gliding.

He falls in behind an early-morning organic rubbish collection. The binmen of Rome tip baskets of food waste into a filthy wagon as it trundles through side streets, and Gallio meets no patrols at this time of day in these places. He rubs his beard, wonders how good is too good to be true. He'd spent the night in the abbey gardens, after the Christians had given him food and a key to the washroom at the café. In the mirror above the sink he'd checked his face for errant nerves, then disapproved of the way he looked. He went back out to find more believers. They loaned him nail scissors and he trimmed his beard.

Paul is under nominal house arrest on the second floor of a two-storey building, in a flat above a kitchen supplies outlet.

This is it, the main drag of the Fourth Regidor, and the shops on either side are blackened and boarded up, the cauterized walls patched with fly-posters for the Circus, *Sold Out* stamped diagonally across the venue and date. For some reason, the fire has left Paul's building untouched.

At the top of the outdoor stairs a plainclothes officer, a dark-skinned Roman in skinny jeans, sits in a rattan chair with his feet against the railings. He's playing *Tomb Raider* on an iPad. Gallio doesn't know if the police are guarding Paul or protecting him, but either way he can't back out. The man lifts his eyes, takes in Gallio's appearance. He nods him through.

In the kitchen a woman is peeling apples into a red plastic tub. She tells Gallio to keep going, as if he looks convincingly in need of spiritual help. In the living room at the end of the hall Paul is writing at a polished wooden desk. His bodyguard faces the door with arms crossed, not a threat but a barrier. Paul glances up, then squares a bundle of papers by blocking them against the leather-inlaid desktop. He looks again at Gallio over the frames of his glasses.

'Antioch,' Gallio reminds him. 'And the King David Hotel in Jerusalem. I've changed.'

Paul nods, takes off his glasses and puts them to one side. 'Don't like people to see me wearing them. Not the Paul my audience expects.'

The bodyguard is never far away as Paul gestures to a leather three-seater sofa he surely can't afford. Gallio sits soft, and Paul takes the matching armchair, which is slightly higher. On the glass coffee table between them, a plate of wrapped sweets and a bowl of banknotes. Paul offers Gallio a sweet. Gallio checks the position of the bodyguard.

'Don't mind him. He won't do anything unless you do.'

Gallio takes a sweet, unwraps, sucks. Ah, sugar. 'You live well.'

'I haven't been convicted of a crime, and I'm a citizen. I have the right to appeal against false accusation without harassment. Are you here to harass me?'

'If you hadn't appealed you'd be free. After James was beaten to death you wanted us to arrest you for your own safety, but it seems like you weren't in danger after all.'

Paul sighs, expressing the heavy burden of his knowledge of the world. Against his will he must inform Cassius Gallio, alas, that the world is largely unjust. 'Now I'm here they can't decide what I did wrong. I'm under arrest for breaching the Jerusalem peace, apparently, which sounds more convincing than conspiracy to make a dangerous phone call. What is it you want?'

Cassius Gallio remembers Paul as the centre of attention on the conference stage at Antioch. He did so enjoy his following, and Gallio can imagine Paul relishing the entertainment of his trial. They can't convict a citizen without a trial, and at his hearing he'll persuade the judge and jury that belief in Jesus is a rational position to take, that black is white and death is the beginning not the end. He may be expecting applause.

'You've done a fantastic job, Paul. First and foremost I came here to congratulate you. The Jesus believers appreciate your leadership, in which there's so much to admire.'

Gallio makes a point of admiring the leather furniture in which they sit, the reflective finish of the coffee table, the rock-solid bodyguard. The disciples strive to live like Jesus and are difficult to imitate, problematic as role models. Far easier, now and always, to live like Paul. Not like Peter, in prison offering solace to the damned. Not like John, wherever he is, hunted and poor.

'You've made a name for yourself at the centre of civilization,' Gallio says, 'where none of your enemies dare touch you. Academics quote your letters and defer to your theology, even when they don't agree.'

'Please,' Paul says. 'I can't take all the credit.'

Paul has a sophistication the disciples lack, which means Gallio isn't certain what he's thinking. Paul spreads his hands to mean he accepts Gallio's flattery, or he doesn't. 'A greater power is at work. Now if you tell me what you want, I may be able to help.'

'I need to set up a meet with John.'

'You and everyone else. I don't think you realize what you're asking.'

'He's in Rome, isn't he?'

Paul steeples his fingers, but the gesture is too studied, buying time. He uses the tips of his fingers as a sight, along which he aims a steady gaze into Gallio's eyes. 'You have to understand, John isn't . . .' Paul dissolves his steeple and taps his head. 'He has suffered. Your people don't know where John is and neither do I, because since the fire Rome has struggled to cope with the homeless, the raving, the unwashed. In this city one delirious voice praising angels sounds much like any other. The situation is very sad.'

'Paul, you can trust me. I know your secret, and the secret of the disciples of Jesus.'

'That's a lot of secrets.' Paul looks Gallio over, his ragged clothes and his rough-cut beard. 'A lot of knowledge for a vagrant, or is it a deserter?'

Cassius Gallio senses that the time is now, and this is the only chance he'll get. John is the last disciple he can save from death, even if he wants to die.

'I came here straight from Addis Ababa,' Gallio says, be-cause he hasn't forgotten how to lie. 'My next mission is here in Rome, but with Peter facing public execution the CCU has to be careful about making contact with a high-profile Christian like you. That's why they sent me to talk to you. No one in Rome remembers who I am.'

Paul's gaze doesn't waver. He brings back the steeple, and covers his nose.

'Valeria sent me to ask about John,' Gallio says, 'because we're reasonable men, Paul, you and I.'

Cassius Gallio has speculated every day in the boats from Patras to Rome, and again last night as he slept beneath the stars at the Abbey of the Three Fountains. If there is an explanation for his second failure as a Speculator, he has decided, this is where the unraveling starts: Paul is Valeria's puppy, he is her little dog. Always has been.

Yes. All the way back in time to Damascus. Cassius Gallio has rearranged the pieces and now the picture is clearer. After his tribunal and his exile, Valeria had been promoted to the vacant senior Speculator post in Jerusalem. As an ambitious CCU operative she'd have liked the look of Paul, a home-grown killer, and Valeria could plausibly have planned to recruit Paul, luring him away from the Jews. Damascus was the opportu-nity, away from Jerusalem. Gather the information, assemble the pieces. Yes.

At the public library in Venice Gallio had looked up the area weather reports, and at the relevant time in that partic-ular year a storm had pummeled the mountain ranges north of Israel. Paul with his entourage must have suffered, possibly hit by lightning. An opening. He arrived in Damascus dazed, blinded, and his recuperation provided perfect cover for negotiations behind closed doors, in which Valeria suggested an arrangement from which both stood to benefit. They put their heads together and devised the story of the miracle revelation, a brilliant invention that led to Paul's acceptance by Jesus sympathizers everywhere.

Baruch had been right—Paul had a secret life. If Gallio had listened to Baruch more closely, and they'd uncovered Paul's duplicity earlier, they could have undermined the Jesus belief. Now Gallio feels humbled but determined: Baruch was right about Paul, but he didn't go far enough. Since Andrew, Gallio had seen the truth, and though he's daunted by his fight against the what-will-be-will-be, he can out-speculate them all. Only Cassius Gallio understands that John must be denied his glorious martyrdom.

'Paul, you told Valeria where the CCU could find the disciples,' Gallio says. 'Our map on the computer with the lights. You fed us information, and without you we wouldn't have known where to start.'

'Ingenious.' Paul picks up a sweet, puts it down again. He looks at his watch, shakes it, holds the face against his ear. He un-straps his watch and places it on the table. 'Interesting theory, except I haven't helped the CCU find John. According to you I've turned in the others. I know everything about the disciples, then when it comes to John I suddenly know nothing.'

Paul has his own motivation for killing the disciples, over and beyond the leather furniture and free escorted travel to Rome. The disciples of Jesus inconvenience him. They're his competition, so the quieter the disciples the stronger the voice of Paul, and one day Jesus will be whoever and whatever Paul decides he is in his letters and lectures. Valeria has helped Paul's reputation to build, encouraging the public disagreements between him and Peter, trying to divide the enemy. She supplied Paul with centurions to feign conversion, and safe passage on his epic pedestrian treks. She once provided armed protection when he was threatened by Jewish militants. Paul is civilization's man.

'Yet Valeria can be outwitted, can't she?' Gallio says. 'Whatever you do, with Valeria's support, belief in Jesus continues to grow. The Christian faith feels as inevitable as that premeditated escape from the tomb, as Jesus at work. You're a triple agent, Paul. Valeria thinks you're working for her, to divide and rule the disciples. In fact you're working for Jesus.'

Paul holds out his hands, his innocent preacher's hands.

'Did you come all the way here to tell me that?'

'You push information in both directions. You told Valeria we could find Jude in Beirut, but you told Andrew where I was in Greece. It was a CCU tracer in the phone, but the information still got through to Andrew.'

Paul stands and goes to the window. He clasps his hands behind his back, appraises the road in which he lives. 'You took a risk coming here.'

He pulls the curtains closed.

'Open them. Closing the curtains is a giveaway. They'll know.'

Paul brushes back the curtains, strokes the edges as if to make sure they hang straight. From the outside he'll look distracted, one of history's deep thinkers taking a break from the meaning of life. 'You don't have any evidence. This is pure speculation, and there are hundreds of ways people know things, especially these days. Jude had his name in the papers.'

'You're not the only person who can change allegiance,

Paul. I can't make you trust me, but you too once converted. You stoned a Jesus believer to death in the street, now you write several letters a day exalting his name. I understand what you're doing, and I want to help. Peter is the beloved disciple, isn't he? Jesus is coming back before Peter dies.'

Paul grimaces. 'And how would you be able to help?'

'Tell me where to find John. I promise I'll kill him, because it's what you all want. I'll make it grim. Then the stage is set for Peter and Jesus.'

Paul gives Cassius Gallio an address that leads to a bakery off the Via Veneto called La Dolce Vita. The woman behind the counter wipes her hands on her apron between every task, possibly between every thought. The shop is empty.

Gallio has the password, also provided by Paul: *Jesus is love*. At first he can't say it, but he makes the effort. 'Jesus is love,' he coughs to clear his throat. 'Sorry. Jesus is love.'

The words turn out to be sayable, but they make his tongue soft and bring tears to his eyes. The woman wipes her hands, thinks hard, approves of what she sees and hears. She pulls up the hinged counter. 'Bottom of the stairs, turn right. We have a cold store. Knock three times.'

The light switch is a concave button that sinks into the wall and starts a timer as it pulls back out. The timer ticks like a watch on fast-forward. Gallio is halfway down the wooden staircase when the light clicks off. In the dark he retraces his steps. The second time he memorizes another light switch at the foot of the stairs, pushes in the timer and makes it down before the end of the buzz.

He pushes in the second light switch, another timer buzzing

in his ear, then turns right toward the cold store. He listens at the door, the timer runs out, the light goes off. He stands in the dark in the silence until he hears movement inside. He knocks three times, as instructed. No response. He raises his hand to knock again. The handle turns, the door opens inward, a bakery store bright with strip lights.

Claudia says: 'Too late, Cassius. He's gone.'

She's pretty, he remembers, and clever and has lovely teeth, and in Caistor he almost believed he loved her. None of that matters now. He's a deserter who ditched his papers and his CCU-issue phone. The penalty is the same as for sleeping on duty in the field.

'I wasn't expecting to see you here.'

'Hush,' she says, finger to her lips. 'There's not much you can say. Valeria doesn't forget.'

'You knew I was coming.'

Gallio's chest feels suddenly empty, and he breathes in sharply to fill the empty space. It doesn't help, because he sees how this has happened. He was wrong about Paul. Paul is simply a double agent, working for Valeria. The further step where in fact he's working for Jesus was a false speculation. Gallio has overcomplicated, again.

'Paul phoned us to say you were on your way. You're losing your touch, Cassius.'

The storeroom smells of bread and charcoal, of yeast and faintly of open drains. Spilled flour dusts the flagstones, imprinted with random footprints, but the baker upstairs is nervous. Perhaps she knows what has taken place in this room in the past. She thumps her feet against the floor to warn Claudia she has a customer.

'Still running Valeria's errands, I see.' Gallio runs a hand over the steel prep table, looks at his palm for traces of pastry, or dried flakes of blood. 'I bet you always did, even in Caistor.'

Claudia lets the accusation hang. A denial would be welcome, Gallio thinks, the compliment of a lie to at least pretend she slept with him because she liked him.

'No hard feelings,' she says.

'No feelings at all. We used each other. Suffering from shock, both of us. Probably did us good, aided our recovery.'

'If you say so. Why did you tell Paul you wanted to kill John?'

'You're a Speculator, work it out.'

Gallio is surprised by her question, by the time she's taking. Despite everything she hesitates, as if held up by the memory of their nights in Caistor. She's the CCU agent sent by Valeria, but now she's here she remembers the skin-to-skin.

'We're not killers, are we, Cassius?' she says. 'We represent order and the future. We're moving the world along, making it a more reasonable place to live. Aren't we?'

She is trying to think well of them both, but mostly of herself and her decisions in Caistor and the job she came back to do.

'I don't think we used each other,' Gallio says, taking this chance to let her know. 'Or not only. That wouldn't be an accurate description of what happened, in my opinion. And I was there.'

Claudia claps her hands, a cloud of flour dust rising to the strip lights. 'I don't know, and I think I probably don't care. I was sent to fetch you, that's all. No time to waste. So come along quietly, because you're back where you started. CCU is the only family you have.'

•   •   •

Ground Zero is an alcove at street level of the ruined Circus Maximus. This is where the great fire of Rome is thought to have started.

'They made it look like a cooking accident,' Claudia says. 'Picked the perfect spot.'

Printouts of the missing and dead flap on temporary fencing like the struggle of a living organism. Cotton flags overlap with cardboard placards: *We Love You, Why?* but Cassius Gallio is distracted by a photocopy of a teenage girl, Alma's age, cheek against cheek with a lolling dog. He steadies himself on a bamboo scaffold, and looks up its fretted length into the blueness of the holiday sky. Birds swoop into nests high in the ravaged monument, for them a year like any other, and not the worst season to be alive.

A scab of time has grown here, protecting tourists from the horror, one more stop for the gawping barbarians on their Roman visit of a lifetime. Already the fire is history, though security remains tight. To one side of the Circus main entrance two centurions in feathered helmets buckle their leather skirts. They're from Eastern Europe for the coach tours, and they share a cigarette before their shift in front of the cameras. The real thing is provided by Securitas employees with scanners beside the turnstiles. Everyone gets checked, even Claudia. She can jump the queue, flash her ID, but she has to walk Gallio through the scanner. On the other side she ignores the hawkers offering private guided tours.

'Second tier,' she says, and follows Cassius Gallio up crumbled steps to an archway where he blinks into the brightness of the damaged grandstand. Valeria is waiting midway along a stone terrace, in the shade of a dyed sail usually deployed during performances. Her face is in orange shadow.

Claudia stays at the end of the row, formally out of earshot, sunglasses fixed in place.

Gallio takes the seat next to Valeria and for a while they win at keeping silent, a trusted Speculator tactic. Whoever speaks first will say too much, and is therefore usually the loser. They watch the banked seats in other sections of the stadium, where security teams launch search dogs along the rows. Low-income employees sweep the sand of the arena. If some are undercover agents, and Gallio assumes they are, he can't tell who is working for Jesus.

'Remember when we came here on leave?' Valeria speaks: she loses. 'Years ago, soon after we met in Jerusalem. We planned to take on the world, you and me.'

Cassius Gallio does remember, though he won't squander his advantage by saying so. Strange that back then she was younger than him, and that had seemed to matter, but now her age is irrelevant. They had sat in exactly these seats and he had failed to say he loved her while crocodiles chased a Parthian and at some point they watched a crucified lion.

'The two of us together, Cassius, once you'd left your wife. Now you've finally become a deserter, but in a more official sense. Sorry, but that's the choice you made when you boarded a plane for Patras.'

'I came back. Here I am in Rome, reporting for duty.'

'You couldn't keep out of Claudia's pants, could you?'

Of course she knows; information is her specialism, because knowledge is power.

'I have high hopes for Claudia,' Valeria says, 'despite her lapse in Caistor, and with luck she'll survive you unscathed. As I did. You, however, deserted your post and lost your tracer. Unfortunate. We recovered your phone from beneath an altar in the

Agios Andreas in Patras, along with your documents. Now we pick you up in Rome, running round and threatening to kill the disciple John. What happened to you, Cassius?'

'I can explain.'

At the end of the row Claudia is sunning herself, holding up her face to the light.

'You disobeyed my orders. I wanted you to locate Matthew in north Africa, but you developed a strange fascination with Caistor. Then you disappeared without permission. I brought you back too soon from Germany, I think, and the tribunal was right about you, Cassius. You're unhinged. You forget which way is up.'

Cassius Gallio is aware of his weathered and beaten clothes, his beard and hair grown long. 'I'm undercover. I'm an active Speculator.'

'I hardly recognized you, and you don't have the right to use that title.'

'I've been on the road, looking for Jesus. That's what you asked me to do, and if finding him was simple you'd have done so before now. You needed me. You still need me. I know more about these people than anyone else you've got.'

After the crucified lion they'd seen a gladiator's nose sliced off by a short–sword. How the Circus laughed that day. Gallio remembers the sound of forty thousand people in hysterics, and a gladiator scrabbling for his nose. The joke was probably funnier because earlier they'd put out his eyes. Tomorrow is Peter's turn, and Valeria should know she's making a mistake.

'I think Jesus is coming back. The Circus gives him an opportunity to make a spectacular reappearance.'

'And this intelligence comes from where? You spoke to Jude and Bartholomew and Andrew. None of them offered a specific place or date. Even Simon failed to confess to Baruch, and by all accounts Baruch did not ask nicely.'

'So why the security?'

'Not for the second coming, I can assure you, but what the second coming might stand for. An attack of some kind, most likely a bomb. We know from Jude that whichever disciple Jesus loved is at the centre of their big event. When Jesus comes back, whatever that means, it's going to happen in the beloved disciple's lifetime. Peter confirmed this information under questioning. It was something Jesus told them, and Peter was his favourite. Now Peter is about to die, so if the attack is going to happen it has to be soon.'

'And John?'

'Can't find him anywhere. Let's face it, he may already be dead. Rome can be a tough city if you don't have money. Peter is the last one.'

'What happened to religious tolerance? Just out of interest. That used to be a priority of ours.'

'We should have crucified the twelve of them, right at the start. Tolerance makes us look weak, but tomorrow Peter comes to the Circus and everyone will see how intolerant we can be, when we make the effort. No secret assassins, no local mobs. Civilization will take responsibility for killing Peter the disciple of Jesus, as a lesson to anyone who chooses to favour superstition over reason.'

'You've misread the enemy. The disciples aren't a danger in the way you think. They have a strategy and you're being played for a longer-term result. The disciples of Jesus want to die.'

'Nobody wants to die. You've been on the road too long.'

'It was the same with Jesus, and Lazarus before him. This goes back to Jerusalem. Death works in their favour. Andrew admitted it.'

'He's a liar. Their belief system is based on lies, a fact you choose to ignore. No one walks on water, or dies and comes back to life. Of course they're scared of death, otherwise they wouldn't be human.'

'It's not too late to stay Peter's execution. Out in the territories they're using the crucifix as a symbol of their support for Jesus, if you can believe that. Listen to me, Valeria. You brought me back as an expert.'

'No one else wanted the job. No glamour, no glory.'

'I'm advising you to keep Peter alive. Change the plan and question him further.'

'Too late. Much too late. Peter deserves his fate, because coming to Rome was a suicidal act.'

'My point. That's my point exactly.'

Cassius Gallio wants eye contact but Valeria looks away, and she must be weighing up whether he's right. She's a born Speculator, as he is; she can't help but speculate. Gallio pushes home his advantage. 'Was Peter an easy arrest? I bet he was.'

The low-income workers sweep at the sand, and they sweep. They level out the arena, then level it again. Valeria lets a silence develop. Cassius Gallio loses.

'Terror isn't their strategy. Dying is their strategy.'

'You're not making sense. You're a deserter, which means you gave up on the reasonable approach. The disciples don't want to die.'

'Yes, listen. Killing them is counterproductive at every level.'

'That doesn't sound very likely. Not at every level. Not in our business.'

'Which is why we fell into their trap. We assume that dying can't be positive, but for them it is, and death is the only plan they have. They were never going to stage an attack.'

'And the fire?'

'Bad luck. Coincidence, I don't know. The fire means you have to kill Peter, or now that you want to kill Peter you have your justification. Everything ties in with their plan, or they cleverly make connections after the event. They're brilliant opportunists.'

'You've seen the list of victims at Ground Zero, the photos taped to the fence. If Jesus or his god is responsible, someone has to pay.'

'We don't know they're responsible, not for the fire.'

'The odds look good, though. According to you Jesus had himself killed, and then killed the disciples to grow his religion. Why would he bother showing mercy to people he doesn't even know?'

'These are his calculations, not mine.' Gallio thinks he understands what Jesus is doing now, but he can't see as far as the ultimate why. 'I don't know how he works them out.'

'No one can think that far ahead.'

Valeria waves Gallio's theory away, pushing out his thoughts to merge with the empty air of the stadium. She has senatorial committees to placate, decisions to implement that are not her own. She isn't always free to speculate. 'Soon the twelve disciples of Jesus will be dead, meaning the principal eyewitnesses to his unbelievable miracles will be gone. Without first-hand accounts to back them up, as admissible in a court of law, the events become lies then fiction. No one will believe they ever happened.'

Gallio gestures around, taking in the empty seats for forty thousand witnesses. 'They've set you up perfectly. Major public event. His beloved Peter alive and at the heart of civilization. Aren't you worried Jesus may have plotted this?'

'We've doubled security. Every operative we have has been briefed and issued with his picture.'

'Think about it. You're bringing together a huge audience who'll be reminded by the taunting of Peter, who looks like Jesus, that Jesus himself is supposed to be dead. This is his method: he makes his exploits unforgettable with witnesses and you're providing him with forty thousand live YouTube uploads. A beloved disciple to save, a sell-out occasion at which to reappear, a frustrated Messiah who loves a show. Who could fail to be impressed?'

Valeria leans forward in her seat, takes a renewed interest in the arena. A steward bites the corner of a triangular sandwich, head back, pulling in his stomach to avoid falling crumbs. A pair of petrol-headed pigeons swoop in for the clean-up. Then Gallio sees what Valeria wants him to see. His daughter Alma is in the arena of the Circus Maximus. She looks older, too old for the Ave helium balloon she holds in her hand. Her personal guide points out items of architectural interest, while a man in jacket and sunglasses follows them with a finger to his ear.

'In the arena,' Gallio says, sitting back. He breathes out with disbelief. 'You are unforgivable.'

'She's a lovely girl, very excited to be in Rome. When you went missing in action I felt it was our duty to provide for your family.'

'Where's her mother?'

'Safe in Jerusalem, but also quite content. We've booked Alma in for a series of sessions with the leading physiotherapist in Rome. Comes highly recommended, reckons he can cure that limp she has.

'You're threatening me.'

'What's the point of our Roman lives if not to help when we can? You'll have to trust in my good intentions.'

The guide is showing Alma the portcullis gate through

which the lions arrive, and he indicates with broad gestures how lions and also hyenas first turn to the left whatever prey is placed before them. Strange, but true.

'Once upon a time you were a decent Speculator, Cassius, and the CCU remembers that, but on this particular case you lost your bearings. The problem and the solution are much simpler than you want to make them.'

'So how does Jesus qualify as Complex Casework?'

'We're tidying up loose ends. That's all we have left to do.'

Valeria pats Gallio's arm, as if comforting a child frightened by a story. Poor thing. None of his fears are real. Gallio watches Alma limp into the tunnel to the underground stables and chariot house, always popular with visitors. He loses sight of her.

'I hate mass persecutions,' Valeria says. 'They're messy and counterproductive. Better to target twelve leaders than thousands of innocent followers.'

'What happens to me if I'm as wrong as you say? Another tribunal?'

'I shouldn't think so. You're deniable, Cassius. I told you that from the start. You don't exist. However, I do have one more job for you, which includes the opportunity to save your skin.'

She reaches into her bag and pulls out two embossed tickets for the next day's performance. 'Solid gold,' she says. 'Completely sold out.'

'As Jesus would have wanted.'

'Enough. There's no way you're getting in without a ticket. I've doubled security.'

'I hadn't looked that far ahead.'

'No, I thought not. You have a day, one day, in which to capitalize on the knowledge you've gained about the disciples of

Jesus. Find me John, however you can. Bring him to the Circus tomorrow and we'll take him off your hands.'

'What if I don't?'

'If you run again, I have Alma.'

'I'll find you John. I'll do my best.'

'That would be good, the last of the twelve. Bring John to the Circus, Cassius, and you can walk away.'

XI

Peter

———

Cassius Gallio spends the night in the garden of Claudia's suburban Roman villa. She has an organized garden, with shrubs in borders and trees in pots, but also many blocked sight lines that allow a vagrant to take advantage. She would be furious, presumably, if she knew that her former lover was asleep beside the compost bin.

Early the next morning, before dawn, Gallio is crouched behind a miniature cypress tree when the first lights in the house come on. Through the lit kitchen window he sees Claudia's husband the architect searching through cupboards for cereal, in the fridge for milk. He finds what he's looking for. He leaves the house before the sky has fully lightened, because after-the-fire is boom time for architects in Rome. The misfortunes of others will provide.

A little later, once the sun is up, Claudia and her two young daughters sit at the kitchen table for breakfast. Through the window Gallio approves their impeccable manners. Alma doesn't join them. In Jerusalem Valeria had assigned Claudia to Gallio's investigation, sent Claudia to keep an eye on him in Hierapolis and Caistor, and later it was Claudia she dispatched to intercept him at the bakery on the Via Veneto. Claudia is Valeria's fixer and Gallio's best guess, his only guess, is that Claudia will be responsible for Alma. John the disciple of Jesus can wait.

Cassius Gallio scuttles round the side of the house in time for a partial view of the front door where the girls kiss their lovely mother goodbye. The children join the neighbour and her son to walk to the bus stop, but the younger daughter dashes back for a forgotten lunch box, snatches another kiss and she's on her way.

Gallio waits ten minutes, goes round the back and knocks at the glass of the French windows. Claudia has nothing to fear, he thinks, because she can see all of him in her garden before she has to open the door. He has nothing to hide. She sees him, stops, moves forward and slides open the doors. She checks left and right outside, then bundles him into the house.

'Fuck,' she says. She shuts and locks the door and leans back against the glass. She's wearing pajamas. 'Fuck I don't believe this.' She screws up her nose, looks at him. 'You need a shower.'

'Have you got Alma?'

'I'll fetch you a towel.'

He wonders how close he is to the limit of the warmth of her welcome. After his shower he hears her moving about in the kitchen, and he flits quickly through the upstairs rooms. The two girls share, and he admires their shelves packed with bedtime stories. No sign of Alma. The bed in the marital en suite is unmade, and on the dresser a framed photo catches his eye, a studio portrait of the smiling family. A life like Claudia's could have been mine, Gallio thinks, but it wasn't to be. He blames Jesus, he blames himself.

Downstairs Claudia is dressed, black jeans, grey woolen polo neck. She looks attractive in grey, and clever, like the first time he saw her. Bare feet, toenails painted black. She sets up the pot for stovetop coffee, and for some reason, maybe the same reason, the kindness of Claudia affects him like thinking about Jesus. His eyes start to brim. Cassius Gallio has a problem with kindness, obviously. With love.

'Let's start at the beginning,' Claudia says. 'How did you get my address?'

Gallio pulls himself together, blinks a couple of times to hide his weakness. 'I'm a Speculator.'

'Me too. I'm supposed to be hard to find, not part of the story.'

'Took some numbers off your phone in Caistor. Then there's a procedure. The Internet. We both know how to do it.'

'I trusted you.'

'You put a tracer in mine.'

They sit on high kitchen stools on opposite sides of her kitchen island, which is narrow enough for them to hold hands, should they choose to do so. Gallio drinks the coffee, strong and good. 'Nice house.'

'You're scaring me. Why did you come here?'

'To find Alma. You work as Valeria's fixer.'

'I'm not a nursemaid.'

'Busy time. All hands to the pump. You'll have other jobs, probably secret, but I thought you might also be keeping my daughter.'

Claudia scratches at the marble counter with the polished

nail of her index finger. The counter is clean, so she has nothing to pick at except deep-set grains in the stone. She wipes the flat of her hand over the smooth finish as if to sweep away crumbs. No crumbs, but she sweeps them anyway with a flick of her hand, as far across the kitchen as imaginary crumbs will go.

'You're paranoid,' she says. 'You can only take speculation so far. When your conclusions stop following logic you become as deluded as anyone who believes in life after death. And sometimes you're deluded even when every individual step looks reasonable.'

'Which is why we need the CCU. To make sure every complication stays tidy and explicable.'

'Exactly. Mysteries can be explained. Explanation makes the problem go away.'

'Has the CCU ever asked you to kill anyone?'

'Don't be ridiculous. I made the same pledges on graduation that you did.'

'I killed Jesus.'

'Did you? No one's convinced about that. You're a special case. You thought you killed someone but you didn't.'

On Claudia's side of the island there's a drawer beneath the counter. She pulls the drawer out far enough to slip her hand inside. She wouldn't, not here, surely? Gallio darts out his hand and clamps her wrist.

'Let go of me.'

'What's in the drawer?'

To have a mind like Cassius Gallio's is a curse. He lets his suspicions find a shape, and Claudia of all people can get close to him. After Caistor Valeria knows that, though she wouldn't have planned anything too exotic because Gallio isn't a disciple. So maybe a muted clip from a silenced CCU-issue Beretta. Valeria would be confident he'd follow Claudia somewhere quiet, should she ask. Like a bedroom, for example. Valeria has created the conditions.

'I have nothing dangerous in the drawer, Cassius.'

'I think you do.'

'You have a vivid imagination. Too vivid. Your story isn't the big story here.'

'Bring your hand out very slowly.'

She does so, though he uses his strength to keep her slow. In her hand she has a buff-coloured padded envelope, A4 size, which she lays on the counter. He lets go of her wrist and she rubs blood back through to her fingers.

'Sorry.'

She bangs the drawer closed. 'Money,' Claudia says. 'Paul's bonus, in cash, once Peter is dead.'

Cassius Gallio peeks inside, sees several bricks of notes. He doesn't need to count it, but it's more of a stash than he spent on Judas.

'You knew all along,' Cassius says.

'Some of it. I've speculated the rest for myself. Valeria had to have an inside contact for us to find the disciples so quickly.'

'Her inside man was Paul. We both worked out Paul was working for Valeria.'

'She learned from the past. You ran the same ploy with Judas, only Valeria embedded Paul more deeply.'

'Why are you telling me this? I'm a deserter. I make colossal mistakes, and end up sleeping in your garden. My judgement is suspect.'

'I don't remember Caistor as a misjudgement. Speaking for myself.'

Claudia sweeps at the counter, and she leans in and sweeps

at the counter once more. She checks her phone, sips some coffee. She bites the inside of the corner of her lip, works at the soft inner flesh like Judas had in the Antonia. Whatever she's about to say, the effort involves eating some of herself up.

'I'm telling you because of Caistor. The CCU has not been kind to you.'

'Valeria called me back from Germany. I'm grateful to her for giving me a second chance.'

'She couldn't find anyone else.' Claudia offers nothing to cushion the truth, not even the smallest lie. 'You were asked to look for Jesus as if he were alive, but Valeria reasonably assumed he was dead. She wanted you for a specific purpose of her own. Basically she faked a manhunt using a washed-up Speculator, and Paul exploited the charade. He could let it be known the CCU was looking for Jesus, making the resurrection more credible, which suits Valeria's strategy of running Paul as a Roman client apostle. By this stage the story of Jesus is more powerful than the living human being, and Paul's version of the sect can prosper on the story alone, as long as the disciples aren't alive to disagree with the details. And, of course, as long as Valeria and the Complex Casework Unit pull the strings.'

'What about the second coming, and the promise Jesus made to show himself in the lifetime of one of his disciples, and to stage a once-and-for-all public appearance?'

'Paul can explain that promise away, with Valeria's help. The second coming is symbolic, he says. It represents individual enlightenment when the world changes for whoever becomes a believer. Not *the* end of the world, as the disciples understand it.'

'Which is convenient, because personal Armageddons don't threaten civilization.'

'There you have it. The Jesus belief is tamed by Paul taking the place of the disciples, and at the same time Valeria gets her personal revenge by luring you into a ridiculously empty quest. To anyone in the loop you look stupid. You're a Speculator running around searching for a long-dead terrorist. Cassius, you're a laughing stock.'

The backs of Gallio's hands look old on the worktop, the whorled knuckles, the prominent veins. Valeria brought him back to seek out a man she knew was dead. She'd contrived a mission with no possibility of success, even though the pursuit itself had given a purpose to his days, the endless days. He at least had that, and maybe his time was better spent on this than looking for nothing. Cassius Gallio remembers his dream of glory, the vanity that had blinded him to the truth. Well played, Valeria.

'I've spent too much of my life on this,' Gallio says. 'I should have accepted the fact that Jesus died. Look again in the obvious place. That's what my stepdad always said. Jesus was crucified and Jesus died.'

'The CCU analysts made a percentage chart, and the highest probability is that the man who died on the cross was Jesus. He did die, like so many others, and his body was stolen from the tomb with the collusion of individuals working for the occupying army. That computes as the most likely explanation, given the conditions, and to make it happen the disciples needed someone's help.'

'It wasn't me.'

'Your soldiers were paid off.'

'After the event. Baruch paid them on behalf of the Israelis to say the disciples stole the body. They wanted to stop the resurrection story from gaining traction, and Valeria knows what Baruch did and why. It came out in the interrogations we did at the time.'

'Baruch is dead. Also convenient. No one can check with him who he paid and who he didn't. You could have taken a bribe to help set Jesus free, which then makes you a prime suspect as the murderer of disciples. You want them dead because they know you were involved, and now you're trying to clean the slate. Valeria can pin this on you without breaking a sweat, if that's what takes her fancy.'

'You're speculating, so speculate about the body. The body, Claudia. No one ever found a body.'

'You're fixated on his corpse. Move on. Even if Jesus survived the cross he'd have died soon after from his injuries. That's the strongest probability.'

'No mysteries,' Gallio says. 'Just like the CCU promised us. You don't believe I killed the disciples, but we both have a suspicion about who did. Doesn't look good for me, though, I see that now. Baruch is dead. Soon Peter will be dead, then John. If I die next no one is left alive to remember Jesus.'

'Except Paul.'

And Paul works for Valeria. He portrays Jesus as a non-political pacifist eager to pay his taxes. With Valeria's help Paul travels the world, speaks at conferences, writes his letters, and together they encourage converts of the acceptable sort. Paul's type of believer, short on the radical tendencies of the original Jesus movement. Paul advises his correspondents to respect the rule of law and put in a solid day's work for the benefit of the civilized economy. Instead of miracles, he opts for conference theology with regular breaks from spiritual engagement for complimentary light refreshments.

'And he gets handsomely paid,' Claudia says, patting the soft envelope on the counter between them. 'You've seen how he lives, and every time a disciple dies Paul's influence increases. I can't say he comes very well out of this.'

'I'm a loose end, aren't I? I was at the tomb. I can't explain what happened but I was there, like the disciples were there up to the crucifixion and then afterward for the life-after-death appearances. Valeria has to kill me to protect Paul's version of Jesus. That's why you're telling me this.'

Claudia holds up her hands. 'I'm going into the drawer again. Don't grab me. I haven't got a gun.'

She pulls out a Circus ticket and slides the stiff card across the counter. 'Check the seat number.'

Gallio recognizes the row and seat as the place next to the pair of tickets Valeria gave him the day before. Jesus is not alone in planning ahead.

'If you turn up without John, and if Jesus fails to make an appearance, and if we don't all die in a terrorist attack, then I'm supposed to do the cleaning.'

'I was right. You're my assassin.'

'Except I'm telling you about it now. That usually means it isn't going to happen.'

'You're young, you're starting out. Making independent decisions could go very badly for you.'

'So I'm changing my little portion of the future, as the least I can do. I used to believe we were the good guys, and I jumped at this mission. If we'd found Jesus or explained the resurrection we'd genuinely enlighten an unsatisfactory mystery that misleads as many people as it helps. Now I find out that Valeria's idea was to replace one version of the superstition with another, and by killing lovely men like Bartholomew. I liked Bartholomew.'

'I liked him too. He was a force for good.'

'He was skinned alive. It doesn't end there. Valeria brought Alma to Rome, and she shouldn't play her games with children. That's why I'm about to disobey orders. I have daughters of my own.'

'Thank you,' Gallio says. 'I think. Just checking, but it has nothing to do with me?'

'You're not wrong as often as Valeria thinks you are. Let's leave it at that.'

'What happens if I do find John, and bring him to the Circus?'

'Everything is mapped out. After Peter is dead I make the payment to Paul at a drop-site outside the city, where fewer people are likely to recognize him. Just me and him and the bodyguard, and Valeria will be there too if you've found John.'

'Then what happens?'

'I hand over the envelope to Paul, no one the wiser. Valeria takes John off your hands. I doubt they'll be going on holiday.'

'I mean what happens to me?'

'You could run before we get there, between the Circus and the pay-off. I'll say I couldn't stop you.'

'She has Alma.'

'Tricky. Depends how much revenge she feels is adequate, but I doubt we can rely on her compassion. Anyway, never pays to look too far ahead. Maybe Jesus appears at the Circus Maximus to save Peter's neck. He genuinely comes back from the dead, not once but twice, and the world as we know it ends and neither of us has to worry about Valeria and the CCU. Silver linings.'

'Could happen.'

'Could do. But if it doesn't, you're in luck. I know where they're holding Alma.'

The SOS Children's Village is to the southwest of the city, about half an hour by Fiat minicab door to door from Claudia's villa. The sign on the driveway reveals what the village really is: an orphanage. Valeria is looking to the future, and Cassius Gallio is suddenly as concerned for Judith as he is for poor fatherless Alma. Though he mustn't rush to judge.

The orphanage is eight bungalows grouped between large houses in a leafy residential area. Six children live in each building, and the orphanage is full. Cassius has borrowed a yellow high-vis waistcoat from the coat stand inside Claudia's front door, and he walks slowly through the compound acting as if he belongs. Keep it slow, he thinks, and a fluorescent jacket makes him invisible. Don't mind me, I just work here.

Through the windows the furnishings in each bungalow look sparse but clean. The kids inside play computer games or they're on Facebook, while others enjoy the fresh air at the play area. Gallio is impressed, and would like to know who pays for this.

At the playground Alma is catching smaller children as they come down the slide, and her leg is visibly more flexible than it was. The physiotherapy is working, and Judith was right—Alma can receive better treatment in Rome than Jerusalem. Maybe. Gallio doesn't know what Valeria is thinking, not when she makes unspoken threats to feed Alma to the Circus, but he believes people are basically good, or have good intentions. He looks at the bungalows constructed for forty-eight orphans: the world is full of unintended results.

A flurry of children run for the gate. Not again, Gallio thinks, but yes—Jesus is also here. He's carrying lollies between his fingers and an armful of DVDs. Gallio watches him hand out his gifts and, predictably, with children Jesus is funny and approachable. As one of the older ones, Alma mocks a bow and links arms with Jesus as far as the orphanage office, and while they're inside Cassius Gallio threads himself into a picnic table and settles down to wait. Time goes by, and he notices a change

in the weather. Clouds are moving in, grey and elegant, the colour of Claudia's sweaters.

Before too long Alma and Jesus reappear from the office.
They seem inseparable, his hand in hers, and she brings him
to Gallio's picnic table. Alma and Jesus sit down on the opposite side to Cassius Gallio. Alma pushes a straw into a lunch
box carton of orange juice, sucks the juice through to check the
straw works, then hands the carton to Jesus. He drinks, one
big suck and swallow, smacks his lips with satisfaction. Alma
settles her head on her hands on the tabletop, gazes up at his
luminous face.

'Hello John,' Gallio says. He hadn't been looking, but here
John is. It must be.

'Matthew, is that you?'

John has an unconvincing beard, as in the images pinned
to the incident-room wall in Jerusalem, but his Jesus-look radi-
ates from sharp cheekbones and a faraway gaze. He sucks on the
straw, more cautiously this time.

'I'm sorry,' Gallio says. 'I'm not a disciple. Matthew is dead.'

'I hadn't heard,' John says, 'but I'm not surprised. Another
one gone ahead. Who are you?'

John peers intently, straining his Jesus-brown eyes, and only
now does Gallio realize that John can barely see. He blinks hard,
leans forward, grasps Gallio by the elbows. He stares at the grain
of Gallio's face, and Gallio is more obviously himself, up this
close.

'I'm sorry I couldn't be Matthew.'

Years ago in Jerusalem John had been first to arrive at the
empty tomb with Peter, and these two disciples let the others
know that Jesus had disappeared. Maybe John's eyesight was
failing even then.

'John, I have a question to ask you. It's important. When did you last see Jesus?'

'I'm nearly blind,' John says. He releases Gallio's elbows. 'I see him all the time. Is it Jesus you're looking for?'

'I don't know. I was.'

John fumbles for his juice, and Alma places the carton in his hand. He sucks at the straw and swallows until the carton pulls in on itself. When he puts the carton down it falls over. John takes Alma's hand, leans forward and aims his gaze vaguely over Gallio's shoulder. 'Have you come to kill me?'

'I'm not an assassin.'

'Someone wants to kill me, though? You'd expect me to die?'

'Presumably, at some point. Like anybody.'

Gallio looks at his daughter, ear squashed against her arm, her thumb rubbing across the top of John's hand. He wishes he could make himself known to her, but there's so much to explain. She deserves someone who can take care of her, who isn't unstable and doesn't tell lies.

'Jesus is dead.'

'You're mistaken,' John says. 'Jesus is coming back.'

'So Andrew told me. As did Bartholomew, and also Jude. None of you know when or how.'

'Jesus never went away. This is an orphanage run for the state by the Church. The children here are safe in the hands of Jesus.'

Cassius Gallio knows from Jude that Jesus promised to return while at least one of his disciples was still alive, whichever one he loved most. He's running out of options, the disciples now down to the last pair standing, with Peter's execution scheduled for later that day. Gallio checks his watch, but he hasn't worn a watch in years. He reads the time off his phone. A couple of hours until trumpets, when the Circus Maximus will open for public gratification.

'Is Peter the beloved disciple?'

'Jesus loved us all.'

'But one of you he loved more than the others. Jude said so without my prompting.'

'He gave Peter the keys,' John says. 'He singled him out and called him the rock. Is that what you mean?'

Yes, that would be enough. For Cassius Gallio the story of Jesus is finally coming together, and Valeria has shown too little respect for the subtlety of her opponent. Jesus predicted that Gallio would seek out Alma, his only daughter, so he sent John to the orphanage where the two men were most likely to meet. This is the work of the same Jesus who arranged the fire of Rome to create the conditions for Peter's public execution. In the years since the alleged resurrection the world's most modern secret service hasn't managed a sniff of him. Jesus could be in Rome right now, and Valeria wouldn't have a clue, because no one can appear and disappear like Jesus.

'Is Jesus planning his second coming for the Circus?'

John smiles, his face lights up. Then the smile becomes a wince, and he blinks rapidly. 'I'd very much like to have seen that.'

'But I suppose you can't, because you're blind.'

'No,' John says. 'When Jesus comes back I'll probably be healed. But I couldn't get hold of a ticket.'

Cassius Gallio uses the last of his Patras euros on a taxi, but the roads are blocked a long way out from the stadium. Fans ring cowbells and wave flags for their chariot teams. They break into

297

chants, not always good-natured. Circus posters say *Eat Chariots Sleep Chariots Drink Coca-Cola* but Rome is drinking Italian wine, and plenty of it. Nearer the stadium, on foot, Cassius Gallio and John navigate random tailgate parties, and raised bottles salute them for embracing the spirit of games day—a man who looks like Jesus, in a sleeveless high-vis jacket, leads a man who looks like Jesus who is blind.

John attaches himself two-handed to Gallio's elbow. They have left Alma in the care of the orphanage, because now that Gallio has John he has less to fear from Valeria. Faced with the choice of taking John to the Circus or kidnapping his own daughter, John is the percentage decision. For the time being Alma is in a safe and caring environment, and one way Gallio can save himself is to be the Speculator who delivers the final disciple. If John is right and Jesus reappears at the Circus, then he'll deal with that when it happens.

The air temperature dips, unusual for this time of year. John will sense the chill but he can't see, as Gallio can, other signs that make him anxious. Gallio spots apostles in stained-glass windows, and sculpted disciples in the alcoves of Roman chapels. For the murdered disciples, death is not death. The disciples dominate the Vatican skyline, flanking a triumphant Jesus, mocking their versatile assassins. Simon carries a saw and Thomas a spear and Jude an arrow, their victorious marble whiteness made brighter by the bank of dark cloud descending. John tightens his grip on Gallio's arm, aching with small-boy excitement.

At the Circus Maximus, increased security means only half the turnstiles are open. Gallio ditches the high-vis jacket because John attracts enough attention as it is, and they join a queue for the bag search. Every bag gets checked. They don't have any bags.

A temporary steward, a woman in a blue suit and white shirt, pats them down. She has no idea how long it will take to get everyone in.

'Fifteen minutes,' she guesses. They join another queue, and for anyone with limited vision, Gallio thinks, the outside of the stadium loses detail and becomes a dark mass with an incomplete upper tier of arches, a symbol of Roman ambition defeated by time. After fifteen minutes Gallio stops a second steward who says 'Fifteen minutes for sure.' Fifteen minutes later the queue begins to move.

Cassius Gallio and John have tickets for the popular third tier, but nearer the front than the back, on the opposite side of the stadium to where Gallio met Valeria the day before. Not the best seats, but good enough for an unobstructed view of the second coming, which if the Circus ever gets started may bring the world to an end by teatime. Gallio excuses himself and his partially sighted friend along the row, making people stand and suck in their stomachs. At their designated places they make themselves comfortable. John puts his hand on Gallio's arm, then on his knee. Claudia's seat, on the other side of Gallio, is empty.

'Bet you can't believe your luck,' Gallio says. 'A spare ticket out of nowhere.'

'Bet I can.'

'Look at this place, it's packed.'

John can distinguish between light and dark but not much else, so Cassius Gallio describes the changing shapes made by a troupe of willing majorettes. They finish their routine as a perfect square and bow to scattered applause. The band of the Ninth Legion marches in, another prelude to the main event. If Jesus has planted a bomb, Gallio thinks, the casualties will be incomparable to those of any atrocity before or since. He talks John through Carthaginian drummers, a motorcycle display team, and from the upper tiers behind them some anti-Semitic chanting.

A steward at the end of the row points Claudia to her seat, and gives her a cushion to bring to John. A convert, Gallio suspects, who on his daily-guided tours will include a lurid description of Peter's execution, complete with the number of spectators in attendance and an incontestable date. He will fix Peter's story on a sharpened point in history, and he'll ask aloud why this religion among so many rivals survived to the present day. Possibly because the stories told by the disciples are true, he'll suggest. Jesus did come back from the dead. His disciples were witnesses, and Peter was so convinced by the reality of miracles he died for his beliefs in this very place.

Otherwise, apart from John and a sympathetic steward, few of Rome's believers could have landed a ticket. The performance is a sell-out, the first full-length programme at the Circus Maximus since the fire, and a once-in-a-lifetime opportunity to see Peter, the favourite disciple of Jesus. He will be alive then dead, all a man can ever be, with as a bonus attraction the possible second coming of a Messiah, and for true value for money proof of a resurrection.

A blare of copper horns, silencing forty thousand voices. The Circus has a producer called the editor, who controls the running order. Today, the editor has decided, the early part of the entertainment will be understated about pain and death. A singing competition is won by the son of a government official. A theatre company performs an extract from a contemporary play—the plot a timeless mix of coincidence, mistaken identity and a moral dilemma, but with the twist that demigods can intervene to advance the action. At the Circus Maximus the demigods of both sexes are young, oiled and intervene half-naked.

'We could leave now.' Claudia leans in close to Gallio, whispers into his ear. John is on his other side. 'Get him out while we can. Beat the rush.'

'He's blind, not deaf. In any case, we're staying for Jesus.'

'You mean Peter. You're getting the two of them mixed up.'

'For Peter, then.'

But before Peter there's chariot-racing, early rounds of Greens vs Reds and Blues vs Whites. The Blues crash, but the races never turn brutal until after the editor decides to spill some blood. With every new act and entrance, Gallio is terrified of seeing Alma. He knows about Valeria's ruthless streak, but he can believe she's crucifying Peter because she thinks it a reasonable step to take. Peter's public crucifixion is a deterrent to say look, look again, Jesus isn't much help to his friends. Targeting Alma doesn't count as reasonable in any comparable way.

At close to four o'clock a carpet of flares announces the imminent arrival of the show's star victim. The tunnel of smoke clears and the countdown begins: the beloved disciple of Jesus is in the arena. Peter carries a cross, and like Jesus he falls. No one vaults a barrier to help him, not in the Circus Maximus, with security as tight as it is.

A guard of four soldiers whips Peter into taking up his burden. Peter is the rock but the weight of the cross sways him, a fisherman on deck in a storm. His clothing has soiled in prison to shades of brown, and he is honestly unarmed for the fight. Grey-haired, bent-backed, Peter stumbles but does not fall, not again.

He suffers, but suffering is the price of salvation. For Peter eternity is within reach, where pain will have no meaning: he bears his burden because the soul will decide, not the body. He reaches the centre of the arena, drops the cross flat into a splash of sand. The soldiers offer him a gladiator's trident to defend himself. Peter turns the weapon away, refuses to entertain.

John will hear the dogs even from the third tier. At opposite ends of the stadium handlers lean back against savage beasts straining at the leash, yowling, snapping, keening. John will supply his own visions to fit the sounds, but at the Circus Maximus he'll also sense the feeling that's growing among forty thousand spectators: Peter's stadium meekness is unsatisfactory.

The bank of clouds is lower, darker. Peter refuses to defend himself and now this: no one wants rain.

Peter kneels in the centre of the arena. He prays. When dogs pull to within inches of his face, lunging at his eyelids, Peter doesn't flinch. He doesn't run and he doesn't fight, which is curious then dull. The Circus crowd respects courage but Peter looks limp and timid, unlikely to provide a decent afternoon's sport. He is a coward, and for the editor of the Circus Maximus Peter presents significant narrative problems.

An outbreak of booing, sporadic at first but increasing in volume. Slow handclaps. The editor releases a reserve of Christians, bundling them into the arena, about thirty women and children he'd been keeping back for later. He allows the crowd to settle, then gives the order: let loose the dogs.

His initiative is rewarded. These secondary disciples are less accepting of their fate than Peter, and half of them run. The runners survive, because the dogs leap at the faces and throats of the Christians who imitate Peter, those who fall to their knees and pray. Vicious, lazy, the dogs sate themselves on the sincere believers, but won't move for the lesser Christians who, lacking in faith, run to save their lives. Everyone gets what they want.

The Circus today is misfiring. The production should feel like a show of strength, but on a darkening afternoon the prevailing mood is weakness. Horns. The editor has seen enough. Handlers with sticks beat the lethargic dogs and surviving Christians from the arena. In come the sweepers, who scrape bloodied sand into wheelbarrows and replace it with fresh. The renewed blondness of the arena is a promise of blood to come.

The editor needs to make Peter entertaining and the best he can do, with a performer Peter's age who lacks fighting spirit, is crucifixion. But not a standard crucifixion, which would bore a knowledgeable crowd. The soldiers lay Peter down, and his lack of resistance allows them to arrange his arms and legs along the wood of the cross, which is flat to the ground. They nail him where he lies, and as the blood spurts, the booing fades. This is mildly diverting. A heavy bass drum beats time to the fall of the mallet. The editor wrests back control of the spectacle, though the crowd is familiar with the opening moves of a crucifixion. He will have to add value.

Oh that's good, though, that's an inspired variation. The Circus soldiers dig out a slot for the upright. Two of them haul on a rope, another crawls under the rising wood and pushes it up with his back until the cross, with Peter attached, is upright on its end and Peter is crucified *upside down*. Applause, from every section of the stands.

Excitement shivers through the stadium. A god worthy of esteem will have to react, if he has any pride, in front of forty thousand reasonable spectators who will be obliged to accept his existence. Come on, Jesus. You will never be offered a better opportunity than this. The veins swell in Peter's inverted neck and head. His eyes, inches from the arena sand, roll into the top of the sockets. He lifts his head, tries to, but can't reverse the blood pressure, the whites of his eyes filling out.

The stadium waits on god. Peter has an eleven-inch nail through each of his feet, Gallio notices, whereas for Jesus a single nail was enough. For Peter two nails are needed to take the weight. Peter's knee joints dislocate, and through curling toes Cassius Gallio feels for the underground warning of an earthquake, the tremble of the dead rising to welcome Jesus. For a bomb, an explosion, a terrorist atrocity. The spectacle is Peter crucified upside down, but the tension is the waiting for Jesus to intervene.

A low rumble, and Gallio looks to the heavy black clouds for Jesus descending. John clutches Gallio's arm. Claudia keeps her eyes on the stands, scans for unusual movement in the tribunes. And again, a low rumbling sound, and Peter's ankles pop, yes the undertone is louder and it is, Gallio now realizes, the stomping of forty thousand pairs of feet acclaiming the editor's work.

Peter's head bangs against the wood of the inverted cross. His neck distends, ridged with obvious ligaments, and Cassius Gallio remembers, too late, that Peter is famous for botched miracles. He is the disciple who could not walk on water. He put his foot on the surface of Lake Galilee and waited a moment before applying some weight and seeing his foot go under.

Peter is dying, and Gallio stares at a disciple's public death, convinced he has a lesson to learn. He leans forward, and John holding tight is pulled forward with him. The upside-down crucifixion of Peter, Gallio speculates, reveals the mind of Jesus. This is the thought that Gallio allows to develop. Up is down and down is up. Right is left and the last are first. Death is life. Defeat is victory. Nothing in this world is as it seems.

He doesn't understand. Nor do forty thousand paying spectators in the Circus Maximus. The distractions that follow, with upside-down Peter as the ailing centerpiece, seem trivial by comparison. Chariots race laps round the inverted cross, but the dying body of Peter holds the eye. The editor of the games has misjudged the audience, and his customers start to leave. At first single seats empty, gapping the stands, loners making for the exits. They ignore the gladiators and the talent contests. Then couples, excuse me please, coming through, before entire rows shift and break. Civilized people, educated to know how the world works, are unsettled by a victim who neither fights nor flees. This is unnatural behaviour. Why would anyone behave like this?

Before long Gallio has John on one side and Claudia on the other, but otherwise they're alone in the stadium, watching Peter die. A crucifixion can take hours, and Cassius Gallio endures the death of Peter as an unforgettable picture, an eleventh grotesque killing to which Jesus doesn't object. The floodlights click off, leaving a brief silver afterglow. Gallio waits for the end, and even from a distance he recognizes the final moment when Peter's limbs ease and his head relaxes and his chest ceases to heave. His body falls spent against the cross, and Peter the beloved disciple of Jesus is dead. He is dead.

So now they know. Jesus is not coming back, either in person or as code for a major event. A steward appears, the production is over, but they look beyond his official jacket at Peter's body ignored in the scuffed centre of the arena. This is a reality check for Cassius Gallio, but for Christians, the no-show of Jesus is a shambles. Peter's cross abruptly tilts in its slot, skews Peter's feet sideways, refuses a neat alignment with heaven.

'Where will we go?' John says. 'What will I do?'

Claudia stands up, but Gallio won't be rushed. With Jesus he distrusts any sense of an ending, and none of the claims made by the disciples have yet been disproved. They never said where Jesus would come back, or specifically when. Gallio is disappointed by Jesus's absence from the Circus Maximus, of course he is, but he can still think rationally. He turns toward John.

'You're the last disciple alive.'

Cassius Gallio touches the side of John's face, runs his fingers over John's eyebrow and along his boyish cheekbone. 'You must be the one, the disciple Jesus loved.'

'Enough now,' Claudia says. 'Nothing they say is true.'

XII

John

" "

The Greek island of Patmos smells of thyme and warm sea breezes. John the disciple of Jesus keeps hold of Cassius Gallio in his usual way, gripping him by the elbow, neither of them clear about who's the guide and who the guided. They pass a mulberry tree where barefoot children laugh, climb a ladder, collect berries into baskets. Mulberry juice stains their arms and legs, and in their game of tag they leave blood-red handprints on exposed brown skin. John doesn't see what Cassius Gallio, who was never chosen by Jesus, can see any day of the week.

From a distance unkempt old men can look much the same. Up close the differences between Gallio and John become more apparent: Gallio has milky blue eyes and John is blind, while

Gallio has a slackness at the sides of his mouth. Arthritis has dried his knees and knuckles, and last night a useful tooth loosened in his head.

Gallio coughs up phlegm, spits to the side of the path. Jesus has not come back, though John hears voices that insist on their daily walk. From the cave past the mulberry tree along the path to the cliff edge, where Cassius Gallio and John the disciple of Jesus wait exposed to the eye of god.

'Sorry,' Gallio says. Another morning, another beautiful day on which to break the discouraging news. 'Not a cloud to be seen in the sky.'

When they first arrived on the island, years ago, they lived more confidently in hope than now. Gallio kept John close because after so much time, such intense speculation, he was jealous of his right to encounter Jesus. Jesus has promised to return in the lifetime of his beloved disciple, and John is the last disciple standing. Therefore he is the beloved.

Cassius Gallio used to watch the clouds on John's behalf, each as eager as the other for the weather of Jesus to cover the sun. Mostly, on a Greek island, the clouds stay away, or appear as distant lines like text in an unknown language, gradually washed out as dawn turns to day. The early morning Aegean sea, Gallio thinks, is more lovely against the blue Aegean sky than seems strictly necessary.

As a group of three they had left the Circus Maximus after dark, half a moon slipping onto its back over the lights of the eternal city. John was the beloved disciple, and as the taxi found a thread through the post-stadium streets John said kill me now. Those were the words he used.

'Please. Now is as good a time as any.'

'You expected Jesus to appear, didn't you?'

'The set-up was perfect,' John said.

Claudia had to lean round from the front seat, so that unlike in England she could hear every word.

'The Circus was a piece of theatre like the crucifixion,' she filled in the gaps left by John, 'only this time the important people, the rulers of the world, could have witnessed the power of Jesus.'

'But Jesus couldn't save Peter,' Gallio said. 'Evidently.'

From Claudia's kitchen to Alma's orphanage to the Circus Maximus, for Cassius Gallio this has been the longest day. 'You're the last disciple, John, and Jesus promised to come back in your lifetime.'

'So kill me and bring him down. Hurry him up. I'll join the others and you'll find Jesus. That's what you set out to do.'

'Why rely on us?' Claudia said. 'Get your own hands dirty. If you want to die then kill yourself, like James did.'

'James was bludgeoned to death in the street.'

'Do it now.' Claudia taunted him from the front seat. 'Force Jesus to show himself. Throw yourself out of a moving car.'

Gallio reached across and pushed open the door, because he could appreciate Claudia's speculative logic. The wind of the city rushed in. The driver braked.

'It's not my life to take,' John said. He reached for the door, missed the handle, grabbed again and pulled it shut. Outside the car, as the driver went back to driving, monuments gathered pace, back to the speed limit and beyond. Life will go on.

'Out of the question,' John said. 'I might be wrong about the time and place. Jesus makes the decisions, knows when and where.'

'Not to mention how,' Claudia said. 'Falling out of a Roman taxi can't contend with crucifixion.'

'Or skinned alive,' Gallio said. 'Or sawn in two.'

'Jesus needs someone else to provide the requisite horror, doesn't he? None of you act alone. To push your religion forward you need some of us, those who aren't disciples, to be assassins.'

Cassius Gallio had once heard Lazarus make the same complaint about his best friend Jesus. He could never do anything by himself.

'Jesus used me to stage his execution,' Gallio said, not as an accusation but as a statement of the sad facts of the matter. 'I took responsibility for killing him. I lived with the guilt of executing a man whose record never warranted a charge of terrorism. Then it turns out he may not have died. Jesus hasn't been fair on me, and neither have you, his disciples. Including you, John. You collude in the various deceptions.'

'But today is John's lucky day,' Claudia said. 'We can give him what he wants. John, we're taking you to your killer.'

'Fate will do the rest,' Gallio said, giving up on his training, on every pledge he'd made to civilization. He could do no more. He would deliver John alive, which would go some way to atoning for his desertion, even though it meant Valeria came out ahead. Valeria was always the winner, but Cassius Gallio was fatalistic about that too.

'I appreciate your kindness,' John said. 'I'm grateful to you both.'

The tour-boats started as dots on the horizon, the dots became ships, and from the ships came landing-boats heavy with pilgrims in search of John the beloved disciple. Cassius Gallio assured these earnest believers that they were misinformed. John the former disciple of Jesus was last seen in Ephesus. He had been assassinated like the others, yes, equally horribly— boiled in a vat of pagan cooking oil, according to widespread reports.

'We found a man not far from here who lives in a cave. He says his name is John.'

Gallio insisted the John on the island of Patmos was another John. This John believed in Jesus, true, but he was not the beloved disciple. Not after all this time. And John is a common name. Some of the pilgrims were heartened, made their excuses and left. Others believed what they wanted to believe, and competed to show their devotion.

'We too are disciples of Jesus,' they said. 'But we are the least of all the disciples.'

The pilgrims shared food and soap and images of Jude impaled by arrows against a verdant pastoral background. Gallio couldn't begin to explain in how many ways their version of Jude's death was wrong. They had woodcuts of Simon sawn in half crossways with a manual bow saw, and Bartholomew on a beach carrying his skin in his hands. They believed whatever pleased them, and as disciples the next generation of Christians, and the next, were impostors. No one could replace the original twelve, individually selected by Jesus. The Patmos visitors were aware of this, Gallio thought, because they were unrelenting in their pursuit of John. He could stand in for Jesus. He could pick out a new set of special disciples, who would be only too willing to serve.

In his failure to do this, John of Patmos was a disappointment. He sat in his cave and he waited. He waited some more and he continues to wait, until the pilgrims and more recently the professors can't be sure it's him. Is the disciple John here? Is *Jesus* here? The questioners want the glory of being certain, but to this day Cassius Gallio refuses to compromise. He concedes that both John and Jesus may once have visited Patmos, but neither is here right now.

'And Satan?'

Gallio despairs, almost, but despair is unproductive so occasionally he'll throw out a story, disinformation in the tradition of Jesus. A myth hides the man himself from sight, Jesus knows this, and Gallio will freely admit that here on Patmos he once saw, with his own eyes, the disciple John collect an armful of hay from a field. John knelt down in front of the hay and prayed, and the hay was transformed into the purest gold. Yes John did exactly that, here on the island of Patmos. John melted the gold down and minted an armful of golden coins.

'Then what? What did John do with the money?'

The researchers and academics are desperate to make connections, to speculate, to move on to what a story means and why it matters.

'He gathered the gold coins together,' Gallio said, 'every last one of them, and he hurled them into the sea.'

The taxi drove against the headlamps of construction lorries carrying sand and gravel for the never-ending renovation of the city. Beyond the tourist highways, where no one would think to look, the final lit windows in the glass Siemens building darkened one by one. It was getting late.

The gateway to the Abbey of the Three Fountains was quiet, apart from traffic noise from the flyover, and the daytime trickle of visitors was a memory. In a sweep of full beam the taxi

U-turned toward the city, leaving Gallio committed to John and Claudia. He acted as if he belonged, but was grateful for the night's half moon that silvered the tree-lined avenue to the abbey building. He wouldn't want to die in total darkness. Lamps at ankle level illuminated the path leading to the raised terrace in front of the arched abbey doorway. At the top of the steps, he could see Valeria waiting.

'A pathway,' Gallio said, 'I'll guide you along it. At the end of the path we have some steps. Keep hold of my elbow. Don't be afraid.'

'Is it the assassin?'

Along with Valeria, up on the abbey terrace, Cassius Gallio could make out two more figures, dark in the shadow of thick stone walls.

'Yes,' he said. 'All of them are here.'

The disciples have disciples with disciples who over the years become implacable. Cassius Gallio can't deter them from building their monasteries, from ringing their ecumenical bells. When John hears the faithful called to prayer he hides in his cave, a hollow in the rocks beside the path. The cave has room enough for two but Gallio prefers to wait outside: Jesus will descend from the clouds, according to Jude, and Gallio would like to be the first to know.

As luck would have it, a contour in the rock beside the cave entrance is a perfect fit for the shape of Gallio's back. That's where he sits, shaped into the island stone and warmed by daily sunshine. Sometimes, especially if he falls asleep, believers will leave him money or handwritten messages: *Please, God, let me find myself in Jesus.*

Cassius Gallio is not John's keeper; that would not be a reasonable position for him to take. More accurately he remains constantly alert to ways in which a beloved disciple could die. Accident, illness, violence. Gallio watches John closely around traffic and water. Strangers have his attention—any of them could be Satan, or a killer from Rome, or both—and Gallio sleeps less well when John catches a cold. He can't be certain that Jesus will appear, but if Jesus does appear, in the final instant of his beloved disciple's lifetime, then he'll find that Cassius Gallio is at hand.

He lives every day as if the world might come to an end, as does John, which is not as exciting as it sounds. Eat, watch for clouds, sit outside the cave. Sleep. Avoid evil, because on Patmos with the monasteries and churches that's the dominant mood. Despite a memorable episode of food poisoning, and a nasty chest infection, John is healthy and strangers are kind and Gallio wakes to endless sunny days by the sea.

John complains that life isn't fair. His brother James—his brother!—was beheaded and went first to sit at the right hand of Jesus in heaven. They killed James an age ago in Jerusalem, so the right hand is taken. As is the left hand. Thomas is on the left hand, or possibly Jude, and the two seats outside those are filled by Philip and Bartholomew, and the next places along by Andrew and Matthew and Peter. One disciple after another fast-tracked to paradise, with John left a vacant chair at the distant end of the table.

'Next to Judas?'

'Even Judas got there before me.'

John feels abandoned. Of the original twelve disciples, only John is absent from the kingdom.

• • •

On the terrace of the Abbey of the Three Fountains, Paul stepped out of the shadows and John embraced him. The short bald man and the blind disciple, solid in each other's arms, even though by Valeria's accounting they weren't supposed to be fond of each other.

'In your own time,' Gallio said. 'Let's get this done.'

He was impatient, wary of any delay because in the open he felt exposed, out in the light: fat-winged flies bashed into the low-level glass of the lamps. Left, right, above, below. Gallio scrutinized the grounds of the abbey. If Valeria had called in backup then her hired assassins were behind the hedges, or moving tree to tree. He watched for black to detach from blackness, as evil would, from the dark of the barn or the lodge, shadows with knives, clubs, a pump-action shotgun.

Nothing moved, nobody took aim from the darkness. Or not that he could see.

Paul's bodyguard, the third person to arrive ahead of them on the terrace, was armed. The curved blade of his sword was dulled with blacking, a professional touch, Gallio thought, and proof that Paul trusted no one.

'Break it up, gents.' Valeria had seen enough hugging, or shared some of Gallio's operational anxiety. 'We're busy people, with problems to solve. No time like the present.'

In the uplight she looked years younger, the Valeria Gallio had once almost loved in Jerusalem. No jacket, no bag, no weapons. Paul and John broke apart but held each other at arm's length, like friends before a long separation. Or afterward, reunited.

'I missed you,' Paul said. 'Now I have to go.'

Claudia coughed, held out the padded envelope containing Paul's fee. 'I brought your money. You can count it if you like.'

'Which one is the assassin?' John asked. He pulled away from Paul and raised his chin.

Part of growing old is the forgetting. The days grow longer then shorten then lengthen again. On Patmos Cassius Gallio loses track of how the starlings come and go, flocking as they depart, flocking as they arrive with a sound like circling bells. The sun goes down and the sun comes up. Light reflects from the sea onto the underwing of a seagull. A black cat jumps from a seaside trellis, lands safely on all four feet.

The Jesus church continues to grow, travelling along the trade routes on the words of dead disciples, promising that Jesus will have dominion over the earth. It looks like he may. For every one of the original disciples there are twelve more, and those twelve breed another twelve, blowing across the region like seeds. The Jesus believers are many but mostly harmless, allowing the first to remain first, leaving the rich and powerful unchallenged.

Some of the stories that reach Patmos are ludicrous. Cassius Gallio hears about memorials to Peter in Rome, of all places, a basilica over his tomb and a piazza that can welcome eighty thousand believers to prayer.

'Is there singing?' John asks, and the Vatican has a choir of twenty tenors and basses and thirty boy choristers and yes John we can confirm that there is singing, along with domes by Michelangelo and stonework by Bernini, sunlight through arches onto pillars.

'Sculptures?'

'In bronze, in marble, in purple alabaster.'

John laughs. This is not what Jesus had in mind, or not that he ever said.

'They pay their taxes,' Gallio reminds him. 'At least some of them do.'

'I'll take John now,' Valeria said. 'Thank you Cassius, for finding him and bringing him here. I'm grateful for all you've done, and I'll keep my promise. You can go, leave us, disappear.'

Valeria was offering Gallio the extinction he had longed for in Caistor, and for most of the time in Patras. Cassius Gallio could disappear and his name with him, a Speculator who never existed.

'Unless you give me a reason to change my mind the CCU will leave you in peace. Your work is done. For the avoidance of doubt, should anyone ask, I see no one here at the abbey but us.' She gestured round the terrace, at Claudia and Paul and Paul's bodyguard. 'Just the three of us, you and me and John.'

'The last surviving disciple of Jesus,' Gallio said. 'It took us a while, but we got there in the end. Every disciple located, and all dead apart from John. You don't worry it was too easy?'

'The full set, exactly. When no disciples are left alive, Jesus can't come back. Or none of his sympathizers can tell that particular story, not in good faith, about Jesus returning at the latest in the lifetime of his beloved disciple. His prophecy collapses, and with it the dangerous idea that he's a mystical genius. With John we have the twelve. We're done.'

'Here I am.' John opened his hands toward her, lifted up his arms. 'You win. We've been hopeless at protecting ourselves.'

'I'd have to agree,' Valeria said.

'Be careful, you're falling into their trap.'

Despite Gallio's efforts in Caistor and in Patras, he found he couldn't walk away from the story of Jesus. He saw the same patterns repeating themselves, but this time Valeria was at the centre, overconfident as he had been in Jerusalem. Gallio had once outwitted Jesus, because a corpse does not escape a sealed tomb. Valeria was satisfied that eleven disciples of Jesus had not chosen to die—and if they didn't think this through Jesus would trick them again.

'I know you were responsible for killing the other disciples,' Gallio said. He wasn't expecting Valeria to confess, but she would listen to his reasoning. She was a Speculator too, and Gallio was worthy of her attention if he could unfold the how and the why.

'Personally?'

'You have your people,' Gallio said. 'Operatives like me, like Claudia. We don't see them and they don't see us. You'll deny them, because that's the agreement, but you made it to regional chief of CCU because you respect how complex a case can get.'

'I didn't kill the disciple Simon in England. How did I kill Simon? I didn't kill Andrew in Patras or James when he jumped from that roof.'

'Simon in Caistor was an unexpected bonus, courtesy of Baruch, and in Jerusalem with James the riot police followed your orders. They have comms equipment, like the rest of us. They radioed for guidance, then used their batons because that's what you told them to do.'

'How did I get James off the roof?'

'Paul made the phone call,' Gallio said. 'When James picked up, Paul kept quiet. That was a signal.

'James wanted to die, as did the others. Paul helped James by letting him know when the time was right, a dark evening when you were jacked into the HQ radio. Paul started the process with the phone call, then you finished the job.'

'I enjoy your agile mind,' Valeria said. 'If it wasn't for Jesus you could have been one of the greats. Explain to me how I killed Andrew.'

'You had your people in the Patras mob, easy to disguise during Carnival. In their costumes and masks they incited the locals and ramped up the aggression. They were the ones who had the cross ready, and the bindings. The mastermind assassin was never Paul, nor was it Jesus, or Satan. It was you, Valeria, though you were helped by Paul from the start. You sent us after Paul in Antioch to give yourself time to kill Thomas in Babylon, then you tipped off Paul and let him run from his hotel before we could make his life awkward. He's a paid informer and he told you where to find the disciples. My role was to make it look like we found them by ourselves.'

On the terrace of the abbey, John was a picture of serenity, rejoicing that finally his time had come. Paul, however, was showing the strain. He didn't know where to stand; it was as if he wanted to avoid Gallio as the truth came out. He moved into the shadows, banged the back of his head against the stones of the abbey. He slapped his hand over his eyes, ran the palm flat down his face. He mumbled to himself, the same sounds over and over, and this was not the composed style of prayer favoured by James on the monitors. Paul clenched his fists and squeezed his old eyes shut. He released his jaw and uncricked his neck, reminding Gallio of Baruch whose soul was never at rest.

'You'll find no evidence of civilized involvement in these deaths,' Valeria said. 'With the single exception of Peter, who was punished for organizing the fire of Rome, an unforgivable act of terror. As for the other disciples, they were randomly murdered by whichever excitable locals they upset most. Infidels can be vicious. That's how history will remember this.'

'You're probably right. Until Peter you kept it clean. We achieved the result we wanted while maintaining our reputation for tolerance. You constructed and followed a brilliant piece of reasoning, which I respect. But you're also wrong.'

Paul was louder with his repetitive prayer, moaning the words over and over oh lord oh lord. John joined him and held his hand, as encouragement. Claudia held the envelope with the money, but this was never a story about the money.

'Paul has given me valuable assistance,' Valeria said. 'I admit that. We understand each other, and recently we both saw that the disciples had outstayed their welcome. They and their story-telling had to be removed to make way for ideas less damaging to the stability of modern life. We'll replace superstition with community values. The resurrection becomes a symbolic idea rather than an absurd and exceptional fact.'

Valeria sounded so reasonable. Cassius Gallio pressed a fist to a twitch beside his eye. So reasonable yet mistaken. No one understood the cunning of Jesus but him. 'Paul isn't betraying the disciples,' he said, 'he's helping them out. If Paul wants them dead he's on their side. Believe me on this.'

'You're unbelievable,' Valeria said. 'Claudia, tell him his speculation doesn't make sense.'

'I think it does,' Claudia said, 'at least until the point about dying. Valeria, you killed the disciples with the help of Paul. But they didn't want to die, because that would mean they were manipulating the CCU. Which makes the disciples smarter than us.'

'Remember the tomb in Jerusalem,' Gallio said. He needed to convince them both. 'Valeria, you were there when Jesus supposedly died, and whatever took place on the Friday and the Sunday we never successfully explained. These are clever people.

Jesus picked disciples sharp enough to keep up with his scams and hoaxes.'

'Paul is my asset,' Valeria said. 'We have everything under control. He's my agent, and has been for years.'

'Which puts him beyond reproach,' Gallio said. 'He has the perfect cover. Valeria, open your eyes and see what's in front of you. He doesn't work for us; he works for them. Paul is a triple agent. He's the father, the son and the holy ghost.'

'I think my time has come.' John's voice wavered as he stepped forward, unsure who was tasked with the actual killing. 'None of us can wait forever.'

John spends hours at a time in his cave, hidden from heavenly sight, and over the years Cassius Gallio has occasionally failed to chivvy him outside.

'Another glorious day,' he'd say, which was unlikely to cheer John up. 'Your loss, but at some stage you'll have to forgive him for keeping you alive.'

'How long before you forgave him for what he did to you?'

'Fair point. He's not an easy man to forgive.'

Inside the cave John writes by candlelight, except he doesn't physically write because he's blind. John dictates and Gallio writes down the seven miracles of Jesus that John remembers best. John remembers the last supper and resting his head against the shoulder of Jesus, and he sees now that Jesus was pitying him for the suffering to come. The memory offers insufficient comfort—Jesus knew in advance but still he left John behind, to live and breathe in a cave on Patmos while his mind is back in Israel. He exists in both places at once, opening gaps in time that let through unsettling thoughts.

'Write them,' he says, and Gallio records the thoughts of John, however extreme or apparently senseless. First he thinks in stories, then in images of natural disasters and harpists and carnivorous birds. He spews out numbers, threes and sevens and twelves, and the voice in his head wants to multiply his findings by a thousand. Gallio writes down every word, from the miracles through to the final reckoning, not to please John but to inform the millions who will come after.

They both seize on the insolence of this idea, understanding that every sentence of John's Gospel and John's Revelation is a snipe at Jesus. The beloved disciple is leaving a testimony for others to read, after he is gone. With every paragraph John scorns the notion that he'll live to see the end of the world. Writing is his act of revenge, his doubt in the prophecy that Jesus will return in the lifetime of one of his disciples.

'Credit where it's due,' Gallio says. 'Jesus isn't all bad.'

Whenever John annoys him, Gallio defends the record of Jesus, in particular his treatment of John. In Galilee John was among the first disciples called, and in Jerusalem Jesus trusted him to lay the table for the last meal the disciples ate together. From first to last, unlike some of the others, John was given specific tasks to achieve. He was selected with Peter to run and discover the empty tomb. He was chosen even among the chosen.

Gallio doesn't know why he bothers, because there are nights in the cave when he considers blocking John's airways. He watches the disciple while he sleeps, and at almost any time Gallio could lean heavily on John's face and he could press down and keep on pressing and force Jesus to make himself known. To return or not to return. Either way would end John's misery at being left behind, and at last Cassius Gallio would know.

Except he's an ex-Speculator, formerly attached to the Complex Casework Unit. He's a guardian of enlightened values and a champion of reasonable thinking. Cassius Gallio isn't a killer, so in Patmos John wakes up come the morning. The two men go for their walk, look for clouds and leave Jesus to choose his moment. Or not, as the case may be.

On the surface, without question, Paul was a Jesus believer. But behind that facade of letters and prayers, Valeria was confident of Paul's allegiance to her and the CCU. Gallio was now suggesting that in actual fact Paul worked, more secretly again, for real for Jesus. Valeria had chosen not to be worried by the spread of churches and congregations, or by how Paul had connected, under her protection in the name of Jesus, Ephesians with Galatians with Corinthians and Romans.

'He encourages Jesus believers to love peace and pay their taxes,' Valeria said. 'Exactly as we agreed.'

Gallio could sense Valeria's exasperation, her inability to accept that a fatal mistake had been made. As a young woman she had misread Gallio in Jerusalem, when he wouldn't leave his wife, but since then she'd pretty much known what she was doing. Being wrong was a feeling she'd forgotten how to recognize.

'The number of believers doesn't matter,' she said, 'as long as they don't pose a threat to Rome.'

'So you never believed in a Christian terror threat, or Jesus triggering the end of the world?'

'I couldn't rule out those risks, not until now. Paul is ours, but we needed to rationalize all twelve disciples to be sure they didn't have a plan of their own in motion.'

'Maybe, but who is actually winning here?'

Valeria turned to Paul. 'Tell Cassius about Damascus, when I recruited you. You've been against Jesus from the start.'

Paul ignored her, his lips drawn thin, his head rocking forward and back. He found a rhythm like a monk in active contemplation of the invisible, but he was trying too hard as if the invisible ought to be easier to see.

'He was caught by a storm in the mountains,' Valeria said. If Paul refused to take responsibility for his past she would tell the story herself. 'He was badly shaken, but he recovered and the real change in him was the secret deal he made with me. Once we reached an agreement he was brilliant. He invented the bolt of lightning and the appearance of Jesus. The miracle revelation on the road to Damascus was mostly his idea.'

'You were so impatient,' Paul said, but as if Valeria was worth only a fraction of his attention. The rest of his mind was elsewhere, and not at ease, but Valeria was easily dismissed. 'You didn't listen to me. In Damascus you were so sceptical you'd have disbelieved in anything.'

Valeria grabbed the envelope from Claudia and pulled out a brick of banknotes, shook them in the air. 'Tell John, tell everyone—this payment is for information that led to the death of Peter.'

'He has gone ahead,' John said. 'In glory.'

Paul recited a prayer out loud and John filled the gaps with Amens, until the prayer between them became a chant.

'He has gone ahead.'

'In glory.'

'To share the table of Jesus. Amen.'

'This isn't right.' Claudia looked from Paul to John and back again. The line was deep in her forehead. 'They're not supposed to be friends with each other.'

Paul shivered violently where he stood, then lay down on the stones of the terrace. He tried to make himself comfortable, clamped his fingers between his thighs. He lay curled up on his side, face drained of colour and teeth clenched, his brain unable to control his body. 'I'm sorry,' he said. 'I don't think I can do this.'

The bodyguard balanced his blacked sword against the wall and on one knee he attended to Paul, his hand reaching out for Paul's shoulder but not quite touching. Gallio saw for the first time the love the bodyguard had for Paul, that he had always loved him.

'You're saying Paul played us.' Claudia wanted to believe in the infallibility of the CCU, but she had a Speculator's open mind and the terrible truth was making itself felt. Her faith had not been rewarded. 'Shit. Paul was playing us while we thought we were playing him.'

'All the time,' Gallio said, 'since the beginning. The most effective way to spread news of Jesus was to hitch a ride with the dominant secular power, accelerating the Jesus story in every direction. That's right, isn't it, Paul? You were always aiming at two billion Christian believers worldwide, a number that never stops growing. Look at him. You never turned him, Valeria. Most of those people found Jesus thanks to Paul.'

Gallio had an urge to kick the traitor where he lay. The bodyguard stood and moved between them, one eye on Valeria, who took this opportunity to pick up the sword. She examined the blacking on the blade while the bodyguard lifted Paul to his knees, made sure with his muscular hands that Paul could kneel unaided.

'Enough speculation,' Valeria said. 'Everyone step away from John.'

'You're not thinking straight,' Gallio said. 'Watch them, Val, be careful. They're experts in deception.'

'John,' Valeria said. 'Move away from the others. Now, please.'

Paul was making a visible effort to hold himself together, humbled at the end on his knees, a short bald man shimmering with fear. He was letting Jesus down but he was only human, and he couldn't help himself. Gallio instinctively glanced skyward, but saw stars and half the moon, not a cloud in god's heaven.

'I have stepped away,' John said. For the second time that evening he lifted up his hands, offering himself to Valeria as the last of the disciples of Jesus.

'Listen, Valeria, think.' Gallio watched the bodyguard. 'Did you *want* Paul in Rome? Are you sure you were in control of that? He led us to the minor disciples before Peter. He kept us away from Peter until the end, meaning the most famous disciple was available for a grandstand death for which we're clearly responsible. And which via a huge audience will reach the greatest number of people.'

'I have not been deceived,' Valeria said, but the words ate at her pride, opened up the possibility of their untruthfulness in the act of being spoken. 'John is the last of the twelve.'

'You think you're being reasonable, and you are,' Gallio said. 'That's your weakness. Everything we do is what Jesus wants.'

Jesus had plotted every cause and effect, guiding the disciples and their assassins to this moment in the abbey and beyond. The abbey, the museum, the free admission, the knowledge that visitors would come here not just now but for countless lifetimes into the future.

'Every dead disciple becomes a martyr,' Gallio said, 'and brings Jesus new converts. Together we can turn this round, but only by not doing what Jesus wants. We should do nothing, or nothing he'd expect. Doing nothing at all, especially right now, is our safest course of action.'

'None of us can refuse his work,' Paul said, his voice squeezed by the tightness of his breathing. His body was at war with itself, or with his brain. 'If Jesus is the son of god.'

On his knees he took half a shuffle toward Valeria. He swayed where he knelt, wanting her attention, but unable to force his body any closer. Cassius Gallio recognized the wildness of defeat in Valeria's eyes, another Speculator outwitted by Jesus. She knew. Suddenly she knew she was losing everything. Thanks to Jesus she could see her career shrivel in the white heat of Gallio's revelation: I have been wrong. The brilliance of Jesus blistered her sense of herself and burst holes in her faith that reason would prevail. Only she couldn't be destroyed like this, not Valeria, not a regional director of the CCU.

Sword in hand, Valeria would seize back control as Cassius Gallio had once sworn he'd restore sanity by finding the body of Jesus in Jerusalem. Wrong and wrong again.

Gallio lunged at Paul, to save him from the death he so fervently desired. Paul's bodyguard had orders for exactly this situation, the only specific instruction he'd ever received, and the day had finally come.

He blocked Gallio, making sure he couldn't reach either Paul or Valeria, then expertly used Gallio's momentum to turn and hold him arm-locked with his wrist at breaking point. Gallio tried to shout out, but the bodyguard's free hand pressed hard over his mouth. Cassius Gallio was powerless to intervene.

• • •

On Patmos, the martyrdom of Paul joins the pantheon of legendary deaths suffered by the eleven murdered disciples. In the stories that reach the island Paul dies extravagantly, as an equal with the apostles of Jesus. The pilgrims bring pictures, and Paul's assassin is a muscular brute in white marble, or a black angel with ragged wings. Cassius Gallio spends years politely considering the visual evidence, the postcards of paintings and sculptures, but he sees little these days that can't be faked.

According to legend, Paul was beheaded at a site close to Rome but outside the city itself, and with each bounce of his severed head a fountain sprang to life. At the Abbey of the Three Fountains the three water sources are about ten paces apart on a downslope. To achieve the velocity for this length of carry, Paul's head must have been cleaved off with appreciable force, in anger.

At her tribunal Valeria presented a different version of events. Paul's untimely death was the fault of Cassius Gallio, a rogue Speculator who assassinated an embedded CCU agent in an ignorant rage. Check the archives, she said, Gallio had a history of mental instability, and a fixated belief that a minor Israeli insurgent was capable of returning from the dead. She conceded that her error of judgement was to have brought Gallio back, but she couldn't have predicted the long-term damage to his powers of reason caused by earlier setbacks in Jerusalem. The tribunal disagreed, and noted that the archives also suggested the two of them had once been romantically linked.

'That's not true.'

The members of the tribunal decided, on reflection, that it was their duty and no longer hers to judge the truth. Paul had measurably advanced the interests of Jesus, whatever secret plans she might have devised for him. Valeria was found guilty of neglecting due diligence in her recruitment of Paul as an undercover agent. The arrogance of her method suggested she was either a traitor or a fool, and Valeria was nobody's fool. In sentencing, the tribunal was deliberately generous, giving Valeria a brief window in which to exercise her free will as a high-ranking guardian of secular behaviour. She bled to death in the bath after cutting the veins in her wrists.

Claudia avoided the fallout. She was young, and could prove she'd disobeyed Valeria's illegal orders to assassinate Cassius Gallio. There was, after all, some justice in the world. In Rome Claudia worked hard, kept her life simple and was promoted through the reorganized Complex Casework Unit. Now she speculates about threats to civilization wherever they may arise, though discounting the island of Patmos. The intelligence community knows of twelve disciples of Jesus, and extensive records exist for twelve spectacular deaths. Paul makes up the twelve, taking the place of John, and Claudia underlines the numbers in official ledgers. Twelve disciples, twelve dead bodies. Done and dusted, nothing more to see here, move along now please. Every time Claudia hides John from sight she recognizes a quiet act of love, of Caistor remembered.

Claudia sometimes sees Alma in the Roman markets, growing older, laughing with her mother as she barters for kugels and Mandelbrot, the two of them enjoying the benefits of life in a progressive world city. Alma's leg was strengthened by extensive physiotherapy—at least that's the most obvious cause—and she joined the regular army soon after her mother agreed to settle in Rome.

On Patmos, John meditates and falls into trances and remembers and generally wrestles with a fate he struggles to understand. His anger gives him strength, whereas Cassius Gallio mostly aches. His knees, his hips, his old man's body subsiding. If nothing else, Gallio can write, and he writes for as long as John hears voices. John hears a word that sounds like millstones, and on another day a word like trumpets; he has bright visions of structures of glass that shine like gold, or of angels in the midst of heaven. Yes, Gallio tells him, he can see the angels. He can make out their vapour trails over the white island of Patmos, every sunny day during the summer months.

Cassius Gallio refuses to be the first to go. He can't risk missing Jesus, but with every year he is physically weaker. Sometimes he mishears John's stories, as if they're true, or forgets that after so much time most of what remains is story. Any life, he finally thinks, can be told as a sequence of miracles, even his own. How extraordinary that the crucifixion of Jesus should have been allocated to a young Speculator whose zealous guarding of the tomb made the escape of Jesus more memorable. Or what a coincidence that of all people Valeria was in a position to remember his plight and call him back from exile. Cassius Gallio has lived these and many other miraculous accidents, if he chooses to remember them, until the cause and effect of his life starts to deceive like a plot, a life mapped out.

It is true that occasionally Cassius Gallio is comforted by what John is able to believe, a vision of eternity where everything is now, and now is everything. At the same time he's proud never to have called on Jesus for help. He resists the divinity of Jesus as an explanation for the path of his life, and if Jesus would like to correct him then he'd better move soon. Time feels short, and one day on their walk to the cliff Cassius Gallio falls. He falls down, as if at imaginary feet.

John lifts him up, but Gallio is too old and frail to be righted. John makes space in the cave, and lays down his friend on woven mats, warms him with woolen blankets. Gallio will not close his eyes, he will not. He speculates to the end, and beyond the end, and beyond, until John takes pity and reaches out. Cassius Gallio takes hold of John's hand and presses it to his feeble chest. At last, comforted, he closes his eyes. In the darkness he grips the hand that Jesus faithfully held, once upon a time.

About the Author

RICHARD BEARD is the author of six novels, including *X20*, *Damascus* (a *New York Times* Notable Book), *The Cartoonist*, *Dry Bones*, and *Lazarus Is Dead*, and three works of nonfiction. He has been short-listed for the BBC National Short Story Award and long-listed for the *Sunday Times* EFG Private Bank Short Story Award. He lives in London.